THE DELIRIUM BRIEF

It is a very bad idea to try and soul-gaze the Eater of Souls. I manage to catch him under the arm before he crumples, and save his pint from spilling for the second time in a minute, and I'm pretty certain I managed not to take a bite out of him but dammit, it's a *really* bad idea to take me by surprise that way. Clearly an adept, he takes it on the figurative chin and bends over, retching. I wave the bartender back: 'I think he just tried to inhale his beer,' I tell the guy. McKracken leans against the bar and takes a deep breath, eyes squeezed shut. He's actually in good shape, considering what he just tried to do. If an unwarded civilian caught me by surprise like that they'd be waiting for an ambulance right now.

'What *are* you?' he manages.

I shrug. 'Bob Howard, Detached Senior Specialist grade one, Q-Division SOE, at your service.'

BY CHARLES STROSS

Saturn's Children
Singularity Sky
Iron Sunrise
Accelerando
Glasshouse
Wireless: The Essential Collection
Halting State
Rule 34
Neptune's Brood

The Laundry Files
The Atrocity Archives
The Jennifer Morgue
The Fuller Memorandum
The Apocalypse Codex
The Rhesus Chart
The Annihilation Score
The Nightmare Stacks
The Delirium Brief
The Labyrinth Index

THE
DELIRIUM
BRIEF

CHARLES STROSS

www.orbitbooks.net

ORBIT

First published in Great Britain in 2017 by Orbit
This edition published in 2018 by Orbit

1 3 5 7 9 10 8 6 4 2

A CIP catalogue record for this book
is available from the British Library.

ISBN 978-0-356-50831-3

Typeset in Sabon by M Rules
Printed and bound in Great Britain by
Clays Ltd, St Ives plc

Papers used by Orbit are from well-managed forests
and other responsible sources.

Orbit
An imprint of
Little, Brown Book Group
Carmelite House
50 Victoria Embankment
London EC4Y 0DZ

An Hachette UK Company
www.hachette.co.uk

www.orbitbooks.net

In memory of
David G. Hartwell, 1941–2016

Laws are like sausages, it is better not to see them being made.

— Prince Otto von Bismarck

PART 1

GOD GAME INDIGO

1: THE PRODIGAL'S RETURN

It's twenty past ten at night and I'm being escorted through the glass-fronted atrium of a certain office building in central London. I'm surrounded by a knot of soberly dressed civil servants who are marching shoulder-to-shoulder in lockstep to keep me from being recognized, or maybe to prevent me making a run for it if I lose my nerve. We are waved past nodding receptionists and security guards who hold the turnstiles open for me as if I am expected – because I am indeed expected. *Unfortunately.*

This afternoon my minders took me to a barber. They said I was overdue for a trim; protests about my male pattern baldness fell on deaf but determined ears. (I still think closing the shop, kicking everyone else out, and stationing guards inside the door was a bit excessive, though: who ever heard of a top secret haircut?) I'm wearing my funeral suit and tie, and my shoes are dazzlingly polished. (*Just pretend you're acting a role*, she said, straightening my collar; *concentrate and remember your talking points.*) I look twenty years older than I feel, and I feel ten years older than usual – mostly due to jet lag. They emailed me a set of notes just before I caught my flight home, and I did my best to memorize them on the plane from Kansai. But right now I feel like it's seven in the morning, and I'm yawning because I'm waking up, not going to sleep.

Minder number three – Boris, a tech-side middle management guy I used to do the odd job for: until today I hadn't seen him in years – hits the button for the sixth floor. The glass-walled lift slides silently up into the lofty heights of Broadcasting House, rising past open plan offices full of serious-faced journalists and program managers peering into computer screens. As we pass a coat of arms saying 'Nation shall speak Peace unto Nation,' I go over points seventeen to twenty-two again, mumbling under my breath. Then I rub my sweaty palms on my woolen suit jacket.

I have got the Fear. Why the fuck couldn't they find *somebody else* to do this?

I imagine Lockhart or the SA or some other drop-in authority figure explaining it to me calmly. 'You *know* why it's got to be you, Bob: it's because of the scaling laws.' The threats the agency exists to deal with grow exponentially, doubling in scale on an eighteen-month cycle, like a nightmarish version of Moore's Law. But our cohort of qualified senior staff only grows linearly. The clusterfuck at the New Annex a year ago killed a bunch of senior officers, and the disaster in Leeds has put so many others on paid leave pending hearings that everyone in the field is currently operating above their pay grade. We're all taking on tasks we're not trained for, often without backup or oversight.

As for this job, we're a secret government agency: we don't even *have* a public relations department. Which is why we're scrambling to improvise tonight. When the order came down from on high that someone was to come here and do this thing, it ended up on *my* desk simply because I was senior enough, and available. (At least that's the official explanation. Part of me can't help thinking that a more rational explanation is that God or Management hates me and wants me to suffer.)

My handler clears her throat just behind my left shoulder, and I jump. 'Try not to sweat so much, Bob, the makeup guy will want to redo everything.' I *hate* it when Mhari sneaks up on me like that. She makes me really uncomfortable: about ten percent of it is knowing that she's actually a vampire, and the rest of it is down to our uncomfortable personal history. The only consolation is knowing that having to work with me makes her even *more* uncomfortable, and only about ten percent of it is because I'm a necromancer. At least we're both trying to be professional about it, and we're mostly succeeding. She reaches out briskly and brushes lint from my lapel, and I try not to flinch again.

When they went looking for someone to represent the agency in public and picked me, they weren't just scraping the bottom of the barrel: they were fracking for oil in the basement. My biggest qualification for this job is that I haven't stepped in any operational dog turds lately. I'm Mr. Clean: nobody's going to blame *me* for the disaster in Leeds, I was out of the country at the time. So they briefed me and gave me talking points to memorize, and sent me videos of the Great Man toying with his prey, to watch as in-flight entertainment on the way home. Which, in hindsight, was probably a bad idea: I'm so keyed up I need the toilet again and I'm due on-air in about ten minutes.

'Remember, he only really takes the gloves off when he's interviewing policy makers,' Mhari reassures me. 'You're a line manager, not an executive, so by sending you out like a sacrificial goat with a sign taped to your arse saying KICK ME we're calling his bluff. He can't crucify you on-air for setting policy without looking like a bully, so he'll have to settle for asking you lots of hard questions to which you are expected to plead ignorance or pass the buck. He can't even badger you until you change your story – remember the Iraqi WMD scandal and the way Dr. Kelly committed suicide when the press turned on him? So you'll be fine. Just remember it's not personal: he's not interviewing *you*, he's interviewing the organization.' She bares one delicately curved canine, ivory outlined against crimson lip-gloss while I boggle at her appalling mixed metaphor. 'I'm buying the drinks afterwards. Everyone okay? Boris?'

Boris nods lugubriously. 'Am understanding there are good club late license around corner,' he slurs. (Boris has permanent damage to his speech center from one too many run-ins with the brain parasites that cause K syndrome.)

A couple of harried technicians glare at us for blocking the lift doors until Mhari smiles at them and sharply knuckles my spine to get me moving again. 'Where are we going?' I ask. The level we're on features lots of floor-to-ceiling beech and invisible recessed handles on doors that curve to match the walls. The carpet is eerily sound-deadening, but I can sense the murmur of many minds all around us, whispering and intensely focused.

'Studio A. Which is right ... here ...'

Boris and the other guy (a blue-suiter in civvies, fooling no one: he stinks of cop) wait outside while Mhari pushes me through the door into the production suite and follows me inside to stop me escaping. I turn and frown at her. She's far better at looking professional than I am. With her mercilessly coiffured blonde hair, tailored black suit, watered silk blouse, and sky-high heels, she looks like Taylor Swift in boardroom drag – a version of TayTay that runs on type O negative and has a severe sunlight allergy. 'Can't *you* do this?' I ask plaintively, one last time: 'Take one for the team?'

She spares me a brazenly unapologetic grin as she points a finger at the ceiling: 'See the bright lights, sweetie? I'd go up in flames.'

I'm about to tell her that they use LED spotlights these days and they're not powerful enough to set fire to her PHANG-sensitive skin when I spot the producer. He's half-risen from his seat, clearly fascinated by this exchange. He leans forward and peers at our ID badges. 'Ah, you must be Mr. Howard and Ms. Murphy from the, er, Ministry of Magic?'

That makes even Mhari twitch. 'Special Operations Executive, Ministry of Defense,' she says sharply. 'There is no "Ministry of Magic."' She holds out her hand for him to shake. Her nails are the same color as her lips: they look dipped in fresh blood.

'Can we take any questions arising from this interview to the Defense Secretary?' he asks hopefully.

Mhari looks at me. I look at her: '*No comment*,' we chorus in unison. Then I add, 'We're just the performing monkeys: if you want a policy statement you'll need to send the organ grinder a memo.' Mhari manages to keep a straight face. *Drinks on me* indeed.

'Well then, assuming you're not going to offer me a last minute substitution I've got you down to go live six minutes into the program, off at twenty – the Big Man's in the studio already, running through the warmup highlights.' Just the biggest news interviewer in the country, the chief presenter on *Newsnight*, waiting for me. 'You haven't done this before, have you?' He shows me all the kindly concern of a hangman sizing up a client. 'Really, it'll all be over before you know it and it won't hurt *at all*. Let's get you hooked up ...'

There's a glass door fronting a surprisingly cramped office with a plain gray backdrop, brilliantly illuminated by camera fill-in LEDs. Through the door I see a famous silhouette: the barely tamed hair and fiercely hooked nose. He was scheduled to retire last month but I gather he decided to stay in the saddle a bit longer *just for us*. I may be the Eater of Souls, but this guy is the Consumer of Cabinet Ministers. And now he's beckoning to me! 'Go on in and take the chair to his left,' says the producer; 'when it's time to go live the camera will give you a red light, and when the red light goes off I'll cue you to slide the chair back and leave. Just try not to run the next guest over.'

The green light over the door begins blinking. The producer starts making urgent shooing motions at me, and Mhari mouths *break a leg*. So I go through the door and I sit down in the hot seat, wishing it was electrified so I could get this over with faster. I wipe my fingers carefully along the underside of the seat frame, then peel back a tab of adhesive film, leaving a coin-sized self-adhesive disc behind. My pulse spikes. The chair is wheeled, rolling on a track: 'Move eighty centimeters to your left – perfect!' The producer's voice comes in through the bud in my right ear. It's not the only wire I'm wearing: there's a lapel mike too, and I half-suspect it doubles as a polygraph so they can tell when I'm lying. 'You're going to be on camera three. Jeremy will lead in to your item in about ten seconds. Okay, I'm shutting up now.'

Then the red light comes on above the camera, and I'm live on a Monday evening special crisis edition of *Newsnight*.

Hi. My name is Bob Howard, and I do secret work for the government.

This is my workplace diary. People in my line – anyone with 'active duty' flagged on their personnel file – are required to keep one. It's a precaution against loss of institutional knowledge. If you're reading this, either you're in an Oversight position (probably an Auditor or a magistrate of the Black Assizes tasked with investigating my activities) or, more likely, I'm dead and the powers that be want you up to speed on my job toot sweet.

Side-splitting stuff, eh?

Let me tell you a bit about myself. As I said, I'm Bob Howard, age 39, position: DSS Grade 1, that's short for Detached Senior Scientist or Deeply Scary Sorcerer or something, nobody really cares (in the Laundry they're more or less the same thing), and my life sucks right now.

I got into this gig because when I was working on my master's thesis in image processing in the late nineties I almost summoned up a manifestation of outer chaos by accident. This led to the Laundry making me a job offer I wasn't allowed to refuse. (Apparently you're only allowed to demolish Wolverhampton if you're a property developer like Donald Trump. Crawling eldritch horrors don't get planning permission unless they're Trump's hairpiece.)

That was about fifteen years ago, in more innocent, less embattled days. So I spent a couple of years in tech support hell before getting bored, stupidly volunteering for operational duties, and ending up as Dr. Angleton's understudy. Dr. Angleton *really was* a Deeply Scary Sorcerer, and when he got himself lethally entangled with a monstrously powerful vampire elder I inherited all of his duties, some of his powers (I'm still learning how much), and very little of his seventy-plus years of wisdom and experience ...

Although I've been learning. Boy, have I been learning! I've spent most of the past year scurrying around clearing up the messes he left behind. He clearly wasn't planning on dying any time soon, so not only did I have to pick up the slack on his more recondite duties, I also had to check the padlocks he'd left on a lot of metaphorical closets with skeletons in them. Angleton did not keep one of these diaries, oh no: he kept his notes on a magically warded electromechanical data store built during the late 1940s, and a lot of those notes said things like, *demon bound under rear quadrant of supermarket car park with level six ward, half-life eighteen years, check back early next century*. So I've spent the past nine months trotting around the globe, pacifying the unquiet dead with extreme prejudice, and inadvertently being out of the country when all hell cut loose in Yorkshire.

But I digress. Nearly a decade ago I married a fellow employee, Dr. Dominique O'Brien.* You might have heard of her. Mo used to be a troubleshooter: whenever the organization had a spot of trouble she shot it until it stopped twitching. When that got too much for her they reassigned her to the Home Office for a while. Now she's back in-house as a freshly minted Auditor, which means she holds people like me accountable for our work with the power of life or death. For many years Mo carried an occult instrument, the White Violin, as her main operational tool. The trouble with occult instruments is that they sometimes have their own agendas; it wasn't too keen on sharing her, so eventually it tried to eat me. She managed to get rid of it somehow, but now she's afraid that as Angleton's heir *I* might absent-mindedly eat *her* in my sleep. As we keep undergoing the kind of personal growth experiences that involve new and exciting magical abilities – like an interesting tendency to absent-mindedly mumble death spells while waking up – I have to concede that she's got a point. This has been a time

---

* Her being a fellow employee is arguably my fault, but as there were tentacle monsters and terrorists involved she chose not to hold it against me.

of changes for both of us and we have about a decade of unexamined marital baggage to rethink, and consequently we're currently living apart.

Did I mention that my life sucks?

Speaking of which: let's have a round of applause for management responsibility! Because, after years of dodging it at every opportunity, I have had management responsibility forced upon me, whether I want it or not. And if I find the joker who nominated me for the role of Departmental Public Relations Officer I will –

No, I won't eat them. That would be unprofessional.

(I won't even put the frighteners on them. I might remonstrate with them politely. I could explain the errors of their ways and suggest, more in sorrow than in anger, that although I have been promoted into a very senior dead man's shoes I don't look good in a suit, I don't suffer fools gladly, and if they *really* want a spokesman they ought to hire someone who's trained for it, rather than being better qualified for fighting off a zombie invasion or fixing a broken firewall.)

Because I'm management now, I have to face facts. Hiring a real PR person would involve approving a budget, going through the HR recruitment and candidate selection cycle, managing the new employee's enhanced security background check and in-processing, then bringing them up to speed on what exactly we do in the agency. (Which involves working around people with titles like *Senior Staff Necromancer*, *Applied Computational Demonologist*, or *Combat Poet*. Lots of newbies flee screaming at that point: our first month attrition rate is sky-high.)

So let me sum up the ways in which my life sucks right now: I've had a bunch of extra responsibilities dumped on me for no extra pay, I've had to move out of my home because my wife's violin tried to murder me, morale is in the shitter because of the disaster in Leeds, and for the pièce de résistance, they made me wear a suit and sent me out to be grilled live on TV, because we don't have the budget for a public relations fixer!

Yeah, it all sucks, but I suppose it could be worse. At least *this* time my line manager isn't trying to sacrifice me to an elder god. But it's still only May, so I suppose there's time for that to change . . .

Jeremy smiles his trademark smile at me, simultaneously sympathetic and pitying, like a headmaster carpeting an unruly schoolboy. 'Some would say that the truth is out there: well, tonight we're going to see about that. My next interviewee is Mr. Howard, from the Ministry of Defense's hitherto extremely secret agency for dealing with the sort of thing you expect to meet in an episode of *The X-Files* – alien abductions, supervillains, UFOs, and' – he pauses momentarily, as if he's just tasted something lip-wrinklingly bitter – '*magic*.' Skepticism boils off him in waves so thick it makes the air around his head shimmer.

I smile, nod, and avert my eyes from my own image in the screen on the opposite wall. *Jesus, I look like a life insurance salesman*. 'Yes, Jeremy,' I hear myself saying, 'although we prefer to call it applied computational thaumaturgy. There's a lot of mathematics involved.'

'So rather than smoke and mirrors you use clouds and servers?' The grizzled eyebrow creaks upwards towards the receding hairline. That's a good pun: obviously scripted in advance. I nod again.

'Yes. It turns out that mathematics has side effects in the real world. This agency, SOE, has been investigating this effect ever since Alan Turing did pioneering work on it in the 1940s at Bletchley Park. Computers are tools that do much more than share cute cat photos, and they can be lethally dangerous in the wrong hands.'

So far so good. I'm on the approved message track, regurgitating talking points acknowledging stuff that's already out there in public. My brief is to make the Laundry sound boring; encryption bad, hacking bad, misusing computers bad, Home Office *rah*, National Security *rah*, War on Tentacular Terror, *rah*. But in the back of my head I am uncomfortably aware of all the tasty minds crowded around me in this building, fuzzy shadows of warmth and sustenance in the studio control room and the offices beyond. I can taste the focus of the producer, feel the chilly (and inedible) ramparts of Mhari's vampire shell, the armored fortress of solitude sitting across the table from me –

What?

Paxo smiles at me like a kindly uncle, or maybe a crocodile with a gold tooth, as he says: 'It has been alleged –' *oh shit*, I think – 'that the disaster in Leeds was the result of an SOE operation that went wrong, that your people invited the attack that killed over nine thousand innocent people and shot down three airliners and two fighter jets. Is that true, Mr. Howard?'

Fuck! The fucker's wearing a heavy duty ward! Which means I can't read him or trivially control him – the small leather bag he's wearing on a cord around his neck, under his shirt, is the thaumaturgic equivalent of a bulletproof vest.

I wipe the smile and do my best impersonation of a granite cliff. 'Absolutely not.' I take a breath. 'SOE does not recklessly endanger national security or put lives at risk.' I think I can see where this line of questioning is going, and it's nowhere good. 'We were invaded without warning by a hitherto theoretical threat. We responded immediately and alerted the Police and the Army in accordance with our standing orders. The handling and outcome of the conflict are a matter for the Commons Select Committee to investigate and the Public Enquiry to report on, and I can't comment further.' Phew.

The Crocodile nods and he's dropped his smile, which is a bad sign: the gloves are coming off and I wonder, horrified, *how the fuck did the BBC get their hands on a level six defensive ward?* – as I realize *this is a setup* and meanwhile he's leaning forward, closing in for the kill –

'Perhaps you could explain to the viewers why the surviving invaders are being treated as *asylum seekers*, Mr. Howard? Wouldn't terrorism charges be more appropriate? Or a war crimes investigation?'

Shit! That's not supposed to be public knowledge. Which means there is a leak somewhere. As the scriptwriters on *Yes, Minister* observed, the ship of state is unique in that it's the only vessel that leaks from the top down. Our oath of office should prevent anyone inside the tent from pissing out ... which means someone in the government is briefing against us, probably at cabinet level. We are *totally* off the talking points now: nobody briefed me for this. *Fuck! Time to pass the blame.*

'The ... survivors ... of the attacking force include a number of slaves and other victims who were there unwillingly. The Home Office has conceded that in some cases there is a case for them to claim refuge from persecution.' *Pass the blame.* 'I'd like to remind you that the enemy military made extensive use of human sacrifice and other forms of necromancy to power their attack.' All of which is entirely true, but –

'I'm not talking about the slaves, Mr. Howard. Why is

the All-Highest, *their leader*, claiming asylum? Can you explain?'

Fuck. Fuck fuckityfuck fucksticks really bad *swear words.*

'Let me emphasize this: what came through the gate in Malham Cove was the last surviving military force of a nation that had just lost the magical equivalent of a nuclear war. Also their dependents. And slaves. They can't go back: sending them back means sending them to their certain deaths. The enemy All-Highest who ordered the attack is dead. The current All-Highest was *not* in charge of the attack, and on inheriting the position immediately ordered the unconditional surrender of the, ah, attacking force.' That is, the Host of Air and Darkness: the surviving armored cavalry forces of the Morningstar Empire. Don't say *elves*, there's nothing terribly Tolkienesque about this bunch and the good PR would just make them harder to handle. 'Accommodating their *unwilling victims* was a precondition of the surrender. In return, the current All-Highest is actively cooperating with us in restraining their military forces. None of them are able to, ah, *go back*. The world they came from is – it's been overrun by alien horrors.'

Not to mention that sending them back would risk drawing the attention of the undead nightmares they were fleeing, who might well pick up the trail in our direction and decide not to stop at eating just one civilization – but I can't say that on live TV news, people might complain to Ofcom about the nightmare fuel.

'But – *asylum*, Mr. Howard?' The eyebrow is at full extension. Time to shut this down.

'I'm sorry, it's not my job to set policy. That question is better directed to the minister responsible.'

Paxo is indignant. 'A minister responsible for a department that didn't officially exist until the week before last? That's simply not good enough, Mr. Howard!' *Bastard*. 'I'm sure we'll get some better answers when we have a cabinet minister in charge. But one final question for you: can you explain to the viewers why you are reportedly known to other members of your agency as the "Eater of Souls"?'

For a moment I see red: blood splattered all up and down the blue-screen back wall of the studio. But no, that would be *bad*, and worse, it would be unprofessional. Also, the ward he's wearing under his shirt collar is powerful enough that I *could* break it, but I'd probably set fire to his hair in the process. It would look bad on camera. And also-also – I suddenly realize this is the wrap-up question: I get the last word in so I can select what to give him.

I summon up a sheepish smirk: 'When I was junior, I used to put my foot in my mouth rather a lot. The nickname stuck.'

And the light on the camera goes out.

The government's occult secret service goes back further than most people realize.

Our oldest handwritten records were left behind by Dr. John Dee, the noted mathematician, alchemist, and astrologer who worked for Sir Francis Walsingham, Elizabeth the First's spymaster. Back in his day, everything ran on a nod-and-a-wink basis. It was part of the Crown Service and established by Royal Prerogative, which basically means Lizzie Tudor wrote a letter saying 'make it so' and appointed Frankie the Fixer to run it. The Invisible College (as it later became known) operated as an informal gentleman-dabbler's club until the Second World War. Then wartime expansion and the systematization provided by the Turing Theorems led to the incorporation of the Laundry as a division inside the Special Operations Executive, when Winston Churchill wrote an 'action this day' memo using the authority vested in him by His Kingliness George the Umpty ...

(You get the picture.)

Now, back in the day the Invisible College ran entirely on ritual magic. But ritual magic doesn't work reliably, because ritual magicians tend to succumb to Krantzberg syndrome, a very nasty spongiform dementia caused by microscopic extradimensional feeders (parasites attracted by magical manifestations of information processing). Over time they nibble the practitioner's cerebral cortex into lace, which tends to bring the practitioner's career staggering to a palsied conclusion. And that's assuming they don't inadvertently succumb to the greater feeders, such as feeders in the night: predators which make themselves at home in neural networks like, oh, the human cerebral cortex, and take over the body to go in search of more brains to chow down on. (Thereby leading to myths, legends, and *Shaun of the Dead*.)

There are a handful of cognitive infections that grant ritual practitioners a degree of immunity to eaters – PHANG syndrome (vampirism) is one of them, and the for-want-of-a-better-word elven invaders seem to have come up with some kind of occult vaccine. And then there's little old me. (I'm ... let's say 'unique' and tiptoe away from the subject.) But all these mitigating techniques have severe drawbacks, and as a result there are old ritual magicians, and there are bold ritual magicians, but there are no old, bold magicians. They don't survive, and they tend to have unique skill sets, thereby defeating the first principle of bureaucracy: that nobody is indispensable.

In contrast, computational magic *does* work reliably, for pretty much anyone who can punch a keyboard and follow a checklist, because eaters don't seem to have a taste for silicon or germanium: which is why it's the go-to discipline for organizations.

Mahogany Row, the successor to the Invisible College, continues to this day to keep track of and provide a framework for the high-level unique practitioners. However, the rest of the Laundry is an ant farm full of computational demonologists and IT managers. Indeed most staff, to the extent that they're aware of Mahogany Row, think it's just a senior management stratum – even though the organization as a whole exists to support it. Because a big chunk of the Laundry's postwar mission was to keep the lid on the mere existence of algorithmic thaumaturgy, we ended up with a bloated head count – we'd spent decades giving everybody who stumbled on the truth a job where we could keep an eye on them. (Or, more accurately, where they could keep an eye on each other.) The iron law of bureaucracy doesn't help: everybody working to ensure that the organization continues to pay them a salary, rather than necessarily achieving its objectives. So it has become progressively harder to keep the ball rolling, with the result that we finally and unambiguously lost the plot in Leeds.

You can hush up a massacre in an office park or a hideous manifestation at the Albert Hall with DA-Notices and dark muttering about terrorist attacks and hallucinogenic gas. But it's impossible to cover up airliners being shot down, an invading army rampaging through the suburbs of a major city, and a traffic jam of main battle tanks on the nation's motorways. Once the situation escalated to COBRA, the Cabinet Office emergency committee, and the government invoked Article Five of the North Atlantic Treaty (calling for support from NATO forces following an attack on a member nation), the mess in Leeds became the number one global rolling news headline and still hasn't died down. It even beat out an eighty-meter-tall daikaiju that invaded the Yokohama Hakkeijima Sea Paradise theme park and duked it out with the Japanese Self-Defense Agency, as a result of the incursion at Puroland that I was sent to help deal with –

Nope, the events in Leeds aren't going back in the closet any time soon.

Nor has the aftermath gone unnoticed. There are smoking craters all over Yorkshire, an animé convention full of collateral damage in pointy ears, and the remains of a heavy cavalry brigade mounted on unicorns (*shudder*) corralled behind razor wire on Dartmoor, eating their heads off under the guns of half the Army's remaining Challenger MBTs. (And *don't* ask me about the, ahem, 'dragons.') They're arranging a snap summit meeting of all the heads of NATO member states later this month, and that's something that simply *does not happen*. A large segment of the press and public are baying for blood, calling on the government to nuke the bastards, convene a war crimes tribunal, or arrest them for terrorism. Only the inconvenient fact that the current All-Highest is pleading for asylum from something *even worse* is giving anybody pause for concern.

I come out of the *Newsnight* studio feeling like SpongeBob SquarePants after a trip through the dishwasher: wrung-out but still somewhat moist. Mhari and Boris are waiting for me. 'Am being impressed,' Boris rumbles once we're out of the glass doors and into the passage leading to the lifts. 'Jeremy are not eated despite copious provocation.'

'This way,' Mhari says tensely. Her heels click as she

walks into the lift and holds the door for us. 'That could have gone worse.'

I lean against the wall and close my eyes as the floor sinks beneath me. 'Thanks for the vote of confidence.'

'No! I mean it.' I open my eyes as she shrugs. Her jacket shoulder pads rise and fall stiffly. 'You spend time in the piranha tank, you've got to expect to get bitten.'

'Piranhas am not biting fishes: reputation undeserved,' Boris says pedantically.

'Doesn't matter.' Mhari raises a finger: 'But I'm calling it a qualified success. For starters, Bob managed to avoid looking rumpled for almost fifteen minutes. I think that's a personal best.' My hand unconsciously moves to loosen the knot of my tie and she bats it away: we're still in Broadcasting House, there must be a dress code or something. Another finger rises: 'Two, he went five rounds with the *Newsnight* rottweiler without wetting himself, babbling state secrets, or losing his temper and eating Paxo's soul.'

I frown. 'I wouldn't have done that: it's far too stringy and bitter.'

Mhari raises a third finger. 'Three: now we know *for sure* that someone's briefing against us. Which means—'

'Wait,' I interrupt, 'you thought someone was briefing against us *earlier*? And didn't warn me?'

Mhari gives me a look. 'In the current clusterfuck, who the hell knows?' she asks. I have to admit she's got a point: in the past four weeks there have been three ministerial resignations, a vote of confidence in the Commons that the government barely won by the skin of its teeth, there's been one mini-cabinet reshuffle already (with rumors of more to come), and the Scottish Independence referendum has been postponed until next year. In other words, politics has gone nonlinear and nobody seems to know what's happening any more. 'But now the Auditors have reasonable cause to start investigating,' she concludes. 'So that's something.'

Her expression wavers somewhere between uncertainty and fear: *nobody* likes being carpeted by the Auditors, even if they're not under suspicion themselves. But before she can continue the lift hits bottom, and she stops talking because there's no telling who might overhear us in the BBC headquarters' lobby.

'Drinks am on you,' Boris reminds her as we head towards the doors at the front of the atrium. I don't dignify this with a reply and neither does Mhari. We're both gloomily silent. I can't speak for her, but I'm keeping my thoughts to myself because I'm brooding and irritable. I'm coming down from the adrenalin high of being grilled live on the nation's flagship TV news program, and the crash is something special.

It's spitting with rain, so Boris valiantly steps forward to flag down a taxi while we wait on the plaza out front. Finally, I glance at Mhari. 'Babbling state secrets?'

She stares into the nighttime London traffic, eyebrows lowered in a minute frown, as if trying to decipher messages encoded in the flicker of passing headlights. 'There's a ten-second delay on the live broadcast loop. That's why I was there: to hit the red button if you fucked up, and cover for you if they spotted you planting the bug.'

'Thank you for that vote of confidence.'

'You didn't need me.' She hugs herself against the after-dark chill: she seems to be shaking. In front of us, in the rain, Boris has lowered his head and is speaking through a cab's open side-window. Mhari's cheek twitches slightly as an ivory fang's sharp point pushes against her plumped lower lip. 'Eater of soles. Heh. Well done!' After a moment I realize she's laughing silently.

'I'm never going to live that down, am I?'

It's close to midnight when the taxi drops us off at the Hilton Olympia. Hiltons are reliable and terminally un-hip, so the bar is blessedly free of the hipster crowd who swarm the lobbies of boutique hotels from Hoxton to Hampstead these days. In fact it's empty except for us, and a couple of international men of mystery busy downloading internet porn on their phones as they try to medicate their jet lag with vodka martinis.

(Welcome to my life these days.)

Boris grabs us a booth at one end of the bar. A waitress materializes as Mhari slithers onto the bench seat opposite us. We order: a whisky soda for Boris, a Bud (the Czech kind) for me, and a Bloody Mary for Mhari, because she's not *totally* humorless about her condition. My beer evaporates slowly as Mhari and Boris dissect my interview in painstaking detail. I wave for another just as Mhari gets around to asking the question I've been avoiding for the past hour. 'Do you suppose it's on iPlayer yet, Bob? Do you want to watch it? Your very own fifteen minutes of fame?'

'How about we don't go there?' I raise my new beer. *Glug.* 'I'd like to sleep tonight, thanks. Watching me make an arse of myself on TV will *not* help. *Beer* will help.'

'You didn't make an arse of yourself—' Mhari cocks her head to one side and looks pitying, which irritates the hell out of me. 'That's not a good place to go, Bob.'

'Yes, well: I don't normally go places where I get laughed at by four million people, do I?' I shrug, then put my bottle down, loosen my strangulation device, and unbutton my collar. This time she doesn't try to stop me: okay, so apparently I'm off duty at last. 'It was a total clusterfuck, he was wearing a class six ward. Who ordered *that*?'

Mhari looks at me sharply. 'You're sure? Class six?'

'Yeah. Someone got to him, in addition to briefing against us. Can you—'

She jerks her chin sideways. 'Boris?'

'Am on it,' he says without looking up as he thumb-types away. 'Am emailing the SA nows.'

'Any other surprises?' she asks me, and I shake my head: 'No, but that one was bad enough as it is. It threw me badly.' I scan our surroundings again. You can never be too sure, but nobody seems to be paying any attention to us. 'What was the sticky about, anyway?' The gizmo they wanted me to plant on the underside of the interviewee's chair.

Boris is inspecting his glass in obsessive detail.

'Nobody briefed me on *why*, just on *what*,' Mhari says calmly. 'You did your job, I did mine, that's all.'

'But it's a really bad idea to play that kind of game,' I complain. 'What if it was—'

She looks at me impatiently. 'You did just fine. What you don't know they can't get out of you if they put you under oath and start asking questions. Anyway, they had three victims in that chair yesterday and another scheduled to go on fifteen minutes after you left. If you did it right it's sterile.'

'Who do I raise it with? Through *proper* channels?' I add sarcastic emphasis. I'm not a goddamn errand boy these days and if they want someone to do a plumbing job we've got an entire department for that. Burning your shiny new PR guy's cover by handing him a gray task on his first time out is really not how we're supposed to operate, unless you're planning on firing him the very next day. Although on second thoughts, we're so short-handed right now –

'Send a memo up-stream: am will forward it,' Boris offers. I stare at him. *Okay, so that's why they sent you along, is it?* I nod.

'Beer,' I say grumpily, and take a long pull from my bottle. 'If I'm going to make a fool of myself in public, at least I deserve a beer afterwards.'

'You didn't make a fool of yourself: I think you did quite well,' Mhari says. 'Now can we please change the subject?'

'Make that *two* beers, and I'll just stand in the corner in my jester's cap.' I really hope she's trying to keep my morale up: the last thing I want is a permanent public relations assignment.

'You should talk to Mo,' Mhari suggests unexpectedly.

Stung, my mouth runs ahead of my brain: 'I don't need your that's a *good* idea actually ...' I get as far as pulling out my phone before a glance at the screen tells me it's a bad idea: it's six minutes past midnight already. I might be living in Beer Standard Time, but Mo has just spent last week off-grid in a cottage down at the Village, getting away from it all. She's back at work this week, and I'm certain she'll be burning the candle at both ends catching up with the backlog. She won't thank me for waking her up in the middle of the night for a drunken chat. 'Tomorrow, maybe.'

'*Definitely* tomorrow.' To my surprise Mhari reaches across the table and grabs onto my fingertips. 'This isn't good for either of you. You should *talk* to her.'

I pull back, but her grip tightens. After a moment I stop. 'Why the sudden concern?'

She hesitates momentarily. 'I like Mo and I have to work with you. She's been in a bad place recently and you weren't there for her, and now you're heading for a bad place too, and—' She lets go of my hand and shrugs again, her shoulder pads miming a vampire princess's bat-wings – 'I'm just concerned.'

I can't hold back a slightly bitter smile. 'So, no hidden agenda.'

'No, Bob, no hidden agenda.' Her answering smile is full of history. Hers, and mine (we were an item for a while, back before I met my wife). 'As I get older I find friendship gets ever more precious.' She's my age, but she could pass for late twenties. She used to be pretty but when she got PHANG syndrome she turned supermodel glamorous: it's as if she's aging backwards, living along some sort of *femme fatale* eigenvector that's iteratively converging on *Big Sleep*-era Lauren Bacall. 'I can see where we're going more clearly these days. I don't want to hit eighty on my own.'

'To friends.' I raise my drink to cover my confusion. The beer's running low so I wave my hand for a third (and final) bottle. Mhari has always been better than me at people skills. It's taken me this long to appreciate her for what she is, now that we're not going at each other like a pair of cats with their tails tied together.

'Absent friends,' grunts Boris, surfacing from his whisky. He waves for another.

'Friends dead, alive, and undead.' Her eyes glance side-long around the bar, scanning. When she's sure it's safe, she continues: 'You realize this isn't over, don't you?'

I put the empty bottle down. Can't get away from it, can I? 'Yes.' The waitress is on her way: either it's a quiet night or my Obtain Bar Service feat just leveled up alarmingly. When she departs I continue. 'Someone in the Cabinet Office will have seen it for sure. Questions will be asked, it'll be on the PM's morning briefing, and I'll be up before the beak, won't I?' Boris chuckles and Mhari giggles. 'So I assume we'll be debriefing first . . . ' Then, right on cue, Mhari's phone buzzes.

'Yup: looks like we have a meeting scheduled for nine hundred hours, Room 406, chaired by the Senior Auditor.' Mhari frowns. I wince slightly at the specter of the SA. He's not someone you want to get on the wrong side of. I must look aghast because she adds: 'Mo is on the invite list, so I'm pretty sure this is not about you.'

'What?'

'Trust me, if the Auditors were planning a Bob roast they wouldn't invite your wife to the barbecue.' Then Mhari glances up from her smartphone screen, and despite the reassuring words she looks troubled: 'He's booked half the Audit Committee, plus Vik Choudhury and a couple of heavy hitters from the Executive Committee. It's all very Mahogany Row: I can't figure it out. But they wouldn't roll the Senior Auditor out to chair it if this was anything less than critical, don't you think?'

'Well fuck.' I pick up my third (and, I remind myself, final) beer. 'You know what this means.'

Boris looks at me, then Mhari looks at me, and we chorus: 'The reward for a job not fucked up is *another* job.'

I finish my beer and dutifully stagger off to my hotel room, while Mhari returns to the office – she works the night shift these days – and Boris heads home. I assume he has a home. Right now, I don't. I live out of a suitcase pretty much constantly. I'm traveling so much that Accounts don't even blink at my subsistence claims any more. I'm in London so little that it's cheaper to pay for the odd hotel night using loyalty points than to find a permanent room somewhere, and I'm still hoping to patch things up enough to go home.

But in the here and now, I am coming to hate liminal spaces like airport terminals and hotel rooms.

Sleep takes a while to arrive. I can dimly sense the minds and dreams of the other hotel guests around me: walls and floor and ceiling are no barrier to souls. It's kind of sooth-ing. Some insomniacs count sheep. I keep separate tallies of shaggers, porn channel junkies, and insomniacs. Eventually I manage to tune my brain to the slumber channel and drift off for a few hours, untroubled by the usual nightmares.

Morning arrives much too soon in the shape of a bleeping hotel alarm clock and a DJ on Capital Radio yattering excitedly about somebody's new album, and how the London stock exchange is reopening and Sterling seems to have arrested its slide because the Chancellor is pointing a firehose of Treasury money at the smoking wreckage of West Yorkshire. It is still unclear whether the Secretary of State for Defense is going to fall on his sword; he seems to be trying to hang on, but the Prime Minister has just said that he 'has complete confidence' in him, and you know what that means. I turn the radio off and shamble in the direction of the shower cubicle.

This is an office day rather than a public speaking gig, so I throw the suit in the suit carrier, pull on combat pants, tee-shirt, and hoodie, and check my email and calendar schedule over a full cooked hotel breakfast. I'm still yawning as I check out and catch a bus to the office, and I'm nearly there when I realize I've forgotten to shave and my shaver is in the bottom of the suitcase left in the left-luggage room back at the hotel. *Great.*

Our temporary headquarters is the New Annex, which we moved into for six months just over five years ago. It's still in use even though Facilities have been unable to get the bloodstains out of the walls and its security is terminally compromised. The first HQ redevelopment stalled due to site contamination, then the fallback plan – a new headquarters up the M1 in Leeds – was trashed less than two weeks ago, along with the rest of Leeds city center. London property prices are so nose-bleedingly insane that we can't even find temporary quarters in the capital, so we're stuck with the New Annex even though it's unfit for purpose and should be demolished.

But the past weeks have brought changes, some of them externally visible. We didn't have armed police standing by the entrance before, making it obvious that we are something more important than a fly-by-night call center operation. Now we've got two of them, and they're not your regular SO19 bods, either: they're wearing matte black Imperial Stormtrooper gear with Metropolitan Police badges, full face helmets, and *really* scary-looking guns instead of the usual assault rifles. They check me for tentacles and I show them my warrant card, then they let me in. Security, we haz it: *rah*. Only I fumble and drop my card, bend to pick it up, and realize I showed them my driving license by mistake.

The main staircase is closed off above the ground floor so I have to take the indoors fire escape up to the fourth floor to get to the designated meeting room. It's a steep climb so when I reach the second-floor landing I pause to dump my suit carrier and messenger bag in my office, then grab a mug of what passes for coffee from the kitchenette next door to the number three briefing room.

'Hey, Mr. Howard! Have you got a minute?'

I manage not to spill my coffee. It's one of the new guys, from Facilities: young (was I ever that young?), eager (was I ever that enthusiastic?), and unaware that it is a *really bad idea* to startle a DSS before he's had his morning coffee. 'Yes?' I demand, my pulse slowing, quite proud of myself for neither grunting nor snarling.

'Um, hi, I'm Jon, and I'm supposed to be auditing the network cable runs for the Ops offices in this wing because there's this overdue requirement for a structured cabling refresh, and I need to get access to your office so I can inspect the junction box and make sure it's properly terminated?'

Jon has a hipster beard and wears thick-rimmed glasses and a check shirt with a button-down collar that doesn't quite conceal his tattoos, but in every other respect it's eerily like looking at myself in a time-shifted mirror set to fifteen years ago. I find it oddly depressing. He seems eager to please, and killing him would result in altogether too much paperwork of an excruciatingly dull variety, so I just shake my head. 'I've got a meeting in five minutes, but I can fit you in afterwards – knock on my office door around eleven thirty?'

'Sure!' He nods happily.

A thought strikes me. 'By the way, if I'm *not* in my office you mustn't try to gain entry without me. I keep hazardous materials there. Stuff that might scramble your mind if you get too close.' Actually it's all in a secure document safe full of catatonia-inducing memos, protected by wards that will set fire to the contents if anyone meddles with them, causing the badly maintained sprinklers to go off, but there's no need to tell him that. 'Also, if you need to gain access to Mr. Angleton's room – down J Corridor and along, it's at the bottom of the stairwell next to the chained-up fire exit – fetch me. Same warning applies, except he used nukes while I make do with hand grenades.'

It's not until I'm back on the fire escape, trudging upstairs to my meeting with the SA and other members of the Mahogany Row Oversight board, that I realize the kid's got my old job.

Mahogany Row refers both to the furnishings on the executive floor of our original HQ building* and to the folks

---

* Now a hole in the ground, soon to be a shiny new investment opportunity for offshore property speculators.

who use those offices: senior management, Auditors, external assets, Deeply Scary Sorcerers, and other questionable types. I'm technically one of them these days, although I'm fucked if I know why. The main qualifications seem to be exhibiting an aptitude for ritual magic or executive leadership, and not dying on the job. At least that's how the organization got started, back when it was the Invisible College and nobody really knew how this stuff worked. The Laundry as it now exists sprang up during a wartime emergency and was subsequently re-purposed to provide backup for the Deeply Scary Sorcerers. Anyway, I have never felt at ease in the thick-pile carpeted corridors and offices full of antique furniture and paintings from the Government Art Collection. It feels like a very exclusive gentlemen's club, and I'm the kind of oik who would be blackballed if he wasn't useful to have around.

I make it to Room 406 on the spot of nine. Dr. Armstrong is already sitting at the front, calmly sipping tea from a fine china cup. There's a big TV screen and DVD player on a stand in one corner, presumably so we can all have a good laugh at me making a fool of myself. As I hunt for a seat that doesn't make me feel uneasily exposed the door opens again. This time it's Persephone's turn to do a double-take, which doesn't give me any kind of happy fun feeling. Persephone Hazard likes to dress like a mafia heiress from Marseilles, living *la dolce vita* with a Beretta in her handbag – which just goes to show that appearances are deceptive: she's the most powerful witch in London. (Also, I happen to know that she carries an FN Five-seveN with an AAC sound suppressor and a 20-round magazine full of microengraved banishment rounds. Berettas are for amateurs.) She nods in my direction, then engages Dr. Armstrong directly. 'Did you see the news this morning?'

The SA smiles his saintly smile – the one he rolls out just before he brains you with a sledgehammer – and says, 'I must confess I never turn on the television before the sun's over the yard arm.'

'It wasn't me!' I protest, before I realize that given a twenty-four-hour news cycle *it might very well* have been me.

But I'm in luck. 'No, it wasn't,' 'Seph agrees. 'Your performance on *Newsnight* would have been a vast improvement over this morning's headlines.' Her fine nostrils flare. 'What *is* the world coming to?'

'I'm sure I don't know,' Dr. Armstrong says placidly. 'Help yourself to tea and biscuits, dear. We may be some time.'

I force myself to sit down. 'Seph is really rattled, but it's not my fault. She's one of our heavy hitters, a deniable external asset who generally tackles the kind of assignment that on old reruns of *Mission: Impossible* is tagged with 'the Secretary will disavow any knowledge of your actions.'

'I thought this was the post-mortem for the media outreach event,' I say as the door opens again and Vik Choudhury slides in. 'That's what's down in my calendar.'

'Seph rolls her eyes as Dr. Armstrong shakes his head, more in sorrow than in anger. 'Oh dear, no! I'm afraid we've been pre-empted by events.'

That does not sound good. 'Was it something I did?'

'Your drop went just fine,' Vikram assures me. To 'Seph, and the other attendees: 'Mhari delivered her payload to the edit suite and Bob successfully bugged the underside of the studio's number two visitor chair. And now we've got six SPIN DIAMOND grids transmitting from the newsroom, thanks to your masterful distraction.'

'I don't see why you couldn't just substitute the contract cleaners—'

'It's a *newsroom*, Bob,' Persephone sniffs. 'They weren't born yesterday. Security vetting the cleaners goes with the territory.'

'Well. I hope it was worth it. That kind of op usually ends in tears, in my experience – too much chance of blowback—'

'Too late to worry about spilt milk, Mr. Howard.' Dr. Armstrong stares at the ceiling, steepling his fingertips. 'This meeting is starting late,' he adds, 'so we are not yet on the official record. But can I request a change of subject?'

Gulp. Even 'Seph has the decency to look bashful. 'Sure,' I say.

The door opens again, this time to admit a stranger. 'Bob, this is Chris Womack from Administration and Policy.' She's a tall woman, mid-fifties at a guess, a no-nonsense senior Civil Service type. I stand, and we shake hands. 'Chris, Bob is Dr. Angleton's replacement. You can trust him implicitly, subject to keyword clearance.' Which tells me in turn that the Senior Auditor trusts her implicitly.

'I saw you on *Newsnight* last night,' she says, smiling guardedly, which makes me feel so much better.

'What can I say?' I shrug. 'Opportunities to make a fool of myself in front of such a large audience only come along once in a lifetime.'

'Bob enjoys playing the departmental jester,' says Persephone. She smiles. 'Don't worry, Bob, you get to do this again.' *Ouch.*

'Absolutely.' Ms. Womack's smile widens. 'You did quite well,' she adds, 'for a first-timer. Let me know if you ever feel the urge to go into public relations full-time.'

'I'll be sure to do that.' Shortly after a squadron of pigs are observed taking off from Heathrow Airport.

The door opens again and this time my brain freezes as eyes meet across a crowded conference room. The late arrival also freezes as the SA smoothly takes over: 'Chris, this is Dr. O'Brien, Dominique, this is Chris Womack, our Chief Counsel. Mo is the newest member of the Audit Board—' My wife raises an eyebrow at me and I nod, then pull the seat beside me back from the table to make room for her. My pulse is running too fast. *Mhari was right*, I realize. But there's too much to say, it's forming a pile-up behind my tongue, and anyway Dr. Armstrong is still speaking – 'time to call this meeting to order now we're all here—'

She sits down next to me and leans sideways to whisper in my ear. 'Your office, after we're finished here?'

I nod. The SA is continuing: 'Crisis containment and management in the wake of this month's events have broken down. The usual mass observation protocol simply doesn't work for an incursion on this scale. Also, the activation of PLAN RED RABBIT and the subsequent need to brief the Cabinet Office emergency committee and bring the full civil contingencies apparatus up to speed means that awareness of the agency's existence is now widespread.' *That's* an understatement and a half: the crisis hasn't been out of the headlines for weeks. 'Pointed questions are being raised in the House of Commons, there have been ministerial resignations and a vote of confidence that narrowly failed to bring down the government, another reshuffle is planned, and it doesn't stop there. Maneuvering by various factions in the cabinet suggests that a leadership coup within the leading party in the coalition is likely if the Prime Minister isn't seen to clean house rapidly. Chris is here to brief us on the past week's political developments, our position in terms to the Constitutional Reform and Governance Act – which is anomalous – and the likely implications for the organization.'

Ms. Womack stands up. 'Thank you, Mike.' (*Mike?* I boggle at the familiarity.) 'Well, folks, this is what we've been afraid would happen all along: an intrusion on such a large scale that local assets were unable to contain it, resulting in widespread loss of civilian life, exposure of the agency to public scrutiny, and extreme pressure on the government to be seen to be doing something about the crisis.' She actually *smiles*, a slightly embarrassed expression, and it's at this point that I know for a fact that we're screwed. Mo takes my hand under the table and squeezes it; I squeeze right back. At least we're in this together.

Chris continues: 'It's been glaringly obvious that this day would come, sooner or later – hopefully later – for the past half century, so we have a backgrounder on the likely course of events to hand, regularly updated, and a fallback plan to execute. Here it is, if you'd all care to sign for it.' She slides a clipboard onto the table. It's one of those briefings you have to sign in at. As the clipboard circulates, she continues: 'In the immediate future, there'll be a lot of media interest and a whiff of scandal and prurient curiosity over a hitherto-secret security agency coming to light. Expect digging and doxxing of any identifiable faces associated with the organization. I'm afraid that means Mr. Howard is particularly exposed, although that masterful display on *Newsnight* might just convince the uglier elements of the press that he's not worth bothering with. But the personal attention *should* – we hope – die down within another week or so, at least until the Defense Select Committee starts holding hearings.'

A murmur runs around the table. Then the clipboard gets to me. I sign with numb fingers then slide it in front of Mo.

'That's not the real problem I'm here to talk about today. The big short-term issue is what the government is going to do with us – about the Laundry, I mean. Historically we were founded under the Royal Prerogative, as was the rest of the Civil Service or Crown Service, as variously defined. CRAG (2010), the Constitutional Reform and Governance Act, put most of the Civil Service on a sound constitutional footing and defined their obligations to uphold the law, and more importantly, laid out the exceptional circumstances under which civil servants might be licensed to take extrajudicial actions – for example the armed forces and our sister agencies, MI5, SIS, and GCHQ. As a rather peculiar unadmitted Crown entity, the Laundry exists in something of a gray area.

'The historic lack of oversight has given us a degree of autonomy unavailable to our sister agencies, but all that's about to come to an abrupt end. At a minimum, we can expect the Committee to recommend that we be brought under the oversight of the Joint Intelligence Committee with defined limitations like the other security services. We can also expect primary legislation to regulate computational thaumaturgy and related fields and bring in criminal penalties for misuse. The Consumer Protection Regulations that superseded the Fraudulent Mediums Act and the Witchcraft Act (1735) in 2008 don't really cover us, I'm afraid. But if the Cabinet are paying attention – and unfortunately we know for a fact that the Cabinet *is* paying attention – we're about to become a political football.'

The clipboard makes its way back to Ms. Womack and she briefly checks that we've all signed the form. Then she opens up her briefcase and pulls out a stack of document wallets. 'One copy each, please. Read and return to this room no later than five o'clock this afternoon; you'll need to sign them back in. They're warded, eyes-only.' Which is to say that *really bad things* will happen to any eyeballs that belong to people who haven't signed on that clipboard and who even glance at the table of contents.

'What exactly *is* this?' Persephone asks, tapping her secure document wallet suspiciously.

'It's a legal analysis of our organizational position, going forward.' Chris frowns at her. 'In it you'll find our worst-case analyses of how the government can fuck us over. The bad news is, one likely outcome of the current situation – if they try to cram us into the existing CRAG framework – is that our core mission becomes irrecoverably compromised. But the good news is, we have a contingency plan. It's called PLAN TITANIC. And you'll find a synopsis at the end of this file.'

'What's the elevator pitch?' 'Seph pushes.

Chris counters with another question. 'What's the most important part of the organization, from an operational standpoint?'

'It would be—' Persephone's eyes widen. 'Mahogany Row?'

Mo sits up. 'You're talking about a lifeboat, aren't you?' she says. Chris is silent, but her face speaks for her.

'Seph fans herself with the TOP SECRET file. 'You're talking about abandoning the sinking ship . . .'

Elsewhere:

It's a busy morning at the general aviation terminal at Stansted airport, and another Falcon 7X executive jet arriving from Denver draws no unusual attention. Neither does the small convoy of vehicles waiting for it on the apron. There's a stretched black BMW limo with darkened windows for the VIPs, a pair of black BMW SUVs with equally blacked-out rear windows for security, and a car in airport service livery for the immigration and customs concierge service that the jet's owner is paying for.

The immigration officer is waiting alongside as the air stairs drop. She spends less than a minute scanning passports. The visitor holds a diplomatic visa and you *don't* want to keep people like that waiting: they generally have friends in high places who will make your boss yell at you if you hold them up. Her counterpart from Customs is equally efficient: entry forms are collected, 'Are you carrying anything illegal? Any drugs, endangered species, or plant material?' is asked, and the all-clear is given immediately. The officers are long gone by the time the Reverend Raymond Schiller sets foot on English soil again for the first time in nearly two years, and leads his staff in offering up a pro-forma prayer of thanksgiving.

Outwardly, Schiller is the very image of a successful televangelist. He's tall but trim, early sixties but spry, his silver hair immaculately coiffed. He wears a conservatively cut charcoal suit and a navy blue tie, a small lapel-pin cross the only obvious adornment. His smile is kindly; his blue eyes twinkle so brightly that it is almost impossible to imagine the damned soul screaming behind them.

As Schiller slides into the back seat of the limousine and straps himself in, his personal assistant Anneka takes her position opposite. A prim ice-blonde in a gray skirt-suit and white silk blouse, she sits with her knees clamped as tightly as her lips. She could pass for a lawyer or a corporate marketing director on the way up, but in the curious parlance of Schiller's sect she is a handmaid, chosen by God to be Schiller's helpmeet and cellphone carrier. Schiller has certain requirements that his handmaids must meet, and Anneka is a paragon. The personal protection officers and other staff – accountant, paralegal, personal chef, and poison taster – take their seats in the SUVs behind. Schiller watches as the jet's other passenger, a representative of the government agency he subcontracts for, nods affably, then walks away towards the embassy car that's waiting for him. Finally, satisfied that all is well, Anneka locks the heavy armored door and secures the briefcase.

There's a brief crackle of static from the intercom, then the driver says, 'We're ready to move when you are, sir.'

Anneka glances at Schiller: he nods minutely, and she touches the intercom button. 'Proceed in convoy as planned. Please notify us when we are fifteen minutes out from the apartment, or in event of unforeseen delays.' As the heavy bulletproof limousine begins to move she pushes a switch beside the intercom button, disconnecting the microphone. A faint, jaw-tensing buzz of white noise begins to leak from the windows all around, and Schiller relaxes infinitesimally.

'Sweep please.'

'Yes, Father.'

She raises her briefcase and opens it. Its contents would be of considerable interest to the customs officer, if performing his official duties was not actively discouraged when admitting a certain class of visitor. It's not just the Glock 17 clipped inside the lid – civilian possession of which carries a mandatory five-year prison sentence in the UK – but the MilSpec electronics in the lower half. Anneka plugs the case into the cigarette lighter socket, then conducts a thorough and exhaustive scan of the limousine's interior for wireless surveillance devices as the convoy queues up at the exit gate from the General Aviation area. This takes some time, and they are on the approach road to the M11 motorway by the time she unplugs the case, closes it, and ducks her head at Schiller. 'We are alone, Father.'

Schiller smiles almost wryly. 'We are never alone, Daughter.' It's his little joke and she delivers an appreciative smile on cue. 'Are there any new messages?'

Anneka's Blackberry chimes and she raises it to eye level. 'No high-priority messages in the past hour,' she recites. The bizjet carries a satellite picocell to keep its passengers in touch over the ocean, but even Schiller's wealth can't insulate him from the leasing company's tiresome requirement to shut down all passenger electronics during final approach and landing. 'The Secretary of State sends his very general best wishes, of course, but nothing confidential. There's an update from Alison: she's working to confirm that all designated attendees will be present at your briefings tomorrow. Bernadette McGuigan would like to bring you up to speed on the current state of targeted operations at your earliest convenience. And there is a personal greeting from Mr. Michaels's secretary.' She pauses momentarily, pupils dilating slightly. 'Requesting the pleasure of your company at a garden party on Saturday, RSVP. At an address somewhere in Buckinghamshire.' She lowers the smartphone, looks quizzical. 'Father?'

Schiller nods thoughtfully. 'Let the Prime Minister know I'd be delighted to attend. Reschedule any conflicting engagements.'

Anneka nods dutifully and begins to thumb-type rapidly. She doesn't notice Schiller's smile sharpen slightly, sliding briefly into a predatory mask. Jeremy Michaels is a very astute player: he does not issue social invitations to just anyone. If he has realized what is going on and decided to acquiesce to Schiller's plan, then that is very good indeed, and the acquisition Schiller has come to the UK to facilitate will run much more smoothly. Takeovers are always easier if the people at the top of the target establishment are willing collaborators.

Some invasions barely warrant the name.

2: THE COMSTOCK OFFICE IS CLOSING

Now hear this:

It has become glaringly obvious – Chris Womack's briefing backgrounder went into great detail on the subject – that the legal and political ramifications of the Laundry being outed are drastic, open-ended, and worrying.

Q-Division, SOE – our official name – has come to the attention of the Cabinet Office. And the CO promptly had a fit of the vapors when they discovered an inexplicably overlooked branch of the Civil Service, unregulated under CRAG (2010), acting in the gray area reserved for the military and security services (but without their constitutional enabling framework and oversight).

It would have been bad enough if said organization consisted of four pensioners in a Nissen hut, playing cards and reminiscing about the Malayan Emergency. As it is, we have over 9,000 employees, £1.2Bn of Crown Estate properties, a small but terrifyingly proficient special forces detachment associated with the Special Reconnaissance Regiment (the successor to the SAS), and a remit to conduct covert operations all over the world. We don't cost *quite* as much to run as GCHQ – if only because we don't launch our own spy satellites – but there are any number of things about the Laundry which are deeply unpalatable to anyone from a government service background, starting with our lack of accountability and going on from there.

Governments are machines for producing and implementing legal frameworks. We don't have one, and the Civil Service's reaction to this is much like Superman's reaction upon discovering that the lump under his mattress is an entire paving slab of Kryptonite ...

... And this is before you throw panicking senior politicians and their backstabbing rivals and murky international alliances into the mix.

That the nation needs an occult defense agency is obvious to everyone who's seen the smoldering wreckage in Yorkshire (although to be perfectly honest this excludes a considerable number of Home Counties MPs, who don't really believe the UK extends north of Watford Gap). That the Laundry is doing a good job in this role is much less obvious, in light of the aforementioned smoldering wreckage. That the Prime Minister has been *personally embarrassed* by our failure to prevent an attack by a psychotic *alfär* general has already been made crystal-clear to us. And because this is now a political problem, the usual political syllogism applies:

(a) is a problem: Something Must Be Done,
(b) is Something,
(c) Therefore (b) Must Be Done.

The only questions remaining are, who gets to decide what Solution (b) is, and how are we going to implement – or survive – it?

Schiller's cortege drives around the M25 to an anonymous office park on the outskirts of Harrow, where GP Security

Systems have a suite. While he and his immediate retinue – handmaids, bodyguards, drivers – enter the building, other staff off-load his team's luggage and peel off in different directions: some towards the apartment he is renting in London, and others to a different site in rural Buckinghamshire.

This is of little concern to Schiller. He moves at the heart of a soft machine, its limbs and heads and bodies smoothly coordinating around him to ensure that his needs are anticipated and taken care of. Polite, respectful receptionists and smiling senior managers await him in the glass-fronted lobby of the office. He is ushered straight into an elevator that has been held for him, whisked to the boardroom suite on the sixth floor, offered refreshments and paid respects as Anneka conducts her routine sweep for bugging devices and then attaches a noise generator to the window glass to block laser microphones.

Finally Anneka tips him the wink and Schiller takes his seat. 'Ladies and gentlemen,' he announces. 'May I have your attention?' Half a dozen senior managers and executives turn their heads. 'I believe a brief prayer of thanksgiving is in order, then we'll begin. Thank you, oh Father, for the gift of life, the continued mysteries of creation, for guarding our thoughts against evil and our bodies against sin, for granting us the boon of thy grace and redemption. Thank you, oh Father, for showing us the way ahead, for giving us the book, and the key, and the word of thy law. Thy will be done, and thy kingdom on Earth be ours to build in the future as it was in aeons past beneath alien skies, amen.'

All heads are bowed, lips moving in prayer, for all those present are true believers and security-cleared initiates of at least the Middle Temple mysteries. (Employment Law forbids discrimination on the basis of faith, but GP Security

Systems is a wholly-owned subsidiary of GP Services; unbelievers tend not to stick around, let alone achieve seniority.) Schiller finishes, then sits in silent contemplation for a minute before clearing his throat. 'Miss McGuigan.' He looks across the table. 'How far along are you with the arrangements for Operation Hospitality?'

Bernadette McGuigan, who is skinny and intense with milky skin and coppery hair, lays a proprietary hand on the plain cross embossed in the leather cover of her day planner. 'It's coming along, Father. I've requested quotes from three private venues that can match your schedule and preferred location. Two of them are also-rans, but I've been sure to let them all know it's an open tender. On the personnel side, I've got Martin vetting local catering firms and I'm taking charge of security myself. They've all signed the NDAs, and the usual sources confirm that there's no chatter about the draft plan. I propose to use only our in-house resources – I'm going to outsource a handful of low-level non-sec jobs to subcontractors in order to free up our own people.' She gives Anneka a brief side-eye: 'It's been impressed upon me that Temple rules apply.'

Schiller nods, satisfied. 'Only the Elect are called to serve as Soldiers of Light,' he murmurs. Heads nod. 'Good,' he adds briskly. 'What do you foresee as scheduling choke-points at this time?'

Bernadette stands. 'I've got it all charted out,' she announces, picking up a laptop remote controller. 'Projector, please . . .'

For the next half hour the meeting is devoted to critiquing McGuigan's project time-line. Her work is sound, and although Schiller requests some minor changes (as much to leave his mark on it as anything else), the review doesn't take long: the main benefit is that by the time she finishes explaining everything, everyone at the table is intimately familiar with Operation Hospitality, its goals and deliverables.

'Thank you.' Schiller twinkles at her as she returns to her seat. 'Next agenda item: I believe this is yours, Mr. Taylor.' All eyes turn towards a bullet-headed man in early middle-age, whose tailored suit doesn't do much to conceal his background as a bouncer. 'What *is* the state of our threat surface in this country?'

Garry Taylor's smile doesn't reach his eyes. 'Dangerously exposed, boss. Not enough communicants to cover all bases, no way to hasten expansion beyond the obvious—' he coughs and covers his mouth apologetically – 'sorry, but without special dispensation we're limited to working with what we've got, and even with your blessed additions we're stretched thin on the ground. Against which, there is the enemy's situational awareness to reckon with. I've been running searches on the names our friends in the OPA* gave us, and I have some bad news. Hazard and her pet thug are inaccessible but at least they keep to a low profile; their known associate Howard is now a public figure, he's even getting TV exposure as a spokesman for the target. If he identifies you in public that would be a, well, that would be an unacceptable risk of exposure. So I've detailed a sub-contractor to identify his handles – family, friends, vices, anything they can get through the usual – and shadow him. If you want us to put them in the hospital for a few weeks—'

'No, that won't be necessary,' Schiller says flatly. 'Just keep out of sight and log all his contacts. Only exception is if a name on the OPA's Termination Expedient list comes

---

* The Operational Phenomenology Agency, a secretive US government agency known to their friends as the Black Chamber and to everybody else as the Nazgûl.

up. If that happens—' Schiller shrugs – 'I wash my hands of them.'

'Understood, boss.' Garry makes a note on his Blackberry. 'Will that be all?'

Schiller's smile is thin as a paper-cut. 'Howard and his fellows will get their just reward in heaven; with our Lord's strength and the cooperation of our fellow Americans we will prevail.' For a moment his eyes flash emerald with a glowing, unhuman fervor: 'Victory is near; let's not mess it up this time.'

As it turns out, Mo and I do not get a chance to put our heads together in my office right after Ms. Womack drops the bomb, because we both get dragged off to different crisis meetings. In my case it's a session with Vik and 'Seph to discuss how we're going to cover the long-term absence of several senior personnel from External Assets and Active Ops (let's not use phrases like 'suspended on full pay pending a public enquiry, possible criminal charges to follow'). We also discuss how best to shelter certain lower-level personnel who may have inadvertently come to the attention of Very Important People – we don't want them to be called to account for stuff they're not responsible for.

Consider the salutary example of Dr. Alex Schwartz, former pencil-necked geek, now vampire. I will freely admit that I don't like the little toe-rag – the first time we met he nearly punched me through an office wall, *and* he's a bloodsucking fiend – but some of the more excitable tabloid columnists are calling for him to be tried for treason, which is a bit rich for my taste. Even if sanity prevails he can expect a long and promising career as a political punch-bag and an object lesson in why we do not allow junior officers to negotiate peace treaties with hostile alien empires. But hanging him out to dry won't save us from a witch-hunt, won't set any kind of good example for the rest of us, and will deprive the organization of a little toe-rag who made the best of a really bad job and shows considerable promise for the future. And so on.

I stumble out of the meeting room with a list of bullet points echoing around the inside of my skull, the beginnings of a really special headache, and a rumbling stomach. As soon as I get past the Faraday-shielded wallpaper and into the corridor my phone vibrates. It's a text from Mo. She's running late too, and suggests catching up in the canteen. I groan.

Actually, I groan prematurely. When I get there I discover that it has been upgraded since the last time I was in town, in a desperate attempt to staunch the lunchtime exodus and thereby make life easier for the guards on the front door. They've repainted the walls, replaced the chairs and tables with ones that date to the current century, *laid carpet* (Facilities are clearly living dangerously), and as for the menu ... oh my goodness, it's come over all gastropub. Of course you still can't have a beer or a glass of wine with your lunch, but the food itself is subsidized and the portions are plentiful. Being under siege by eldritch horrors clearly has a silver lining, so I go and fetch myself a latte and something that claims to be bruschetta with a topping of mozzarella and rosemary, then go find a corner to lurk in.

Ten minutes later I'm doing my daily updates to my twitter feed – we're required to maintain a boringly vague social media presence these days, just so we don't stand out like a sore thumb when foreign agencies sweep the net in search of spies – when Mo approaches. She puts her tray down and pulls out her chair as I try and think of something to say. 'Well?' she asks, unwrapping the paper serviette from around her cutlery.

I shrug and bite off a mouthful of flatbread and smashed tomatoes in olive oil while I put my brain in gear. It buys me a couple of seconds. 'I gather congratulations are in order,' I try.

A frown flickers across her face, just a microexpression but enough to make me wince. 'Not you, too?'

I mime thumping the side of my head: 'A knight's move up the org chart is usually considered grounds for congrat- ulation, but given the square you've landed on, I can see why you might be conflicted about it.' It's not much of an apology but she nods warily, then takes a sip of her mineral water, and pokes at her chicken Caesar salad, checking it for threats. I try not to twitch. She may be back from med- ical leave but she's still broadcasting WHOOP WHOOP RED ALERT stress signals on all the emergency frequencies I can pick up. 'Bad meeting?'

She nods and swallows convulsively, leaving her fork hanging in front of her mouth. 'You could say that.' She pauses a moment, makes the food disappear – a very good sign – then continues: 'Dealing with a lot of follow-up and loose ends left over from Operation INCORRIGIBLE, to say nothing of Leeds.' She dry-swallows, then reaches for her mineral water. 'I'm not looking forward to that,' she adds: 'my first time on an Audit Board and it has to be *that* one.'

Oh yes, that would explain her mood. The Auditors will be all over the mess in Leeds. Power to bind and release, enforcement of oath of office, that sort of thing. Authority to lay charges before the Black Assizes, our very own Star Chamber, potentially unlimited penalties: sobering stuff to say the least. Never mind the House of Commons Select

Committee on Intelligence. 'There's a difference between intentional malfeasance and failure to recognize and respond to an unprecedented threat optimally,' I remind her. One's a soul-stripping offense, at least potentially; the other is just grounds for additional training and supervision. 'This isn't an Iris Carpenter scenario.'

I was trying to reassure her but I've obviously said something wrong because Mo jolts as if I just kicked her under the table and glares, eyes narrowed: '*What* did you just say?'

'Uh?' I boggle. Iris was my manager from hell a few years ago: *very* good at her job, except she'd somehow fooled her oath of office (the *geas* by which all Laundry staff are bound) into letting her lead a congregation of the Church of the Black Pharaoh. I rub my upper right arm self-consciously: it still aches occasionally where her hellspawn offspring took a chunk out of me and ate it, consuming Bob sashimi as a kind of unholy communion. (I survived: that's enough.) 'I'm just saying, this isn't an Iris situation: we have met the enemy and it ain't us. There is no treason here, the SA is breaking you in gently.' Iris disappeared into one of the organization's deeper oubliettes shortly after her abortive summoning turned the UK's largest graveyard into a zombie rave. I haven't heard anything about her since I got pulled off the COBWEB MAZE committee, so I suppose she's still in prison. I'm not generally vindictive or vengeful, but if she's on the outside she'd better hope she never bumps into me, is all.

(I haven't forgiven her for the thing with the baby and the sacrificial altar.)

Mo uncoils slightly. 'Well,' she says, 'that's all I can say for now.' Her eyes swivel sidelong: 'This is no place to talk shop.' Even though it's a canteen in a regional headquarters building of a top secret agency, loose lips are discouraged outside meeting rooms or warded offices. 'Especially about this morning's stink bomb.'

Uh-oh: I see where this conversation is going. 'Well, I've been doing a bit of thinking,' I admit, then pause to polish off my bruschetta.

'Thinking is dangerous, Bob.' There's a drip of my wife's old, dry affection there, under all the stress-bunny anxiety and borderline PTSD.

'Do you want to make another go of it?' It slips out without my thinking it consciously, and I freeze, watching her freeze as she watches me right back. Her expression is haunted. (I *think* that's the right word for it.)

'We can't go back to the way we were,' she says, but there's uncertainty and regret there, so I push, hoping I'm not trying too hard –

'What about the spare room? We could clear it out and put a really heavy-duty ward on it—' The spare room in our house is a joke. Officially it's a bedroom, but this being London, that needs clarifying as 'bedroom 2, suitable for small child or gerbil.'

Mo's lips thin: 'It's too small, unless we throw out a bunch of junk, and even then ... not viable, love. Anyway, it's not safe for you to move back in: what if you sleepwalk while I'm going to the bathroom in the night?'

'But you're an Auditor, dammit! That's hardly defense-less, *I* should be afraid of *you*—'

I manage to stop myself before I can say anything inexcusable.

Mo shakes her head. Around the canteen I see people pointedly ignoring the married couple raising their voices in the corner. It's as if we've got our very own invisibility field. 'No, Bob,' she says tiredly, 'mutually assured destruction is *not* a reasonable basis for a marriage. Sooner or later one of us will get over-stressed, there'll be an argument, and it'll be the kind of domestic that starts with thrown crockery and levels up to grenade launchers. Only we don't max out at "high explosives, handle with care" any more. This isn't *Mr. & Mrs. Smith*. We've got to find a better way.'

'Do you have any ideas?' I ask.

She gives me a guarded look that screams *nothing up my sleeve, nothing to see here*, then goes back to digging in her salad. I watch her in frustration. Presently she says, 'On the subject of your being the Eater of Souls, I want to do some digging in the archives, follow up a couple of loose ends. There's nothing else exactly like it but maybe TEAPOT ...' She trails off into thoughtful silence, then pauses. 'In the meantime, we could try counseling? See if that shakes something loose.'

'Counseling.' I know the word but I don't know what it means, at least not at a gut level. 'Um. What? I mean, why? It's not like—' I swallow – 'I still love you.'

'Yes, I know.' She puts her fork down and reaches across the table for my hand. I have an unaccountable feeling that I somehow said the wrong thing, although I'm not sure how. 'But that's not why marriages end, is it? At least, not always. A lot of the time it's because one or both partners have gotten into ways of behaving that the other can't live with, or because one or both are going through a period of personal growth and the other isn't keeping up or isn't on the same track, or because they're both stressed out. And that *last* one applies to us like nothing else. We've hit an impasse. It's not even about us both sleeping with a loaded gun under the pillow. Metaphorical loaded gun ... It's the responsibility, Bob. We need to talk about me being an Auditor and you being what you are and it just isn't happening and the longer we leave it the worse the pressure will get, and even if we find a way to live together we'll end up squabbling because of the stress.'

I don't understand exactly what she thinks we need to talk about, but maybe that's half the problem. So I nod and try to look as if I understand, because listening is half of the solution. 'Going to need a security-cleared counselor.'

She raises a warning finger. 'Not Pete.'

'Friends don't make friends debug their marriage?'

'Correct – not if they want to stay friends, anyway. And we don't have enough of them.' She takes a deep, shuddering breath and suddenly I wonder just how much this conversation has taken out of her. Has she been lying awake at nights, rehearsing its script endlessly, the way I have? 'I'm glad you're taking this so well.'

'Hey—' I reach for a light-hearted quip but the quiver is empty – 'I'm glad you still want to try.'

'Let me see if I can find a suitable counselor first, then thank me.' She pushes her tray back, only half-eaten, and gives me a tired smile. 'I don't want to go on this way.'

'Neither do I.' I stand up. 'So let's not.'

One of the problems associated with inheriting a new and senior position by virtue of the law of necromantic succession – that is, dead man's shoes – is that I am now expected to work at executive level. In a regular government agency I'd be in a Senior Civil Service grade, and if this was a private sector organization I'd be a vice president. If you're the janitor and the stores cupboard is bare, you shrug and blame your manager; if you're the VP in charge of Facilities and the stores cupboard is bare, you are responsible and you just fucked up by failing to organize resupply. I actually have – this is quite terrifying – signing authority and a budget line all of my very own. It's terrifying because I can use it whenever I feel like it, except that I've got to keep Accounts in the loop, on pain of being taken aside for a quiet word by the SA himself if I screw up. On the other hand, being able to sign a hotel bill on my own cognizance after a hard day's work stabbing chupacabras in Belize is like a breath of fresh air conditioning.

When I'm not conducting goat-sucker population control exercises, part of my new job is to digest a book of accounting rules several centimeters thick. (This is the abbreviated training-wheels version, you understand, for the *very junior* Vice President In Charge Of Janitorial Supplies.) Another part of my job involves spending two-hour sessions holed up in an office with the long-suffering Emma MacDougal from HR. Emma is tutoring me on how management works: not the MBA everything-is-a-process employees-are-perfectly-spherical-interchangeable-blobs variety that all the smiling sociopaths in suits are getting in the private sector, but how this *very eccentric* job-for-life corner of the Civil Service works internally, with a specific emphasis on house-training the newly minted sorcerer. Apparently I wasn't expected to hit this grade for another five years, but CASE NIGHTMARE GREEN and vacant org chart boxes are calling, so needs must.

It's *not* my favorite part of the job, but I can't see a way around it. If my office needs redecorating I can't moan at my boss any more, I *am* the boss. So I need to know how to fill out the right magic scrolls to summon Facilities, recite the correct incantation to invoke Painters and Decorators, and propitiate the demons of Accounts by documenting peeling wallpaper and rising damp. Which is to say, I'm learning a whole lot about how this organization works, in ways I'd barely even noticed before.

It's quite humbling, really. I was intimately familiar with the endless upgrades to the structured cabling runs that keep our in-house networks running, but I had little or no idea about how my proposals for work got turned into the budget items, job specifications, and contract tenders that resulted in people in overalls coming in to lift floor tiles and install runs of Cat5e cabling. Bureaucracy is like an iceberg: nine-tenths of it is below the waterline, and if you spend all your time rubbernecking at the tentacle monsters while you let the ship of state drift, before you know it the canteen will be out of teabags and the engine room crew will go on work-to-rule.

This is a long and rambling way of explaining why I don't get to leave the office until well after 6 p.m.

I spend the first half of the afternoon with Emma chewing over the high-level org chart and procedures for submitting job requests to IT Services from outside (the irony is not lost on me), and then I spend a couple of hours with Boris and Vik analyzing the reception my appearance on *Newsnight* got. We have had a dozen or so write-ups in newspapers (nothing making the front page), a minor 'Boffin puts foot in mouth at new agency' tag on *The Register* which got picked up by *BuzzFeed* for some reason, and three requests for interviews from local radio stations, all of which were politely turned down on my behalf before they reached my inbox. The request from the *Today* program on Radio 4 is a lot harder to ignore, but I gather policy (per the SA and the shadowy coterie of senior administrators who rule on such things) is to (a) play for time, and (b) spread the misery around, so they're going to try and break out of the twenty-four-hour news cycle, then send Mhari round to flash her choppers at them. She can't plead incendiary tendencies under arc lights to dodge a radio interview, can she? *Hah.*

I get everything nailed down by five o'clock, but then realize I've barely had time to check my email all day, so I head back to my office. And that's when I find I have a visitor.

'Ah, Bob, do come in.' It's the SA, sitting primly in my visitor's chair. 'Are you terribly busy right now?'

Cold sweat breaks out up and down my spine. 'No, not really—' *Oh god what have I done –*

Dr. Armstrong looks thoughtful. 'I have a little errand for you.' A momentary pause. 'You are not in trouble,' he adds.

'Uh—' I manage not to startle. 'Oh. An errand.' I walk to my desk, stiff-legged with relief, and sit down, then hit the DO NOT DISTURB light switch. 'Do tell.' *Bastard, thanks for taking a year off my life like that.* It's unfair of me to blame Dr. Armstrong for my own guilty conscience, even when I know I haven't done anything, but he's the Senior Auditor: he doesn't pay house calls, as a rule.

'I have a little out-of-the-office errand I was going to attend to this evening but I've been delayed and I was wondering if you could take care of it for me? It's just a short diversion on your way home.'

'I suppose so.' By home, I hope he means the hotel, otherwise it's in the opposite direction from where I'm going. 'What is it?'

He leans toward me, intent. 'This is not to be discussed outside your office or mine, and your report will be classified Secret and prepared under NOELEC protocol.' I have to write my report using a manual typewriter or a pen, in other words, on handmade paper inside a warded containment grid. I'd be seriously annoyed if this didn't flag the SA's 'little errand' as highly sensitive. 'Understood?'

I nod. 'What's up?'

Dr. Armstrong glances sidelong at the door. 'I received a signal from an old acquaintance this afternoon,' he says, 'using a prearranged code. He's in London and he wants to talk to someone. I—' For a moment an expression of savage frustration flickers across his face – 'I'm tied up with setup for TITANIC for the foreseeable future. Burning the midnight oil. It couldn't come at a worse time, in fact it's probably connected, but I need someone reliable – you – to go and listen to the man, hear what he has to say, and report back to me.'

A contact with a prearranged code that gets the SA's attention can't be anything trivial. I tense. 'I can do that, but you'll need to give me something more. Otherwise I won't know when to pay attention.'

The SA nods, shadowing his eye sockets. 'His name is Bill McKracken and he's a US Postal Service Inspector. He flew in from New York on a red-eye this morning and he's due to fly out from Heathrow late this evening.' I wince. (I've done the London/New York day trip myself: in economy class the jet lag is brutal.) 'He just felt like a chat, for old time's sake.' Dr. Armstrong's smile is terrifying.

'You said he's a postal inspector. You mean the, uh, he's one of the Comstock people?'

'The Comstock people don't exist, Bob.' He doesn't meet my eyes. 'He's just a postal inspector.' He slides a folded sheet of paper onto my desk, covered in his cramped, neat handwriting: 'There you go. I'll take your report later tonight or first thing in the morning. Ta-ta.'

The SA unfolds from his chair like an origami giraffe, waits for me to switch off the DO NOT DISTURB sign, then leaves without a backward glance. And that's when I realize that things are even worse than I imagined. Because the 'Comstock people' don't officially exist, and if they're jetting in from New York to ask for our assistance things must be really bad.

Long ago, in the late nineteenth century, there lived a certain American Postal Service Inspector named Anthony Comstock. While serving in the Union army during the US Civil War, Comstock was shocked – shocked! – to discover the profanity and ungodly behavior of his fellow soldiers. He responded like any other self-righteous, blue-nosed killjoy by creating the New York Society for the Suppression of Vice, which did exactly what you'd expect it to: lobbying for a law to criminalize the transport by mail of 'lewd materials' including anything to do with sex education, abortion, contraceptives, or the prevention of sexually transmissible diseases. And, having gotten his law passed by Congress, Comstock was given a commission by the Inspector General of the Postal Service to enforce it, which he did with enthusiasm, acquiring for himself and his inspectors the status of federal agents with the right to open the mail.

While the original Comstock Law was overturned some time in the 1950s, the US Postal Service Inspectorate still exists to this day. It's a small federal agency with obscure but remarkably far-reaching powers, who mostly keep an eye out for people stealing from the mail or using it to transport narcotics, child pornography, and other contraband. And one particular task that Comstock took on is still an active part of their remit – although not many people know that the Occult Texts Division goes back that far.

Now, here's a very weird thing: the defense establishment of the United States of America is so complicated, not to say baroque, that many different agencies can accomplish any given task. Want to invade a small Caribbean island?

Who you gonna call: the Army or the Navy's Army, which is to say, the Marine Corps? Want to call in an air strike? You could ask the Air Force ... but the US Navy has lots and lots of fighter jets and tends to get annoyed if they're left out. And the Army of the Navy has its own Air Force, the USMC Air Corps, and *they've* got aircraft carriers. It's the same, if not worse, in the world of covert operations and intelligence. Nobody is quite sure how many espionage and counter-espionage agencies the US government runs, but there are at least nineteen and, by some accounts, more than thirty.

And then we get into the super-black world of occult intelligence agencies like the Laundry.

Generally, when we deal with the US government, we find ourselves dealing with the Operational Phenomenology Agency, also known as the Black Chamber – the original 1920s organization, of which the NSA is a spin-off – and known to their detractors as the Nazgûl. The OPA are not nice people. In fact, mostly they're not people at all, except in the loosest sense of the word. OPA doctrine calls for the binding and control of 'occult intelligence assets,' demons by any other name, and their deployment as agents of the state, loyalty guaranteed by the choke-chain of a fate worse than death should they ever fall short of instant unthinking obedience to their handlers.

The OPA are not the only American OCCINT agency. Comstock's office began finding copies of the *Necronomicon* in the mail during the 1880s. With the growing popularity of theosophy and Eastern traditions in the late nineteenth century, the Occult Texts Division took a proprietorial interest in the spread of esoteric materials, seeking to track and prosecute the exiled spawn of Innsmouth, the masked followers of the *Liber Facierum*, the True Initiates and

Hidden Seekers of the hairy stars and the final conjunction of the heavens. They don't discuss their successes, but some say that they were instrumental in preventing the serial killer H. H. Holmes from completing his necromantic murder palace in Chicago. Their fingerprints have been found on correspondence relating to the cases of Albert Fish and the Manson Family. If the OPA are a ghastly hybrid of all the worst elements of the CIA and the NSA, with a strong stench of demonology on top, then the OTD is the counter-OCCINT air freshener in the room. But a bathroom air freshener can only do so much to stave off the stink of a pile of rotting corpses, and the OTD is so small and beleaguered that many people doubt they even exist any more.

I stumble bleary-eyed onto the pavement outside the New Annex just before seven, late enough that even the police on the door have gone home. I have my messenger bag slung over one shoulder; the suit carrier I left to fend for itself in my office. I hang a left along the high street, catch a bus most of the way back to my hotel, then detour into the hole-in-the-wall pub where, per the SA's instructions, I can expect to find my contact from the US Postal Inspectorate's Occult Texts Division.

It's becoming extremely hard to find a good pub in London these days. Partly it's the housing market: real estate speculators love to buy up the title deeds to a pub and redevelop the land it sits on as something more profitable. And partly it's the knock-on effect of smoking bans and drink-driving laws. Pubs have to make their money somehow, so they can either go gastro and turn into a boutique restaurant dining experience, or go swill-house and pack in the inebriate herd. The upshot is that you can't find a decent, quiet hole-in-the-wall where you can have a low-key conversation: either they're trying to upsell you a fifty-quid-a-head artisanal pork pie (serving this week: Peppa Pig's Uncle Bertie's left haunch, marinaded in a drizzle of preschoolers' tears) or it's so packed you need an oxygen mask to breathe and are reduced to texting your neighbor by way of conversation.

The SA's note directs me to one of the former. The bar is pointedly stool-less and the tables all boast clipboards with multi-page menus changing by the hour, and the kind of incredibly hard seating that causes your legs to go to sleep within half an hour if you're there for a leisurely drink rather than to gobble and go. The tables are, predictably, crammed, but the bar isn't too bad, and there's a guy standing there who fits the description. He's wearing an airline-rumpled nondescript suit that shouts Fed in an American accent, with buzz-cut hair, six o'clock stubble, and a despondent expression. A fiftyish face that's been lived in for too long, like a once-handsome shopping mall on the downslope to demolition. He's swaying gently over his pint of London Pride but it's not drunk-swaying, it's I-can't-stay-awake wobbling. Every minute he gives a little myoclonic jolt and stretches his back, as if forcing himself not to fall asleep. Poor bastard probably shipped over in cattle class and has been awake for going on forty-eight hours. Oh, and the cheap briefcase at his feet is wearing a grade six ward, which seals the deal.

I wander up beside him and wave a purple drinking voucher at the manager. 'Pint of Spitfire,' I say, then turn to see my barside companion's eyelids fluttering. 'You must be Bill. Dr. Armstrong sent me.'

My contact twitches wildly, nearly knocking his half-full glass over, then glares at me. 'Who?' he demands.

'Are you Bill McKracken?' I ask, flipping open my wallet so he can see the warrant card.

'I—' I can see his brain strip a cog as he hesitates on the edge of a stutter – 'yeah, I am.' His watery blue eyes focus on the card and flicker alert. 'Mr. Howard. Huh. I've heard of you.' He glances at my face, his expression shuttered. 'Who did you say sent you?'

I slide the wallet away as the bar manager shoves a pint of Spitfire in front of me and makes my twenty vanish. 'Dr. Armstrong, our Senior Auditor. He sends his regrets but he's tied up in a meeting this evening. I'm here in his place.' I raise my pint to him. 'To see you don't miss your flight home. Cheers.'

A certain tension drains away from his shoulders. 'I was getting worried. Hell of a way to come for a no-show.'

'We've been a bit busy this week.' He nods vigorously. All his body language is a bit off, with the kind of uncoordinated exaggeration of someone who's losing fine motor control from being awake too long. 'What brings you over here?' I ask, checking the time. If we're to get him to Heathrow for a nine o'clock check-in we'll have to leave soon.

'My manager sent me to courier a message for your C-suite crisis team. Hand-to-hand, eyes-only, because the regular networks are all compromised. I'm supposed to deliver it in person, so—' McKracken looks at me – 'I apologize in advance,' he says, then hits me in the face with a soul-gaze.

It is a very bad idea to try and soul-gaze the Eater of Souls. I manage to catch him under the arm before he crumples, and save his pint from spilling for the second time in a minute, and I'm pretty certain I managed not to take a bite out of him but dammit, it's a *really* bad idea to take me by surprise that way. Clearly an adept, he takes it on the figurative chin and bends over, retching. I wave the bartender back: 'I think he just tried to inhale his beer,' I tell the guy. McKracken leans against the bar and takes a deep breath, eyes squeezed shut. He's actually in good shape, considering what he just tried to do. If an unwarded civilian caught me by surprise like that they'd be waiting for an ambulance right now.

'What *are* you?' he manages.

I shrug. 'Bob Howard, Detached Senior Specialist grade one, Q-Division SOE, at your service. Like I said, the Senior Auditor was unavailable so they sent me in his place.'

'But you're not, you're not—' He looks at my face, everywhere but my eyes, as if frantically searching for something he's lost.

'I'm Dr. Angleton's replacement,' I say gently, and his face pales.

'I shouldn't have done that, should I?'

'No,' I agree with him, 'you shouldn't. But you've got my undivided attention. Now. What can I do for the Comstock division?'

McKracken clears his throat discreetly, glances round, then makes a curious hand gesture: obviously triggering a macro of some sort, for the noise of the pub flattens and fuzzes until I can no longer identify individual voices. 'The short version is, we're fucked.' He raises his briefcase to the bar, dials in a combination, mutters something under his breath – I feel the very nasty wards on the case relax – and opens it. The contents are disappointingly mundane: toilet kit, spare socks, boarding pass and passport, a battered Dell laptop covered in inventory control stickers, and a brown manila document mailer. This he passes to me. From the heft, it contains some sort of file. 'This is the long version. Codename DELIRIUM. Everything about how the enemy within sneaked up on us and whacked us and what they're trying to accomplish, not that we can do anything about it – it's gone too far.'

I accept the envelope and slide it into my messenger bag. He glances at it dubiously for a second, then nods. 'This will be in front of our executive within twelve hours,' I promise him. 'Now. What's gone too far?' I pick up my glass, take a mouthful of beer, and wait.

McKracken closes his case and pulls himself together with a visible effort. 'We're being attacked via a new vulnerability channel: privatization.' His shoulders slump. 'For the past few decades a bunch of congressmen have been pushing a bill to privatize the USPS.' He means their Post Office. 'It's going to happen sooner rather than later.' I manage to keep a straight face. (It may have been driven off the front page by events in Leeds, but there's currently a scandal brewing in the news about how little money the government made from selling off the Royal Mail last year.) 'When that happens, the Inspectorate's duties go with it and will be fully under the authority of the new owners. The private carriers, UPS, FedEx, and their rivals, are covered by Homeland Security. So it's a way of selling us out.'

'If it happens.' I try to look on the bright side.

'No, it's gonna happen. The fix is in. The Inspectorate has been disbanded and defunded, via an amendment to a fisheries bill that Congress passed on the nod. They blindsided us with this – we had less than a week's advance warning, it just came out of nowhere, bam! Only it's not a true privatization – the Treasury will keep a controlling shareholding and most of the shares go to a holding company that already exists, a front owned by the OPA that's called GP Services. That's short for Golden Promise.'

I nearly drop my glass: 'The – what—'

I have a flashback to fimbulwinter striking Colorado Springs, years ago: driving through a blizzard towards the airport only to be turned back by Highway Patrol officers.

Johnny McTavish and 'Seph Hazard in a safe house, look-ing angry and tired and alive in a way they never were in meetings, like they'd woken up and remembered what it was like to measure themselves against dead-eyed worshippers chanting foul hymns in a desecrated mega-church before a silver-haired preacher with flickering emerald-bright eyes. Me, and a giant woodlouse from hell in a fish tank in the basement of a church, mindlessly singing lullabies to its worshippers through the spawn it had grafted to them in place of their tongues.

'GP Services is a subsidiary of GP Systems, which is owned by Golden Promise Ministries out of Colorado Springs, which was set up over a decade ago by one of the OPA's deniable assets, a stringer called Schiller.' I startle involuntarily. 'Did you know of him?'

'We met,' I say before I can bite my tongue, and McKracken's eyebrows rise.

'Welp, that'll make this easier. He disappeared a while ago, but his corporation is still rolling and they're taking point for a series of operations the Nazgûl appear to be running, and apparently the Nazgûl are willing to burn about three billion bucks just to shut down the US Postal Service Inspectorate's Occult Texts Division.' He taps his briefcase. 'As to why they're making a play so big right now ... it's part of a grand strategy. The Black Chamber's true master is finally stepping out of the shadows and moving to consolidate power. And you need to tell your bosses that my agency is burned. Steps are being taken to ensure that the Black Library doesn't fall into their hands, and a bunch of us are taking retirement, all kinda ensuring that continuity of institutional experience is lost, if you follow my drift. At this point that's all we can do, unless you know a way to un-root a congressman who's been got to by the Nazgûl ...? No? Didn't think so. Anyway, we can't fight back actively, but that envelope contains a synopsis of everything we know about how they made their play, everything about the relationship between GP Services and the Operational Phenomenology Agency that we've been able to dig up, and how they're trying to take over the governments. Ours first, then yours. It's our worst-case scenario. The monsters have taken over the Black Chamber, and their dread master is using a fake outsourcing bid as a lever to liquidate the opposition agency and pave the way for his return as we approach the Grand Conjunction.'

'Are you—' I swallow. Unaccountably, my throat is dry: I chug my beer – 'are you going to be all right? Do you want to talk to someone about asylum?' Although fuck knows how much standing we've got on that subject since Alex pulled that stunt with the Host ...

McKracken snorts. 'I've got my pension; Friday is officially my last day on the job. Figure I'll move out somewhere cheaper to live, catch up on all the fishing I haven't had time for. Montana maybe. Somewhere where,' his voice drops to a confidential murmur, 'there's a survivalist community who have an inkling about what's coming, if you know what I mean.'

We finish our drinks and I escort Bill to Paddington – which is well out of my way home to my digs – and see him onto the Heathrow Express. Back to the gathering storm on the East Coast. I wish him luck, but if half of what he said is true, then he might have been wiser to ask for asylum.

The idea that the Black Chamber is willing to spend billions to take out a minor and eccentric rival agency leaves me shaken. That they're using Raymond Schiller's outfit as a front to do so is even worse. Schiller's dead, but the thought of the thing he served gives me the cold shudders. The idea that the Nazgûl are working with the Sleeper cultists in service to a greater evil ... well fuck me, and here I was hoping to catch some sleep tonight. Instead, it looks like I'm heading back to the office to type up an urgent report about the end of the world. Again.

The pavement is nearly deserted and the traffic has thinned out from the usual rush hour rumble and daytime congestion. It's getting into summer so the London air is the usual oppressive mixture of humidity, dust, diesel fumes, and the collective body odor of ten million people crammed in a city that hasn't discovered air conditioning. Or maybe that's just me, impatient and looking forward to a hotel shower. But in any case, I'm shaken and worried and not paying nearly enough attention to the over-familiar streets around the New Annex.

Which is why it takes me way too long to realize I'm being followed.

I am enough of a native to catch the bus where possible, to avoid the stifling summer congestion of the tube (no air conditioning and worse crowding than the Tokyo subway) and the wallet-bleeding cost of taxis (which seem to burn pure single malt Scotch, judging by what they charge). The nearest stop is a quarter mile from the New Annex, so I get off along with a couple of other passengers and walk briskly towards the corner of the high street. It's late enough that the pavement is nearly deserted. My thoughts are with the suitcase in the left-luggage lock-up at last night's hotel. I'm not sure what I was hoping for: another short-notice assignment out of country, perhaps, or maybe an overnight invitation from Mo. Either way it was a wash, so I might as well sleep under my desk tonight, grab the bags tomorrow, hit Expedia for a last-minute hotel bargain, and check myself in somewhere for a couple of nights –

That's funny, the part of me that never sleeps registers, *didn't I see that guy before* –

Fuck it, what do I have to do to get away from work?

Two men about fifty or sixty meters behind me on the other side of the road cross over hastily to keep me in view when I turn the corner. One of them is unfamiliar but something about the other reminds me of somebody I half-noticed back in the pub. Or maybe it was earlier this evening: I didn't really register it at the time. Now there's a woman with a pram twenty meters ahead, and that's when I know I'm in trouble because something is wrong with the baby: I can't hear its mind. The thing about babies is that what they see is what you get: a constant stream of random sensory impressions and emotions with the volume cranked up to eleven as long as they're awake. While they're asleep? Violent, chaotic dreams. Adults are much quieter. This one's either in a coma or dead or warded up to the eyeballs, or, and I know this is paranoid, it makes me feel like something I encountered in a hotel in Denver a few years ago –

I open my inner ear and hear the sleepy crunching half-thoughts of blind, segmented nightmare parasites possessed by a vast and bottomless well of faith.

Fuck, it is them. And I pick up on something else at the same time –

Fuck. They're tailing me.

It's a classic box tail with a twist: there are the usual two blokes behind me, but rather than another two in front there's a mother-and-baby combo instead. I don't know why it took me so long to pick it up: maybe it was the bus journey and then the mostly empty pavements and I'm just not paying enough attention. But that's not the only thing that's wrong with this picture. Normally a box tail is all about making sure you don't lose your target in a crowded city, but something about this one has *snatch* written all over it, if not *hit*. I can see it all unfolding in my mind. If I try to break the box I'll have to get past her, whereupon she'll make a loud scene (baby snatchers are perennially popular) and her two 'white knights' will close in. If I try to break past them, she'll start screaming that I was stalking her. There's probably a fake police van and a couple of bodies in equally fake uniforms shadowing us, waiting to make the pickup, but I can't sense them this far away (not through bricks and concrete and dozens or hundreds of bystanders), so all I can see is the immediate threat.

They're clearly coordinated and they're converging on me, and they probably saw me pick up Bill's package – which means it's an intercept and they'll make their move before I get to the New Annex.

Fuck.

The New Annex is a secure government site. We have CCTV on all the approaches and armed officers outside the front door these days. But the plod clocked off at six and I'm out of range of the site surveillance and *secure* is not the same as *secret*, as the residents of 85 Albert Embankment in Vauxhall* can testify. And after my *Newsnight* slot I'm very much not secret at all. I'm not sure how they traced me to the office in the first place, but to have a snatch squad on the pavement waiting outside for me to leave is bad: very, very bad indeed.

And it gets worse. I can't tell what's in the pram, but the adults are all using MilSpec wards. MilSpec wards like the

---

* Where correspondence addressed to 'James Bond' will be responded to with a polite note that Mr. Bond is a fictional character and in any case would have retired long before his employers moved to these premises.

one Jeremy was wearing when he interviewed me, not something knocked up in a spare half hour by an amateur warlock. I can count the number of organizations able to make that kind of kit on my fingers without cheating and using binary arithmetic, and after this evening's fun and informative pub chat I don't need to make any guesses. I abruptly feel so sick I wonder if I'm going to throw up. It's the adrenaline spike from being hunted – I've been here before and it's something you never get used to. But at least I'm not paralyzed. I know what to do and I've done it before: I need to evade and escape, then take them down before they hurt anybody.

It's late enough that most of the shops on this street are shuttered. There's a kebab joint up ahead on my side and an off-license on the other side, but neither of them have multiple customer exits, which makes breaking out of the box problematic. Nor am I armed, at least in conventional terms. I palm my phone, hoping they can't see me in the failing daylight, and dial the first number on my contacts list. Ten seconds of suspense carries me fifteen meters further towards the next crossing, and I'm in luck: the phone rings twice, then she answers. 'Yes?'

Mo sounds tense. Unexpected mid-evening phone calls from separated not-quite-an-ex-at-this-point will do that.

'I'm in a box tail heading towards the New Annex front door, I just made a pickup for the SA and I think the oppo are planning on lifting me. Please alert the duty officer, CODE RED.'

'Bob – understood.' Her voice catches. 'Keep the call open for updates, I'll be on the land line to the Duty Officer.'

I switch to speakerphone and slide the gadget back into my pocket without hanging up. Mo is a total professional and will get the ball rolling in the time it would take me to authenticate myself over the phone to whoever's on the ops desk. Every second counts now. I walk ten more meters, estimate another ten meters of pavement ahead before the pelican crossing, note that the lights are against me (not that there's much traffic), and observe that the lead element of the trap is stopping and not pushing the WALK button. The two behind have just crossed the road at a brisk clip, dodging between two cars that have slowed to weave between speed pillows, and now we're all in a classic kill zone. Out of the corner of one eye I see a white van turning into the main road behind me.

I stop in the middle of the pavement, ten meters short of the mother with pushchair and unidentified contents, and take a deep breath, knowing that this is going to be really unpleasant even if I'm wrong –

I'm not wrong.

There's no such thing as telepathy ... at least not for the likes of me. There are some really nasty brain parasites that can blur the boundaries between their victims' minds, and there are destiny entanglement rituals as well, along with all the concomitant risks, but I've got no way of peeking inside someone else's skull and pulling out anything but the owner's current sensory impressions and emotional tone. Especially when they're warded. But as I focus hard and crank up the metaphorical gain, I begin to burn through their wards and pick up a common sense of feral intent and frightening dedication. I take in one of them sliding a telescoping baton out of his coat sleeve as the other raises a spray can, and they're both watching me with anticipation. *Can't be having that*, part of me thinks, and then that part of me *yawns*, a sensation like a deep sea angler fish spreading its jaws infinitely wide, and I bite down on their minds.

Yes, they have high-powered MilSpec wards. They crunch all the same, a mild fizzing note of bitterness and gunsmoke tarnishing the desiccated fragments of their souls as they go down hard. There's something wrong with them: they taste gray and drained, half-eaten from the inside out by something that got there before me. I gag as I swallow their minds, feel their last thoughts spiraling down in surprise and dismay as I shred their souls. They have pepper spray and a baton with a three-centimeter ball of tungsten on the end, but that doesn't save them. What I do is clearly self-defense within my terms of engagement. Even so, I feel sick to the tips of my toes and take an involuntary step towards the bodies. I don't get enough practice at killing people to not feel bad about it; I hope I never do, although that's looking like a forlorn wish these days.

The vehicle turning the corner is stickered up to look like a police van, one of the regular ones with seats and no light bar used for ferrying bodies around rather than snatching people, but the driver is just as intently focused on me as the box tail duo –

There is a flat crack-crack behind me and something tugs sharply at my hood.

I reflexively reach my imaginary jaws behind me and bite down hard as my heart starts pounding and I dive at the pavement. This one's soul squishes. They've got a stronger ward and there's an indescribable sensation, somewhere between wasp-stung-my-tongue and the memory of standing by my father's graveside and letting a handful of soil trickle onto his coffin (which is odd, because he's still alive). As I hit the ground there's a clatter as pushchair girl collapses, dropping the suppressed pistol. The baby buggy topples over into the road.

I hear a screech of tires and an engine revving as the

white van takes off. It side-swipes the pushchair, then careens round the corner, running a red light. The pushchair is flung into a shop doorway: there's no baby, but a life-sized doll and something else, a horribly familiar olive-drab casing. *Claymore mine.* This isn't good, this is very bad indeed: it may have started out as a snatch but they were willing to use massive lethal force if it failed, high risk of collateral damage. The van was there as much to evacuate the survivors as to collect the captive.

'Oh fuck,' I say and my voice comes out shakily.

'Bob? Bob? Sitrep!' Her anguished voice is muffled through my fleece.

I roll over on my side, breathing hard, and reach for my phone. My right upper arm is a searing ache, an old injury coming out on strike in sympathy. There's a siren in the distance, then another. The phone screen is shattered where I fell on it but it's still working. I'm gasping for air, skin clammy, and my hands are shaking. 'It was a hit. Shots fired, three down, UXB on-site, I've been, I've been—' I reach up and fumble at my hood – 'shots missed me, but get me backup *right now.*'

It's one thing to go into a fight expecting it, another thing entirely to come through a hit by the skin of your teeth and not lose self-control. Pram woman missed me but one of her shots punched a neat hole in my hoodie, missing my carotid artery by about five centimeters. There's a wall beside the shuttered corner shop and I roll again and sit up halfway, then lean against it, feeling gray and dizzy. If I hadn't been moving towards my other attackers, turning and ducking, she'd have landed a double-tap in my center of mass. It's as much as I can do to listen to the sirens getting closer, keep a weather eye open for signs of a follow-through, and concentrate on keeping what's left of my shit together. I don't want to lose control: I could accidentally shred the souls of everyone in all the buildings around me if I let myself slip.

It's going to be a long night.

Time speeds up and everything seems to move very fast for a while once the real police arrive on scene, which they do, mob-handed, within five minutes. I have my warrant card out when they get officious in my face, which short-circuits no end of shit until they get the message that I'm a Victim Of Crime. But at that point they turn all checklist-solicitous in a very unhelpful way. About two minutes later the real police arrive: an Armed Response Unit with the new kit – ward-inscribed body armor, mirrored helmets, and scary-looking automatic weapons, issued at short notice from some depot or other where we've been sitting on a stockpile of heavy kit. I resist the urge to say *where were you when shit got real on my doorstep* because that sort of thing really isn't constructive, and anyway, it's not their fault. I finally start to unwind once I'm sitting in the back of an ambulance, clutching my messenger bag, and surrounded by machine guns pointing outwards. Which is a sign of how bad a turn my life's taken recently, if you think about it.

The ambulance crew check me out on the way to A&E and verify that I have a minor graze on the right side of my neck, a scraped knee, and that I'm uninjured but showing signs of shock. They think it's because I've nearly been shot, but I know better. Either way it's enough for them to light up the Christmas tree on the roof and drag me off to a hospital where I can expect to spend six hours sitting on a bench watching an endless stream of heart attacks and drunken party animals take priority. I try to argue, but they're firm: discharging a patient who subsequently goes into cardiogenic shock is really bad for their customer performance metrics, sorry guv'nor. I am considering pulling my warrant card on them, regardless of whether it's bad form or not, when my phone rings again. It's Mo, and she's got her shit together.

'Where are they taking you?' she demands. I tell her which hospital. 'Right. Go with the flow and I'll have a car pick you up at the Acute Receiving Unit door. The DO's lining up a secure safe house and I'll get the on-call doctor to visit you there. I'm on my way back to the office right now to audit the lockdown, but I'll come visit as soon as things settle down.'

'Why, what's going on?' I ask, weak and shivery and somewhat slow on the uptake.

'Someone tried to kill a senior member of staff,' she says drily. 'Do pay attention, we take a dim view of that sort of thing. Sit tight and I'll send you a babysitter.'

Mo's idea of a taxi service for her husband in the wake of a snatch attempt is an SO19 sniper team. The heavily armed cops are lurking around the hospital entrance when I arrive, scaring the crap out of the smokers clustered under the awning. Nor did she mention in her call that the DO's 'secure safe house' is an entire floor of a terrifyingly luxurious apartment block in the East End (upstairs from a bulletproof lobby with a very comprehensive security system). Apparently it belongs to the Sovereign Wealth Fund/Oil Sheikh equivalent of Airbnb. It's so heavily warded that I can't sense any minds in the flats above and below me – it's almost like we're alone in the building – and there are more armed police in the lobby. It reeks of diplomatic passports and numbered bank accounts.

I'm dizzy and so tired that I'm beyond surprises as I

enter the safe apartment's front door and shuffle along a hand-woven Adraskan rug that's probably worth more than I earn in a year. I assume it's 'Seph's bolt-hole: it's far too luxurious for normal agency business. At the end of the hallway I find myself in a living room the size of an aircraft hangar, if aircraft hangars came furnished in Louis Vuitton with a view of the Thames. The bobbies with bazookas are camped outside the apartment door; I gather they have orders to start World War Three if anyone without a warrant card tries to get in. I plant my bag on the sofa, then for some reason I decide to make myself useful and set out in search of the kitchen in order to make them a placatory cup of tea, but I get about as far as a Louis XIV chaise in purple crushed velvet and gold leaf before my knees turn to water and I sit down, just for a minute.

I'm still there a quarter of an hour later when Johnny McTavish bounces in.

'Wotcher, cock!' he says cheerily. 'How's life treating you?'

'I'm fine,' I try to say, but it comes out as an inarticulate gurgle.

'Heh!' He looks amused. Johnny is about two meters of special-forces-surplus muscle in stone-washed denim, despite which, he's not dumb. You don't get to be Number Two in the Hazard Network by being dumb; the monosyllable is Johnny taking time out to evaluate me. The entryphone buzzes. 'That'll be the flying doctor service for you, I'll bet,' he says helpfully, and disappears. He returns with a medic in tow. Fussing and blood pressure monitoring ensues. One adrenaline shot later (and a sermon on the side about bed rest, fluids, and not overdoing things) and I'm feeling a lot perkier. 'Well then,' he says, pulling up a gratuitously ornate chair and crunching onto it. 'What's all this about? 'Ave you picked up some new fans from bein' on TV?'

I stare sullenly at the nighttime London skyline, the stench of rotting minds catching in the back of my throat. 'It's those fuckers from Denver. They had a Claymore mine.'

'But they're dead and you're not, me old mate. So what's wrong?' He pauses expectantly.

I close my eyes. 'Their souls had third-degree god burns. Also, one of them tried to shoot me when the snatch failed.' I can't stop hearing gunfire, feeling the sharp tug at my collar and the hot burn on my neck. I swallow. 'They bungled it, but they nearly had me. I think they followed me all the way to and from the pub, but I was too dozy to notice until it was nearly too late.'

I hate guns. I can use them, but I don't like being around them: they add this terrible random-act-of-no-god-at-all angle to any fight. *Bang, you're dead*, even if you weren't the person the shooter was aiming for, even if it's an accidental discharge. At least I only kill people I *mean* to kill, when I grab them with one or another of the Eater of Souls' notional appendages.

Johnny looks at me warily, as if I'm made of fine bone china and he's afraid I'll break. He's got this rough-diamond-geezer pose that I think he copied from a Bob Hoskins gangster movie. It's actually about as authentic as a three-pound note. He's got a chip on his shoulder a mile high about not being middle or upper class, but there's a very sharp mind behind the abrasively casual exterior, and you don't get to be a staff sergeant in the Légion Étrangère without a good working grasp of how people are put together, and more importantly, how they fall apart under stress ... much less rise to be 'Seph's Number Two. Right now the way he's looking at me is setting alarm bells ringing in my head. 'What do you think is going on?'

Now a second set of alarms go off. Johnny is an External Asset, kept at arm's reach from the agency, officially deniable and off-the-books but working directly for Mahogany Row. He and 'Seph turn up for meetings in the New Annex but they're not on our regular payroll and they don't carry warrant cards. Ostensibly retired, 'Seph founded and ran the Hazard Organization, about the most terrifying private sector occult intelligence organization I've ever heard of (and one I'm very glad I never ran up against in an adversarial capacity). 'Seph and Johnny retired a decade ago, winding up the company and moving to a life of comfortable luxury in London, and today they're part of the organization's plausible deniability capability, so if they're being dragged into this something deeply alarming is going down.

'The agency is under attack, isn't it?' I dry-swallow. 'The Black Chamber are making some kind of move on a global scale. How long have you known? And for how long?'

'Long enough.' Johnny walks over to the floor-to-ceiling picture window and stares moodily out at the darkness. He's backlit, and I'm momentarily aghast at his reckless self-exposure until I realize he's not the real target here. He turns to face me: 'Interesting you say it's the Nazgûl. Productive meeting?'

I nod. 'The SA sent me. They're making a move on the Comstock office – details are all in the bag.' I nod wearily towards the sofa. 'Big wheels turning. Do you know what's going on?'

'I don't believe in coincidences.' His tone is flat. 'This Monday at nine eighteen a Falcon 7X landed at the general aviation terminal at STN and was glad-handed by a reception party: full red carpet, small armored convoy, very select VIP treatment you may be assured. The Money gets to side-step the E-borders palaver although the Border Force still checks their passports and visas. And let's not mention the State Department hitchhiker they had along for the trip, whisked off to Grosvenor Square before you could snap your fingers. But of course we don't get notified routinely because we're not the Police or Security Service. So today's cock-up is that it turns out we can keep penniless Syrian war refugees out but when Raymond Fucking Schiller knocks on the door he's given a posh handshake and the keys to the kingdom and nobody tells us for days.'

'But he's dead,' I say, mouth on autopilot, or maybe it's the shock talking.

'Turns out he isn't, not so much. Pete's been keeping an eye on the Golden Promise Ministries as part of his brief. They toned down the rhetoric and Schiller hasn't been seen in public pounding the pulpit; it's been one aspiring guest preacher after another. And there's been a significant internal reorganization of his Church's innermost circles, dissolutions and reformations and restructurings and suchlike. Some of it's our fault for killing off his brain-parasites' brood-mother. But he's had time to procure another egg-layer so he could be up and running again in the ole tongue-eating game by now. Or worse. Meanwhile his compound is still active and there are certain interests he invested in and they're ... well, he hasn't been declared dead so his corporations go marching on.'

'That's what Bill was saying. GP Services is fronting for the OPA.' I lick my lips. 'But surely Schiller himself is out of the game? I mean, we—'

I do *not* say *we killed him*, because, firstly, that's not something you say in a nonsec location you haven't personally swept for listening devices and warded against some of the more irritating occult bugs. Secondly, I didn't personally verify cessation of metabolic activity or put a stake through his heart. I was flash-blind from taking out Schiller's guards when Persephone went for the man himself. According to the RAINBOW appendix, 'Seph closed the Gate he'd opened to an alien world while Schiller was still on the wrong side of it, in the Temple of the Sleeper in the Pyramid. The world in question lacks a human-compatible biosphere, so it's not unreasonable to assume he died. But another thought strikes me immediately after I realize all this, and it's not a welcome one:

'If Schiller's back over here and the tail was his work? And the Nazgûl are involved? It's not just the American government that's under attack, is it?'

'Not a clue, me old cock!' Johnny makes what is clearly his best effort to show good cheer. 'The fact that Golden Promise Services Corporation are up to their armpits in outsourcing contracts and the OPA are making cannibal whoopee on their sister agencies is neither here nor there. But when someone with 'is photo on their passport flies in and a couple of days later someone else tries to snatch you off the streets of London, that's kind of suggestive, innit?'

'I was on TV the evening before,' I say slowly, slotting an unwelcome realization into place. 'Was I there as bait?' Did someone set me up with Paxo on *Newsnight* just to tell Schiller's people that I'm about? (I knew the 'let's bug the BBC newsroom' mission was too Mickey Mouse to be the entire story.) My nasty paranoid imagination supplies a plausible scenario all too easily: The armed cops on the door of a clearly compromised worksite put up a neon sign saying BOB WORKS HERE, but they clock off at 6 p.m. because bad guys only kick the door down during office hours. Meanwhile I've just ploughed through a day of meetings carefully contrived to keep me busy until the

SA sends me to run his little after-hours errand, instead of sending the cops to haul the helpful Mr. McKracken into protective custody –

No, Bob, don't be fucking stupid, the Laundry wouldn't set you up as a tethered goat, they'd never do that to anyone senior and you're a valuable high-level asset –

'Dunno, Bob, not my brief, more'n my job's worth to go drawing conclusions.' He whistles surprisingly tunefully, shoving his hands deep in his pockets. 'Although it isn't just Schiller who's got the knives out for you. You being our public face to the nation and all that, it could be anyone, really. And it would be really fucking stupid of Schiller to do something so gauche as to try to put a hit on his least favorite Laundry employee the week he sets foot back on old Blighty, wouldn't it? Not saying what you're thinking is impossible, like, but say wot you will about him, Schiller isn't stupid. Smart money is on you being the wrong target: he sent them after your contact, and they followed you because 'e passed you the file the SA wanted. Let's face it, it'd be pretty fucking dumb to send only three-and-a-bit brain-scorched gunmen to take down the Eater of Souls, right?'

I take a deep, shaky breath. 'I could have killed everyone within a quarter-kilometer radius.' That's an underesti-mate, probably, but I know better than to go full Angleton in the middle of a city. (I practice rigid self-control. It leaves me with unresolved anger issues, but those are the breaks: with great power comes a great tendency to mangle Spider-Man quotes.)

'If it's any consolation, the SA knows that.' He ponders for a few seconds. 'What d'you think would have happened that time in Denver if you'd had your current mojo when we walked into the New Life temple while Schiller was running his summoning?'

I let my breath out. 'I'd have dropped the hammer.' Necromantic rituals are really easy to break if you're the Eater of Souls, just like house fires are really easy to blow out if you just happen to detonate a few kilos of C-4 inside them. Of course there won't be much of the house left afterwards – but that's not the point.

'Right, right.' He punches the palm of his left hand for emphasis. 'Nobody in the big tent would be stupid enough to hang you out as bait, and Schiller – or his people, or whoever fielded those grunts – are too professional to take the bait. Which means we're probably looking at something else, it's not about you, you just 'appened to be in the wrong place at the wrong time. Not that that's a surprise, knowing you. You sit tight, read yer file and write yer report, and I'll see it gets to the big man as soon as you're done—' The buzzer rings again – ''Scuse me.'

Johnny disappears from my field of view and I slump back on the sofa. I hear quiet voices from the vestibule, then feel the arrival of someone with another high-level ward. Two sets of footsteps approach: Johnny's heavy boot steps and someone lighter and faster. 'Bob? Are you all right? Bob?'

It's Mo, she's upset and frightened, and that's when I get really afraid.

3: GOD GAME
INDIGO

I force myself to my feet, dizzy and nauseous notwithstanding, as Mo breaks into an uneven trot. Time stops, or goes a bit blurry for a while. 'I'll just be minding my own business out back,' Johnny grumbles in the background.

When I come back to myself I've got a double-armful of my wife, and she's hugging me hard enough to hurt, and sniffing. 'Don't you dare get yourself killed!' she scolds me, voice catching somewhere between laughing and crying.

'I'm—' I'm wheezing – 'touched.'

'Touched in the head,' she grumps, but her grip around me loosens. If she was that fragile when she was carrying the white violin she'd have been an hors-d'oeuvre for horrors years ago, but she's shaking. That medical leave she's back from, I wonder if it was worse than she's letting on? *Add a sudden change of job* – 'What … what exactly happened?'

'Let me sit down …' Somehow we find ourselves hip-to-hip on a white leather sofa so big it could be the end product of a really bad taxidermy job on Moby Dick. 'The SA sent me to talk to an informer and I was jumped on my way home.'

'I got that,' she says impatiently. 'You mentioned a snatch.'

'They were tailing me, I'm not sure for how long. Then

they set up a box, three plus a bomb in a pram – the pram was an insurance policy, I think. There was a van in the frame. I think they meant to take me but they were armed—' I feel her shiver as I continue – 'and I'm not sure whether they were after me or the brief.' I tilt my chin towards the messenger bag on the sofa.

'Right. Right.' She tucks herself against my side and buries her chin on my shoulder.

'How not-all-right are you?' I ask, hoping she'll tell me something meaningful.

'I'm—' she sniffs – 'not very all right at all, it's the relief more than anything else, I mean, you're not kidnapped or dead—' she sniffs again – 'during is easy it's after that's harsh, that's what my counselor keeps telling me.'

Counselor? What? I've been so up to my ass in lost temples to nameless evil and laying to rest the thaumaturgic equivalent of leaking radioactive disposal sites that I can almost half-kid myself I've got an excuse for not knowing, but – 'We—' I pause and rephrase – 'I haven't been doing a good job of keeping an eye out for you lately, have I?'

'Makes two of us,' she mumbles.

Johnny reappears. He's carrying two tumblers half-full of amber liquid that promise unguarded words and sore heads on the morrow. 'I shall just leave you two lovebirds in 'ere,' he tells us as he hands over the water-of-life. 'I'll be out front with the guard detail if you want me, polishing the guns. Master suite's all yours; if you want the second bedroom—' He hesitates momentarily – 'I'll take the sofa.'

He ducks out discreetly enough, but just the mention of the second bedroom is a real buzzkill in view of our recent difficulties. Mo sniffs and straightens up self-consciously. 'I'm staying the night,' she says, as if challenging me to contradict her; 'Spooky can cope, he's just a cat.'

'You can stay,' I say as gently as I can, 'if you feel safe.'

Her immediate hand-wave takes in the apartment. 'Feel those wards?' I nod. 'The agency is renting it. It isn't regular Crown Estate, but it'll do for tonight: the security was installed by a minor Saudi prince who was afraid of being strangled in his sleep by the vengeful ghost of his third wife.'

'Was he?'

'No.' She shakes her head. 'Slipped and drowned in the bathtub between rounds of golf at Gleneagles. Or maybe he fucked the wrong kelpie.'

'Should I be afraid of Saddam-style cheesecake murals on the bedroom ceilings?'

Her shoulders slump and she leans against Moby Dick's carcass. 'Same old Bob.' She sounds somewhere between nostalgic and sad.

'When the going gets tough, the tough desperately evade the issue,' I throw back at her. She *is* tense. I haven't seen her outside of meetings for ages – Dr. Armstrong all but ordered me to stay away – and I don't like what I'm seeing now in close-up. If you see someone every day you maybe don't notice the minute incremental changes, but take a few weeks out and they become glaringly obvious, and what's obvious to me right now is that she's been to a very dark place and I'm not sure she's out of it. Judging by the way she's reacting, what happened to me tonight hasn't helped. 'Okay, so not really excessively bad taste, just ten-centimeter shag carpets, a mirrored ceiling over the black silk sheets on the water bed, and an implausible collection of kangaroo-shaped sex toys ... ?'

She chuckles weakly. 'Never stop trying to cheer me up.' She knocks back a good-sized mouthful of Talisker, goes cross-eyed from the effort of trying not to spray it everywhere, and holds her breath before taking a whooping gasp. Then her mood slumps. 'I'm a bad woman, Bob. I'm about as supportive as a plank: I really ought to try harder. You deserve better than me.'

'And I'm about as perceptive as a plank so maybe we deserve one another.' I sip at my glass and the liquid evaporates before it reaches the back of my tongue. 'We've got to start somewhere.' *Change the subject before you get maudlin, Bob.* 'How does it feel not having the violin in tow all the time?'

'Like walking around naked in public.' She shivers again. 'It was weird and frightening at first but now it's almost liberating. I don't have to worry about keeping Lecter under control any more. The worst has happened, it's all history. If it hadn't nearly broken me I'd be doing just great.'

There doesn't seem to be much I can say to that so I put my arm around her and we sit in silence for a couple of minutes.

'Why are you here tonight?' I eventually ask. 'Aside from the obvious?'

She half-turns into my chest and wraps an arm around me. 'You gave me a bad fright. Also, Dr. Armstrong told me to come.' And there you have it, I just about have time to think, before she adds: 'Not that he could have stopped me with anything short of a direct order.' *Oh.*

'Um. Why?'

More hugging ensues. It's embarrassing – we're acting like teenagers – but neither of us is inclined to stop. 'Something about putting an armed guard on the stable door to stop the horse thief if they make a second attempt, I think. He said Johnny will babysit you until he can organize a personal protection detail. Maybe tomorrow.'

'What?' The words, *I'm the Eater of Souls, I don't need*

no steenking bodyguards, die before they reach my lips: the sore patch on the side of my neck aches and I remember a searing moment of near-panic, the realization that I could have lost control.

'Don't worry, they're not coming back tonight. But if they try it they'll have to come through Johnny and me.' The way she says it reminds me Mo is formidable with or without the violin. I remember the incident report on the attack on the New Annex, detailing the damage Judith Carroll inflicted on the ancient vampire sorcerer before he rolled over her. She was an Auditor. Mo is her replacement, and they have capabilities we mere mortals don't know about. Best not to ask too many questions. 'One more piece of work to do, and I'm done for the night: how about you write up your report on the SA's meeting while I examine whatever it is that your attackers were so keen to get their hands on?'

That's a no-brainer. 'Sure.' I lean over, grab my bag, open it, and pass her the envelope.

Her finger circling cautiously over the seal as she checks it for unseen wards or invisible occult finger-traps. 'Who was it . . . ?'

'A fellow from the US Postal Service Inspectorate. He's taking early retirement and thought we ought to know why.'

'Oh dear.' She frowns as she opens the envelope and removes a fat sheaf of printouts. 'This is going to take some time.'

'I'll be over there.' I stand up and shuffle towards the inhumanly clean desk at the other side of the room, tugging my bag along. I had the foresight to pack a couple of biros and a notepad, but I'm not looking forward to tomorrow's writer's cramp: I don't normally handwrite anything longer than my signature these days.

'Oh, and one last thing,' she calls across the room: 'I asked HR to book us a slot with a relationship counselor for early next week, one with a security clearance. Are you okay with that? It's in your calendar, we can change it if you want.'

'I can't—' I stop and rephrase. 'I don't see any reason why not, as long as work doesn't get in the way?' I heft the bag. 'But first . . .'

She chuckles sadly. 'Work *always* gets in the way, love, that's our problem. But we're not going to fix things by sitting around in a safe house waiting for the end of the world to fall on our heads.'

Night in the capital.

There is a row of six Georgian town houses with shared walls on one of the avenues near Sloane Square in London. Taken individually they are astronomically valuable pieces of real estate, any one of them worth tens of millions of pounds. An onlooker might suppose that they're owned by sovereign wealth funds or minor Middle Eastern royalty, like so many others in the center of the world's most expensive city.

But of course, the onlooker would be completely wrong. They're all owned by the resident of the house in the middle of the row. She's had the attic spaces combined into a single open studio workspace, she rents out the lower three floors of the other five houses for income – and she's a witch. By which I do not mean the crystal-chakra-healing kind of witch, but the consorts-with-demons, walks-between-the-raindrops, stops-hearts-with-a-single-word kind of witch. She's Baba Yaga with a laser beam, guaranteed to blow your mind. And right now Persephone Hazard is furiously, incandescently angry.

'They let *who* into the fucking country?'

It's late evening and Ms. Hazard has made an emergency exit from a gallery opening in Knightsbridge – a cocktail reception full of investment bankers looking to diversify into a new type of portfolio, WAGs with money to burn, and hopeful artists trying to get a handle on their market – in response to the news about the attack on Mr. Howard. Not only is her weekly evening off duty a washout, she has barely had time to walk in the door (never mind unpinning her hair, removing her display jewelry, or kicking off her aching Jimmy Choo couture heels) before the doorbell rang. Zero the butler admitted the guest directly, which is exceptional and would normally be bad form, but under the circumstances Persephone is more annoyed with the cause of the visit.

'Raymond Schiller,' repeats the Senior Auditor, as Zero assists him with his raincoat. He looks suitably grim. 'Or someone who claims to be the Reverend Raymond Schiller, which is not necessarily the same thing, whether or not the biometrics and the documentation matches: he hasn't been seen in public for more than twenty months, after all.'

'Someone or something,' Persephone snarls in a low tone. Then she collects herself and raises an immaculately threaded eyebrow: 'Can I offer you refreshment?'

'I wouldn't say no.' Dr. Armstrong allows Zero to steer him towards the drawing room. Persephone stalks over to the cabinet, removes a bottle and two fluted glasses, and pads after him. (Somehow, without her ever pausing, her shoes have parked themselves neatly by the front door for Zero to deal with.) 'It's a troubling development.'

'Oh, do please go on: I love your understatement.' Zero seats the SA on an antique armchair where he waits patiently while Zero moves another chair into position by his left elbow. The SA looks tired and, for want of a better word, stressed. Persephone hands him a glass, transfers the other to the same hand as the neck of the bottle of Moet. She makes a strange gesture with her free hand and the cork vanishes, allowing a perfumed mist of vapor to rise from the bottle. When she pours into her guest's glass, it doesn't dare to fizz up and overflow; she fills her own flute and sits down, then raises it in a toast. 'To survival.'

'To survival,' echoes Dr. Armstrong, then takes a sip.

Persephone downs a too-big swig of champagne. '*Fuck* Schiller and all his works.' The vehemence and venom is personal, and the atmosphere in the room chills as she curses the adversary. 'What's he doing here this time?'

'Officially, he's here on behalf of certain powerful entities in the current US administration. Sponsors in the Department of Defense, high-end Investor's Visa, funny handshakes with the ambassador in DC, and someone from the State Department hitched a ride in his Gulfstream. Apparently he's due to attend a garden party at Chequers this Saturday afternoon. Guest list is very short, starts with the Prime Minister, and includes a couple of other top cabinet briefs.' Armstrong gives the news with the stiff-upper-lip treatment reserved for word of an execution or a terminal prognosis. Persephone is so appalled that Zero tenses, moving to clear his suit jacket from fouling his belt holster, before she blinks and nods at him to stand down.

'Fuck me, the Prime Minister, *how*? I thought we headed that off at the pass two years ago?'

'Insufficient data.' Armstrong's voice is flat. 'But I'd like to note that Schiller's operation was always on the approved contractors list and for the past two years has been operating as a direct proxy for the OPA. It turns out that he's got a current security clearance with the US government, fingers in all the right pies, and a couple of tame congressmen on his string – the K Street mob, the Family, that sort of thing. And there's worse. There seems to be some kind of shift in the power balance between the hidden players in progress. I got a call this morning using a long-established emergency code from the Comstocks and sent Bob to investigate. Apparently they're undergoing a hostile takeover, and our contact wanted us to know the inside scoop. Then parties unknown nearly killed Bob. He had a very close call.'

'This—' Persephone pauses. 'How is he?'

'He performed acceptably.' The SA waits for her guarded nod before continuing. 'I've got him stashed in the new safe house with Johnny to babysit for him; Dr. O'Brien is on her way to join them. She'll take his report and we'll have something to go on in a couple of hours.'

'Huh.' Persephone crosses her legs and leans forward, rocking slightly, deep in thought. 'Was it a hit by Schiller, or an attempt to deny us intelligence?'

'Let's not get sidetracked by operational minutiae.' He takes another sip. 'We're desperately short of friends in the current cabinet, otherwise I'd look for an off-the-record briefing with a minister who could play our corner convincingly. But the business in Leeds has poisoned the well: very nasty, difficult to get them to see past the immediate fallout to the big picture. I'm very much afraid that Number Ten is actively hostile towards us and will welcome an offer emanating from the other side of the pond without fully understanding the nature of the strings attached, or looking beyond the hand he's shaking to ascertain whether the owner of the limb it's attached to is human—'

Persephone sneezes champagne bubbles, hastily banishes it with a gesture before it can spray across her lap. 'You cannot be serious!'

Armstrong shrugs. 'We have to be realists. It wouldn't be the first time we've – our – this government has – reacted inappropriately to a situation they are unfamiliar with. I suppose that's where Schiller comes in, on the other side. He was here a couple of years ago and laid the groundwork, with his missionary circus: some of the cabinet actually like him.'

Persephone lowers her glass and looks at him thoughtfully, eyes narrowing. 'You suspect the Nazgûl sent him for us.'

'If not the Nazgûl or their master, then the Sleeper.' He inclines his head. 'Schiller's kept such a low profile for the past couple of years – why move in now? I think the answer's obvious. Everything points to it.' He swallows. 'If the beings directing the Black Chamber these days deem that the situation has settled in their favor, then, well, we're a logical follow-on target. They are moving into some sort of end game, taking over all OCCINT operations in North America as a prelude to consolidating power over the entire government, and our current crisis is the perfect opportunity to expand into Europe. And that's the *best* case. Because otherwise, the Sleeper is coming for us.'

'Yes.' They sit in silent contemplation for a minute. Schiller's Church harbors an inner circle that worships the Sleeper in the Pyramid, and indeed Persephone was instrumental in preventing him from awakening his alien Lord a few years ago. The Laundry believed that Schiller had died, but now he was back, with unknown but presumably greater capabilities ... 'Do we have a plan for that? For what to do if the Sleeper came through when he returned and has taken over the OPA?'

'Not really: we'd be screwed,' the SA says flatly. 'But I don't think the situation is necessarily that bad yet. Schiller may be a puppet, the Sleeper may be stirring; but if the Sleeper were fully awake and present then its effects would be visible from orbit. As that doesn't appear to be the case we might as well focus on what we know how to fight: inadvisable political initiatives and all-too-human cultists. Which is a very good thing, because there's no force on Earth I know of that can stop the Sleeper except another Elder God.'

Persephone's expression is stony as she raises her glass, drains it in one swig, and refills without offering her companion any. She's so badly rattled that she forgets to suppress the consequential burp. She has met Schiller, heard him preach his variant theology, seen the consequences. 'You remember my report about the, the clinic? I still have bad dreams about that.' Even though her earliest memories were forged during the Balkan war and she has survived many traumatic incidents, the combined spinal injuries/ forced maternity ward for Schiller's victims in the clinic in his mountain compound was a stand-out. 'About not being able to do anything for them. Or worse, about waking up there myself, paralyzed like one of those caterpillars that parasitic wasps lay their eggs in.' She gazes into an inner distance. 'Speaking entirely hypothetically, assuming he isn't in fact the living vessel of an ancient evil, would anyone at Head Office be terribly upset if a grand piano fell on him? Because I am *so* very tempted.'

'A grand piano.' Dr. Armstrong smiles faintly, and slowly swirls his glass. 'I wish.' He raises it to his lips. 'I disapprove of wet work on principle, but I believe I could find a way to make an exception in his case, if appropriate circumstances emerged.'

They sit in tense silence for nearly a minute, both lost in thought, before Persephone speaks again: 'So let's go back to basics. It seems to me that our proximate objective is to establish what we are dealing with. Identity, intention, and execution: who is the enemy, what they want, and what their capabilities are.'

The SA nods wordlessly.

She looks at him sharply. 'This lack of input isn't like you, Michael.'

He carefully removes his gold-rimmed spectacles, pinches the bridge of his nose, and takes a deep breath. 'You're absolutely correct.' The kerchief in his suit pocket is a lens cloth, and he busies himself cleaning his glasses for a few seconds. 'I've been a little overwrought lately. On the back foot.'

She waits.

'Ever since that terrible night when we lost Judith, and so many others—' He wheezes unhappily and replaces his spectacles – 'We've been thrown into a succession of crises while woefully understaffed. One damn thing after another, all of them Never-Happen events, culminating in last month's disaster in Leeds. I'm sorry to say I've been reacting without thinking. And that's always a mistake.' The SA visibly pulls himself together. Persephone watches, fascinated and appalled.

Finally he regains his composure. 'If I don't give you any explicit instructions, I won't have to lie about them or otherwise mislead a Commons Enquiry. So. What were you about to say?'

Persephone retrieves the champagne bottle and fills up his glass. Then she begins checking off points on her fingertips. 'Item: Adversary, returned from the dead, presumed either a stalking-horse for the Black Chamber or a genuine independent player – which could be worse – shows up with a gilt-edged ticket to visit the PM at home. Other capabilities unknown but presumably he won't be any less of a nuisance than he was a couple of years ago, not with CASE NIGHTMARE GREEN in train. Item: the agency's profile is so deep in the ordure that we need a periscope to see daylight right now. So we're vulnerable to power plays and short on friends in the administration. So I have to ask: is there a domestic political threat you're not telling me about?'

The SA raises an eyebrow.

She takes a deep breath. 'Let me rephrase. Did you see Bob's performance the other night?'

'On television?' Dr. Armstrong nods. 'Do go on, please.'

'According to Bob, Paxo was heavily warded and knew far too much about us.'

'The Cabinet Office has a bottomless drawer full of high-level wards,' Dr. Armstrong remarks, deceptively casually. 'Ever since the Mandate tried to brainwash the Chief Whip, all ministers, senior civil servants, and spads are supposed to carry one at all times.'

'You should watermark them.' Persephone is carefully non-judgmental. 'So we know who to look at next time one goes missing, along with the classified briefing papers. Or to check that the ward in question is one of our own and not, for example, one supplied by a rival organization.'

'Duly noted. Please do continue ...'

'So: the Intelligence Select Committee will be starting its closed-door hearings on Q-Division SOE next week. And the cabinet reshuffle is continuing incrementally. There are rumors—' She swallows – 'that a ministerial portfolio will be created with authority for the supernatural, in view of the significant threat to national security exposed by recent events. Not to mention the recent outbreaks of superheroes, rains of frogs, beer casks full of blood, and other tabloid end-of-the-world headlines.'

The SA nods reluctantly.

Persephone closes her eyes, then opens them again. 'Get me a guest list for that garden party,' she says abruptly.

'A guest list – are you planning to send someone? You don't mean to go yourself . . . ?'

'No, that would never do. Someone might create a scene, you know. But we do need to know who else is attending. That'll tell us which direction to keep a weather eye on.' She shrugs minutely. 'Could black-bag Schiller's base while he's there, too, but that's another caper entirely.'

'What do you suspect?' The SA leans forward, holding his glass by the stem. 'Tell me, Persephone.'

'Never attribute hostile action to the enemy when even your own side want you dead.' She frowns furiously. 'You've been Civil Service almost all your career, and consequently insulated from what's going on in the private sector. You're looking for threats from the Black Chamber and the Sleeper. But that's not the only problem we've got right now. I go to the same gallery openings as those people, and I know how they do business. I need that guest list because it will tell me at a glance whether we're in the sights for privatization and outsourcing.'

Dinner is a stack of takeaway pizzas, escorted to the doorway by an apologetic cop. Johnny pays for it. Mo and I take time off from writing our reports to eat, hunched like vultures around a breakfast bar the size of an aircraft carrier in a kitchen that's all Italian marble and chromed steel. We gossip uneasily and try to avoid speculating about the evening's events. But eventually Johnny's phone rings and after a brief call he tells us that 'Seph isn't coming round to brief us after all: we're to finish the reports and he'll see they get to the SA by midnight. So we do just that, and after I turn in I spend a couple of sleepless hours staring at the ceiling before somehow my eyes close and it's morning again.

Mo, as was pretty much inevitable, took the spare bedroom. When I surface for breakfast I'm chagrined to see she's drawn an alarmingly comprehensive ward on the door in conductive ink, augmenting the already-more-than-adequate defensive grid embedded in its frame. Mo's boundary issues with the Eater of Souls raise their ugly head: she's terrified of me sleepwalking and mistaking her for a midnight snack. I wish I could say this was unreasonable of her. She's left a circle labelled KNOCK HERE, so I do, and ask, 'Coffee?'

'Did someone say coffee?' she mumbles.

'It's in the kitchen,' I tell her, then shuffle through the living area to the breakfast bar, where I start hunting for the wherewithal to deliver on the promise.

Typical. This furnished flat, renting for something north of £2000 a night, comes with a cheap filter machine and no coffee or other supplies in the spotless walk-in refrigerator. Luckily there is a Café Nero across the street, so after checking on our guards Johnny nips out. Breakfast consequently consists of reheated bacon and egg rolls, coffee in cardboard cartons, and stomach acid. I'm rubbing my itching chin and cheeks (furnished flats don't come with shavers either) and Mo is futilely trying to fix her bed-hair when my phone rings.

''Lo,' I say.

'Mr. Howard.' I sit up: it's the SA. 'Are Dr. O'Brien and Mr. McTavish with you?'

'Yes—' They're both looking at me – 'they're here.'

'Good. I've read your report and the briefing Mr. McKracken gave you. I'll be round shortly to explain what's going on. In the meantime, please don't leave the flat.'

'What?' demands Mo as soon as I hang up.

'It's the SA. He's coming here.' Why does she look momentarily appalled? It's a sign of yet more history we don't share: Is it something dodgy about the Auditors, or else a deeper unease ...? 'We're to stay indoors until he arrives.'

'Right ...' Johnny regards the Café Nero paper bag and the remains of its contents with distaste verging on resignation. 'Like that's going to work. Ah well.' He drains his coffee cup. 'I made sure the neighbors didn't see me, anyway.'

'Neighbors?' Mo asks.

'Neighbors.' Johnny grimaces. 'I didn't want to worry you last night and I'd rather leave it to 'is self to fill you in this morning.'

The entryphone buzzes for attention, and Johnny marches off to negotiate with building security and the armed guard on our front door. Mo looks at me looking at her. 'What?' we ask each other simultaneously. I shrug, and she looks archly amused. It's one of those marital telepathy moments that you start getting after a few years together, and I feel a sudden pang of acute isolation. 'Johnny's holding out,' I say, just as she tells me, 'We're about to find out.'

She's right: Dr. Armstrong marches in, and he's carrying a Café Nero paper bag too. 'Good morning!' He smiles and places it on the breakfast bar. Then he sees the detritus: 'Johnny?'

'Before you rang, guv, I took precautions.' Johnny, padding after him, slides onto a leather-topped bar stool.

'Jolly good.' The SA manages to sound like an absent-minded headteacher when he does that; it makes me wonder how deep Angleton's influence on the organization ran, but he doesn't give me time to woolgather. 'I brought croissants and coffee, so dig in,' he says. 'All right. You've probably worked it out already, haven't you?' he asks Mo.

'What? The reason for this unaccustomed ... luxury?' An ironic shoulder-waggle (she's holding a fresh coffee cup) takes in the apartment as a whole.

'I'm guessing a room in the Ibis was out of your price range,' I joke.

It falls flat. 'Not exactly.' The SA glances at Johnny. 'Incursions? Probes?'

'Nothing. It's as if 'e ain't even here.'

'Well then.' The SA stares at his coffee cup as if he can't remember what to do with it. Then he glances at me. 'We leased this apartment in a hurry yesterday, when we first learned Schiller was in London. We had no indications his people – or anyone else – would attempt to snatch you. But—' he's watching Mo, I realize – 'it was the logical place to put you under the circumstances.'

'Wait. *What* circumstances?'

Johnny recoils slightly and Mo's eyes widen: the SA looks as imperturbable as ever. 'The entity identifying itself as Raymond Schiller is very unlikely to suspect that you are in the very same building, two floors up, wouldn't you say? In a secure, heavily warded apartment with another empty secure suite between your floor and his ceiling.' The old bastard actually looks pleased with himself.

'How is this a good thing?' I ask tensely.

'Well—' Johnny raises an eyebrow at the SA, who tips him the nod – 'seems to me, guv, that what we're dealing with probably isn't exactly the same old Raymond Schiller, is 'e?'

The SA looks away. 'We haven't confirmed that yet,' he says quietly. 'We do know that Persephone shut down the gate he used to get to the Temple of the Sleeper, presumably trapping him in a pyramid on a lifeless world with only his undead god for company. There is no evidence of him being present anywhere on Earth during the next four months. Some bits of the UK/USA intelligence arrangement still work normally for us, even though the OCCINT community weren't wired into the treaty process, and according to our colleagues in the Doughnut his metadata logfile simply flatlined during that period. No mobile phone usage, no personal bank or credit card activity, no appointments with his visiting hairdresser, nothing to indicate he was alive.'

He clears his throat. 'But then, eighteen months ago, signs of electronic life reappeared. Schiller doesn't carry his own phone, but his social graph, the pattern of calls he places, is distinctive. For the previous four months a law firm owned by Golden Promise Ministries handled his affairs under power of attorney; as soon as the calls started, power of attorney went back in its box. Cards unfrozen, private appointments resumed. Just like returning to everyday life after a long stay in hospital or a stretch in prison.'

'Who knew?' Mo asks tensely.

'Not many.' Dr. Armstrong's voice is softly reassuring. 'We did not think it appropriate to spread the knowledge far and wide. A cell was established with a watching remit, Johnny and Persephone leading, the Reverend Peter Russell supplying specialist analysis on request. He wasn't briefed,' the SA adds. 'By the time Schiller reappeared Bob was already fully occupied by the OPERA CAPE project.'

I resist the impulse to groan and clutch my head theatrically.

Mo says it for me, with quiet vehemence: 'Schiller didn't come back from the Sleeper's Temple under his own power. So we've known for – what, at least eighteen months? – that the Sleeper in the Pyramid was, if not fully engaged, then at least able to act through a proxy in our world?'

'Yes,' says the SA regarding her with a saintly calm that would amount to suicidal daring if he was a lesser mortal. I know what the tightening around her lips and the warning glint in her eyes means, and if I was in her sights I'd be diving for cover. 'We've been rather overstretched lately,' he says, as if making a huge concession. 'We are in a time of crisis after all. Would it have helped to give you more things to worry about while you were dealing with Lecter, or while you—' he's looking at me – 'were tidying up after James?'

I stare at him in disbelief. 'I might have rebalanced my priorities accordingly,' I say through gritted teeth.

'Yes, well, water under the bridge, spilled milk, and so on.' (Imperturbable, yes, but dismissive isn't like the SA at all. Is he getting a trifle defensive, perhaps?) 'We don't have enough high-level resources to allow ourselves to be distracted. In the absence of clear evidence about Schiller's purpose in coming here we are not in a position to act directly against him – yet. He has, you will note, cordial relations at the highest levels of government.'

Johnny snorts.

'Be that as it may,' the SA continues, 'we have a known agent of an external threat who is now in our back yard with an invitation to a private reception at the Prime Minister's country residence this weekend. We are not in a position to get close to him at that event—' the shadow of a frown crosses his face – 'insufficient cleared assets of the right profile, I'm afraid. But we *are* in a position to keep an eye on the guest list and monitor comings and goings to the apartment he has rented for his stay in London. And if circumstances demand it, to mount an intervention.' He flashes his pearly choppers at me in something not unlike an impish smile: 'I intend to determine the enemy's objectives and then neutralize him once and for all, but only after we have acquired sufficient evidence to convince even the Cabinet Office that he's an unsuitable playmate for Number Ten.'

Mo is looking at him as if mesmerized. Finally she speaks up. 'Excuse me. By what authority do you act?' She adds, hesitantly, 'This sounds to me as if you're taking on executive responsibility.'

'Indeed, and normally that would be a breach of the Chinese wall between audit and operational arms.' Now the SA's imperturbability slips, at least enough to allow a slightly waspish note to sneak into his voice: 'Need I remind you that we are currently overstretched? Also that the nature of this investigation is so sensitive that it would be inadvisable to brief additional personnel?'

The penny drops. 'The Wilson Doctrine,' I say. It's the long-standing rule that the security services do not spy on the communications of the government itself, in the person of the Prime Minister and the cabinet. It's not a law, exactly, but breaking it isn't something to be undertaken lightly –

'The Wilson Doctrine has been effectively a dead letter for some time now, because of the Five Eyes' approach to blanket data retention, but it has not yet been formally repudiated by Downing Street, so it remains on the shelf as a stick to beat the unwilling mule with.' The SA hesitates. 'After the briefing by Ms. Womack, she shared certain new guidelines that the Steering Committee has been preparing for myself and the Audit committee.' He glances at Mo apologetically. 'I believe everybody present has a need to know.'

Mo clears her throat. 'The Steering Committee sets operational policy for Mahogany Row, with legal input from the Assizes' Chambers,' she tells me, then gives the SA a questioning look.

'Yes.' He nods. 'While Mahogany Row is part of a service not regulated directly by CRAG, we are constrained by the need to work within our existing guidelines and requirements. The Audit Committee's job is to ensure that the service, and senior staff and associates who are part of MR, including External Assets—' a nod at Johnny – 'comply with the regulations and laws governing the service. But if MR is to split from the Civil Service—' I startle: that's a much blunter description than Ms. Womack used – 'then we're going to be so short-staffed that we'll all be wearing multiple hats for a while. So there are provisions for us to operate in multiple roles, subject to crosschecks.

'So. I am taking personal control of this operation, which I'm designating GOD GAME INDIGO, on my authority as a DSS(3)—' two levels above me, one level above Angleton – 'and you, Dr. O'Brien, will be my number two, in charge of both internal and external assets. Additionally, in your capacity as a staff Auditor, you are required to call me out if you think I am exceeding my remit.'

Mo looks appalled. But the SA hasn't finished: now he looks at Johnny, and then at me. 'You are all on the inside, as is Persephone. Because you are part of Mahogany Row you are already privy to GOD GAME RAINBOW and CASE NIGHTMARE RAINBOW, and I need your particular skills. But because you are known to the target we need to bring in some clean faces as well. Along with Persephone, we are the entire fully briefed team so far. I think—' he pauses – 'it would be expedient to bring in at least two PHANGs; if nobody has any objections I propose to pull in Ms. Murphy and accept her recommendation for one other. We brought you here last night, Mr. Howard, because it was an emergency and in my judgment the short-term risk of direct exposure to the target was minimal. But after we find a better safe house for you you'll be staying well clear of this installation unless you're specifically needed here. We'll install a surveillance team drawn from regular Laundry line personnel, but the threat surface will be kept as small as possible and the line/PHANG staff will not be given full GOD GAME RAINBOW clearance.'

'What *exactly* is our objective?' I ask.

'We're going to stake out Schiller, find out what he's up to, and stop him,' says the SA, at which point I almost jump up and hug him. He raises a warning finger: 'But before we stop him, we need to find out what he's trying to accomplish, how powerful he is, and how far his influence extends. We thought we'd blocked his attempt to influence the government two years ago but we were wrong; this time we can't afford to make any mistakes. So it's vitally important that we don't tip him off ...'

Johnny and I skulk out of the rear service entrance of the apartment block wearing dark glasses and hoodies, like rock stars in rehab sneaking past the paparazzi – at least that's the flattering version of it. A waiting police car whisks us off in the direction of Chelsea, to a row of unnaturally quiet town houses where the defensive wards are clustered so thick they make the hairs on my arms stand up. 'You'll like the Duchess's pad, guv,' he tells me, 'she does enjoy 'er bit of posh.'

(Behind us, Mo and the SA wait for the surveillance team's first shift to move in, then leave via the front door. None of the building's other residents have any idea who they are, so subterfuge is pointless. But the two of us are known to Schiller and his associates, so discretion is mandatory.)

Johnny shows me to the front door, which he opens – he has a key. I try to ignore the potentially lethal summoning grid under the welcome mat, but he notices my discomfort and smirks: 'Duchess says you can't be too careful in this end of the big smoke. Just last month, the chairman of Barings what lives round the corner got 'isself and 'is lady wife burgled by your proverbial blokes in balaclavas; they cleaned out half a mil in jewelry. Now, if 'e'd had security like this—' a quick jerk of the head prompts me to glance at a small framed print hanging across the lobby from the door – 'been another story, right?'

I glare at the framed print hanging on the wall opposite the front door. The insensate nodule of existential emptiness trapped in it stares back at me with ravening intent for an instant before it recognizes what I am and hastily finds something else to hunger for. 'Entrapment is illegal,' I remind Johnny as I study the ward binding the demon. (It's pretty solid, but if there's a house fire. . .)

'If you'd ever 'ad a man come through the door with a gun, me old cock—'

'Been there, done that.' (Although I feel pretty safe here: only an utter idiot would try and burgle the home of London's most powerful witch.)

Persephone Hazard's front door opens into a small vestibule, which could easily be mistaken for a porch if not for the presence of the aforementioned trapped demon and a number of other fascinatingly lethal surprises. An archway leads through into a narrow hall, and off to one side I see that centerpiece of the classic Georgian town house, a morning room.

Johnny goes straight in, calling, 'Duchess? Oh, hi Zero. It's me and Bob. Gang's all here.'

Zero, the butler, ushers us both into the morning room. It's decorated in coordinated Laura Ashley prints and antique furniture. If not for the tasteful indirect LED lighting and the electrical outlets I could picture a mid-Victorian

MP's wife and her brood of daughters sitting around, drinking tea and receiving visitors. (Well, minus Johnny, me, or Zero the butler, who looks more like a bouncer at the kind of night club you don't get into unless you have a Twitter following and a bank balance in seven digits.) 'She's upstairs, in the lab,' Zero tells us. 'I'll just let her know you're here. Would you prefer tea or coffee?' No 'sir' I notice: he's not that kind of butler.

Coffee is procured while we wait: Jamaican Blue Mountain. A few minutes later Persephone emerges. This morning she's dressed down, wearing jeans and an old army sweater with shoulder and elbow patches: her lab gear, going by the burn marks. She looks my way and smiles, not unpleasantly. 'Bob, because of the circumstances – Schiller and his movable circus being in town – the SA asked if I could put you and Johnny up in the spare rooms. If you've got luggage in a lock-up somewhere, give Zero the tickets and he'll collect it while you're in the office.'

'Wait,' I say, then stop. I had some vague idea about actually staying in my own spare bedroom, if Mo and I can clean it out: that's warded too. But then my brain catches up. 'Are your wards certified by Facilities?' I ask doubtfully.

'Who do you think chaired the working group that drafted the common criteria for safe houses?' Her smile takes some of the sting out of the put-down. 'Anyway, you shouldn't go home just yet. If someone's hunting you, you don't want to lead them to Dr. O'Brien.'

She's right, dammit, but she didn't answer my question. 'Are you sure this is safe?'

'Mr. Howard.' Her expression is that of a particularly long-suffering primary school teacher towards a very slow learner: 'You know what you are. You know what I am. And you've seen Johnny in action. If you're worried about civilian casualties in event of a rumble, I own the properties to either side. And?' She points to a discreet plastic clamshell on the wall by the doorway: 'That's a panic button. I have the Diplomatic Protection Group on speed-dial: we're less than a hundred yards from embassy row. You'll be more exposed entering and leaving the New Annex for meetings, but while you're under my roof you're very welcome to ask Zero for a ride.' Persephone likes her cars. She has a Bentley Mulsanne turbo and her name is on the waiting list for a Tesla as soon as they begin selling them over here.

I swallow. 'I don't want to be too much trouble, but—'

'Nonsense.' There's that smile again: fey, slightly manic. 'This house was a hotel for a few years before I moved in and renovated it, did you know that? It'll do us good to open up a couple of the guest rooms. And anyway, it's a much better location than your place – you live too far out in the sticks for what's coming.'

'What's—' *Uh-oh.* 'What's that supposed to mean?'

'You're on the public radar and your hands are completely clean – you weren't even in the country when things went to pieces up north. So you're one of the public faces of the organization, like it or not, Mr. Howard. Which means when you're not working on your own projects or helping out Dr. Armstrong in his executive role, you can expect to be summoned to testify in front of the Commons Select Committee on Intelligence. Who I gather will begin holding closed hearings this afternoon. You're on the list for later this week and you need to begin getting your ducks in a row right now.'

As I learn when I finally get to check my calendar, the Commons Select Committee hearings are indeed due to kick off that afternoon. I'm not going to be called to give evidence for another two days.

It's late morning when Zero drops me off outside the New Annex, but work waits for no man and I've got a ton of admin to catch up on before I can start working out what exactly I'm going to tell the MPs. Luckily there are no murderous cultists or tabloid photographers waiting to doorstep me outside the office, which is a mercy. The cops are back on door duty with their mirror-visored helmets and matte body armor, but they pay no particular attention as I enter. I head for my office, sit down, sigh loudly, and poke at my inbox and schedule. It's nearly twelve o'clock, I have a mild headache, and after a minute or three I diagnose an excess of blood in my caffeine stream, so I head to the break room. People get out of my way, either because I have become a giant cockroach overnight or, less unreasonably, because I look like death and I will reap the soul of anyone who gets between me and my coffee.

I grab a mug of institutional paint-stripper and stalk back to my den, just in time for my monitor to ping. It's the SA: he wants me to drop by his office for a, a – *what the fuck is a media performance review?* I wonder irritably. It's in my Outhouse calendar, though, along with other flagged attendees: Mhari and Vikram. And that's my evening fucked, because it's blocked through until 8 p.m. tonight. Then I spot the start time and swear. I have twenty-five minutes to dash to the canteen, swallow whatever's on offer, and get to Dr. Armstrong's office.

I luck out. There's no queue in the canteen when I get there and they've still got some food on the hot counter. I wolf down a steak and kidney pie with baked beans, and at least my stomach isn't rumbling when I dash for the staircase to Dr. Armstrong's office on the fourth floor.

'Ah, good afternoon, Bob.' The SA himself answers the door. I enter and collapse on his sofa. The SA's office is like the den of a somewhat eccentric Oxford don, his sole concession to modernity being an antique 1990s green-screen computer terminal perched on one end of his blotter. (Angleton doubtlessly chewed him out in his own inimitable way for courting disaster through Van Eck phreaking, but hey: that was long ago and in another country, and besides, the barrow-wight is dead.) The office itself is slightly disturbing. It occupies a four-meter-deep slice of the New Annex floor plan but is at least seven meters long, and Dr. Armstrong keeps the window bay permanently shrouded with blackout curtains. It's no weirder than Angleton's office, which swapped buildings once while nobody was looking, but this is the sort of thing that leads sane Laundry employees to give DSS-level practitioners a wide berth. I'm probably heading that way myself, come to think of it.

The door opens again and Vikram Choudhury enters. Vik doesn't have an occult bone in his body unless you categorize management as a black art. 'Bob.' He nods. 'Dr. Armstrong.' He's staggering slightly under the weight of a huge armful of stuff; after a moment I realize it consists entirely of newspapers. He wheezes slightly as he deposits them on the SA's coffee table. 'I thought we could – oh, hello.' An otherwise unremarkable section of the wall opens and Mhari steps out. She closes the panel and straightens her jacket, as if it's perfectly normal to enter the SA's sanctum via a secret door that can't possibly lead anywhere inside the building's real-world floor plan. 'Bob,' she smiles impishly, 'Dr. Armstrong, Vik, is this us?'

'Yes,' says the SA. 'Please make yourselves comfortable. Mr. Choudhury, what do we have here?'

Vik folds himself into the middle of the sofa, Mhari bags the visitor's chair, and the SA himself pulls his ancient wooden banker's chair out from behind the desk so that he can loom over the occasional table like an amiable thundercloud.

'The *Daily Mail, Daily Express,* and the *Daily Mirror.*' Vik separates the tabloids as he unfolds them. 'Also the *Sun,* the *Metro* ... and that's all the significant tabloids.' He starts a new pile: broadsheets this time. 'The *Scotsman* and the *Yorkshire Post,* to represent the regionals. Finally, the big four: *The Times,* the *Independent,* the *Guardian,* and the *Telegraph.*' He looks as serious as a heart attack. 'If we each pick three, this will go faster.'

'What are we supposed to be doing?' I ask.

'Combing them for coverage,' Mhari tells me. 'Any mention – substantive news, human interest pieces, scurrilous gossip, editorial, and other lies – basically anything about you, Bob.'

I stifle a groan. 'Why would you want to do that?'

'Because you're our public face now, Bob.' The SA speaks with the compassionate tone of a doctor giving me a terminal prognosis. 'We want to see what the papers make of you, with a chance to discuss it. Do bear in mind that when you're up in front of the Select Committee, this reportage is going to inform their first impressions of you. We could pay a clippings agency to do this for us but we'd still have to read what they sent – and this way, paid out of my pocket, it's entirely unofficial.' And thereby invisible and deniable. *Hmm.*

'But isn't it all about the Facetweets and interwebbytubenet these days?' I protest. 'These are just loss-leading birdcage liners put out by billionaire tax exiles to offset their double-Irish Dutch cheese sandwich tax arrangements, right? Clickbait for crumblies.'

'Old people vote,' Mhari says, with mild asperity, 'and there's an election coming up. *Do* try to keep up, Bob.'

'We're not campaigning for office, though—' I stop dead as my brain finally catches up with my tongue. '*Oh.*'

'Yes,' says Dr. Armstrong. 'And there's an ongoing cabinet reshuffle right now. Get skimming, there's a good lad?'

'It shouldn't be too painful as long as you avoid the op-eds about which reality star is getting what bits of their anatomy surgically enhanced in the run-up to their celebrity wedding,' Mhari adds cruelly. Now she knows I'm going to be unable to avoid them.

Because I've wasted time carping I end up with the bottom of the pile and have to spend half an hour wading through the *Express* ('Does the Spirit of Diana Make You Fat? Are Elves Communists?'), the *Mail* ('Elven Scum Are Coming for Your Daughters!'), and the *Sun* ('Phwoar, Get a Load of Santa's Lovely Helper's Jubblies!'). This forcible dunking in the collective subconscious of the British public leaves me feeling dirty, but I'm relieved to discover that I rate zero column-inches in the *Mail* and *The Sun*. There is a short piece on page 11 of the *Express,* wherein the ink-on-paper equivalent of a talk-radio shock jock expresses dismay that in last night's Paxo Roast the great man didn't interrogate 'the boffin from the Ministry of Magic' with red-hot pliers and pilliwinks, but as I don't even rate a name check I've got to concede that the SA might be taking my meteoric rise to national celebrity status a bit too seriously. So I'm just getting ready to breathe a sigh of relief when Mhari excitedly says, 'Ooh, that's interesting!' and punctures my balloon.

'What is?' I lean towards her.

'It's the *Telegraph* business section.' She holds up a quarter-page piece, solid text and a very unwelcome and familiar photograph. 'Did you guys know about this?'

The SA leans forward and adjusts his half-moon spectacles. 'Oh *dear*,' he says very softly. 'Oh dear me.'

'What is it?' Vikram asks tensely.

'American Televangelist in Outsourcing Deal with Serco,' reads Mhari. 'Dr. Raymond Schiller's GP Security has just inked a thirty-six-million-pound initial contract to handle domestic security operations on behalf of ...'

She keeps on reading, but I know instantly that we're fucked. GP Security is now officially in bed with one of the biggest government outsourcing corporations in the UK, and you don't have to be a genius to put two and two together.

I spend the next couple of days drinking bad coffee, making list after list of things I'm not supposed to say in public while bearing in mind that the people I'll be briefing on the committee under parliamentary privilege have all got security clearances that theoretically cover most contingencies, living on canteen food, and going home to Persephone's town house to crash for a few hours each night. My accounting procedures and project management standards homework is unaccountably neglected: can't think why. In between I snatch time to chew over the DELIRIUM file contents with Mo and the Senior Auditor a few times, but we don't reach any firm conclusions about it. It's disturbing, true, but not that different from any number of other public-private partnership stitch-ups. This sort of thing happens all the time in the state sector these days, and the only thing that makes this case different is the unacknowledged remit of the agencies involved.

Then it's suddenly four o'clock on a Friday afternoon, and instead of the usual weekly wrap-up meeting, I'm enduring a grilling in a conference room in Whitehall.

My interrogator is the Right Honorable Lord Swiveleyes of Stow-on-the-Wold, a retired Big Cheese from MI5 who is eking out his political afterlife in the Lords – and he is slowly driving me mad. He has a maddeningly rhythmic cadence that's *just* too slow, as if he's trying to lull me to sleep, but it's entirely deliberate, then every so often he speeds up abruptly and throws me a curveball. I *hate* being cross-examined by barristers.

I'm tired because I slept badly – stayed up too late giving my revision notes a final once-over, then had too many nightmares about being interviewed live on TV by a gently smiling journalist with a giant extradimensional woodlouse for a tongue – but I can't afford to lose track in front of the Defense Select Committee. It would be Very Bad Form – possibly bad enough that they'd consign me to the Tower of London, given the way this session is going. If only I'd woken up this morning, headed for Heathrow, and hijacked an airliner to Syria. (Yes I *know* they're supposed to shoot them down when they're hijacked these days. Not that they're flying a normal service again, after the events in Yorkshire: but that's the point.) I'm standing under the spotlights in my monkey suit, trying not to admit that anyone in the organization I work for broke the law. *Any* law. Because they're out for blood – and mine will do, if nobody juicier comes to hand.

They hauled me in for two reasons. Firstly, I'm senior enough to represent the organization in public, and secondly, I'm junior enough they think they can squeeze me for gossip before they go on to interrogate higher-level folks using the ammunition I negligently left lying around. So it's a no-win situation for me, and for the organization. Oh, and because I've been on TV, they (or their staffers and spads) know who I am. So there is no escape.

The worst part? *They keep asking the same fucking question*, over and over, from different angles. (Who do they think they are, Paxo?)

'Where exactly were you when you first learned of the existence of *elves*, Mr. Howard?' my tormentor repeats for the fourth time, hunching forward over his microphone. (He pronounces the word *elves* in portentous tones, as if he thinks they're some kind of TV special effect.)

I try not to roll my eyes.

'I was first made aware of the existence of a gracile hominid species distinct from our own kind – *Homo sapiens sapiens* – seven months ago, in a weekly briefing paper circulated by our scientific liaison department. Professor McPherson of the Natural History Museum's Department of Paleontology delivered a lecture to some of my colleagues describing the recent discovery of a ritual burial site in the Republic of Ireland. Approximately a thousand years ago—'

There is a brief muttering among the assembled MPs, civil servants, and assistants behind the horseshoe-shaped ring of conference tables that focus around the podium I'm standing at. 'Silence, please!' calls the chair. 'Please continue, Mr. Howard.'

'Thank you. As I said, I came across this report in a weekly news bulletin that crossed my email inbox, but I confess I only skimmed it at the time and didn't pay close attention.'

And the inevitable derail happens: '*Why not?*' The Keen Young Thing on the edge of the front row demands triumphantly, as if I just confessed to treasonable negligence.

'As I'm sure the Right Honorable member is aware, the Division has a variety of roles and responsibilities. My personal duties at the time had absolutely nothing to do with tracking new discoveries in paleontology. I am certain everyone here is as up to date on the deliberations of the Commons Select Committee on Intellectual Property Rights as I was, *at that time*—' this doesn't even provoke a titter: they're *really* looking for blood – 'on a discovery by another department that was assessed by those involved as being of purely historical interest.'

'But you *would* agree that your organization was aware, on some level, of the existence of *H. alfarensis*, Mr. Howard? As much as seven months ago?'

Oh for fuck's sake. 'Individuals within the organization were aware that another hominid species, *presumed extinct*, had persisted into the historical record.' I put a heavy emphasis on the presumed extinct. 'This isn't unprecedented. The hobbits, *H. floresiensis*, died out about ten thousand years ago; elves, we thought, had become extinct somewhat more recently. I'd like to emphasize that there was *no* evidence of anomalous technology or occult capabilities associated with the Specimen B burial site. All we had was an Iron Age ritual burial of an executed – beheaded – non-human.'

Keen Young Thing subsides in a mound of disappointed pinstriped tailoring. To his right, Lord Swiveleyes bloats up slightly, then starts to drone on again. He goes straight back into interrogation mode: 'How do you account for your department's unaccountable lack of follow-up, Mr. Howard, in light of the discovery of Specimen B?'

I'm running low on fucks given, so help me. If he'd just bothered to *read the after-action report* he'd know all this – 'Hindsight is wonderful, and in the wake of this month's events we now have a context for understanding the discovery of Specimen B which was absent at the time of discovery. The Morningstar Empire ceased exploring the ghost roads when their own world descended into a thaumaturgically enhanced world war, approximately a thousand years ago. The Host, our intruders, survived and entered a period of suspended animation for the intervening centuries in an attempt to out-wait the aftermath. It is currently believed that Specimen B was a forward reconnaissance asset – a spy or special forces operative – who was stranded in dark ages Ireland when the balloon went up. Isolated and cut off, they were unable to pass for human and so resorted to theft to keep body and soul together, until a local war band or tribal leader hunted them down and executed them. I emphasize that this is merely speculation: after a thousand years there's no way to be sure, and the Host's records are fragmentary.'

I pause for a moment and catch my breath. 'The existence of *H. alfarensis* was noted by our Operational Oversight group and assigned a low threat probability because no incursion had been noted more recently than the Norman invasion. Nevertheless, contingency plans that had been drafted purely speculatively – I will note that PLAN RED RABBIT was a methodological training exercise, not a real war plan – were reviewed and kept up to date accordingly.'

'But why didn't you—'

And so on and so forth, all bloody afternoon.

The clusterfuck in Yorkshire was a Never Happens event, like an airliner crashing or a surgeon amputating the wrong leg: something that supposedly can't happen unless institutional procedures fail or aren't followed. This enquiry *should* be about determining which of these cases apply and producing findings so that we can draw up new guidelines that ensure it never happens again.

But this particular mess went above and beyond the call of duty, rising from the dizzy heights of fuck-uppery – an air transport operator dropping a loaded 747 – to the moon-shot-level insanity of losing over twelve thousand lives and several tens of billions of pounds' worth of property damage to an invasion by hitherto-mythological beings. It's the worst disaster on British soil since the Second World War. And in case that isn't bad enough, there's a general election coming up on May 18 next year and we're already featuring prominently in the campaign ramp-up by all parties.

In such a febrile atmosphere, they're not going to settle for a bloodless enquiry finding along the lines of mistakes-were-made (here's a checklist, try not to do it again); nothing short of a public gibbeting will slake the bloodlust. I just hope it's not my neck in the noose when it happens.

Saturday evening: the Prime Minister's Garden Party.

There is a sixteenth-century mansion near Ellesborough, in the middle of a country estate surrounded by woods at the foot of Coombe Hill. The house has a long and prestigious history: it contains a large collection of memorabilia associated with Oliver Cromwell, and once guarded a royal prisoner. Remodeled in the early twentieth century to restore the original Tudor paneling and windows, it was subsequently donated to the nation to serve as the Prime Minister's rural weekend retreat.

This weekend the PM is in residence, throwing a garden party for selected members of the great and the good. Security is tight. As Raymond Schiller's BMW crunches to a stop at the end of the graveled drive, close protection officers from the Metropolitan Police wave it to one side, then politely inspect both its occupants and the underside of the vehicle. Schiller puts up with the formalities in good humor, rolling down his window to allow the officers to identify himself and Anneka. Checklists are updated. 'Good morning, sir,' says the sergeant, finally moving to hold the door for him. 'You're expected: please go right on inside.'

Chequers Court is small and unimpressive by the standards Schiller is used to. The billionaire donors and tycoons he rubs shoulders with generally took the antique stone piles of the English aristocracy as a starting point for their fantasy palaces, rather than the destination. Consequently, the reception laid out in the Hawtrey Room feels curiously like stepping into cramped middle-class 1950s suburbia. It's a surprisingly small room with drab carpet, chintzy overstuffed armchairs, and occasional tables that might have been sourced from a Martha Stewart franchise shop. The oak-paneled walls lend an oppressive, tight feeling to a room that isn't very open in the first place. But the furniture and oak paneling are four hundred years old, and these aren't Martha Stewart reproductions: this is the real deal. Schiller takes a deep breath and reminds himself that he's not being shuffled off into the parlor frequented by the PM's chauffeur and security detail when they're on call.

Well-dressed domestic staff approach and offer Schiller his choice of tea, coffee, or a very acceptable Merlot; for Anneka he requests a glass of mineral water. They are politely steered towards a pair of wing-back chairs close to a cold stone fireplace. 'The PM will be along in a few minutes,' murmurs the butler. 'His last meeting has overrun. If there is anything I can do to make you comfortable, please don't hesitate to ask.'

Schiller smiles. 'I'll be fine,' he says, resisting a naughty impulse to test the outer limits of the butler's willingness to serve. (Schiller's little master is hungry, for there have been no opportunities to feed since they flew out of New York.) He relaxes in the chair, sips his glass of wine, nibbles canapés from an eighteenth-century porcelain plate, and considers his next move. Anneka stands with one hand on the back of his chair, his vigilant shadow alert for threats. Her water glass sits on the table, ignored.

As it happens, he isn't kept waiting long. The door at the far end of the room opens and Jeremy Michaels struts in, followed by the Cabinet Secretary, Adrian Redmayne, whose expression suggests he has not yet recovered from drinking one too many G&Ts the night before. Michaels is as complacently self-assured in private as in public – when he's oozing false sincerity for the TV cameras – and Schiller forces himself to smile warmly.

The Prime Minister might be a pompous and self-satisfied upper-class twit who married an heiress and counts the Queen as a second cousin, but he's amazingly good at persuading people to do what he wants (like make him leader of a political party, then appoint him to head the government). If Schiller can get him on board with his project everything will flow smoothly; if not, it will be tediously necessary to install a new PM. He still needs to meet with Nigel Irving, the Secretary of State for Defense. He also needs to get the Home Secretary on board, but she's not stupid and if she wants to be the next resident of Number Ten she'll play ball. Today's priority is the Cabinet Office, and this is Schiller's opportunity to take Mr. Redmayne in hand. The highest-ranking civil servant in the land has been attending Sunday services at a church affiliated with Schiller's mission for the past three years, but Schiller believes in adding personal contact to the denomination connection. The only real problem he can foresee is that these upper-class Brits think of religion as an embarrassing weakness, and Irving in particular is a notorious libertine. So he can't count on the Come-to-Jesus glad-handing that works at home to soften up these people. He's going to have to approach the topic sideways, with a smirk and a wink.

'Ah, Dr. Schiller!' The PM is friendly, if not effusive. 'So good of you to visit, and at short notice, too.' Redmayne clears his throat and sidles in for a handshake, mustn't be left out in the cold, then briefly glances sidelong at his boss before looking back at Schiller. Schiller's smile broadens as he squeezes the man's hand reassuringly. The PM clears his throat. 'Adrian tells me you have an interesting angle on the recent unpleasantness up north and that I should give it due consideration.' Michaels is looking at Redmayne with an avuncular expression. It's as if the head boy is indulging his pet snitch, just for once, but the story had better be a good one or tears will be shed behind the bike shed before sundown. Doubtless the PM has got his Civil Service supremo nailed, and has a good idea how much Schiller has paid for this half-hour slot – cash for access comes under the eleventh commandment: *thou shalt not get caught* – but none of that matters as long as Schiller uses his time effectively.

'Thank you for making time for me in your busy schedule.' Schiller, who stood for their entrance, waves towards the seats and waits for the PM to get comfortable. 'Very regrettable, I'm afraid, the business in Leeds. But this is what you must expect if you trust an old-fashioned organization untouched by modern management principles to deal effectively with the – I'm sorry, I have to say this – forces of darkness. Without oversight, mistakes are inevitable, and the public at large cannot be expected to understand the difference between a rogue agency failing disastrously and a responsibly managed, effective arm of government—' The PM is turning an entertaining shade of puce, so Schiller hurries it along – 'but you're going to change all that,' he completes, and pauses to take a sip from Anneka's water glass.

'I was under the impression that you had a concrete proposal.' He's still polite, but there is a barely restrained impatience to Michaels's tone.

'I do.' Schiller drops the smile. 'As you will have become aware, the US government has its own agencies for containing the sort of threat you confronted so recently. And as Mr. Redmayne has doubtless told you, much of my business is concerned with providing private sector support to the Operational Phenomenology Agency – the name is deliberately anodyne – in combating similar demonic incursions. Which is why you haven't seen one in the United States. We have a twenty-three-year track record of activity in this sector, with a fully security-cleared organization that can offer a full range of supporting security functions ranging from base and perimeter patrols to large-scale exorcisms and witchcraft interdiction. More importantly, we're used to working with the big boys – the OPA alone has a larger budget than your GCHQ, MI5, and SIS combined – and we're used to working as a junior contractor on outsourced agency projects managed by federal and enterprise-level service entities such as Halliburton, Carlyle Group, and Serco, and security specialists like Xe and G4S.'

He pauses to take another sip of water. He has the PM's undivided attention; behind Michaels's shoulder, the Cabinet Secretary is giving Schiller the indulgent smile of a waiter expecting a fat tip from a happy customer.

'Do go on,' purrs the Prime Minister.

'I don't presume to tell you how to handle the current situation,' Schiller says carefully. 'Nor is it my place to make any suggestion over how your security agencies should be managed. But I can't help noting that SOE is entirely self-governed, operating almost completely outside the normal Civil Service guidelines. They are in effect a rogue agency with a strong institutional culture of keeping everything in-house and using no external support organizations. This is both a strength and a weakness; groupthink can lead to failure to respond to new threats in a timely manner, as happened in Leeds. Anyway, you know now that alternatives exist, and as the largest private-sector specialist contractor employed by the US government, my company stands ready to deliver the full portfolio of services you will need if you decide to make a clean break with the past . . .'

The drive from Chequers back to London's Docklands takes over an hour and a half. Schiller spends the time cocooned in the twilit back of the stretch limo, protected by a sound-proofed privacy screen and blacked-out windows. The first meeting with the Prime Minister went adequately well, he decides: the man is pompous and vain, but he understands all too clearly the need to dissociate himself from failure. He'll take the bait, with a little nudging from Redmayne, who is already hooked. By the time Michaels realizes the price it'll be too late for second thoughts. Or any thoughts at all, come to think of it. 'A good day's work,' he says contentedly.

'Yes, Father.'

Anneka sits beside Schiller, outwardly composed, knees close together and head bowed. He can feel her mind, the bright and fervent clarity of her belief in the Mission, her joyful acceptance of the inner doctrine that will bring about the arrival of the New Lord, her dissatisfaction . . . *dissatisfaction*?

'I sense that something ails you, Daughter,' he murmurs. 'Rest assured, you have not failed our Lord: your efficiency is beyond reproach.' A telling pause. 'Or is there something else?'

Anneka draws breath, but then falls silent – a virtuous woman, she is quiet save when he bids her speak – but he can feel the tension fluttering in her chest like a caged bird seeking flight, and he thinks *it would be so easy to set her free*; but then she lets her breath out explosively, and quietly wails, 'Why has our Lord not taken me yet, Father? He claimed Virginia and Sarah last month! They're so *happy* now they know the Lord in all his glory. And Lucile and Mary the month before. They are no more devout than I—' she blushes suddenly – 'I'm sorry I spoke out of turn. But I keep praying and, and . . .'

Oh, *that*. Schiller smiles contentedly and stares at the window opposite, deliberately avoiding direct eye contact with her. Reassurance first: 'You're quite right, you are every bit as deserving as they are. In fact, your patience is an inspiration to everyone who knows you, and will be reflected in the magnitude of the reward our Father in Heaven intends to bestow upon you.' He sees the slight rise of her blouse as her shoulders tense, reflected in the glass, darkly. 'But I thought it necessary to maintain your purity because the stigmata of the chosen may be recognized by those who fear and hate our Lord's servants. Just as the communicants of the Middle Temple are obvious to the prying unbelievers, so too are the chosen of the Inner Temple recognizable to the enemies of the Lord. I place too much value on your ability to travel freely among the unbelievers without detection, as a trusted servant of the Mission, to Elevate you lightly.' Her shoulders begin to slump. He pauses a moment before adding, 'But now we are in England, and our Lord has a very special mission in mind for you. One that none of his handmaids in Colorado can accomplish.'

'A—' Almost a hiccup – 'mission?'

'Yes. And to carry out this mission you must first be Elevated.'

'Oh, Father!' She clasps her hands before her, eyes brimming with the joy of a willing martyr. 'Will you do – will it hurt?'

'Only a little, my daughter,' he says gently. He glances at his Patek Phillipe: *an hour and twenty minutes until we get there. Should be long enough.* 'Unfasten your seatbelt and disrobe, for our Lord desires to return you to the natural purity of humanity before Eve's fall, and for that we must both be naked.'

As Anneka unzips her skirt, the thing that cleaves to the remains of his original sin is already uncoiling and inflating, leaving him headachy and prickly hot as it suckles on his bulbourethral artery. He slides out of his jacket and removes his tie. 'How must we do this, Father?' Anneka asks nervously. It's her first time, of course: as a virtuous girl raised in the chaste bosom of Schiller's ministry, she has never been alone with a man who was not an initiate of the Middle or Inner Temples. (Nor is sex education on the school curriculum in Schiller's compound in Colorado.)

'First we undress, then we pray together,' Schiller reassures her. While she peels off her pantyhose and unhooks her brassiere, he removes his shirt and trousers, then he ducks across the aisle to the wide bench seat opposite. He kneels on the floor of the car and leads her through a recitation of the Lord's Prayer and the Celebration of the Mission. Schiller still wears his boxers, and Anneka is naked save for a somewhat unchaste G-string. Her garment distracts him with visions of a sinful nature, but Schiller has done this before, so many times that the prayers of the ritual come naturally to him in his sleep: and in any case, this is the one situation where such sinful imaginings might be forgiven by his Lord, for the purpose is procreation, after a fashion.

Finally, it is time. 'Recline the seat,' Schiller directs her – Anneka's hand goes to the button that turns the rear bench into a bed almost before he finishes the phrase – 'then render yourself as naked as Eve, close your eyes, and imagine your body to be the tabernacle of the Lord.' As she obeys he shoves his underpants down, hands shaking with the urgent need to obey the commands of his little master, who has not fed for *far too long* and who shares with Schiller a keen appreciation of the fair and virtuous woman who spreads her legs before him. She's virginal, but shaved: evidently she anticipated her long-deferred Elevation. It's almost more than Schiller can bear. He growls softly in the back of his throat, then crawls forward to commence the act of communion that will Elevate Anneka into the ranks of the Inner Temple.

Many years ago, plagued by nocturnal visions of succubi and tormented by sinful urges, Schiller found solace in the Inner Codex of his faith. It came to him after much study that he must become the gateway to his Lord's re-emergence into the world: and so, to open the way, he took a razor blade and cut away his manhood, flensing aside all that which was unclean from his life. Then and only then were his prayers answered by the Lord.

As he lowers himself atop the still-willing Anneka, Raymond Schiller rejoices in his renewed virility. Through long years of bleak despair after his premature self-mutilation, he doubted himself: but then he found his way to the Lord in His Inner Temple. There, his Lord blessed him by making him the first to be united with the little master, the New Flesh that replaces the Sin of Adam. Now it is his duty to guide the handmaids through the eye of the needle, to initiate them into the Inner Temple where all shall dwell in joyous submission to the will of the Lord. Once inducted, the Lord's beneficence takes root in their bodies. Thus impregnated, the Temple Maidens are thereby equipped to Elevate the men of power that Schiller needs beside him to fight the good fight and return the Lord to His rightful place astride the Throne of Earth.

Raymond's New Flesh stiffens gratifyingly as he eases her thighs apart, then squeezes its way into her vagina. She heaves against him and sighs wordlessly as his little master's segmented head pushes inside her for the first time, but her desire for communion stills her initial instinct to resist and by the time the pain begins her limbs are paralyzed. There is a slight rasp in her throat when it reaches her cervix and pushes inside – shedding the grace of her virginity is no doubt uncomfortable. Schiller prays silently for her in sympathy, sharing her last moments of isolated humanity. Then his little master splits, the distal segments pulling away halfway along its length. The proximal segments stay wedded to Schiller's crotch: the rest remain inside Anneka, in whose womb they will take root, to feed and grow new segments in safety.

The limousine's soundproofing is excellent. As the little master shoots tendrils into her pudendal nerve and thence up the spinal cord to take control of her brain stem, Anneka's scream is muffled against Raymond's shoulder. By the time they reach the underground parking garage beneath the apartment they are sitting up again, shaky and drained but presentable. The wet wipes in the console suffice to clean up most of the blood, allowing them to make it to the private elevator. And if Schiller's New Flesh is truncated to little more than a weeping stump, and Anneka's eyes are bloodshot and her expression is slackly pole-axed, well, they will both recover from her initiation soon enough.

PART 2

LIQUIDATION

4: TERMINATION

We British pride ourselves on our lack of corruption in civil life. Nobody takes bribes. We hold that sort of thing in contempt and view it as utterly beyond the pale in polite society. Merely offering something that might be misconstrued as a corporate favor invites prosecution under the Bribery Act (2010).

And if you believe *that*, I've got a very nice bridge you might be interested in buying. (It leads to Brooklyn, you may have heard of it?)

Of course, if I were the government and I *really* had a bridge to sell ...

Listen, there's nothing corrupt about it. At least there's nothing *provably* corrupt about the way outsourcing contracts are handled. That's because corruption is defined in narrow terms to nail the poor deluded fool who slips a £20 note inside the cover of their passport before handing it to the Border Force officer who is checking travel documents with a CCTV camera looking over her shoulder. There's nothing corrupt about the government minister who announces new and impossible performance targets for a hitherto just-about-coping agency that manages transport infrastructure, drives it into a smoking hole in the ground, and three years later retires and joins the board of the corporation that subsequently took over responsibility for maintaining all the bridges on behalf of the state – for a tidy annual fee, of course. After all, the minister is a demonstrable expert on the ownership and management of bridges, and there's no provable link between their having set up the agency for failure and their subsequently being granted a non-executive directorship that gets them their share of the rental income from the privatized bridge, is there?

All of this happens very discreetly. Air gaps, Chinese walls, and plausible deniability are baked into the process. But the general pattern is out in the open for those with eyes to see.

First, identify a department with an essential function or significant capital assets on the books. Second, define ambitious performance targets they can't possibly meet with the resources available, hire a bunch of non-exec directors to 'provide valuable insights from the private sector' to the board, and in case that's not enough, cut the budget until they fail to perform. Third, the minister moves on and a new minister parachutes in, with lots of heroic rhetoric about radical change and accountability. Fourth, the non-exec directors leave, returning to their private sector posts with the large outsourcing company they originally came from, taking with them everything they've learned about how the agency is run. Fifthly and finally, the work is put out to public tender, and the usual outsourcing contractors, who now know how the agency works in intimate detail, makes a – surprise! – winning bid. Finally, the usual suspects show up on the golf course a year or two later and buy trebles all round.

What greases the wheels is that the capital assets managed by the agency are transferred to the new owners, thus taking them off the government's books, thereby thinning the property portfolio the Crown can borrow against. It looks good to get all that debt off the balance sheet. Meanwhile, tax revenue continues to roll in and some of it is now siphoned off to rent back the former government assets.

You might think, 'That's insanely inefficient!' and you

would be right. But you're not seeing it through the wonderful rose-tinted lenses of high finance. Viewed in the right light, a little sprinkle of free market pixie dust can turn the drabbest of public sector services (sewerage, for example) into a rainbow-hued profit vehicle. Certainly, sewage farms are something you can float as an investment: they're valuable infrastructure and once you own them you can rent them back to the government until people learn to shit in their hands.

No, I'm not bitter or anything about the Post Office fire sale, or the roads, or the way they're flying kites about turning the fire service and police into employee-owned companies. I couldn't care less whether the nation's air defense interceptors are maintained by a blue-suiter or by a former blue-suiter working as a private sector contractor at five times the hourly rate. The worst case for any of the above is that parcels don't get delivered, buildings burn down, or Vladimir Putin parks a tank in Downing Street. Stuff breaks, people die, maybe there's a small nuclear war, boo hoo.

But if they pull that stunt on the Laundry or an equivalent agency the worst-case outcome is drastically worse, because the adversaries we face are not remotely human. And the DELIRIUM brief that Bill handed me gives us a working example of exactly that happening, in the shape of the shutdown of the US Postal Service Inspectorate Occult Texts Division by the Operational Phenomenology Agency, aka the Black Chamber, via a private sector cut out in the shape of GP Services.

This is how it went down, according to our leaker:

GP Services (and other companies) have been lobbying Congress to privatize the US Postal Service for years now.

There are any number of beneficiaries: the private parcel carrier services, the phone and cable networks and internet service providers, and the obvious corporate interests who can do without the nonprofit competition. And there are any number of politicians who can make political hay by being seen to cut government spending on a basic infrastructure service that doesn't turn a profit and that isn't able to defend itself politically. Nothing has officially happened yet – the inertia of the US government is astonishing – but it's obvious that the fix is in: too many people want the Post Office to die. And so they're already chewing lumps off the periphery of the still-living organism.

Taking on the outsourced contract to deliver the mail is one thing, but there are related tasks which can't be so easily privatized. The US Postal Service Inspectorate's role is mandated by Act of Congress, so *someone* has to do it. But a private corporate mail service is something else, and they're monitored by Homeland Security. So as a cost-cutting measure the Inspectorate is one of the first units to be axed, and its residual assets transferred to corporate contractors with a security clearance. Eighty percent of its staff are downsized and the remainder, the folks who manage the remaining assets, are replaced by private sector contractors employed by GP Services. And of course GP Services supplies contractors to the OPA.

And then there was one fewer agency standing between the public and the things that want to eat their souls.

Monday morning.

Raymond Schiller is a traditionalist in many ways, both in business and in faith. Not for him the modern conveniences of teleconferencing, hot-desking, and virtual workspaces: he insists on in-person meetings with his sub-ordinates, on emails printed out and presented to him for a response dictated and transcribed by one of his handmaids, and on office suites that can be swept for bugs and secured against surveillance by the agents of apostasy.

The GP Services headquarters in the UK is located in a windowless warehouse-like shed near the cargo terminal at Heathrow. There is a wilderness of rectilinear roads, surveilled by cameras and patrolled by armed police, entirely within the perimeter security cordon of Europe's largest airport. It's inconveniently far from the center of the British capital by ground transport, but Schiller's serviced apartment is close by Docklands airport and a charter hel-icopter is waiting to whisk him across London in privacy and comfort – and if security is a priority, a major airport is the next best thing to a military installation.

Schiller travels with Anneka and his new PA, Bernadette, who is to be Anneka's replacement once she starts her assignment elsewhere. Bernadette is a bubbly, outgoing Ulster redhead whose enthusiasm has not yet been mod-erated by the induction into the Inner Temple that is her destiny. She is a member of the Outer Temple of the Golden Promise Ministries, it is true, and is sincere in her dedica-tion to helping bring about the Second Coming, but it is one thing to worship the True God and something quite different to nurture a graft of the True God's flesh in place of your private parts, so Schiller and Anneka are circum-spect in her presence.

As they transfer to the limousine, Anneka checks his phone for messages. 'Tom Bradwell has arrived and is in conference room B,' she says tonelessly. 'James MacDonald is on his way. Mr. Carroll from Q4 Services is incoming according to his assistant. The first of today's meeting should start on schedule.' She continues in similar vein for a minute. All those named are senior account managers for companies that specialize in tendering for and providing private sector services to various British government agencies. They're here for a briefing and then a day of discussions about how they can work with Schiller's organization on the bid he's assembling.

'Are there any hitches?' Schiller asks.

'I'll check for no-shows and chase everyone up once you go in! It's no problem, really,' Bernadette volunteers. The limo door swings shut, locking out the throbbing of helicopter rotors and the smell of jet fuel. 'If Anneka has her phone I can text her updates ahead of each—'

Schiller makes a cutting gesture. 'There will be no phones allowed in the meeting,' he tells her. It's an observation, not censorious, but her face stiffens all the same. 'Security,' he says gently.

'Is that a problem?' Bernadette asks nervously. Anneka glances at Raymond, lizard-eyed. *Is this one going to be trouble, Father?* she thinks at him, with an unthought subtext of fingers tightening around an unprotected throat. *Do you want me to . . .*

Schiller smiles. *That won't be necessary*, he replies. He intends to Elevate Bernadette sooner rather than later – once his Lord has regrown enough body segments. Indeed, now he is in London he intends to Elevate handmaids as fast as the flesh can manage. 'We have rivals,' he tells Bernadette. 'Also, some elements of the security services may not approve of us purging the ungodly.' Bernadette nods, comprehension visibly dawning, and Schiller feels Anneka relax beside him. She's willing to kill for the faith – perhaps too willing, he thinks privately. Killing your own recruits is *not* a good long-term growth strategy.

The limousine drives through an automated security gate, then around the side of the warehouse and into a loading bay. The roller door lowers itself to the ground before an inner door rises to admit the car. As their driver inches forward, the signal on Anneka's phone drops away: the entire building is a Faraday cage, to exclude wireless signals. Less visibly, it's also protected by a security grid: an occult circuit that channels an information flow that subtly corrupts remote viewers and repels extradimensional summonings – with one very specific exception. There are CCTV cameras and motion detectors, and security guards patrol the area with walkie-talkies and paintball guns. Which are loaded with a type of ammunition that would cause extreme consternation if it were to become known to the Laundry.

Schiller and his assistants leave the car and walk across the cavernous floor to an office block that fills half the warehouse. The elevator whisks them straight to the conference rooms on the third floor. Schiller marches into conference room B with a confident smile on his face. Three of his guests are already waiting. 'Gentlemen! Welcome to GP Security Systems. I'm glad you could make it at such short notice. Anneka, do you have the briefing packs for our guests?' His handmaid is already reaching into her briefcase for the slim document wallets. 'This is the deployment plan for our new UK venture. I'd like to stress that this is highly confidential, and extremely urgent: elements of it need to be actioned no later than close of business today, and I expect none of you will be going home tonight – possibly not for a few nights, although if everything goes to plan we should be fully up and running by Friday, with enterprise-level operations ready to open for business the following Monday. So once you've had a few minutes to look at it, I'll take you through the details point by point, answer any questions, then you can go back to your departments and set the wheels in motion this afternoon.'

It's Monday morning and I have no inkling that things are about to completely go to shit as I walk towards the New Annex entrance on the high street. I'm only partially recovered from Friday's grilling, and I'm not looking forward to the week ahead. I'm wearing my suit – there's a strong likelihood of my being called back in front of the Commons committee – and my mind is on the quickest route to the coffee station, and then the mid-morning departmental meeting, when the robocop gate guardians suddenly turn towards me. 'Identify yourself, please,' says the one on the left (mirror-polished visor on helmet, fashionable MP5 carbine with about six dozen cameras and laser-thingies clamped to its business end) while the one on the right watches his back.

This is a first, so I slowly pull my warrant card out of my pocket. 'Bob Howard. I work here,' I say, semi-redundantly as the cop examines my pass, paying special attention to the mug shot. *Oh good, they're actually* doing *something for once*, I think, just as he reaches out and takes the card. 'Hey!'

'Mr. Howard, please step this way,' says cop number two, who has taken a step sideways and is now facing me alertly. *This way* is indicated with the muzzle of a gun, and it's not in the direction of the front door.

'I've got a meeting—'

'And we have a warrant with your name on it.' Before I can quite register what's happening, cop number one is behind me and has clamped my left wrist in a handcuff. 'Come along quietly now.'

The crystal clarity of the moment congeals around me: the body-armored cop in front of me with the gun, his buddy behind me reaching to grab my right wrist and yank it behind me, the muffled silence of their warded minds. And I am on edge, jittery and tense and spiky. *It's another snatch – no*, I realize, they *really are* cops. Cold sweat and the tension between my shoulder blades as I register the presence of a police van parked across the street, a real one with a mobile cage in the back. *Come along quietly.* What are my options? Instinct screams: *this is some mistake!* Training nudges me to break the wrist lock before cop number one can get me properly cuffed, to break the lock and then break their minds – I don't think they have a clue how much danger they're in – but then I get past the immediate reaction, second thoughts kick in, and I force myself to relax my right elbow and allow the guy to pinion my wrists behind my back. These aren't cultists – I can feel that much for sure – and it follows that they're following procedure and there is no reason to escalate: this isn't a life-and-death situation.

'What's the warrant for?' I ask.

'It's for you,' says cop number two. 'Here's what's going to happen: we're going to run you down the station and the desk sergeant will book you in and read you the charges. Then you get to phone a friend who can organize a lawyer for you.' Cop number one gives me a push in the direction of the back of the van, then takes hold of my right arm.

'Yes, but what am I being charged with?' I repeat, puzzled, as cop number one slides my warrant card into a ziplock evidence baggie.

'Fuck knows, your name just came up on Charge and Book. Come on, the sooner we get you to the nick the sooner you can talk to a lawyer.'

There is a monkey cage in the back of the police van, with a not-terribly-well-padded chair. I let them lead me into it and they strap me in – there's a seatbelt – then the regular uniforms up front drive off at a snail's pace while the robocops go back on door duty. Nobody's feeling terribly talkative, the driver up front presumably because this is a routine job and life's too short to get the cargo riled up, and me because I don't trust myself not to get mouthy and make matters worse. As the initial shock of being arrested wears off I find I am increasingly annoyed – this was *not* how I planned to spend my Monday morning – but I'm acutely aware that my problem doesn't lie with the boots on the ground but with whatever jobsworth issued the arrest warrant, or more likely mistyped a name in the Met's database. Very *Brazil,* much Terry Gilliam.

A couple of ice ages later my taxi wheezes and grinds into the walled car park at the back of Belgravia nick. The door rattles open. 'You going to come quietly, mate?' the driver asks hopefully.

'Yeah,' I grunt. I am getting old and stiff enough that having my wrists cuffed behind my back is distinctly uncomfortable.

'This way, mate.' He steers me along a short corridor, through a door, into a reception suite with a couple of bored cops waiting behind a counter. 'Going to search you now. Is there anything in your pockets or bag you want to tell me about first?'

'No, but your mate took my warrant card,' I say. At the words *warrant card* the desk sergeant suddenly takes an interest.

'Come on, let's see this,' he tells the driver. I wait patiently as pockets are checked and a baggie is produced. 'Hey, what's this . . .'

'Ministry of Defense, Q-Division,' I say as he squints through the plastic. 'So are we going to get to the bottom of this or am I going to have to get our Chief Counsel to come in? Because I'm pretty sure I haven't committed any arrestable offenses ...'

Things get extremely interesting for a couple of minutes as the handcuffs come off in a display of something not entirely like professional ass-covering and I am politely invited to come and wait in an interview room and asked how I take my coffee. I'm under no illusions: I'm still under arrest, the door locks on the outside and they took my phone, bag, and anything that might conceivably be a weapon. But it's obvious even to the jobsworths on the front desk that this isn't a routine booking and somewhere else in the building phones are doubtless ringing off the hook. (Or would be, if phone handsets still had hooks.)

After about ten minutes a constable ducks his head in and hands me a mug of something so lip-curlingly awful that when I finally dare to take a sip it's all I can do not to spit it out. Then more time passes, and I'm beginning to think they've forgotten me when the door opens and a very familiar face walks in. Jo Sullivan is one of our security-cleared Metropolitan Police contacts, hence fully briefed on the Laundry – I've even worked with her on a case or two. 'Fuck me, it *is* you,' she says. 'Shit. And my day just keeps on getting better.'

'Yeah, that's a pretty good summary of my day so far. Want to tell me why I'm here?'

'In a minute.' She looks almost amused for a moment. 'Humor me?' I nod, and she ducks out of the door and calls the desk sergeant in.

'This person,' she says crisply, pointing at me, 'has a warrant card. Did he show it to you when you booked him?'

Sergeant Slow looks at her, then back at me. 'The arresting officer had it, ma'am. Mr. Howard here drew my attention to it which is why we called your office—'

'Jolly good.' Chief Inspector Sullivan grins humorlessly. 'Did you recognize the organization he belongs to?'

'Um. One of the spooks ...?'

'Yes. Go on?' She nods encouragingly.

'The, uh, Ministry of Magic?' An expression of horror slowly begins to dawn. 'Is he some kind of wizard ...?'

Jo lets him down gently: 'Sort-of. If you ever see one of those cards again, just refer it to me. Meanwhile, I'd like the names of the officers who apprehended him because I think they need a training refresher in dealing with transhuman arrest situations. Luckily for them Mr. Howard is a professional and not a bad guy so it all worked out okay this time and I'll take it from here, but there'd better not be a next time, for their next of kin's sake. Have you got that file I requested?'

'No ma'am, I'll just go get it ...'

He vanishes smartly and Jo drags out the chair opposite me and makes herself at home. 'Jesus, Bob, what have you gotten into now?'

'I have no idea.' I shake my head. 'I was just on my way into the office when the boys on the door lifted me. They said something about my name coming up on Charge and Book ...?'

Jo frowns. 'That makes *no* sense.' Her eyes flicker towards the door. 'You're lucky I was in town today.' Sotto voce: '*Idiots*. Sorry, Bob. They should have known better.' She's not wrong: if they'd followed the correct procedures for arresting someone like me they'd have called in a full transhuman containment crew and sniper teams, whacked me with a sedative dart, and I'd have woken up in the converted nuclear bunker downstairs that they use for holding supervillains. 'I don't think they knew who you were, or this wouldn't have happened.'

'Yes, well, I kind of guessed that much.'

'So let's see—' The door opens, and Sergeant Slow passes her a printout apologetically.

Jo reads the top line, then starts swearing, quite creatively. I listen with interest, but then she realizes the door's still open and the sergeant is standing there and she stops abruptly. 'Sergeant, please fetch Mr. Howard's phone,' she says. 'Sorry, Bob, this makes even *less* sense now.' My phone appears on the table before me. 'Sergeant, please attend. Mr. Howard, you are under arrest because you are facing an outstanding charge of receiving stolen goods, specifically, a document or documents that were reported taken from the victim of a fatal mugging at Heathrow Airport last Wednesday.'

Fuck, I think dismally. *It can only be Bill McKracken. Poor guy. I knew I should have escorted him all the way to Departures.*

Her expression is hard. 'Smells like a week-old kipper, but I am afraid I am going to have to book you and print you and run you through the usual, then park you downstairs for a bit. First, one question: do you suspect this charge relates to your activities in pursuit of your lawful orders?'

I don't even have to think about it. 'Yes, definitely, although I didn't know about the killing. And I need to report this to the Senior Auditor *now*.'

She points at my phone. 'Be my guest.' Then she stands. 'Come on, Sergeant, we can wait outside the door while he makes his call, it's to a recognized security organization; you can take his phone back afterwards. I hope you didn't have any plans for this morning; things are about to get busy ...'

Jo walks me back out to the front desk and they take me through the routine of being booked into the system. I'm fingerprinted, photographed, have a DNA swab taken, am given the formal police caution, then I'm told the preliminary charges against me. Then the desk sergeant apologetically leads me to the lift down to the subbasement, then into the suite with the bank vault door up front and the nuclear-grade air filters, then sits me down in the underground break room to wait for a responsible adult to show up and sign me out – prodded by Jo's not-so-subtle intimation that this is a bullshit charge and something's obviously gone wrong.

I'm sitting slack-jawed watching the television a couple of hours later, my cup of marginally-less-dreadful coffee cooling beside me, when the SA walks in and takes the chair opposite. 'What's going on?' he asks without preamble.

'Rioting in Glastonbury, apparently three New Age shops have been torched. And there's some kind of demonstration in Brighton. Superpowered vigilantes tried to vandalize Stonehenge overnight, said it's a gate to hell or something. And I've been charged with receiving stolen goods because apparently we missed Bill McKracken being murdered on Wednesday night and *what the fuck* is this all about?'

I'm on my feet and breathing deeply by the time I finish and Dr. Armstrong is looking concerned. 'I'm not sure, Bob, but we'll sort it out,' he assures me, but his hand gestures are slightly fluttery and his words fall kind of flat. 'Josephine sorted you out, I gather?' I nod. 'Good, good. I don't know the details of the case, but I gather your DNA was found on the victim's personal affects and you left a

CCTV track with him on the buses. I'm less clear on how they have you stealing something—'

I groan. 'Oh, I know *exactly* how. It was at the pub. Tradecraft swap. Probably looked dodgy as hell on camera. But it was entirely legit!'

'Yes, you know that and *I* know that, but the other thing – Bob, you're lucky they didn't charge you with murder.'

'*What?*'

'Your doppelgänger boarded the train with Bill – the Heathrow Express – a carriage behind him. If it wasn't you it was someone identical. When they arrived Bill got off the train, fake-you followed him, and that's when it happened. Stabbing and snatch job.'

'But, but . . .' I boggle for a moment, helpless anger bubbling up from under.

'You've got a perfect alibi, of course, because at the same time someone who looked like your evil twin was murdering your contact you were in the back of an ambulance having survived a hit. The fake-you was the rest of your tail, Bob, masked with a glamour.'

'Shit.'

'My thoughts exactly.' The SA looks ill. 'The killer showed us a clean pair of heels. Probably nipped into a toilet cubicle and dropped the glamour, they could have been anywhere in Western Europe by midnight.' He pauses. 'I can brief Jo, of course, and we'll get the charges dropped. You'll need to give a statement, but this is basically just a case of crossed wires. I'm more worried about where this is all pointing.'

'Schiller?'

'Maybe.' The SA glances at the TV screen, which is showing the Russian army conducting a large-scale exercise near the border with Latvia: something about prepping for

Chernobog, Orthodox bishops blessing tank crews and helicopter gunships. 'We live in dangerous times. Nobody saw the All-Highest coming; everybody is wondering what happens next. Superheroes, supervillains, elves and dragons and the wheels coming off. Did you know the FTSE-500 is down nearly ten percent in the past week? The only corporations bucking the trend are the defense sector. The PM just strong-armed the Treasury into approving a one-time eight percent rise in funding for the Police, citing public order concerns. Those aren't the first New Age shops to be firebombed, Bob. The churches are actually full for the first time in half a century. Nobody knows what's going on, and the public want answers, they're looking for someone to blame.' He pauses. 'Jo has promised to find out who pulled the trigger on that warrant with your name on it.'

Churches. 'You think Schiller's people could have ...'

He frowns pensively. 'The Metropolitan Police are an equal opportunities employer. As such they're not allowed to discriminate on the basis of religious faith. So it's not impossible.'

Oh, this keeps on getting better and better. 'I don't like the sound of this.'

'Chin up, dear boy. We'll get to the bottom of it.' The SA stands. 'I'm going to go and find out if I can sign you out, or if I need one of Chris Womack's people. *Don't* give them a statement without a security-cleared solicitor present. And don't assume that just because they're in uniform they're loyal to the same crown.'

While I'm talking to the SA about my spurious arrest, another meeting is happening – this one in Audit House, a Georgian town house in central London. Part of the Crown

Estates, Audit House is used by the Laundry for high-level briefings and off-site administrative meetings that involve personnel from other agencies. Today's session has been called by Morgan Hastings, Emma MacDougal's grand-boss in charge of Human Resources. It's ostensibly set up to be a brainstorming session about efficiency improvements and fixed-cost savings, but the subtext behind the invitation fills Mo with deep foreboding, which only continues to mount as she drinks coffee with the other participants.

The group assembling in the morning room come from various departments within the agency, but they have in common long faces and over-stressed dispositions. Everyone in Operations (and not a few in Oversight) are scrabbling to cover for colleagues queuing up before various boards of enquiry to testify as to their deeds a month ago. HR and Facilities are desperately trying to find a way to recover from the organization's second headquarters move in a row being disrupted, and today's meeting was called to discuss the agency's response to a forthcoming funding review and other changes that fall somewhere on the continuum between unwelcome and critically damaging.

Mo is finishing her coffee while keeping tabs on faces she knows when she senses a familiar presence behind her left shoulder. 'I hate it when you do that,' she says, maintaining a thin layer of control – her cup only rattles on her saucer for a moment – as she turns. 'So they roped you in, too?'

'Sorry.' Her former operations officer shrugs noncha-lantly, but Mo knows her well enough to spot her unease. 'I'm here because somebody has to look out for my people, and I drew the short straw. Not to mention the, uh ...' Mhari trails off, uncertain. Which in and of itself rattles Mo more than her silent arrival, because normally Mhari is admirably decisive.

'The prisoners?' Mo waits.

Mhari nods minutely. To someone who doesn't know her well, she might merely look worried, but Mo recognizes something else in her expression: carefully controlled fear.

'You're afraid the rations won't stretch.'

Mhari nods again. 'That too.' She takes Mo by the elbow, very lightly: 'Do *you* know for sure what this is about?'

It's Mo's turn to tense up. 'It's the inevitable. You know very well we've been overstaffed for decades.' She takes a deep breath, but Mhari gets her punch in first.

'Yeah, but for my people it's not about a final salary pension scheme,' she whispers vehemently, 'it's life or death! Mo, what are they going to *do* to us?'

'I don't know,' she replies, her voice hollow, 'I really don't know. They haven't told the Auditors anything you haven't already heard.'

'Well ...' Mo hears the implied expletive as clearly as if Mhari shouts it in her ear. Nobody's happy to be here today, but the PHANGs have more grounds for anxiety than most. And that's without considering the knock-on implications for the situation behind the fence on Dartmoor. Fear and loathing will be the order of the day when the bad news from this meeting trickles out to the organization at large. No stones will be left unturned, and in addition to the inevitable, it's likely that some nasty wriggling things will be brought to light as a side effect.

The doors to the former drawing room open and people file in, coffee cups still in hand. Rows of seats fill the room and there's a desk at the front, with a projection screen and laptop. Mhari sits down beside Mo, on the other side from Vikram Choudhury. He turns and whispers in her direction: 'Good luck.'

'Thanks, I think.'

Mo settles back in her chair as Mr. Hastings walks to the front. 'Can I have your attention please . . . ?' The quiet conversational buzz gives way to unhappy anticipatory silence.

'Thank you. I'm sorry to spring this on you like this, but Cabinet Office has prepared an order in council that came into effect this morning. As of today, Q-Division is dissolved. A new Cabinet Portfolio for Paranormal Activities is being established, and will take over responsibility for all activities previously under the agency's aegis when it becomes active next Monday. You will return to your departments, return all classified materials to storage no later than five o'clock today, and inform any personnel working under your direction that they are being made redundant. HR is distributing out-processing packs and hardcopy paperwork to your offices right now; all IT logins are revoked as of ten minutes ago. Everyone is to leave in good order, take personal effects only, return all wards and inventory items to their designated secure storage area, and deposit their warrant cards at the front desk. Personnel will be paid through to the end of the current calendar month and there will be statutory redundancy pay and pension and social security contributions. In addition, HR are required to take onward contact details for all out-processed personnel on behalf of the new agency that will come into existence next Monday. The new agency will not continue our obligation under Article 4 to provide supervisory employment for all researchers who independently discover the key theorems. Are there any questions?'

Mo sags in her chair for a moment, then sits up straight again. She feels breathless, as if gut-punched. Around her there's a buzz, not of conversation but of shock and disbelief and denial. Mhari, to her left, is quietly swearing. To her right, Vikram is shaking his head: *no, no*. She looks around, but there's no sign of the Senior Auditor anywhere. She raises her right hand.

'Yes?' Mr. Hastings is looking at her.

'What happens to operations in progress?' she demands, a sense of anger and injustice settling over her. 'We've got people working in the field! Who's going to take over the agency's ongoing business processes? What about remote sites and facilities?' She doesn't stoop to mentioning personnel living in subsidized key worker accommodation or relying on regular supplies of biohazardous material for their sustenance: everybody present can figure it out for themselves. 'This is totally irresponsible!'

Hastings frowns thunderously. 'I don't *know*,' he says, voice cracking with frustration. 'This came down from the Cabinet Office last night. All I know is what I've been told, which is that SOE is being dissolved with immediate effect—'

'Reckless!' someone at the back interrupts, and it's as if a dam has burst: within seconds almost everyone – and they're all senior enough to be able to keep a grip on their tongues – is trying to get their word in.

'Please! Let me speak! Please!' Hastings is turning pink at the podium. For a moment Mo wonders if he's about to have an aneurysm, but gradually the immediate hubbub subsides. 'I'm in this with you,' he adds, and suddenly everyone stops talking. A pin could drop with the reverberation of a kettle drum. 'The government, for better or worse, has decided to dissolve the agency with immediate effect and, to the best of my knowledge, no active replacement to hand. We, as the agency's management, are tasked with shutting everything down in an orderly manner and turning out the lights. What happens next—' He looks at the upturned faces, an expression of something like desperation on his face – 'let's just hope they know what they're doing,' he ends on a near-whisper.

It's a quarter to one and I'm sitting in the break room of the underground custody suite with an empty mug of coffee and the television for company, when a sense of dread steals over me as if an entire colony of black cats just used my future grave as an outdoor toilet.

I shuffle uncomfortably on the threadbare sofa. Cold sweat begins to prickle on my spine and my pulse is suddenly audible, a drumbeat in my ears. The rolling news has revolved back to today's human interest story, something about a goat at a petting zoo adopting one of the feral parrots of Regent's Park, but every nerve is shrieking at me that something is wrong and I need to get out of here *now*.

Then the door opens. I look up. It's Jo Sullivan. She doesn't look happy. 'Bob?' She beckons towards me.

'Yeah?' I stand: 'Has the duty solicitor—'

She shushes me urgently. 'Bob, something's *wrong*.'

'Wha—'

She holds up the melted wreckage of a ziplock evidence baggie. Something that might have been my warrant card has gathered in one corner, and the whole thing is dripping wet. 'I dunked it in the sink when it went up. Bob, what's going on?' My expression must be sufficiently eloquent, because before I can put my mouth in gear she adds: 'It just went up in flames like a broken cellphone battery. Right after I got word that I'm being called in by the chief super this afternoon. Something about a new desk assignment, new responsibilities.' She focuses on me like a kestrel that's spotted a field mouse. 'Do you know anything about this?'

The skin-crawling sensation is back, extra intense. I

extend a finger towards the baggie: 'May I – shit.' It doesn't feel like my warrant card: it feels dead. And I feel *adrift*. That's what this is: it's a lack of certainty, a sense of something missing, like I'm a homing pigeon in a Faraday cage who suddenly can't sense which way points to magnetic north. 'Didn't Dr. Armstrong say he was sending the duty solicitor round? Like, about two hours ago?'

'Bob. Listen to me.' Jo leans close and drops her voice. She's putting on the trust-me-I'm-a-police-officer vibe, trying to take control of the situation, or maybe she's afraid I'll panic. 'Can they revoke your warrant card?'

Huh? 'I d-don't—' I stop speaking and force myself to take a breath. My hands are clammy with a near-panic reaction. *Rudderless.* Oh, this is bad, very bad indeed. 'They wouldn't do that,' I say, with every microgram of certainty I possess, realizing as I say it that it's absolutely true. 'Jo, you remember Dr. Angleton?' She nods. 'You remember I was his understudy?' Another nod, slower this time. 'These days I'm not his deputy any more. They wouldn't cut me loose any more than the Navy would ignore it if one of their Trident warheads went missing. B-but I-I-I-can't feel it any more.'

It's not like me to have a panic attack, not like me *at all*, but I'm not sure what's going on. I sense a great disturbance in the Force, as if a million bureaucratic org chart boxes suddenly became vacant. Or maybe like someone with Admin rights tried to drunk-empty the Recycle folder across an entire storage area network without warning the users. A huge and reassuring weight at the back of my mind has vanished, taking with it a sense of certainty. I probe at it, like exploring the socket where a tooth has just been removed, and realize what it is. There's still *something* there – I have more than one tooth, more than one binding *geas* – but my regular oath of office is missing.

'I'm not bound any more,' I tell her, with rising incomprehension. 'Jo, have they *sacked* me?'

'Don't know,' she says tersely. 'But you're supposed to be in the secure lock-up next door and I'm not allowed to leave you here if you're, if—' She swallows. Suddenly she looks a lot less raptorial. 'Would you mind moving next door?' she asks, almost diffidently. 'While we sort this out?'

I look her in the eye, wondering if I can do this. I know Jo. She's not a friend exactly, but I trust her and respect her judgment and I think she's a very solid police officer, and normally I'd do as she says without asking questions. Well, more questions than usual. But something about this situation doesn't strike me as normal, even for being arrested and held in supervillain nick. 'I'd like to call the SA again,' I tell her.

She glances sidelong at the door. 'There's no signal down here. Promise to go back in the box afterwards if I take you up to the yard?'

Fuck me, I'm going to hell for this, and I don't even believe in hell. 'I promise. Scout's honor, on my oath of office.'

'Wait here, I'll be back in a minute.'

She vanishes for a while, then reappears with another evidence baggie. Then she leads me to the vault door and thence to the elevator. The ride up to the concrete-walled yard up top seems to take forever. I stare at the scuffed metal walls despondently. *If this is a mistake I can just go back*, I rationalize. I don't *have* to fuck over a not-a-friend-exactly in a career-ending way. But that sense of something missing won't go away, and I know in my guts that I'm about to be a very bad boy.

'Here.' She opens the baggie and passes me my phone. 'You've got three minutes, then I'm going to have to take you back down to the cells again and I can't promise I'll let you out any time before your hearing.'

'Jesus, Jo.' I take the iPhone and I touch the home button, and it doesn't unlock. 'Hang on.' I try a different finger. *Enter PIN*. 'Hang on.' I use a long number, not just four digits, and it takes me a moment to get it right, then the phone unlocks. I fire up the OFCUT app and select *Secure Voice Call*, and my phone reboots to a pale glowing Apple logo. 'What the *fuck*?'

A progress bar begins to crawl across the screen. 'Problem?' asks Jo.

I shrug. 'Phone's on the fritz. Got to wait while it reboots.' She nods. Rebooting seems to take forever, but finally it's done and with a sigh of relief I touch the home button, only to see a very unwelcome WELCOME logo. 'Fuck. It just did a full factory reset on me!'

'Then it's not much use standing here, is it?' Jo points out. 'I'll call the SA and keep bugging him until he sends someone, but you can't wait here—'

'Sorry,' I say as I close my imagined mental fist on her mind, and the flicker of horror in her eyes before they roll up makes my stomach churn.

I manage to catch her as she collapses so that she doesn't crack her head, and I lay her out on the ground. She's still breathing, and something inside my head is screaming and raging at me for baiting it to wakefulness, then not letting it eat its fill, but I don't listen to my inner feeder. I think she'll be okay. I *hope* she'll be okay. If she isn't okay ... I don't want to think about that. If I'd known I was going to be in this bind I'd have prepped a binding macro and a no-see-em or two, but that's not the sort of thing you can do safely on the back of an envelope in a lock-up and you have to work with what you've got.

We are not alone in the yard. There are steps up to a back door into the main station where a constable smoking a cigarette begins to turn towards us as she slumps. I wave to him urgently. 'Inspector's collapsed!' I yell. 'Call a paramedic, I've got this!' I kneel beside Jo for a moment as he throws away his butt and scrambles inside, then I unhook her ID badge and lanyard and close my eyes. I can feel him dashing into the station, so after a count of three I follow him, but I zig where he zagged and the instant I turn the corner on the windowless corridor I drop back to a slow walk with my hands behind my back. I surreptitiously tug my sleeves down in case any cuff abrasions are visible, and I let my awareness spread out, feeling for thinkers to either side.

If you ever have occasion to move unchallenged through a big construction site, your disguise needs to include certain totemic elements of the trade: a hard-hat, hi-vis jacket, and a clipboard, for example. Anyone looking at you will assume you're a surveyor or architect's assistant – someone else with reason to be there but who marches to a different drumbeat.

And if you ever need to escape from a police station, your best disguise is to look like a cop. Or, to be more specific, a detective: soberly suited, ID badge visible (but photo concealed by your tie), and walking the policeman's walk, watching everything, giving nothing away. It helps that I can feel the minds around me. I can't read them, but I know which rooms are empty and which hold meetings; I know when someone's going to come around the corner ahead of me or when the lift is going to open.

It takes me about two minutes to work my way through the warren of offices to the front of the building, then out past the front desk unchallenged. The main road outside is busy as usual and there's no sign of any alarm. By now they've probably found Jo and realized I'm nowhere to be found, and possibly they've worked out that there's somebody missing from the enhanced security lock-up, in which case all hell is about to break loose ... but I'm already on the pavement. I see a black cab with its hire sign illuminated and I stick my arm out instantly, and the driver pulls over to let me in.

'Where to?' he asks.

'Sloane Square.' I sit back and tighten my seat belt as he pulls back out into traffic and sets course, feeling another stab of guilt: I have no money and no intention of paying, or of leaving my driver in any immediate condition to tell the police what happened. But Sloane Square is within walking distance of Persephone's house, and I *really* need to touch base with someone who can tell me what the fuck is going on today. If 'Seph tells me I'm off base, I suppose I'll have to go back to Belgravia and hand myself in and face the music. (And in addition to whatever stupid charge got me huckled in the first place we can now add: assaulting a police officer, absconding from custody, theft, and another assault charge.)

But I really don't expect that to happen. Something has gone wrong with the oath of office, and having read the DELIRIUM brief, I've got a horrible feeling I know what it is.

The New Annex is in an uproar when Mo gets there.

She takes the stairs to the fourth floor, to Mahogany Row, through knots and clusters of staff gathered in corridors and talking in hushed, vehement tones. Ordinary work has been canceled; computer screens in the admin areas are dark. Security are everywhere, escorting weepy, angry, and variously emotional employees carrying cardboard boxes.

She passes doors that are sealed shut with police evidence tape, others that glow with the inscribed radiance of activated security wards. She feels numb as she turns the corner, onto the carpet, then sees the SA's office door standing open.

'Doctor—' She gets as far as the threshold before she stops. It's Dr. Armstrong's office door, but it doesn't open onto Dr. Armstrong's office. There's an empty room here, grimy curtainless windows staring like a dead man's eyes at the building on the opposite side of the main road. The floor is worn lino, scuffed and battered and unsullied by furniture. The man himself is nowhere to be seen.

Mo leans against the doorpost for a moment, overcome by a dizzying sense of disorientation and alienation. *This can't be happening.* It takes an effort of will to pull herself together. The beehive, minutes after the queen has died. Something in her handbag is buzzing: it takes her a moment to realize that it's her phone. She opens her bag, stares at the screen for a moment, then answers it, heart in mouth: it's a regular voice call from the SA.

'Dominique.' Dr. Armstrong's voice is a lifeline.

'Yes?' She realizes she's clutching her phone in a death grip. 'What's happening? Did you hear—'

'Yes, I already know. PLAN TITANIC is in effect. Your phone—' His voice sharpens – 'do you have OFCUT or any other agency assets installed?'

'Um, yes, I think so—'

'Don't activate it. I want you to ... ' He pauses for a moment, before continuing: 'Where are you? Are you back at the New Annex?'

'Yes, I'm at your office – did you know—'

'I cleaned it out this morning. Let's see ... you have received instructions about winding up your tasking. I suggest you comply with them. However, first you should check your in-tray. You'll find an inter-office envelope from me with some additional instructions. After you leave the building, meet me at the safe house in Docklands. Observe evasion protocol. Can you do that? Oh, and don't try and get in touch with Bob.'

'Bob? What's, has something happened?'

'I'll explain this evening.' A note of urgency creeps into the SA's voice. 'Don't try and call me back at this number. Check the instructions in your office. We'll talk soon.'

And with that, he hangs up.

Mo, still shocky from the dismissal meeting, stumbles along the corridor to her own office door. The stenciled lettering on the name plate is so fresh that the paint is still nearly tacky. She strokes her finger across the ward on the door, then opens it. As the newest of the Auditors Mo has no people reporting to her, yet. Not having to tell anyone else that they're out of a job is a small mercy, and she sits at her desk with her eyes closed for a few minutes, practicing her deep breathing, before she even bothers to check her in-tray.

There is a thick envelope – almost a parcel – addressed and sealed with a spidery silver sigil, a ward drawn in the SA's own hand. Mo opens it and tips the contents onto her desk, then stares at them. There is the expected letter, of course, handwritten for security. The writing appears, shimmering, a few millimeters above the paper when she touches it, existing in a dimension inaccessible to anyone who lacks the SA's permission to read it. There's a cheap plastic card wallet as well, and a box that looks to contain a cheap smartphone. Mo opens the card wallet and sees her own frozen face staring out of it, next to a familiar coat of arms, beneath a new and distinctly disturbing motto: CONTINUITY OPERATIONS. 'So that's how it's going to be,' she mutters. She opens the phone box next, unsurprised to see that clever fingers have gotten there before her. It's an Android device rather than her familiar iPhone, and there's a Post-it note on the screen that says USE ME. She snorts quietly, amused, and fidgets for a moment until she's found the power button. An unfamiliar logo lights up the screen, then is replaced by the Laundry's coat of arms: someone has been busy installing custom ROMs. Mo sets it aside as it starts up, then turns to the SA's letter and reads, the text scrolling across the paper and fading into the air as she assimilates it.

Nothing in the letter is terribly unexpected. This is her new phone, encrypted and patched and provisioned with OFCUT; a list of GOD GAME INDIGO contacts are already in memory. She's to secure it with a strong password and enter key contact addresses by hand, and must *not* pair it with her old phone or connect it to any agency desktop or use it for any agency business before she leaves the office for the last time. Her old phone may be a personal item but it's compromised, and the next time she activates OFCUT it will be scrubbed clean and reset. (She swears horribly at this point. Her old phone is also her contact number for her mother and sister, not to mention her husband.) The warrant card ... again: it is not to be used until she has left the office for the last time. Indeed, it won't work at all until she has been sworn into the chain of command of Continuity Operations.

Badge, phone, secret agent decoder ring ... Mo slides them into her handbag, then reads the last paragraph of the SA's letter:

> Continuity Operations is most secret. You should presume that CO is under active attack at all times and conduct yourself accordingly: Moscow

Rules apply. Uncleared former co-workers from Q-Division might conceivably be compromised by adversarial factions, and following the dissolution of SOE's binding oath your Audit override cannot be guaranteed to work. You may assume CO clearance and membership for everyone assigned to GOD GAME INDIGO or PLAN TITANIC clearances prior to the organization's dissolution, but not all PLAN TITANIC personnel are privy to the existence of GOD GAME INDIGO.

Destroy this letter after you finish with it. After leaving work, you may go home and collect essentials for an absence of at least one week. Do not over-pack or give any indication to an observer that you are not planning to return. Expenses will be covered for subsistence, accommodation, and replacement clothing. Once you are ready, identify and shed your tail (if any), then proceed to the designated safe house for GOD GAME INDIGO.

Meeting tonight at 10 p.m., or when the gang's all there.

Good luck.

I leave the taxi driver slumped behind the wheel of his vehicle in a side-street, then merge with the lunchtime crowds at the east end of King's Road. It's a routine matter to check for a tail – doubling in and out of a department store, around a block, down into the lobby of a tube station, then up and out of the other exit. Doubtless I'm leaving a fat footprint all over the CCTV records, but they won't start checking them until well after the taxi driver wakes up and I'll be long gone by then.

Of course, this assumes that the organization's assets haven't fallen into enemy hands already. My binding *geas*'s absence is a horrible sphincter-tightening hole in my defenses when I realize this. Oversight *might* have decided to burn me, but you don't burn a senior officer, much less a designated Unique External Asset, trivially. More likely the undertow that sucked me down to the cells under Belgravia are the very edge of a cat-5 hurricane of enemy action. If we're being attacked by the highest levels of government in a horrible kind of Civil Service auto-immune disease, *if* the enemy has uploaded my face to the basilisk guns of the national SCORPION STARE network, then my first warning is likely to come when I burst into flames like a magnesium flare and burn down to a human-shaped cinder in the middle of the pavement.

I realize this as I walk the upper floor of a department store, checking mirrors for secret shoppers following me. But I also realize that it's unlikely at this stage, a rapid and drastic escalation. If they're arresting and holding potential threats, then they're assuming some degree of cooperation: they won't switch to gunning agents down in the streets instantly. When they do ... well, if I have sufficient warning there are countermeasures. On my way out I look thoughtfully at the cosmetics counters on the ground floor, wondering if they've got the basics for CV Dazzle. (It's a set of makeup patterns designed to bamboozle computer vision systems – although they *really* don't go with my current Gray Man suit-and-tie disguise: computers and humans recognize anomalies in entirely different ways, unfortunately.) But I'm not willing to half-kill a shop assistant and steal some face paint just on the off chance, so I slip my stolen ID badge into an inner pocket and slip out onto the street again, crossing my fingers and hoping I'm right about the escalation lag.

My hair doesn't catch fire as I amble along the side-streets near Victoria, then double back towards Westminster with my hands in my pockets and my shirt glued to my back by a sheen of cold sweat, so I suppose I'm right. It's even conceivable that the Police haven't realized I'm missing – nobody but Jo, the SA, and the custody sergeant knew I was meant to be in the secure cell, and Jo won't be talking for a while – but I'm not betting on it.

I walk for nearly an hour and my feet are beginning to ache – polished leather dress shoes feel like shit compared to my normal trainers or insole-padded combat boots – as I turn down a familiar tree-lined crescent and walk past Persephone's front door. If I close my eyes it looks like a beacon of occult power, a giant T-shape with the upper floor spreading along the entire block to either side. I tense up and unleash my will to one side, rattling the wards on her front door. The returning zinger is painful even though I'm prepared for it, like having my forebrain stung by an angry cognitive wasp. I nearly stumble, but manage to recover and keep going. Nothing happens immediately so I walk on, then begin to work my way back around until I can pass her front door again. There's no block pattern in central London, no rhythm or rhyme to the layout and geometry of streets, so it takes me about five minutes (and a couple of embarrassing dead-end cul-de-sac excursions) before I find myself there. And that's when I realize I've picked up a tail, to my utter relief.

'Wotcher, Bob.' Johnny falls into step a couple of paces behind me. He speaks quietly, casting his voice just above the background traffic noise. 'Sitrep.'

'Warrant card burned, arrest warrant out with the Met, broke out of Belgravia and need to go to ground. So how was *your* morning, Mr. McTavish?'

'Fucking awful, mate, it's not just you who's having a bad day. 'Seph isn't home, by the way: spot of bother with the boys from the Border Force, something about her permanent Leave to Remain being revoked and them wanting to haul her off to Yarl's Wood for deportation to Serbia. You may imagine just how well *that* went down, especially on account of her actually being an Italian citizen hence not needing that paperwork to live here. Someone, we surmise, has been hacking government databases. Walk on and take the second left, Zero'll be along in a sec and will pick you up. Don't mind me, I'm just going to check yer arse for cling-ons.'

Johnny stops following me abruptly, turning to check the pavement behind me for signs of a tail. I could tell him not to bother – I've been tasting the minds around me for the past half hour, they all have distinctive aromas and they're all new since last time I came this way – but I humor him.

Another couple of minutes of aimless dogshit-dodging later, I'm walking past a somewhat less up-market row of town houses when a car pulls in ahead of me and pops the passenger door open. 'Bob?' It's Zero, Persephone's butler, chauffeur, and somewhat spurious bodyguard. 'Hop in.'

I don't even break stride. Moments later I'm belting myself in as Zero pulls away from the kerb. It's a boringly plain silver Peugeot hatchback, so down-market I'm astonished Persephone's driver would be seen dead in it. 'There's a mask in the glove compartment. Put it on,' he tells me.

I don't need to be told twice: I open it and grab the horrible, floppy, rubbery Archie McPhee face – Ronald Reagan, if I'm not very much mistaken. 'What the fuck.' I pull it on. 'Mind telling me why?' I ask.

'ANPR cameras also do face recognition these days,' he tells me. 'We don't want to burn the car.'

'But what about—'

'Relax, Bob, there's a class five glamour on it to take care of the human factor. Now sit back and enjoy the ride or something. I'm taking you to see the boss lady . . .'

Mo doesn't keep many personal effects in her office. Partly it's that she's only had an office in the New Annex for the past month, and partly because she doesn't believe in mixing personal and public personas: as it is, there's just a framed photo of her parents and sister, another of her husband, and a box of antihistamines. She scoops them all into her handbag along with the phone, card, and the SA's letter, then pauses in the doorway to look back at the room for a moment.

Which is when Mhari clears her throat.

'What?' Mo turns. Mhari waits in the corridor, looking slightly lost, her boardroom shell cracked wide open by the cardboard box she holds in the crook of one elbow.

'Mo? Can I have a word?'

'Sure. Come right in; my door is open.' Mo chuckles wearily and leads her back inside. It feels very unsettling to sit down in her office chair again, so soon after having steeled herself to stand and leave it for the last time. 'Is it about . . .'

Mhari makes eye contact as she takes the visitor's chair, smoothing her skirt over her knees neatly. A sign of tension, Mo realizes. 'Yes.' Mhari's face is expressionless, a white doll-mask with crimson lip-gloss and perfect wingtip eyeliner hiding the vulnerable skin beneath, but Mo sees the underlying tension, a steel cable wound so tight it's close to snapping in a whiplash of mayhem that will slice through the flesh and blood of anyone who gets in its way. 'About that.'

Mo bites her lower lip. 'When did you last feed?' she asks. She's proud of herself for being able to ask without hesitation or any sign of fear. She doesn't even bother to scribe the glyph of protection unseen below the edge of her desk, because she trusts Mhari implicitly to a degree that would have been impossible a year ago.

'Friday.' Mhari shrugs. 'I can go a while. But the others . . .' She shakes her head. 'No idea, frankly. And that worries me.'

'Did HR say anything about continuity of support for OPERA CAPE personnel?' Mo asks, then freezes as she registers Mhari's expression. 'Oh dear.'

'I might be spooking at nothing. For all I know provisions are already in place.' Mhari glances towards the shuttered window. 'But I haven't been told, and this isn't just a personal crisis. If they haven't made provision for Janice or Dick or John, that's bad enough. But what about Alex and the Host's magi? What are they feeding *them*?'

'Alex can keep All-Highest in line, and All-Highest can—' Mo stops dead as her brain catches up with her mouth. The situation in the camp on Dartmoor is delicate. Three thousand surrendered *alfär* warriors and their servants and dependents sitting in a barbed-wire circle surrounded by tanks are one thing – especially once they've been disarmed and bound by *geas* not to fight back – but *alfär* magi are PHANGs by any other name, and far less tractable. The *alfär* traditionally controlled them by a combination of castration and religious indoctrination, but Mo can't begin to guess what will happen when the blood thirst rises and threatens to overwhelm them. The problem with feeding PHANGs is that the blood needs to come from a live donor, and the V-parasites use it as a bridge to the victim's brain, which they rapidly chew into the lacy wreckage associated with death through V syndrome dementia. The Laundry arranged for a hospice to supply their half-dozen

PHANG employees with blood from terminally ill patients whose lives won't be substantially shortened, but the *alfär* magi are used to a rich diet of healthy brains. 'What have they been doing?'

Mhari's cheek twitches. 'When the Host surrendered, there were a number of slaves who had already been tapped, but not used up. That was less than three weeks ago, and they're already almost gone. According to the last memo I saw the crisis was going to become acute by the end of this week.'

'Do you have any suggestions?' Mo asks tonelessly.

'Do *I* ...?' Mhari's eyes glow red for an instant before she forces herself to sit back. She laughs shakily as her irises fade back to their pale turquoise baseline. 'Nothing good. Cycling PHANGs into storage in a time-frozen containment grid would work, but you're not going to get many volunteers: all it takes is one bigot with a grudge and a flashgun and that's it. It'd be like being handed a life sentence in solitary confinement with no fixed duration, only worse. Even John has something he calls a life – parents, a room he rents, that kind of thing. But there's worse. *Alex*.

'He's out there in the camp keeping Cassie under control, and she's out there in the camp holding down the Host, and as long as he was a sworn member of Q-Division that was fine because he was an agent of the government and there was a clear line of authority back to the Crown. But if they've absent-mindedly fired him along with the rest of us—'

'Oh *fuck*.'

'You said it.' Mhari stands wearily. 'It's like what happened in Iraq after the invasion, when the American occupation government fired the entire army and the police without bothering to disarm them or asking what they'd do.'

Mo surprises herself by standing and, as Mhari pushes

herself up, preparing to leave, she hugs her. 'You take care,' she says, looking Mhari in the eye. 'I mean that.'

Mhari blinks, then leans into Mo's embrace. 'You too,' she murmurs. 'I've got a feeling this is going to be a bumpy ride.'

'I'll have a word with Dr. Armstrong. We'll sort something out.'

Good luck with that.' Mhari pulls back, then takes a deep breath. 'I'm out of here. See you tonight.' And she walks away with her back straight and proud, leaving Mo alone in the darkened office with the dreadful apprehension that more things are broken than meet the eye.

At sites scattered all around the UK, hundreds of projects are coming to an abrupt, disastrous end.

In Grantham, behind a cast-iron door in a high brick wall warded so that it appears derelict to casual observers, a very peculiar institution receives letters printed on paper informing the staff that their funding is being terminated. Two doctors and a (human) nurse exchange heated expressions of disbelief with an equally worried office administrator. Meanwhile, in the secure ward below, the four elderly inmates are happily unaware that orders requesting their transfer to beds in a boringly insecure NHS psychiatric hospital are being dealt with and that on the morrow an ambulance will arrive to rip them away from St Hilda's, their home and the site of their life's work for the past fifty years.

(They are not in fact insane, but merely disconnected from the mundanity of consensus reality, and by the time the staff at their new home begin to realize that they are dealing not with institutionalized basket cases but with deeply scary (and dissociated) sorcerers who are now *extremely irritated*, it will be too late.)

The lost village of Dunwich, down on the east coast, receives a postal delivery twice a week by warded boat. The boat crew have been laid off, and it will be some time before the staff and trainees in the school realize that anything is wrong, as the commissary runs out of fresh milk, the diesel generator runs low, and the bar runs perilously low on cask-conditioned beer. (But that's probably the least serious of the shutdowns.)

Around London, in the windowless factory-like sheds that contain the Laundry's server farms, the racks of equipment that monitor the nation's occult defenses begin to shut down. The staff have been ordered to leave, and the electricity bills will go unpaid. In the early hours of Tuesday morning, a fire in a substation – nothing to do with the Laundry *per se* – causes a local brown-out and trips the backup electric system in data center TANGENT ORANGE. Unnoticed and with no drama, the site switches to internal power and the diesel backup generator kicks into life. But the tanker hasn't been called, the fuel level is perilously low, and nobody is watching, so on Tuesday afternoon the eight thousand rackmount servers that provide SCORPION STARE coverage for London and the southwest will power down hard.

At a temporary office in Leeds, tired and disbelieving emergency workers who have spent the past weeks working sixteen-hour shifts making safe the thaumaturgic debris of an occult war receive their P.45s and out-processing paperwork and are sent home, shaking their heads in disgust and asking who will pick up the pieces, many of which are heavily enchanted and still dangerous to approach. The axe swings for employees who have been injured in the line of duty as well as those who are active: Brains reads Pinky his letter of dismissal – Pinky's eyes are still bandaged, recovering slowly, although he's been discharged from hospital – and swears an angry vow of vindication.

Near Bristol, in a windowless aircraft hangar staffed by a mixture of contractors and RAF personnel, the aircrew in the ready room listen with anger and disbelief as the civilian engineering manager informs them that his entire team have been laid off and they can no longer keep Bird Four flightworthy and in readiness. Heated phone calls escalate to the Group Captain responsible, and may make it as high as the Secretary of State for Defense within a day or so, hampered by the exigencies of secrecy surrounding discussing the existence of an unadmitted strategic nuclear strike capability (albeit one tacitly recognized by the other UN Security Council Permanent Members). Meanwhile, around the country every spare fitter and engineer the RAF can scrape together who has any record of working on similar airframes is being woken up and ordered to head for Filton immediately, in the desperate hope of getting there in time to pick up the pieces, run the checklists, and keep Squadron 666's strike capability from degrading.

All around the UK, the lights are going out and the shutters are falling across the doors of dozens of offices and remote installations. The lights will stay on for a while longer at a handful of sites that are only tenuously connected to the rest of the nation, sites which are isolated by virtue of the perilous forces they work with or by the most draconian of security perimeters: but the orders have been issued, and by Friday evening the Laundry as an organization will have ceased to exist.

5: BREAKOUT

Zero drives me out of the center of London efficiently and calmly. I sweat inside my rubber fright mask every time we pass a traffic camera or a police car, feeling the itch of gunsights on the small of my back. It's never nice being a fugitive, but it's a thousand times worse being a fugitive in your own country. I don't want to talk to Zero about the situation – if I tell him what happened at Belgravia that'll make it much harder for him to deny being an accessory when it comes up in court – so I keep my mouth shut and my thoughts to myself. And I've got a lot of them, mostly tainted with guilt, mostly attempts to second-guess what else I could have done.

I'm still drawing a blank and wondering if I could have avoided hurting Jo when we drive down a concrete trench in the East End and come out in a maze of spaghetti-like roads overshadowed by skyscrapers. Finally Zero turns into the entrance of an underground parking garage – the barrier rises automatically for him: there's no ticket machine and no human attendant – and parks between a bright red Italian skateboard with a bull-headed badge on the bonnet, and something that looks like Porsche tried to make a stretch limousine. 'She'll see you upstairs,' Zero tells me, passing me a card key. 'Eighth floor, suite two.'

'But I—' I rub my face-mask. 'Really?'

'Yes, really.' Zero nods. 'Please move, I've got a false trail to lay down.'

I use the contactless ebony card to open the elevator door, and find myself in a darkly reflective infinite regress, subtly distorted versions of myself mirrored to every side between columns of white LEDs. The doors close and the lift begins to rise without waiting for me to do anything so gauche as to push a button; there *is* a control panel, I eventually notice, but it seems to be emergency controls only. (Secure apartments, I realize: you can only go to the floor you have a keycard for.)

When the doors open I recognize the corridor. I go straight to the safe apartment, open the door, and go through to the gigantic living room at the far end of the corridor. Persephone, standing in front of the window, turns to face me: the flash of surprise that crosses her face is balm for my paranoid soul. I whip off the Ronald Reagan mask – or try to whip it off, the sweat sticks it to my face like a hideous alien parasite. 'If it wasn't for you meddling kids I'd have gotten away with it! Uh thanks, 'Seph. Do *you* know what's going on?'

'The agency is under attack. If you're going to kill a man, aim for the head: you're not the only Mahogany Row staffer with an outstanding arrest warrant.' She raises an eyebrow. 'Why don't you go and freshen up, maybe change into something less instantly recognizable to anyone who saw the CCTV of you making your escape? I'm waiting for the others to get here.' I spot my unmasked reflection in the window. I look like I've been dragged through a hedge backwards. 'Your bag's in the spare room.'

'Thanks,' I say, and retreat in confusion. It's clearly casual Monday for Persephone: she's got her hair tied back and her outfit is more battle dress than cocktail dress, albeit still in black. 'Be back in ten minutes.'

It's more like fifteen, but by the end of it I'm feeling

human again, showered and shaved and changed out of management drag. I slope back into the living room and find we've been joined by Johnny and the SA. Dr. Armstrong smiles. 'Ah, Bob, glad you could join us. Here.' He hands me a surprisingly heavy mailer.

'You know I—'

'– Broke out of a police station, injured a detective chief inspector and a taxi driver, are wanted for receiving stolen goods and assault and, I believe, an entirely spurious murder charge? Yes, Bob, nothing to worry about.' His smile vanishes. 'Sit down. We've got a lot of ground to cover.'

''Aven't we just,' rumbles Johnny, as I do as I'm told, then absent-mindedly open the jiffy bag and pour the contents all over my lap.

'Whoa,' I say, seeing the phone. And, 'What's this?' There's a well-aged leather wallet – not mine – and when I open it it's full of cards. Debit, credit, driver's license, health club, and something else that says CONTINUITY OPERATIONS.

'Pay attention,' says the SA, looking me in the eyes with an expression that makes my blood freeze because I've been here before: '*Ruby. Seminole. Kriegspiel. Hatchet*. Execute Sitrep One.'

And with that, I'm gone. Someone else with my voice replies: 'Subjective integrity is maintained. Subjective continuity of experience is maintained. Subject observes no tampering.'

'Jolly good. Bob, repeat after me—'

Ears hear and larynx speaks but I am not consciously aware of what I'm saying. The SA is uttering words of power and I am repeating them, binding myself to something powerful, something that hums and throbs in the empty space where my oath of office once burned, as a huge, silvery icon flames and takes form against the eigen-grau background of my mind's eye.

'Exit supervision mode.' And then I'm back in my own head, not watching from an abstract distance as the SA nods, guardedly. 'Sorry about that, Bob. Had to repair the damage.'

'I know.' I clear my throat. *Fuck, this is not turning out to be a good day.* 'How bad is it?'

Dr. Armstrong folds himself onto the sofa opposite. 'The picture at ground level is that the organization is under attack from the top down, by our own government,' he says bluntly. 'SOE is officially being dissolved, effective immediately, and all personnel are being laid off. There is no provision for continuity of staff, although Crown assets and property are being secured and a successor agency is due to spin up next Monday – no word on who will direct or staff it, of course, but that's how these things happen.'

Well, that might go some way towards explaining why nobody showed up to bail me out of pokey. (Although now I feel a bit like the prisoner of war being held in a Japanese military prison camp at Hiroshima on August 6, 1945, complaining that his breakfast is late.) 'Schiller?' I ask.

The SA raises a finger: 'Most probably, but we need to rule out other possibilities first. I will note at this point that the original warrant for your arrest, Bob, implies inside knowledge that would only be available to the operation that tried to snatch you. Also, there is a spurious and preposterous Immigration Service Leave to Remain warrant out for Ms. Hazard, and I believe Johnny is wanted on firearms charges—' Johnny whistles tunelessly between his teeth – 'and a number of other Mahogany Row key operatives are the subject of criminal proceedings by the police. This has obviously been in train for a little while now. They're *very* well prepared, whoever they are.'

'Mo—'

'Is safe for the time being.' Dr. Armstrong raises another finger. 'They're not so well prepared that they exhibit any special knowledge of the role the Audit Commission plays within the agency, otherwise—' he spreads his arms – 'I would have been their very first target.' His smile, this time round, is vulpine and frightening. 'So that's their first mis-play. And their second is that there is no sign of special provisions for the PHANGs, the residents of St. Hilda's, and any number of personnel with unusual and exacting requirements.' His smile disappears. 'That is both a weakness on the adversary's part, and a huge problem for us.'

'No provisions for PHANGs?' My mind is spinning. 'They're firing everyone, PHANGs included? But what about—' I stare at him – 'Alex?'

'Exactly. Bob, Johnny, Persephone: welcome to Continuity Operations. The oath I administered binds you much as your previous oath of office did – only the name of the organization has changed. And, ahem, its source of authority, which reverts back to the previous Royal Prerogative. Our first task is to secure our resources and establish our threat perimeter, and as you so perspicaciously observed, this means someone needs to retrieve Alex and the All-Highest before a use for them occurs to the Adversary. Persephone, I need you for another job – low risk but delicate – up north. So it's down to you two likely lads to break into a prisoner of war camp and ensure the two most valuable prisoners aren't used against us.'

'But . . . Schiller?' I will freely confess that my brain is stuck like an old-time vinyl record with a bad scratch. 'If he's back, does that mean he successfully awakened the, the . . .'

'The Sleeper isn't your problem, Bob,' Persephone assures me, only slightly patronizing.

'Anyway, if 'e'd succeeded in waking it fully, d'you think we'd be sitting 'ere?' Johnny adds rhetorically. 'No, it's just Ray with some extra mojo walking about. Worse case, the Sleeper's in 'is driving seat, but it's still sized for a bloke, and he's no less human than you are these days, mate.'

'Thank you *very* much.' I manage not to snarl, but he's right about one thing: if it *is* the Sleeper, it's way above our pay grade – and if it isn't, there's no need to worry about it. Something as big as the Sleeper wouldn't be pissing around declaring bureaucratic war on a Civil Service department. 'Okay, agenda item number one: how to get to our two assets. Do you have any suggestions?'

'Sure do. Duchess . . . ?'

Persephone stares at me thoughtfully. 'Yes, I think it could work.' She snaps her fingers. 'The mask – it'll do, but I need to make some adjustments.' Then she nods thoughtfully. 'And while I'm doing that, you need to go clothes shopping with Johnny.'

I barely have time to finish a mug of tea and set a password on my shiny new hacked-about CyanogenMod phone when Johnny whisks me out the door for a brisk afternoon out, clothes shopping GI Joe style. Anonymity (and immunity from speed cameras) is ensured because Johnny's idea of getting about town is a matte-black Kawasaki Ninja ZX-14. I am not used to wearing a mirror-visored crash helmet – or riding pillion, for that matter, especially on an insanely souped-up sports bike that's not designed for passengers – so after the second time I nearly fall off he sticks within hailing distance of the speed limit. It's a bit like taking a Lamborghini to the corner shop, and by the time we get to our destination I've almost stopped shaking with fear.

"Op off, Bob, we're there,' he tells me via bluetooth as he drops the kick stand, and I stumble away from the terror machine, take a deep breath, and look around the industrial estate in northeast London we seem to have crash-landed in.

'Where's here?' I ask.

'Army surplus.' And with that he shoves open the door to the nearest warehouse-like building and takes his helmet off as he goes inside.

Now, at risk of being accused of sexist stereotyping, I'd like to note that a lot of retail psychology (and sales) depends on the fact that men and women shop (or are trained to shop) in different ways. Broadly: women forage while men hunt. This is *especially* true of clothing, where I've noticed Mo can spend all afternoon searching for exactly the right pair of shoes and end up with a jacket, two bras, a skirt, and an umbrella – while I begin to sweat bullets and edge close to a panic attack if I can't find exactly the correct size of plain black tee-shirt in Marks and Spencer within thirty seconds of entering the front door.

In this case, Johnny is working to a countdown timer and knows exactly what he's going to dress me in. Which is why precisely sixteen minutes after we walked in the door we walk out again with a cheap backpack slung over my shoulder, which includes all the elements to make up No. 13 temperate barrack dress (Army Legal Services Branch) in my size, along with appropriate insignia for a major with a law degree, and a few extras. Some of it is second-hand, some of it is new, but it all fits, and between the glamour Persephone's working up for the rubber mask and Johnny's coaching on how to Talk Officer it might just work.

*

Back at the safe house I discover that the SA has already left. While Persephone is doing something unspeakable to the rubber mask in the kitchen, Johnny sets me to work with spray starch and a steam iron, explaining the requirement for razor-sharp creases with a sergeant-major's sarcasm while he blacks up both pairs of boots. His own costume is, unsurprisingly, already hanging in the wardrobe; I'm pretty certain that when Johnny impersonates an NCO he's doing so from first-hand experience.

I've just about finished the shirt when Persephone walks in. 'Try this for size,' she says, holding out a flaccid mask.

'Must I?' I take the thing and pull it on over my face.

'Great work, Duchess!' Johnny seems to approve.

Persephone cocks her head to one side as she inspects me. 'Yes, I think it'll do,' she says after a bit. 'All right, my work here is done.' A brief flicker of concern as she glances at Johnny: 'Bring them back alive, please, I'll be too far away for backup if it goes pear-shaped.'

'What?' I say, but it comes out muffled because the mask is half-covering my face, and she's already out the door by the time I wrestle my spare face into submission. 'Where's she going?' I demand.

Johnny gives me a very odd frown. 'Ye dinna wanna ken,' he says, accidentally dropping out of his usual fake two-bob cockney and into something not unlike his original Highlands dialect.

'Well *that's* okay then,' I say, and get back to ironing.

Early the next morning I dress in my new duds, mask and all, and follow Johnny – turned out as a sergeant in the Military Provost Guard Service –. down to the car park, where we take Zero's Peugeot hatchback out for a spin.

Johnny is carrying a bunch of paperwork that arrived by courier overnight: the SA's little helpers have been busy, and I get a nice warm glow of reassurance from knowing that not everyone's hand is raised against us – at least, not yet. For my part, I'm trying to look like a major in the Service Prosecuting Authority, which is to say, an army prosecutor. They're both plausible roles for visiting a prison, and as we barrel along the M5 towards Bristol Johnny drills me in what I'm going to say to get us inside the fence and I drill Johnny in what we're going to say in order to get out again.

(What I'm going to say to get us out again is another matter entirely, but we'll worry about that when we get there, shall we?)

Dartmoor is both a national park and a big steaming pile of moorland in the southwest of England. It's piled on top of the largest granite extrusion in the country, and is dotted with tors – low hills – where the underlying rock peeps through the scrubby cover. Finally, despite much of it being the aforementioned national park, other areas are reserved for use by the army as firing ranges. Right now we're on our way to one of those firing ranges where I am led to understand the Royal Artillery have an MLRS rocket launcher and a gang of howitzers set up and zeroed in on a target area just on the other side of one of those granite tors, which some asshole with a warped sense of humor has named Camp Tolkien.

There are wards around the camp. There are guards with machine guns and dogs and a razor wire fence bearing signs in Elvish – ahem, in the *alfär* Low Tongue script – saying DANGER OF DEATH. There are also tripwires and searchlights and other defenses I know better than to ask about. The artillery is there in case of a mass jailbreak attempt, but nobody is taking any chances, even though the

Host surrendered to us unconditionally. Their hierarchical social order is rigidly controlled by *geas*, which means there is a single point of failure, and if All-Highest accidentally chokes on her Cheerios ... well, incoming fire has right of way, as they say.

Okay, so the *Daily Mail* would be really happy to put them all in a field and bomb the bastards, to quote the immortal Kenny Everett; or failing that, to ship them back where they came from because hanging's too good for them. The usual engines of public outrage over-revved and burned out completely in the wake of the events in Leeds. We're so used to shrieking and wailing displays of grief over the military equivalent of an ingrowing toenail that a *real* attack left the media speechless. As for the surrender immediately afterwards ...

I am merely a DSS. I do not personally report to the Board of Directors. (The SA reports to them via an intermediate level; people at my level are reported *on*.) But I am led to believe that obtaining this fragile peace required a personal visit to Number Ten by the *entire Board*, who explained to the PM in words of one syllable the likely consequences if he followed his first (public relations) instinct and repudiated the acceptance of their surrender. (*Hint*: immediate resumption of unconditionally hostile action by the survivors of the *alfär* Host. *Hint*: the undermining of every occult binding ever actioned by agents of the government. *Hint*: violation of the Benthic Treaties and other binding agreements with the Great Powers we do not speak of in public.)

And so to Camp Tolkien, where we keep the elven equivalent of the SS Panzer division that just parked itself on our doorstep, while the people who are paid to deal with the hard questions figure out just what to do with them. (Best non-self-destructive proposal so far: send them to Syria and set them on the Islamic State nutjobs.)

We get through an outlying perimeter checkpoint five miles up the road on the basis of our paperwork and Johnny's rottweiler growl, but we're not allowed to get any closer to the camp than the outer fence. Johnny parks up outside the outer fence between an Army Land Rover and a tank transporter. The guard hut by the gate is a converted freight container that looks as if it just came back from Camp Bastion in Helmand. 'We have to walk from here, sir,' he tells me, dead-pan in character. Typically, the drizzle in Exeter has graduated to a steady cold spring rain.

'Lead on,' I say, and he's off at a quick march to the human-sized door beside the main vehicle gates.

I'm not going to bore you with the protocol for getting into a prisoner of war camp. We progress through a series of circles beneath the eyes of very serious looking men and women with loaded guns and identity checks, a bag search, then a wall of shipping containers, another checkpoint, then an inner wall of raw concrete motorway crash barriers, hastily erected.

Inside the compound there are rows of shipping containers painted desert beige, suggesting the original intended destination was Afghanistan or Iraq, not the wilds of rural Devon. They're customized temporary accommodation intended for troops, rather than jail cells, and they're clumped in small groups surrounded by high fences, although the inmates seem to be relatively free to move around. I see a few of them through the wire mesh, in orange jumpsuits but no manacles or fetters – obviously someone realized that elves and ferrous metals are a bad combination. Anyway, as long as All-Highest orders them to behave themselves their guards won't have any problems.

And if All-Highest has a change of heart, there's always the Royal Artillery.

At one side of the camp sits a complex of window-less containers, linked by walled and roofed walkways: daylight-proof accommodation for the Host's magi, and you'd better believe that those guys are wearing ankle tags and don't go outside without armed guards and restraints.

Finally, at the opposite end of the camp from the entrance is a smaller walled compound: the admin wing. And this is where Johnny and I are directed by the very serious guys with guns who seem to believe that we're here to question the All-Highest on behalf of the Deputy Director, Service Prosecutions.

The guard house is windowless – these folks aren't get-ting to see any daylight except for the exercise yard in the middle – but there's carpet, comfortable seating, and a cap-sule tea and coffee machine for the staff, and a welcoming party is waiting for me: a brisk fellow in a well-pressed uni-form with a captain's shoulder boards and a scarlet beret. 'Captain Marks? I'm Major Oliver, on behalf of the DDSP, and this is Sergeant Smith. I'm here to discuss proceedings with Dr. Schwartz and Ms. Brewer.' And I show him my warrant card.

Captain Marks stares at the card for a moment and I suppress a shudder. It's the new Continuity Operations card and this is the first time I've used it on anyone. For all I know it's something the SA found in his cornflakes one morning and Marks will – but no. 'Ah, excellent! Pleased to meet you.' He sounds genuinely enthusiastic as he offers me a hand to shake. 'My office is right this way, we should talk there.' I follow him to a side room that's just big enough to hold a desk, two chairs, and enough paperwork to account for half a forest. Johnny looms as inconspicuously as he can in a corner by the door. 'What do you need from me?'

'I need an interview room, or something that can pass as one, and both prisoners. What I've got to say concerns both of them so I can kill two birds with one stone.' Despite Marks's outward affability he tenses, so I offer him the clear plastic document wallet containing my faked-up authorizations. I've no idea how the SA arranged for them, but they back me up and strongly imply (to anyone who can be bothered reading them) that I'm here to offer the All-Highest some sort of deal – what the Americans would call a plea bargain. 'As you can imagine, we're still picking up the pieces and trying to work out how to handle this. The thinking is that All-Highest might be motivated to cooperate if we offer to go lightly on Dr. Schwartz – and vice versa – and maintaining their cooperation in regards to controlling the other detainees is an immediate priority,' *and will make your life much easier*, I think at him.

Captain Marks twitches and for a moment I think I nudged too hard. It's much easier for me to reap someone's soul than it is for me to stun them, much less cozen them into doing what I want – there's nothing subtle about my necromantic capabilities. Marks gives me a hard stare, but I've been stared at harder by much more terrifying people; after a moment he takes my folder and says, mildly, 'I've got to double-check this with Andover, but I'm pretty sure interview suite three is available. Give me five minutes.'

'Of course,' I say as he disappears.

Johnny gives me the side-eye. 'A solid B-minus, sir,' he mutters disapprovingly.

'But he bought it?'

'Yes. Just as long as head office slipped the paperwork under the transom at Legal Services ...'

I sweat bullets in silence for a few minutes until Captain Marks returns.

'All checked out,' he says briskly, and finally manages a wan smile. 'Prisoner Number One is finishing lunch right now but I'll take you to interview room three and park you there, then send her round with Dr. Schwartz. If you'll follow me?'

And with that, he leads us into the very heart of the prison, to meet nerd-boy and his faerie queen.

Of course it's not *quite* as simple as Captain Marks saying, 'You check out,' but ten minutes later I find myself sitting at the side of a low table equipped with notepad and recording gear, opposite a two-place sofa. Call it a VIP interrogation room, or a living room with ambitions in the direction of police procedural. Either way it's not exactly an adversarial *you will confess or else: ve haff vays of making you talk* setup. The only duff note is Johnny who is standing at ease with his back to the wall next to the door, doing his best to become one with the magnolia emulsion.

'Tea or coffee?' I ask the vampire on the settee; 'and what do you take?' I ask his girlfriend.

'Er ... do you have any decaf?' he asks hopefully. 'Because that'd be a decaf with milk, no sugar—'

'– I'll have his caffeine, *and* his sugar, twice over!' Cassie takes over seamlessly, and hits me with a smile bright enough to cause eye injuries.

'Right,' I say, and look at Johnny: 'Can you get that?' I ask him. *And check the outer office*, I don't say aloud. Johnny knows what to do.

A moment later we're alone. I smile at Alex, keeping my teeth to myself: the glamoured mask echoes my facial expressions. He's not much to look at. Twenty-four years old, about one-eighty centimeters, skinny at seventy kilos. Dark hair cut in an I-don't-care nerd crop parted on the left, brown eyes trying to grow a beard, bless. I took an instant dislike to him the first time we met, possibly because he thought I was a burglar, but I've got to admit he did a bang-up job in Yorkshire – which is why he's banged up right now, unfortunately. Then I glance at Cassie. She looks to be about twenty-two-ish, with turquoise hair in a pixie cut and high cheekbones. She's taller than Alex, and slightly built: pretty in an elfin kind of way, before you notice that the tops of her multiply-pierced ears rise to short points. She's more Mr. Spock than Galadriel, though; with the right hairdo she could pass for normal. While Alex is dressed in M&S office-casual, Cassie is clearly an invader from the perkygoth dimension: she looks like she just stepped out of a Shadowrun LARP. Which I take as a clear warning sign that she's one hell of a lot more socially aware than her dutiful nerd-boy minder and companion. Here is a woman who knows how to work on people's misconceptions, who has absorbed a shitload of cultural tropes about elves, and who is playing to the peanut gallery for all she's worth. But two can play at that game.

'What's this about, anyway?' asks Alex, a guarded expression on his face. He's not quite in guilty schoolboy mode, but not far off, and if we slide into adversarial mode this isn't going to work, so I lean back in my armchair and try to look nonchalant as I check him out with my inner eye. He seems to be clean: no sign of obvious tampering, beyond the spent *geas* his companion briefly had him under. Then I glance at Cassie and nearly fall off my chair.

'You're not a lawyer! NoNoNo you naughty magus – no, wait, what *are* you?'

Cassie stands so fast that I recoil instinctively and Alex is suddenly in full-on defensive boyfriend mode with added fangs and glowing eyes, and *I'm* still shaking my head and blinking away afterimages because *fuck me so* that's *what the Host of Air and Darkness's binding geas looks like* – 'Wait!' I raise a hand and rip my face off.

'*You!* What are you doing here?' Alex demands, then after a slightly-too-long pause, 'Sir?' He licks his lips. 'Is it something to do with what happened to the oath, yesterday?'

Well fuck of course *he'd have felt it.* Even if the binding *geas* is flaky when it comes to PHANGs. I shake my head, trying to dislodge the sweat trickling down my nose. *No going back now.* 'The government has been rooted by hostiles under cover of the chaos and the agency is under attack by the Cabinet Office,' I say bluntly. 'When I say *under attack*, I mean we've been defunded and everyone is out of a job, except for those who are being rounded up and arrested. There is a contingency plan for surviving this sort of thing and I am here to retrieve you for Continuity Operations. The standard formulation of the oath was broken in the process. I'm meant to swear you in, then get you out of here.'

'Who *is* he, Alex?' Cassie gives me the dirty old man stink-eye and I can feel the fine hairs on the back of my neck prickling under the heat of her gaze.

'This is Mr. Howard, like I told you about,' Alex tells her. Back to me: 'What happens if I don't want to come?'

Decision time. I cross my fingers mentally. 'Then you have a big problem. The government is setting up a replacement agency, but they're not keeping anyone on and they don't seem to have made any provision for feeding you – the PHANGs – during the transition period.' Alex winces at *feeding*: so our boy has issues? Interesting. '*They* may be willing to hang you out to dry, but we are not.'

'This "we" you're using – you mean what? Continuity Operations? What is *that*?'

Cassie punches him lightly on the arm: 'The ones he is *geas*-bound by, can't you see? It's obvious!' She points at something behind my head: 'Can't you *see* them, fang-boy?'

I take a deep breath. 'If you swear the new oath and come with me now, I can take you to Mhari who will explain everything. But we don't have time to go over it now.' *Dammit, where's Johnny? He's taking too long.* I pick up my mask and shake it to try and get the moisture out. 'We've got to get you out of the camp before the enemy get their hands on you.'

Alex's eyes widen and something feral shows in Cassie's expression and for a numb instant I think I've lost them but then I realize that the door behind me is opening and it's not Johnny. I begin to stand up as I turn my head and see a straight-haired ice-blonde supermodel in a black suit that screams *barrister*. She's clutching a stack of legal case notes but something about her feels hinky, and behind her there's another suit, this time male and there really *is* something wrong, it's *in their minds*, they're not hosts to the dreaming tongue-eaters but soul-ridden by something hungry and –

'Who are *you*?' demands the woman. 'What are you doing with my clients?' Raising her paperwork defensively in front of her as the thing in her mind hisses hungrily at me and writhes –

'Stand aside,' the dead-voiced male lawyer tells her and *he's one of them too* and it's making my head hurt with its hunger and I think he's got a gun –

Johnny punches him in the kidneys and he drops the gun as the blonde woman dumps her stack of papers and takes a little step, then tries to kick-box me in the left eye with her spike heel. I dodge and open my inner mouth and *bite* and there's a stabbing electric pain and smoke as the ward she's wearing shatters and she stumbles, but she's still coming and the lump I bit out of her soul tastes absolutely foul and utterly not human at all. I'm trying to remember the Enochian command word for the stun macro I memorized but I fumble it and Suit Number Two is not going down but turns and lays into Johnny in a blur of jabs and feints that Johnny barely manages to block, and his mind isn't normal either –

Then Cassie screams – with rage, not fear – and her hair stands on end and I feel static ripple up and down my skin as she lets rip with all the mojo she's able to draw from the *alfär* Host.

I manage to duck aside and raise an arm to cover my eyes, which is a really good idea because the heat flash feels like an oven door opening in my face. It's terrifying. For a moment I'm standing just to one side as Cassie channels the combined thaum flux of the entire Host of Air and Darkness, such of it as is confined within the giant magical ward that surrounds the camp. It's like holding up one end of a USB phone charger cable next to a 400kV national grid transformer farm. Thousands of *alfär* and a couple of dozen magi, their tame PHANG sorcerers, are all feeding her will, and there's a deafening double bang and a spray of burning red fat across the side of my face as both headless bodies collapse to the floor, arterial gouts spraying from the stumps of their necks.

Shit! Shit! Panic! No, don't panic, if she wanted me dead I'd be ... well. I straighten up and open my eyes and instantly regret it as the vision in my right eye goes red and blurry and something unspeakable trickles down my neck. I take a deep breath, air heavy with the aroma of fresh blood and hot poached brains. Another deep breath.

'Who, who were –?' Alex demands, sounding as almost-panicky as I feel. Then, a moment later: 'Crap, that tastes horrible – what the fuck *are* they?'

I wipe the worst of the blood and gore off the side of my face and peer down at the bodies. There's a familiar-ish silver cross pinned to the lapel of the woman's suit jacket and *something inside her is still alive* – I leap backwards, shuddering, as her blouse twitches like John Hurt's stomach in *Alien*.

'Adversary,' I say unnecessarily. 'Johnny, sitrep.'

'Two down in the guardroom ... Captain Marks, I'm afraid ... Headshot with suppressed pistol.' Johnny pauses to breathe heavily between sentences. 'Jesus, Bob, looks like we got 'ere just in time.'

Jesus ... I am having a flashback to Denver and the streets of London, but these aren't Schiller's tongue-eaten congregation: this is something new and deadly. The blonde not-a-lawyer would fit Schiller's peculiarly specific taste in handmaids, though. I try to ignore what's left of her scalp trickling down the wall. There's something alive in her body. I focus on it. Something alive and thinking, a finger, *no, a tentacle*, of a greater will – her skirt twitches then wrinkles as something cylindrical that's probably white underneath a film of blood begins to worm out from under her hem, and I recognize it as the source of the hideous, disgusting, no-good mind-taste. 'Fuck me, this one's still alive,' I say, just as Johnny raises the silenced Glock with both hands and pumps three rounds into it.

'That one too!' Cassie says merrily and points at the other headless body's tented crotch, where something is twitching and pushing to get out: 'Shoot it kill it burn it with fire! YesYes!'

Johnny unloads the rest of the magazine into the alien nightmare. In the ear-ringing silence that follows when he ceases fire I hear a moaning, hiccuping noise: the vampire is throwing up behind the sofa.

I take another deep breath, force my stomach to shut the fuck up and stop churning, and manage to look as calm and professional as I can with bits of the Sleeper's hit squad trickling down my face. 'Well, I think you've just seen the other side's counter-offer,' I tell Cassie, and force myself to smile as I look Death in the eye and Death cutes at me shamelessly. Then I turn to Alex: 'Would you like some more time to think about it, or shall I swear you in right now so we can be on our way?'

Breaking out of a military prison camp is not supposed to be easy. However, there are two unexpected but useful side effects of our arrival having coincided so neatly with the arrival of the hit squad from the other side: namely, the availability of a couple of headless bodies.

'Sometimes it pays to be subtle,' I tell Cassie, while Johnny tries to scare up a couple of clean towels in the other room of the briefing suite, 'but this isn't one of them.' I smile and Alex flinches slightly. I can only imagine I must look as much of a fright as he does. 'Johnny and I are going to walk out of here disguised as ourselves. And you and Cassie are going to walk out of here disguised as these two—' I bend over and open the dead man's suit jacket, then start going through his wallet – 'if your girlfriend can glam you up. Can you?' I ask.

Cassie's eyes have gone all deer-in-the-headlight and she looks wan and shaky – no surprise in view of the massive jolt of power she just channeled – but she manages to nod. 'Easy enough,' she says dismissively, 'while I have the Host to draw on.'

A horrible thought occurs to me. 'But we're going outside the wire – the binding ward. That's going to cut you off, isn't it?'

She shrugs. 'But by that point we'll be outside the camp, YesYes?' I find the keyfob for a Mercedes. *Jackpot*. 'They won't see us once we are in a car.'

'That's the idea.' I don't tell her about the buttoned-up Challenger MBTs hull-down on the hills around the camp. That kind of heavy metal blocks *alfär* death-spells. Also unlike most NATO main battle tanks, Challengers retain the ability to fire high-explosive shells that can blow up buildings and take out soft-skinned targets, as well as armor-penetrating hypervelocity spikes for kebab'ing enemy armor. If this works we'll be out of range before the tanks get the call ...

'We're both lawyers: you're civilian and I'm military, so we're going to walk out of here casually talking shop, then get in our cars and drive away. You can follow Johnny and me and we'll swap vehicles once we reach – what is it?'

Alex is shaking his head. 'I'm not licensed to drive a car,' he says: 'Low-capacity motorbikes only. And Cassie—'

'I can't drive!' Her face wrinkles pathetically. 'I am a miserable failure at human-ing!'

I count to ten. 'Alex, do you know *how* to drive a car? Where the controls are? In theory?'

'Um.' He gives an annoying bobblehead nod. 'I think so?'

'Well then.' I smile at him. 'We're going to add driving without insurance and taking without owner's consent to your charge sheet, which currently stands at aiding and abetting murder, breaking out of prison, waging illegal war, giving aid and comfort to the enemy, and—' I draw a blank – 'forget it, if you don't feel good about driving you can ride shotgun with Johnny and I'll drive Cassie, or vice versa.'

'Whee! I'll go with you!' Cassie, unlike Alex, seems to actually be *enjoying* this meeting. She's probably bored out of her skull here, and I'm the most exciting thing that's happened all week. I just hope it doesn't all end in tears.

Johnny steps back inside. He's got the worst of the gore off his uniform and he tosses me a kitchen roll. 'You ready to rock, me old cock?'

'I think so—' I wipe my face down – 'can you glam us up now?'

'Done.' Cassie clicks her heels and suddenly she's a straight-haired blonde in a black skirt-suit and Alex looks like a Mormon missionary. I take another deep breath and pull my rubber mask on, then look at Johnny. There's something not quite right about his uniform, but my eyes skitter away whenever I try to see the bloodstains. *Wow, she's good.* 'Is right, YesYes?'

'Is *very* right,' I agree. 'Johnny, you're driving the Peugeot with Alex, I'm taking the bad guys' Mercedes with Cassie. You lead. Once we get off-site to the first services we dump the bad guys' wheels and carpool to the RDV. Right?'

'Sure.' Johnny grins cynically. 'Piece of cake. What could possibly go wrong?'

Nothing *actually* goes wrong until we're almost out the gates of Camp Tolkien, largely because Schiller's missionaries (or their hideous controlling parasites) have cleared the way for us. Captain Marks is lying dead in his office and we pass three other dead soldiers on the way out, two of them armed guards who didn't have time to go for their sidearms before something hit them. (My guess is the missionaries had their own occult mojo to throw around – skin contact, probably. Everyone assigned to the camp wears a ward, but wards will only protect you against minor threats, much like body armor won't protect you from a high-velocity rifle bullet to the face. How they got the pistol through security is a worrying question to raise later, but the way the adversary has gotten inside our decision loop doesn't give me the warm fuzzies. What we need to focus on is getting out of here *right now* so we can make our report.)

So here we are: a military lawyer and his female civilian opposite chatting cordially, while behind them follow a redcap sergeant and a legal aid with a double-armful of papers. We proceed through to the first checkpoint, are signed out, and acquire an escort who leads us to the outer checkpoint and the guard house where we are signed out *again*. There are no searches on the way out, because legal privilege is a powerful magic, and we're actually out in the open-air car park just inside the fence, and I'm trying to spot the Mercedes without looking obvious about it, when our escape plan goes to hell.

I've just spotted the giveaway flash of side-lights on a huge black car a few cars away and Johnny is unlocking the Peugeot when a siren begins to wail somewhere behind us. I catch his eye and nod, then tap Cassie on the shoulder. 'Johnny, Alex? Come with me,' I tell them, and begin to quick-march towards the Mercedes.

Cassie catches on and trots after me. 'WhatWhat?' she asks, an all-purpose interrogative.

'Don't know, let's get out of here.' I open the driver's door, which is ridiculously heavy and solid-feeling, drop into the seat, hit the engine start button, and am sliding the chair forward so I can reach the pedals when Cassie climbs into the passenger seat. Behind me I hear muffled swearing as Alex and Johnny get in the back.

'Ooh, it's so shiny!' she says. 'I've never been in one of

these.' I think she means a Mercedes but after a second I realize she's talking about cars in general.

'Fasten your seatbelt—' I demonstrate – 'and shut the door.' There's a *thunk* as the door closes like a bank vault and I realize it's dark in here, as if we're under water: the window glass has got to be two centimeters thick and the view out the rear window is like looking through a tiny porthole. It's a limo, just not a stretched one; there's a logo on the dash saying S600 GUARD, whatever that means. I shove the car into gear and move off towards the airlock-style double-gated entryway because I've got a very bad feeling about this. The barrier is down and a soldier is coming out of the guardhouse and bending towards my window and then his rifle is coming up –

I don't have time for subtlety: I crunch down on his ward and it shatters and I can feel his mind naked and vulnerable before me for a moment, and I *push* instead of chewing, and he drops like a stone. I think he's still breathing. I hit the gas. There's a thunderous gurgle of fuel draining into an engine the size of a destroyer's, followed by a surge of acceleration, and then we crash into the barrier and it goes flying, chunks bouncing off the windscreen. I hear distant shouts from outside and take my eyes off the road as I stretch my mouth wide and *blow*, and the little mayfly minds around us tumble and dim, and then we hit the front gates and crash right through them. This isn't a regular car: I seem to have stolen an armored limo, a heavily reinforced VIP transporter. Suddenly the picture comes into focus: the attempted snatch in London, another team coming here with a vehicle with a sealed, soundproofed rear compartment, this is Schiller's style now –

There's a screech and tearing of metal and I'm thrown forward for a second, but then the tall gate topples forward into the road, ripped right off its hinges by several tons of armor. It's not a very substantial gate because the real security around Camp Tolkien totes SA90 rifles, but I'm on that and feeling icily detached as I realize there's another Power riding shotgun in the seat beside me, mouth and eyes wide open as she sees how I'm clearing the exit of anyone who might be able to interfere with us. I drive forward across the gate, the Mercedes bouncing heavily on its shocks, and then we're back on the road again and I hammer the throttle wide open just as Johnny figures out how to wind down the screen behind us and shouts, 'What the *fucking* fuck, Bob?' in my left ear.

'Can't stop, clowns will catch us!' Or if not clowns, anyone who's monitoring the CCTV cameras overlooking the exit.

'Challenger's covering the exit road about two kilometers down, you can't outrun it,' he points out, inhumanly calmly. 'This is good for rifle bullets but not for a GPMG let alone the main gun and we'll be under their sights for at least fifteen hundred meters.'

The engine is bellowing and the smooth surge of power is still coming – we're up to 120 kilometers per hour already and I'm finding that tracking the two-lane blacktop ahead is a challenge. Looks like we'll be into the killing zone in another thirty seconds and it'll take us about two minutes to clear it. Maybe less if I can hold this thing on the road. If I wasn't driving and could get line of sight on the dug-in defenses I could take their crews' minds off the job, but trying to delicately nibble on souls at extreme range while practicing high-speed evasive driving is way above my pay grade. And I don't want to kill them: they're only doing their job, and it's a necessary one for the most part. 'Cassie, can your glamour stretch to an invisibility spell?' I ask.

'Nope!' she chirps. 'But I can throw our shadow around?'

'You can what our what?'

'Just drive,' Johnny tells me.

Alex moans, 'I don't want to die!' I catch a glimpse of him in the rear-view mirror and realize that it's cloudy and overcast outside, but he already looks like he's got a bad case of sunburn.

We hit 140 kilometers per hour and I'm sweating bullets and hanging onto the wheel as we rock and roll all over the road. I'm not even trying to stick to my side of the white line; this beast is almost as wide as one of the lanes anyway. The road twists and bends around the base of a low hill, climbing, and there are warded minds on another hilltop beyond it and well off to one side, forming a tight knot of watchful vigilance just over the crest. I punch at them, trying to flick them away, but I can't concentrate on them without risking losing our grip and there's something more than a regular ward guarding them. Cassie is singing something in a weird, breathy voice and after a second or two I realize it's a chant in Old Enochian, some sort of incantation. She feels a lot dimmer than she was back in the camp, and I realize with a sick sense of apprehension that she's cut off from her servants, unable to draw on the power of the Host.

I hold the armored Mercedes on the road as we hurtle around the curve at the crest of the hill, slowing to a sluggish hundred, then hammering the brakes so hard that the judder of ABS kicks in because there's a blind hairpin bend right ahead of us and *there*, that hill *over there*, that's where they're stationed. It's a watch tower overlooking the road, but this time I've got my macro lined up and I swat the men inside and leave them puking over the barrel of their machine gun. Then I've got us down to thirty just in time to slew around the bend and register the ruler-straight road ahead, diving downhill into a valley and then up the far side. I floor the gas pedal and aim at the horizon, watching the speedometer needle creep towards two hundred, then on towards two-fifty, and I can just about see the minds of the tank crew so far ahead, but I can't touch them or recite a memorized trigger incantation, not while I'm trying to keep us alive and on the road.

Something is making my vision blur and I wish it would stop but it's in the seat beside me and it'd be a bad idea to divert my attention and besides she sounds like Björk with a hangover and it's kind of pretty, really, telling me that I'm somewhere else, floaty, fifty meters back or a hundred meters sideways or *up* in the *sky* above the road. Which is *bad*, because trying to keep to the middle of the road while flooring it for dear life is hard enough without being unsure where the road even is; whatever illusion Cassie is spinning up is so indiscriminate it's even fooling *me*.

Then the hillside I sense in the distance flashes white-hot fire. The sky spits thunder behind us and drives spikes into my ears, and I nearly lose control: but I keep my grip on the wheel and we're barreling along at nearly 250 kilometers per hour – over 150 miles per hour in old money – and the hard knot of anger on the hillside is lurching into motion from behind cover and rising to meet the horizon, turret and main gun traversing as the tank commander tries to get a firing solution on us. The tank itself is too far away to get to the road before we pass it, but he can see us and what he can see he can kill, *if* he can see it clearly. We're barreling along the road as fast as a helicopter, and my co-pilot is singing a song of delirium and hallucination to blind the tank crew.

There's another thundercrack and the world turns white for a moment, then the high-explosive shaped charge slams into the ground a hundred yards off to one side. But we're getting closer all the time, and while our angular velocity past the tank is rising we're also following a more predictable path and they're going to get a lead on us and kill us in the next minute if we don't do something. 'Johnny, take the wheel,' I say, 'take the fucking *wheel*,' even though I'm standing on the accelerator and the horizon is closing on us as the tank kicks up a plume of dirt and careens downhill towards the road –

An arm reaches past my shoulder and grabs the steering wheel and we lurch sideways a bit but it's okay, and I close my eyes and force myself to lift my hands. And then in the retinal darkness I can see them: four minds, eager and focused, closing for the kill as they finally get the thermal imager to work properly – Cassie has the optical sights totally flummoxed, bless her – and they're getting closer and I can *taste* them and the wards put up a struggle and force me to really work at them and then – *oh fuck I didn't mean to do that but precision is* hard *and and and oh fuck* I open my eyes and take the steering wheel again.

'You can stop now,' I tell Cassie, and I ease off on the gas because we're safe, and I drive the rest of the way to the nearest town with tear trails drying on my cheeks because I've finally done it, I've broken something that shouldn't have been broken, and I'm really not sure who the monsters are any more.

There is a safe house in a small town in Hampshire. When it's safe to stop, Johnny and I swap seats and he drives the rest of the way there in silence, sticking within speed limits. I sit in the back with my eyes closed, wishing I could turn back time. Latest rap sheet additions: manslaughter times four. I'm pretty sure our Chief Counsel could make a convincing case that it was self-defense, but if it ever comes up in front of a judge I'm not sure I'd want her to, because I know I'm guilty. I should have stopped and surrendered, I should have worked out another way, I should have known better. Only now it's too late.

Someone – a Lamplighter from another cell – has already visited and stocked the house with food and clothing, and there are two bathrooms, so I don't have to wait to shower off the dried blood and tears, although I scrub and scrub until my face hurts. Once I'm done I dress again in sweat pants and a hoodie; I keep nothing I wore but the army boots, and I plan to toss them the instant I can get my trainers back. I don't just feel guilty and heart-sick, I feel *drained*. I've been using the beast in the back of my head without letting it feed properly, right up until the very bitter end of our wild ride. Now there's nothing to do but eat and sleep and hope I don't dream, because this is not the successful mission I'd aimed for.

I walk into the living room at the back of the house, adjacent to the open-plan kitchen. The windows are curtained, as a courtesy to Alex. He's mooching moodily in the vicinity of the kettle: he's found a teapot and milk and is brewing up, because that's what the English do when they've just broken out of military prison one jump ahead of murderous assassins from an alien death god cult, then survived being shot at by a main battle tank. Johnny has buggered off to get rid of the incriminating set of wheels, because we don't actually *need* Raymond Schiller's personal VIP transport, and the instant it's reported missing there's going to be a set of ANPR breadcrumbs leading our way.

'Tea?' Alex asks guardedly.

'Yeah, thanks.' I watch as he grabs a mug from a cupboard and pours. 'You'll be wanting an explanation next, am I right?'

'It'd help. Who *were* those people? And the, the things? What's going on?'

He passes me the mug as the door at the other end of the room opens and the Queen of Air and Darkness walks in, and he begins filling another one immediately: she's already got him trained. 'I'm pretty sure what's going on is that the folks who are attacking the agency sent those, uh, people, to kidnap you. Either or both of you. Incidentally confirming my theory about who the attackers are and why this is all kicking off now. I was sent to make sure that they didn't get their hands on—' I nod at the aforementioned Empress of all the (surviving) Elves* – 'you.'

'Cool!' she says brightly, and bounces onto the sofa next to Alex. He puts his arm around her shoulder protectively as she leans against him. *So it's like that*, I think. 'What happens now?'

'We need to talk about your future,' I tell them. 'Dr. Armstrong sent me.' Alex twitches at the name, as startled as if I'd said *Reichsführer Heinrich Himmler.* (At least he's got enough of a clue to be afraid of the Senior Auditor. *Good.*) 'Short version: the chaos over here shook stuff loose and some bad guys from overseas decided to move in. Said bad guys have friends in *very* high places, everyone's looking for scapegoats, and yesterday the Cabinet Office rammed through an order shutting down the Laundry completely. They're establishing a new agency next week, but that's not good news because it's going to be staffed and run by Schiller's people. Uh … Schiller? Raymond Schiller?' They both look blank. 'Big American televangelist, does subcontract work for the Black Chamber—' more blank

---

* The *alfär* Host run on a hierarchical tree of *geases* – compulsions to obey – leashed to the All-Highest's will. The artillery park outside the camp was there because if the All-Highest dies, the web of power collapses onto the head of the next-highest in the hierarchy. We demanded that she bind Alex as her Second, and he's one of ours, but if he dies as well … let's just say *alfär* social hierarchy isn't great at managing single points of failure.

looks – 'our nearest American-equivalent occult agency, they've been kind of captured by the things they work with . . . anyway, Schiller runs a church and last time we had a run-in with them they were trying out a ritual to bring about the resurrection, only it turns out that if something hands you a piece of magic that says "open can to bring about the Second Coming" you should really ask, "Second Coming of *what*," before you perform it.'

I can see I'm making a hash of this, so I take a sip of too-hot tea before I continue. 'Schiller's people are cultists, a great big very rich religious cult, hiding inside a not-quite-mainstream fundamentalist church. His Inner Temple pray with a Bible that has several extra books and a very different ending. Anyway, he flew in a week ago and has been having loads of meetings with cabinet ministers, even the PM – and then the hammer comes down on the Laundry. Those people who tried to take you are his; I recognize the type. He's big on using mind-controlling parasites to keep his flock in line, and I'm pretty sure she was a handmaid – one of his more fanatical female followers. They tried to tackle me on the streets of London last week, they killed a foreign contact who was busy leaking their operational plans our way, they've got form. So: as of yesterday everyone who worked for SOE is out of a job, those of us who are directly on Schiller's radar are wanted for arrest on faked-up criminal charges, the fox is making a public-private partnership bid for the hen house with the support of the Prime Minister, and they're moving to steal those bits of the household silver that look particularly tasty to them. Like you guys.'

'FuckFuck!' Cassie sounds disgusted. 'What a mess. Why can't humans run a nice sensible feudal hierarchy like anyone else? Then you wouldn't have these problems!'

I decline to derail onto the Wars of the Roses. 'We work

with what we've got. Anyway, it's not as if there wasn't a plan for this sort of thing. The Laundry has other sources of funding and political legitimacy. Dissolving SOE triggered ramp-up of a different core agency called Continuity Operations, tasked with addressing whatever circumstances caused a government to turn hostile, and CO sent me to get to you before the bad guys.'

'Uh-huh.' Alex frowns. 'And what makes you any better than—'

He's interrupted by his maniac pixie dream girl, who punches him affectionately on the shoulder – '*Stop it! You're spoiling all the fun!*' Cassie, unlike Alex, seems to be enjoying the meeting. She leans forward, nostrils flaring as she hams it up. 'I know what we can do for you. What can you do for us?'

I fix my professional smile in place: the one that says *this won't hurt, not a bit*. Ideally I should have done this part as soon as I swore him in, but I was distracted by the extradimensional hypercastrating parasites. 'Cassie, I need to ask Alex a question. Please don't interrupt, no matter how strange it seems.' I don't stop, but roll straight on, and now I dig into my pocket and pull out my warrant card. 'By the authority delegated to me, here goes … *Hertzprung, Sapphire, Ocelot, Baculum*. Execute Sitrep One, Dr. Schwartz.' The words feel like lumps of mercury dripping from my tongue and Alex's eyes go wide, then unfocused.

Cassie tenses and glares at me. 'You—' she begins.

'– Subjective integrity maintained. Subjective continuity maintained. Subject observes no tampering.' Alex's voice is flat and his answers are about what I expected. If they were anything else? Let's not go there.

I push on. 'Very good. Now execute Sitrep Two, Alex.'

Cassie keeps staring daggers at me but shuts up as Alex

answers. 'V-parasites at zero point seven. Interference at zero point three, rising.' The V-parasites tend to render PHANGs insensitive to *geases*. 'Subjective compliance at zero point six six, falling.'

I exhale heavily. 'Exit supervision.' As Alex slumps I look at Cassie. 'You will speak of this to no one. Those words won't work on you,' I add. 'Do you understand why I did that?'

Alex is blinking his way back towards full consciousness as she looks away from me and nods, just a sharp jerk of the chin. 'Your kind's loyalties are variable, YesYes?'

'Yeah, that.' I put the warrant card away. 'Especially since dissolving the Laundry *shut down our fucking oath of office* for a while. I had to confirm that he hasn't been meddled with. It's a necessary precaution.'

'Ow.' Alex's eyes are closed but I can feel his mind sharpening, like a bundle of razor wire emerging from the fogbank on the sofa opposite me next to the miniature lightning cloud that is Cassie. (There is no way in hell that anyone would try to bind Cassie with an oath of office. It's bad enough getting traction on a PHANG's soul-bleedingly sharp surfaces; if you tried to net the *alfär* All-Highest in a *geas* you'd set fire to your head – and that of everyone else in the same web of thaumaturgically enforced trust.) 'What did you just do?'

'Trust but verify, Doctor. Continuity Ops is a rump and everyone is overstretched – even the Auditors – so he delegated the dirty work to me.' Cassie gloms onto him for reassurance and glares at me on his behalf: they're still at the stage in the relationship where it takes a crowbar to prise them apart, and it makes me feel like a heel. 'Cassie isn't bound by our oath, obviously, but we have protocols for working with External Assets and—' at this point I'm pitching to her as much as to him – 'I assume you have each other's best interests at heart?'

They nod simultaneously.

'Good.' I drop the smile and crack my knuckles. 'I assume neither of you want to go back to the camp, and I expect you're not terribly keen on hosting one of those parasitic worms, which is what's in store for you if Schiller gets his hands on you. And unlike Schiller, we take care of our own. So. Are you willing to join us and help fix whatever has broken our government? Because if so, we have an assignment waiting for you.'

6: PARTY
PLANNERS

Meanwhile, Continuity Operations are busy. It's not just me, or the SA and Mo and the other Auditors: this little circus has drafted in all sorts of key players, from the regulars of Mahogany Row to various External Assets. And so it is that the very same day that Johnny and I are breaking out of a prison on Dartmoor, Persephone Hazard makes a call on a very unusual holiday camp in the Lake District, several hundred kilometers to the north.

Camp Sunshine started out as a disastrous experiment in the late 1940s. One of the big seaside resort operators – Pontins or Butlin's perhaps – branched out and tried to establish a holiday camp in the beautiful wilderness of the Cumbrian mountains, just outside the national park. I'm not sure quite why anybody thought this was a viable business plan, but it turns out that the sort of clientele who want to spend their annual works vacation on a week of sea, sun, and organized partying are going to be less than enthusiastic about a trek into the wilderness. Especially when said trek terminates in a dismal camp of prefab huts halfway up a mountainside where it rains sideways six days in every five, and the nearest night life is downtown Penrith on a Saturday evening, twelve miles down a dirt track. Heaven for hill-walkers it may be, but a seaside resort it ain't.

Which is why the Laundry acquired it in part-settlement of a corporation tax bill in the early 1950s, strung a wire fence and some really powerful containment grids around it, and put it to other uses.

Merely visiting Camp Sunshine is problematic; starting out from London, it's faster and easier to get to Moscow. Previously a visitor from head office might fly to Manchester Airport, hire a car, and drive the last eighty-odd miles. But thanks to the total shutdown of air travel two and a bit weeks ago, and the knock-on disruption that followed, that isn't an option. So although she set off shortly after dawn, it's late afternoon by the time Persephone leaves the A6, turns onto a B road, and cautiously points her Range Rover up a series of hairpin bends lined with drunkenly leaning reflective poles and signs warning of road closure in event of snow.

Beyond the top of the pass, there is a gate in a drystone wall that runs alongside the road as it crosses a strip of moorland. Persephone pulls over, climbs down from the driver's seat, pauses just long enough to stretch her back – she's been driving for more than two hours – then opens the gate. As she does so she feels a warning vibration in the ward she wears under her jumper. It's confirmation that her satnav was telling the truth: she hasn't been here before, and Camp Sunshine doesn't exactly advertise its presence these days. She slowly drives across the cattle grid, then closes the gate behind her. There's very little traffic on the road behind her, and there are no witnesses to see when vehicle and driver fade from view as the gate latches shut.

Back in the Range Rover, Persephone peers at the map display, then inches forward in low gear. Wheels spin momentarily on the moist pasture, but then a deep-rutted track appears in the grass. A crudely hand-painted

wooden sign beside the path reads, TRESPASSERS WILL
BE SHOT. Her gaze flickers to the rear-view mirror as she
brakes to a stop. '*Merde*,' she mutters – a bad habit, talking
aloud to herself, but there are no witnesses – and she digs
around in the passenger seat legwell for her handbag, then
rummages in it for a small leather pouch which she hastily
attaches to the backside of the mirror, so that it is visible
through the windscreen. Only when she has confirmed to
her own satisfaction that the sigil inside it is active does she
release the handbrake and drive on again.

(Containment grids and razor wire fences are passive
defenses, whereas the prisoners who live in Camp Sunshine
warrant more active containment measures, and being shot
by mistake is the least of 'Seph's worries.)

Driving across the field, she comes to another gate in a
wall of loose-piled stones. This time she pulls up short but
stays in the Range Rover and taps out a quick riff on the
horn – shave and a haircut – then waits. A few seconds
pass before a red light flashes between the stones, and the
gate slowly swings open. She glances round warily, checks
that all the windows are sealed and the central locking is
engaged, then creeps forward. As she passes the threshold of
the next field the quality of the daylight coming in through
the windscreen changes subtly, as if she has driven into the
penumbra of a storm cloud. Her ward stings, briefly, and
there is a brief bluish flicker around the brightwork on the
outside of the car, as of St. Elmo's fire. Disturbing shadows
flicker at the edge of her vision as she drives across the field,
and even though she knows full well what they are and that
she is permitted to be here, her fingers whiten where she
grips the steering wheel rim.

(This is the main defensive zone around Camp Sunshine.
Instructions for what to do, in the unlikely event of a

breakdown: remain in the vehicle, do *not* open any door or window under *any* circumstances – even if it is on fire – and await the arrival of Camp Security. Being trapped in a burning vehicle would be bad, but leaving the vehicle would be far more dangerous.)

Persephone has the climate control in the Range Rover set to a comfortable shirt-sleeves temperature, but by the time she reaches the gate at the far side of the field, her back is slick with chilly fear-sweat. Something about the shape and motion of the dancing shadows brings atavistic night terrors bubbling to the surface of her mind, puts unease in the driving seat of the mammalian brain. It's intentional: frightened mammals behave stupidly and predictably, providing easy prey for the Shadow Stalkers bound in this place where the walls between the worlds have been deliberately abraded, and the stars shine bright in the upturned indigo vault of the sky at noon.

After what feels like an hour she reaches the gate at the opposite side of the killing field. (Her sense of the passage of time is off, for the field is less than a quarter of a kilometer wide at this point.) The gate at this side is ready for her approach and opens automatically. She revs the engine until the anti-slip kicks in with her eagerness to be out of the zone, then is dazzled by the return to full daylight. She has to brake hard to avoid ramming the outer fence of the camp.

Persephone switches off the engine, reaches for a tissue, and dabs at her forehead. Her hands are shaking slightly. She knew what to expect – Dr. Armstrong provided the credentials and introduced her to the people in Detention Admin for a full safety briefing – but it's still close to overwhelming. To occupy her hands while she waits for the gatekeeper to take note of her arrival, she pulls out her makeup compact and repairs her face, using the ritual of making herself look calm and collected to invoke and bind her rattled calm. The POW camp on Dartmoor is a Potemkin village, built in the glare of media scrutiny to reassure the public that its inmates are secure, but Camp Sunshine is the real deal. A black site, an undisclosed location, the answer to a snare and a delusion: How do you confine the wizards who walk between the rain drops, that which is dead but dreaming, and those who by force of will alone can chew holes in the warp and weft of reality like moths in the fabric of spacetime?

The wooden hut beside the gate in the fence is almost disturbingly prosaic, like a cheap garden shed from a DIY store. 'Seph's working on her eyebrows and just beginning to wonder if they're on their tea break when the door opens and a guard steps out and strolls towards her. He's unarmed, she sees. If the prisoners here ever cut loose, guns won't save you. He's middle-aged, paunchy, with crow's feet around his eyes and salt spreading around the edges of his comb-over. He gestures at her window and she lowers it. 'Name?' he asks.

'Hazard.'

She waits patiently as he makes a show of checking his clipboard. 'Hazard, P.' He makes a note, then walks in front of her car and squints at the number plate, copying it down. Then back to her window: 'Do you have any paperwork?' he asks mildly.

'Yes.' She reaches up and unhooks the leather pouch from around the stalk of the rear-view mirror, then passes it to him. She feels the contents squirm for a moment as it leaves her hand. 'Is it all in order?' she asks.

'Seems to be, yes.' He nods, evidently satisfied, and attaches the pouch to his clipboard. 'All right, I'm signing you in. Take the first left and park around the side of the canteen. When you're ready to leave, I'll sign you out and you *must* take the token with you – you can't leave without it – and return it to Doreen in head office, or whoever gave it to you. Do you understand?'

Persephone forces herself to smile. 'Absolutely.'

'You want the interview room in Hut Six. She's waiting for you.' The gatekeeper hesitates for a moment, then adds: 'You've not asked for my advice but you can have it for free – you shouldn't believe a word she says. You can't trust her. She's poison, pure poison.' He turns his head and spits over his shoulder, then steps back and hauls the chain-link gate open. 'Good luck,' he adds.

Buckinghamshire in the Home Counties is stuffed full of stately houses, the provincial palaces of the landed gentry and those with seats in the House of Lords. The lush foothills and valleys of the Chilterns have for centuries provided out-of-season accommodation and country estates for the ruling classes within a day or two's carriage-ride of the capital. During the twentieth century many of the family seats ended up in the possession of the National Trust, having fallen prey to spiraling maintenance costs and steep postwar inheritance taxes. Those that remain in private ownership are the properties of the reclusive and extremely wealthy – or are available for hire to those who wish to temporarily enjoy the lifestyle of billionaires and dukes.

Nether Stowe House was built as a fortified family manor by one of the endless aristocratic Nevilles that litter the fifteenth century. Over subsequent centuries it spread wings of red gothic brick and softened into flabby architectural middle age. It is surrounded by its former kitchen gardens, reworked as a carefully curated landscape garden by Capability Brown. The building itself was remodeled in the Georgian era as a family home for an immensely wealthy family of merchants, but families rise and fall, and the House changed hands twice during the nineteenth and twentieth centuries, finally coming into the custody of the distant descendants of its original owner ... who, feeling the chill wind of the Exchequer's interest during the 1960s, re-established it as a *very* exclusive hotel.

One does not reserve a stay in Nether Stowe House in the usual manner, via a hotel booking website or by phoning the front desk. Nor does one check in, receive a key to a room or suite, and hand over a credit card to cover incidental expenses. If you have to ask how much it costs, you can't afford it and the very discreet management agency will direct your enquiries elsewhere. But if you are acceptable, the entire mansion and all forty full-time staff are in your employ for the duration of your residence, from the butler to the lowliest gardener's assistant. It's a serviced apartment for sheikhs and presidents – and especially for those who want to make an impression on the visitors they receive during their stay.

Raymond Schiller has acquired the exclusive use of the facilities at Nether Stowe House for a one-month period with a down payment of two million pounds. It's cheap at the cost but there will be other ongoing expenses: the executive helicopter service, the catering and drinks bill, the ongoing cost of security clearing the hospitality workers bussed in from nearby Amersham, the security itself – provided by Schiller's corporation – and sundry others. For the season of entertaining he has planned, it will be necessary to upgrade the house security system, install a picocell and leased line to secure the visitors' mobile phone traffic, and place discreet cameras in all the public and private rooms.

It is also necessary to hire certain other workers, who will arrive and depart discreetly and service those guests who Anneka and his staff deem more likely to respond to sex and drugs than wine and money.

(While Raymond respects those who follow the teachings of the Lord and his various prophets and apostles, he is a pragmatist and understands that he cannot afford to scorn the willing aid of powerful men who are less scrupulous about the state of their souls. And so his staff are under orders to ensure the purity of the cocaine and the STD-free status of the sex workers no less than the quality of the champagne and caviar.)

Finally, certain other preparations demand Schiller's personal attention and the participation of his permanent staff, handmaids, and deacons – all fully inducted members of the Inner Temple. In London, if you have enough money you can obtain the services of almost any imaginable consultant; Schiller's virtuous servants require additional coaching and training, a task that is outsourced to a former high-class madam. With the correct costumes and accessories they will be able to pass, and they are all of one mind in their determination to perform the necessary but somewhat distasteful actions to the best of their abilities: for they know their souls are safe in the Lord's hands, and it is their duty to spread the Lord's seed far and wide, and harvest new souls for the Inner Temple.

Two women sit beside a table in a wooden hut, drinking tea and trying to work out where it all went wrong.

'It's been, what, six years? Six and a half?'

'You get used to it eventually. I'll confess the lack of visitors is troubling – you get bitter after a while, thinking you've been forgotten. But it's also peaceful, and eventually you get used to it.' She chuckles, slightly sadly. 'In the middle ages they used to warehouse the surplus women – at least the better class of women, along with the hard-to-control ones – in nunneries. I'm not under a vow of poverty or chastity or anything like that, and I'm certainly not allowed to pray – but? There's plenty of time for meditation and cloud-watching. And it's peaceful.'

'Peaceful.' An edge of scorn creeps into Persephone's voice. 'And I suppose you prefer it like that.'

'Does it make any difference? We're all doomed, either way. Would you like a top-up?'

'Don't mind if I do.'

Persephone waits and watches while the woman she's come to visit performs the ritual of refilling the teacups. (She was present when the tea was brewed and the milk carton unsealed: her trust is not unconditional.) Her – host is not precisely the right word: disgraced former co-worker might be closer – moves with slow deliberation. There's no need for haste in her condition, in this place. She's got all the time in the world. Detained Indefinitely at Her Majesty's Pleasure is the technical term for her situation, a life sentence pursuant to a criminal trial and verdict handed down by the Black Assizes. Peering at the backs of her hands, Persephone spies the telltale signs of aging. The loosening of the skin, tendons and veins rising into view as subcutaneous fat recedes. Her grip is firm, though, the stream of tea pouring steadily into the cups. 'There,' she says, and lowers the pot triumphantly. 'All yours.'

'Thank you.' Persephone lifts her teacup and takes a sip. It's very British tea, made with milk rather than lemon juice and served in a porcelain cup instead of a glass. She has made an effort to accustom herself to it, but the mouth feel is still subtly wrong to her. 'On the matter of our doom I believe the jury is still out, but the situation is changing at present, and not necessarily for the better.'

'This is bad news, isn't it? Is it anything to do with whatever happened to the binding oath last week?' The woman watches her guardedly.

Persephone puts her cup down. 'When you're contemplating and cloud-watching, do you ever pay attention to the contrails, Iris?'

Iris Carpenter, former Field Ops manager turned traitor, looks surprised, then shakes her head. 'Why would I? A turkey with clipped wings shouldn't stare at eagles, the silly thing would only get ideas above its station—'

'No.' Persephone cuts her off with a wave of her hand. '*Not* what I mean. Would you notice if the contrails stopped?'

'What?' Iris's eyes widen. 'Why on earth are you talking about contrails?' Her teacup rattles on its saucer as she pushes back from the table.

'There was an incident a couple of weeks ago. A black swan. I thought you might have noticed the lack of overflights. That's all.'

'An incident.' Wide-eyed but in no way innocent, Iris stares back at her. She's out of touch, but surely not *that* out of touch – inmates here are permitted *some* access to outside news, albeit only via a heavily censored camp newsletter. 'Another 9/11? No, you wouldn't bother to come here just to tell me that, would you. It must be the oath. Do you really think I . . . ' She trails off as her facial muscles slacken in fear. 'No, I didn't, you can't think—'

'I don't, you can relax.' Persephone smiles, even though there's no cause for reassurance. 'There was a major incursion and it shut down air travel over the whole of Western Europe, but everything's under control, we got on top of it and the intrusion is fully contained.' Across the table Iris is just short of hyperventilating with anxiety. 'It came from an unanticipated source, nothing to do with your people, and you're in the clear. Sit *down*.'

At the crack of her voice Iris drops back into the chair she's half-risen from. 'What?'

'Your co-religionists were not involved. Unfortunately,' Persephone continues, 'there were complications.'

'Complications.' With a visible effort Iris collects herself and folds her hands in her lap.

'We're out in the open now. Mass casualties and total organizational exposure. You may be amused to know that your former office dogsbody Howard had to front for the agency on *Newsnight* last week. Hearings in Parliament, select committee hearings, public enquiries, that sort of goings-on. They were talking about legislative supervision, an enabling act, appointing a Minister. And then the thing that now runs the Black Chamber got to them. Hence the – disturbance – you noticed.'

'You are joking.' It comes out as a horrified whisper.

Persephone can't help herself: she giggles at Iris's expression. 'Oh you! You should see yourself. Anyone would think I'd announced the return of the Black Phar—'

'*Don't take his name in vain!*' Iris stands suddenly and marches over to the door, then stops with one hand on the latch. She takes a deep breath, then another. 'Don't jerk me around,' she says, her voice huskily over-controlled. 'You don't need to yank my choke-chain, Ms. Hazard. You know what I am and you've got me where you want me, here for the past six years: Fine, isn't that enough for you? There's no need to gloat!'

A stillness hangs in the air between them.

'No,' says Persephone, 'there isn't, and I'm sorry, I didn't

THE DELIRIUM BRIEF   213

mean to mislead you. I'm not here to gloat. What I mean to say is, things have gone drastically wrong, and in a way none of us ever foresaw. The Cabinet Office agenda and the public-private partnership process doesn't know anything about ancient gods and nightmares, Iris. Their world is all about austerity politics and balancing the budget in time for the next but one general election instead of winning the war against sleep. We know how to deal with soul-stealing horrors, not death from above by legal sleight-of-hand. Your way and our way – we still disagree about the means, but the goal is survival, yes? The new reality, though, is that we came under the scrutiny of superiors who fundamentally don't believe in anything except the size of their bank accounts and the number of non-executive directorships of public corporations they can retire into when they quit politics. And they've been bought and sold by the enemy without even noticing. Which is why, when an order in council came down from the Cabinet Office yesterday, dissolving the agency with immediate effect, we moved onto Continuity Operations. And that's when whatever was left of your oath finally dissolved.'

Iris Carpenter, formerly a mid-level executive within Q-Division Field Operations (and Bob Howard's line manager), also High Priestess of the Lambeth Temple of the Cult of the Black Pharaoh, and finally a permanent resident of Camp Sunshine, turns to face Persephone. 'Don't you people ever give up?' she whispers; then, louder, 'What do you *want* from me? Isn't it over yet?'

'It's never over until the agency has no more use for us, you should know that. And by the way, we *know* that back in the day you didn't break your oath of office – you bent it, most certainly, so extensively that the working group is still trying to establish how exactly you did it – but *you* still belong to *us*. On some level. The oath is merely a marker. And now we're calling it in.'

Persephone stands up and recites in a singsong voice, 'Oh *dear*, all that tea has gone straight to my bladder! I'd better go and powder my nose right away. I think I'll just leave my handbag here where it's safe. There's a spare exit token from the camp in the side-pocket, I hope it's still there when I get back, I'd be in *terrible* trouble if it goes missing and I only thought to check it when I got back to London.' She nods at the now-gaping Iris and pushes past her, opening the door to the outside world. 'Good luck.'

And then she's gone.

For the next couple of weeks after the escape from the POW camp, I am a fugitive from justice. I'm also hiding from my own conscience, but I won't burden you overmuch with that. But boy have things changed!

In the old days of, say, 1984, if you went on the run you'd try to do everything with cash. Pay for cheap hotel rooms, shop in supermarkets, lose yourself in the crowd. Forged papers were still plausible. Hell, forged checks and credit cards were still a thing. Your biggest risk was being recognized by a cop, either spotting your face from the MOST WANTED poster down the nick, or by running the poster past a bored hotel desk clerk who'd seen you the night before. So you'd do your best to stick to the anonymity of crowds or stay out of sight completely. Oh, and avoiding the cameras was easy: there weren't any. Well, there were a *few* – some big stores had them to deter shoplifters and catch staff stealing from the tills – but there was no mechanism for the cops to monitor them.

Today, we've got networked cameras everywhere.

Everyone carries a mobile phone, but it's a tracking device that can report your location if the cops know your number and can get a warrant. (Which, for a murder suspect, they most certainly can.) Cash? To buy anything, you need plastic, and it will be checked online to the bank for any significant purchase. So you might think that hiding out would be ridiculously difficult, if not impossible – but you're not thinking like a state security agency.

There's a goddam *script* on my phone. Not the software kind; I mean a series of activities for me to perform, in sequence. So after I leave Cassie and Alex in their safe house, I go into zombie mode – you know what that looks like, the guy shuffling along the pavement, head down-turned to gaze into the depths of his glowing Palantir – and obey the instructions a twenty-first-century Lamplighter has installed on my phone. (Lamplighters: they're the dudes who set up the safe houses for the spies in all the le Carré movies and ensure there's milk in the fridge, bugs in the bed-stead, and nobody watching the target. That's a real job within the security services.)

Now, as I've already said, Bob Howard is not my true name. (If you need to ask why I don't use it, you obviously haven't been adequately briefed on powers of binding, *geases*, and how they work.) What the SA handed me in that envelope was: a sterile smartphone with a bunch of extremely paranoid security upgrades and a burner SIM card, a driving license, a passport, debit and credit cards, and a warrant card bound to Continuity Operations. All in the name of, oh, let's call him Bob Howard 2.0: a fresh new working alias. But what I didn't realize at the time was that this represents the very tip of an enormous iceberg of plausible lies.

Passports are issued by the Identity and Passport Service, a rather quiet department that maintains a biometric database of the roughly 85 percent of the British adult population who hold passports. This passport is genuine – so the README on my phone assures me – which means, by extension, the Lamplighters for Continuity Ops must have rooted the IPS database. Otherwise any attempt to use the Bob 2.0 passport will result in my biometrics being queried with that database and linking back to the Bob 1.0 identity. I don't know *who* rooted the IPS – probably our friends from MI5, for their own purposes, or possibly the Police undercover intelligence folks – but realizing it's been done at all is a *holy fuck* moment, because once you've got a genuine verified passport identity, you can get all the other stuff you're going to need if you're hiding out. Driving license? Yup. Credit cards? As long as you can fake out Experian and Equifax, sure: break a leg! What I'm holding isn't a *false* identity – it's a terrifyingly real one that's been injected into the government's own ID verification system and will hold up to official scrutiny unless CESG realize one of the crown jewel databases has been hacked by their own side. Of course, the passport's no good for foreign travel: the instant you enter a country you've visited before on your previous ID, they'll spot the identical biometrics. But as long as I stay within the UK, the only way I'll be recognized is by eyeball, human or mechanical.

So, some nice person has provisioned my phone with a secure password database and a bunch of apps for useful services. Airbnb, Uber, that kind of thing, all linked to a genuine fake credit card backed by real money and a credit history stretching back a decade. It goes further than that. The phone has a Gmail account with a bot that helpfully sends human-looking emails back and forth, and Twitter and Facebook accounts ditto, to generate a plausible internet habit that won't trigger any trawls at GCHQ, because

I'm under no illusions: they'll have figured out that former SOE operatives have gone off the reservation and there will be a full-dress security panic in progress this week. And there's a version of OFCUT that points at secure servers that aren't hosted in the Laundry's usual server farms.

Back to the script. There is a hoodie and a pair of dark glasses waiting for me in a neat bag by the door. I put them on, cringing somewhat. If Ops have been this thorough so far, there's no chance that SCORPION STARE will pick me up, but there are always the other camera networks. I hope there's something about ... oh. Call an Uber, have it take me to *this* shopping center, go to level one and look for *that* hair salon, reservation in the name of Boris Johnson. Make sure you're seen by Dave, he's a trusted resource. So I spend a couple of hours having my eyebrows reshaped and being taught how to wear and maintain a wig and use some very special makeup that makes me look completely different to infrared cameras, then I go back out and, next checklist item: call an Uber, go *there*, pick up keys to the Airbnb flat Bob 2.0 is renting for the next three nights (but moving on from a day early), being sure to arrive before 5 p.m. because a Tesco delivery van is heading your way with food and drink to sign for.

This is the life of the modern spy on the run: we've got an app for that! Stay indoors during daylight hours unless the excursion is mission-critical, because your biggest risk is being recognized by a human being or camera operator. Order food for delivery via supermarket apps. Use Uber to move from temporary house to house at night. Never meet anyone you know face-to-face unless it's absolutely essential, because network analysis is a bitch; if you've got to attend a meeting, get an Uber to an address a couple of blocks away and walk – and check the approaches to the venue for CCTV cameras first, using Google Street View. You can be perfectly safe inside your own anonymous moving bubble of misery, programmed in advance by Lamplighters who have your best interests at heart.

If only I could sleep at night.

While I am being kept in a web 2.0 mediated virtual safe house, using a burner laptop leeching off next door's wifi to follow the news, the world outside is moving on.

The news about SOE being shut down hard has leaked, unsurprisingly. What's perhaps more surprising – at least, to me – is that it has been met in the press with widespread approval: lots of jerks being interviewed on the news saying 'They deserve it,' lots of talking heads commentators saying 'Well, it was so obviously a failing agency that . . .' You can fill in the ellipsis yourself. The fact that *there's no bloody successor agency in place* and the nation's occult defenses are wide open seems to have eluded the peanut gallery; perhaps because the idea that the nation *needs* defending in this way is such a new ingredient in the public debate that nobody seems to be questioning the line from the cabinet, which is that the police and army are on top of things and a new agency is being set up under proper oversight and will pick up the traces in due course, with help from our NATO allies. It's insane, but no more insane than Japan shutting down its entire nuclear reactor fleet in the middle of a heatwave because an extreme tsunami washed over one plant, or the USA invading a non-involved Middle Eastern nation because a gang of crazies from somewhere else knocked down two skyscrapers. In a sufficiently large crisis, sane and measured responses go out the window.

But sanity is in short supply in government these days. Instead, there are ominous smoke signals coming out of Downing Street and the COBRA committee meetings on a daily basis, drumbeats that signal the PM's iron-jawed determination to stand firm in the face of elven terrorist sympathizers and threats to the British way of life. Possibly by introducing a new package of mandatory, child-friendly censorware for all internet users, or maybe by invoking the Civil Contingencies Act (the twenty-first century formulation for rule by decree during a state of emergency). Oh, and a steady trickle of leaks about SOE's reckless and unaccountable waste of public funds, domestic spying and infiltration of bible study groups, and anything else they can find in the classified reports that makes us look bad. (Of which there is rather a lot, given that a large government agency can't possibly exist in the shadows for over seventy years without stepping in the occasional dog turd.)

There's other news, on a global scale, and it's just as depressing. The clean-up operation in Tokyo Bay continues, but there's been another attack near the southwest coast of Honshu. Russia continues to be troublesome. There's been an earthquake in Syria, in the vicinity of Palmyra, which is currently under occupation by Da'esh, and if you know what's buried there that's *really* worrying: those whack-jobs have form for robbing tombs to auction off the antiquities, and if they've stumbled across RANCID MOON I could be putting out the resulting fires for the next decade. Worst of all is the news from the United States, or rather, the lack of it. The political headlines are all saber-rattling over the Iranian nuclear weapons program and some bullshit enquiry into Benghazi in the run-up to a mid-term election. It's almost as if Congress has no idea that a giant occult power struggle for control of the US government is in progress ... or perhaps it's over already, and a ruthless media clamp-down by tongue-eating mind control parasites is the only thing keeping the world from learning about the takeover of DC by gibbering alien nightmares. I hope I don't get sent over there on a fact-finding mission once we've sorted out our domestic headaches: I've got a bad feeling about this.

Finally, the personal news: on my second day I got a terse email from Mo, who also has one of these phones. The cat has gone to stay with my parents, she herself is fine but will be moving around a lot, and these are her new contact details. I grind my teeth a bit, but per the README my wife and I aren't supposed to go to the mattresses together because it would roughly double our likelihood of being apprehended, never mind requiring us to confront all our unresolved baggage in a setting where one of us can't just walk out if things turn bad. (So it's going to stay unresolved for now, itching like hell.)

As for the rest of the agency, Persephone, Johnny, and everyone else I can think of are also on the move, because I'm not the only Mahogany Row name to pop up on the Met's charge and book system. We're not the only people who can root government databases, it seems. Persephone's on a bogus immigration rap, Johnny is wanted for illegal firearms ownership and is flagged as *extremely dangerous, do not approach* (which means if they spot him they'll call in a sniper team). I've been upgraded to assaulting a police officer, aiding and abetting a fugitive, impersonating an officer, murder, murder, and more murder – they've pinned the unfortunate Captain Marks and his guards on me, along with the headless handmaid and her assistant. Oddly, they haven't added the tank crew to my rap sheet, and there is no mention whatsoever of Cassie going missing, probably because they don't want to trigger a national panic.

So all I can do is sit here all on my own, in a rented living room with the curtains shut, surfing the web, swearing at the news, and hating myself.

Isn't life *great*?

It's early evening on a Wednesday night in North London. A woman pauses at the corner of Woodside Avenue and glances at her phone, as if checking a message. She's dressed for the office in a business suit and heels, and carries a brief case as well as a small handbag: unexceptionable, except for the pallor of her skin and her hair, the glossy blackness of which suggests she might be a weekend goth. The hair is dyed, of course. Mhari Murphy doesn't know for sure that there's a warrant out with her name on it, but she doesn't believe in taking any chances. She's hungry and impatient, but not so impatient she's willing to risk watching the final sunrise through the window of a locked police cell.

She checks the time again: 2057. Nearly nine. She starts walking, heading for the driveway and frontage of the hospice. This is London, so although the facility is set back behind a hedge, the grounds are not extensive; however, the red brick inpatient unit is reasonably secluded, with the ground floor rooms facing inwards onto a terrace and courtyard surrounded by flower beds. There are, Mhari thinks, many worse places to die.

The last straggling carers and support staff – administrators, physiotherapists, a chaplain – from the afternoon shift are leaving as she heads towards the hospice. One or two of them climb into cars parked on the street, but most drift towards the nearby bus stops or Woodside Park tube station. Mhari heads for the front door under the short drop-off driveway opening onto the street. The front door opens onto a quiet reception area, not the bustling receiving unit of a front-line hospital. She walks to the desk and waits until a door nearby opens and a nurse comes out to greet her.

'Hello. Can I help you?'

'Hi, I'm Jill Cantor, from the Wellcome Trust – I'm here to talk to Dr. Gearing, if she's available?' Mhari smiles stiffly and raises her briefcase slightly, watching the nurse's eyes track towards it. 'I have an appointment.'

'I'll just check if she's available.' The nurse picks up the desk phone and dials, then waits. She seems to have swallowed the cover unquestioningly: Mhari can see the precise pigeon-hole she's landed in. The black business suit and briefcase make her look like a drug company sales-woman, but it's late in the evening and the Wellcome Trust is a charitable research foundation, and Dr. Gearing is the pain management specialist on team, working night shifts this week, so: Ms. Cantor – or maybe Dr. Cantor – is obvi-ously here about some joint research project, going above and beyond her core working hours because death's hand-maidens never sleep. 'Dr. Gearing? A Ms. Cantor ... yes, I'll send her on up.' She looks at Mhari: 'First floor, ward two, if you ask one of the sisters they'll point you at Alice.'

'Thank you.' Mhari smiles, showing her some melting ice. Then she turns and heads for the stairs up to the first floor.

It must be a quiet period: half the rooms on ward two stand open, empty and waiting. The others are mostly closed, although through one half-open door Mhari glimpses a bedridden figure, two women sitting in chairs to either side, one holding the sleeper's shrunken hand. It's a somber reminder and she finds herself taking more care over her heels, although – unusually for a medical ward – the corridor outside is carpeted to deaden the sound. It must be hell to keep it disinfected, she thinks absent-mindedly, although it's not as if most patients stay here long enough to pick up a bug.

Dr. Gearing is checking a patient's records on a computer terminal behind the nursing station as Mhari approaches. She's in her late thirties, wearing the slightly frumpy business attire that seems to be a thing among junior doctors, like an overworked office administrator except for the totemic stethoscope that signals her status. She glances up. 'Ms. Cantor ...? Can I help you?'

Mhari nods. 'Is there somewhere we can talk in private?' she asks, holding her Continuity Ops warrant card just slightly too far away for Dr. Gearing to read the fine print. 'It's about the midnight supply arrangement.'

Gearing meets her eyes for a moment and nods minutely. 'Be with you.' She finishes typing, then stands up: 'Follow me.'

They end up in one of the empty rooms on the hospice ward, overlooking the patio at the back. Gearing shuts the door and leans against it. 'I heard the news,' she says tiredly.

'The agency was abolished, just like that, with no replacement supply arranged for the, the recipients,' Mhari tells her. 'They're in serious trouble.'

'These recipients.' Dr. Gearing looks at her. 'I was under the impression your research program would be restarted in a few weeks? Or maybe a couple of months, when the new organization has had time to sort everything out. It *is* a research project, isn't it? That's what I was told.' She focuses on Mhari. 'What's this about, exactly?'

'I can't tell you; it's classified. Which is a problem, unfortunately, because I'd *like* to tell you, but I'm not allowed to. I think I'm allowed to say that the ... the cultures that the samples are serving to maintain will be irreparably spoiled if the regular supply is interrupted for more than a few days. It took years to get these cultures established and stabilized, and—'

'Please don't bullshit me, Ms. Cantor, or whoever you are, I'm not buying it.' Gearing's gaze sharpens and she stands up, clearly adamant. 'This has been a very strange research protocol all along, and the whole ... *occult* ... connection with your agency is quite disturbing. As you are probably aware, the supply arrangement imposed on me by our directors breaches the Human Tissues Act and almost certainly wouldn't pass muster in front of a medical ethics review board; unless you can give me a *good* reason to stick my neck on the line for your study I'm going to have to—'

'– Don't move.' Mhari throws her force of will behind the instructions and Dr. Gearing freezes. Then Mhari takes an irrevocable step: she smiles.

'Uh-huh-unh—' Gearing is fighting it, a sure sign of her rising panic. Mhari lets the smile slip, allows her lips to relax back into place, concealing her dentition.

'I'm not going to bite you.' Mhari takes a deep breath, then searches for the right words, a formula that will imply the essentials without breaking confidence, 'even though I'm hungry. But this isn't about me. The agency has been dealing with a, a certain problematic condition, a contagious paranormal disease. As you can see, some of the patients can be stabilized, if they receive regular transfusions. The downside is that the donors ... don't survive. So the optimal protocol is to take donations only from people who are already dying.' Gearing's eyes are wide and dark, terrified, as she meets Mhari's gaze. She's breathing rapidly, and Mhari can't help glancing down at the nearly irresistible pulse in her throat. 'Do you understand? You may reply.'

'Yuh-you're a—'

'Stop! Don't say it. Let's keep this deniable, please.'

Dr. Gearing's face is wan and her forehead is shiny with

perspiration: it's a wonder she hasn't pissed herself. 'But you, you drink—'

'*Calm down.*' Predictably, that sort of order doesn't work, even with PHANG mind control mojo behind it. 'Most of what people think they know about this condition is stuff and nonsense. I'm not going to murder you, I'm not some kind of undead animated corpse, I'm not harmed by religious symbols, it's all rubbish. Well, except for needing regular blood samples. The point is, if the supply arrangement is disrupted a number of people with this condition will be faced with a slow, lingering death or, or, having to face an unacceptable alternative. I'm a civil servant, Doctor, I didn't sign up to become a blood-drinking serial killer. But I can't speak for all the others, if their rations are interrupted.'

Dr. Gearing is shaking her head. 'But if it harms the donors, if they haven't given informed consent, it, it's clearly unethical as well as illegal—'

Implied threats aren't working and she's in danger of losing control. Mhari consults her conscience and takes another step into the twilight borderland between bending the rules and breaking them: 'One of the other civil – former civil – servants who shares my condition is the fellow to whom the All-Highest of the *alfär* Host pledged their surrender. I'm not exaggerating: this little *interruption* jeopardizes our national security. If it comes to the crunch, there are soldiers who will stick the needle in their own arm and draw blood, even knowing that their life expectancy afterwards will be measured in weeks, because it's better than the thousands of deaths that will result if they don't.' Mhari's delivery grows increasingly vehement as she makes her case: 'Do you know the streetcar problem? A runaway tram is hurtling towards six people on the track, but you can throw a switch and divert it onto a siding – where it will kill one person instead? Congratulations, Doc, welcome to my world. It's a classic streetcar problem – except the six people you think you're saving will die of natural causes before the streetcar reaches them, and the person on the other track is carrying a bomb that will wipe out everyone on the tram if it hits them.'

Mhari takes a step back: now she's breathing too fast as well, and trying not to clench her fists. Dr. Gearing stares at her as if she's grown a second head as well as fangs. 'You can talk and move again,' Mhari says curtly. 'I'm not going to hurt you. But I want you to think very hard. I just committed a serious offense in trusting you with this. I'm not just risking a disciplinary hearing or being struck off, my neck is quite literally on the line here.'

She turns and stares out the window, at the moonlit garden where so many of the people who have unknowingly kept her alive for the past year spent their last hours. She feels empty, purged of human feeling. By rights she ought to be appalled at herself for the deliberate breach, but she finds she really doesn't care any more. She has reached the point of questioning whether her actions are more about defending herself than defending the realm, and the irony of surrendering responsibility and dumping the whole thorny dilemma on the shoulders of a doctor who specializes in pain control does not elude her. She seats herself in the visitor's chair, beside an empty bed where her own will to survive has hastened the end of more than one cancer patient's story: and she finds herself at peace as she waits for the doctor to return and deliver the verdict on her prognosis.

It's six o'clock on a Saturday evening at Nether Stowe House and the reception is just getting underway. The permanent staff and Schiller's events team have been working flat-out for days to ensure that everything is ready to run in accordance with the plan drafted by the party planning office. This first session is a black tie event with a very exclusive guest list (no journalists or press photographers will be permitted to approach within telephoto range). While many of the attendees are arriving in a fleet of chauffeur-driven limos provided by GP Services, others – the reclusive property tycoon Burroughs twins, the eldest son and heir of an infamous press baron, a former French president and his supermodel/rock-star wife – are dropping in on the helipad tucked discreetly behind the orchard at the rear of the building.

Nigel Irving, the Minister of Defense, does not rate a helicopter, but the vintage Rolls-Royce Schiller's people laid on for him is a step up from the normal ministerial Jaguar, as is the bottle of posh plonk in the solid silver bucket. It's a nice touch, he has to admit, and he is more-than-somewhat lubricated by the time the car glides to a halt on the graveled drive in front of the big house. (A Minister of the Crown can't accept gifts, but a lift in a friend's car and a bottle of refreshments between friends is somewhat deniable, or can at least be written down as 'party hospitality' on his parliamentary expenses form.)

Nigel is, as is so often the case, alone for the evening. Winifred only accompanies him to public work shindigs these days – she says the other kind give her a headache, although what she really means is *Nigel* gives her a headache – and the girls are at college or on an overseas exchange program, conveniently out of the way. Of course he doesn't have to be here – when you're a Minister you're not short for party dates – but he's heard that Schiller throws *great* parties, and he's been curious for a while.

The chauffeur opens the door and Nigel pulls himself unsteadily to his feet, blinking at a sleekly smiling platinum blonde in a black evening gown. She offers him her opera-gloved hand: 'Welcome to Nether Stowe House, Minister, we're so glad we could welcome you tonight! My name's Anneka Overholt and I'll be your hostess for the evening.' She has an odd accent, transatlantic with a trace of something Scandinavian, and Nigel smiles back, pegging where she's coming from immediately.

'Thanks,' he slurs, then squares his shoulders and offers her his arm. She rests her hand on it and guides him discreetly towards the marble mosaic floor of the entrance hall. 'Charmed, 'm sure.' He stifles a hiccup. The champers in the car was somewhat stronger than expected, or else he forgot to eat lunch again: he's not sure. 'Happy to be here.'

'I've heard *so* much about you,' his companion gushes happily, ice-blue eyes twinkling, and for a moment Nigel's mind sharpens: *I'm sure you have*, he realizes. This isn't amateur hour and the girl's clearly top-drawer talent, not somebody you rent by the half hour off the back of a phone box postcard. 'We have a seafood buffet in the Grand Hall, there's a very accomplished swing band playing in the Prince Regent's Ballroom, and a firework display after dark at the end of the Rose Garden. There are other refreshments in the pavilion on the terrace, and if you want anything – anything at all – I'll see to it.'

'I'm sure you will,' Nigel purrs amiably. She dimples as she smiles, earrings glittering as brightly as her perfect teeth – *gosh, Schiller must own half of Hatton Garden*, he tells himself as he notices the amount of ice she's wearing – and she sways closer for a moment.

'Would you care for refreshments?' she asks, and without looking away she reaches sideways and produces a glass of

Bucks Fizz from a tray presented by a uniformed waiter: 'Something lighter, to pace yourself with, perhaps? The night is young ... '

Damn it, he's had a wearisome week. The fallout from that mess up north is the gift that just keeps on fucking giving, one damn hearing after another, not to mention the headache of dealing with the PM's insensate demands that he shut down this rogue agency *immediately*, a job just concluded this week. He deserves an evening off, especially one on the dime of the transatlantic cousins who'll be picking up the slack. Kicking back with the delectable Anneka is just what the doctor ordered, he decides. 'Thank you! A glass for yourself?' he suggests.

The night is indeed young, and if he's reading the signs correctly it's going to prove a much more memorable affair than the other options that were on his menu – the Defense Electronics Association's annual dinner or some tedious constituency thing. Anneka from the Planet of the Platinum-Amex Playmates smiles at him with a glint in her eye that makes his pulse race as she raises her glass in a toast. 'Your health!' she proposes, then leads him arm-in-arm towards the ballroom.

The ambiance in the public rooms of Nether Stowe House is carefully curated, remaining just on the tasteful and up-market side of riotous. Not that Nigel's anyone to criticize – he was a member of the Piers Gaveston Society back in the '80s when that prize rotter Graf von Bismarck was running it as a live-action re-enactment of *Oberst Redl* – but it's interesting to watch. Lots of distinguished men of business wearing DJs and a fair few older women in designer gowns, but the female age distribution skews a couple of decades younger than the men's and there's something, something oddly *uniform* about the girls, as if they're animated mannequins from the same dress agency window. Servers in dickie bows or old-fashioned maids' uniforms keep a discreet eye on the level of bubbly in the guests' glasses. As Anneka leads him through the grand hall he hears laughter from the top of the sweeping staircase. He looks up in time to see a piece of prize totty leaning over the banister, displaying side-boob and cleavage down to her navel as she giggles behind her hand at something a milky-skinned Adonis in a leather jockstrap has just told her. 'Tonight is your special night,' Anneka purrs in his ear, 'you can have anything you want. *Anything*.' She tugs his arm around her shoulders like a stole. Her glass has disappeared somewhere and she produces a silver pill pot with her gloved left hand, flipping it open to offer him a familiar-looking blue tablet: Pfizer's little helper. Nigel takes it without a second thought, washing it back with the last of his drink. 'Anything at all,' she adds, leaning against him in such a way as to make her meaning clear.

The drawing room seems to be reserved for movers and shakers sad or staid enough to have brought their spouse along for the evening, but as she draws Nigel towards the rear of the house he recognizes a wilder scene, like a grown-up version of the excesses of his student days and certain discreet private events at Party Conference. He spots a couple of fellow Bullingdon alumni, a younger Saudi prince in mufti, and a couple of MEPs who pointedly fail to make eye contact. They're all accompanied by toned and tanned arm candy, mostly (but not exclusively) female, appreciatively hanging on their egos. The band is indeed playing swing, but the ballroom floor provides a stage for a small professional dance troupe who retreat between each set to shed more layers of their outfits. The audience mostly stick to the edges, watching from the sidelines or conversing.

'I must say you know how to make a fellow welcome,' Nigel murmurs in his companion's ear. 'For some reason I wasn't expecting ... well, this.' His wandering gaze takes it all in, a couple billion pounds' worth of distinguished silverback executives and their glittering constellation of *personal entertainers*: a euphemism he can just about convince himself fits. (Political probity dictates that nobody here will admit to paying for, or selling, sex for money, but the young and athletic will doubtless leave with their personal finances improved, and the old and the louche with the other side of the coin bankrolled by their host.) 'It's all rather remarkable.'

'Oh, I can't take the credit for it: it's all thanks to our CEO,' Anneka reassures him. 'He likes to lay on a good spread and send his guests away happy.' She smiles, reaches out, and snags a champagne flute from a passing waitress, and passes it to him. 'Perhaps you'd like to meet him personally?'

'I'd be very glad to, if he's around,' Nigel says affably. He feels a warmly benevolent glow of gratitude towards the CEO of GP Services as Anneka tugs his arm down around her waist, squeezing his fingers in friendly reproach – perhaps he's been trying to move too speedily for her, or she feels this is too public a setting for hanky-panky – but he has to admit to being slightly puzzled. Isn't the fellow reputed to be some sort of god-bothering sky pilot? But this is a terribly worldly sort of party. 'Is he around?'

'He was earlier, in fact – oh yes! There he is now! I can introduce you briefly and then perhaps I can show you around the rest of the house? There are rooms upstairs if you feel like a lie-down or a massage,' she adds, then turns him towards a distinguished-looking fellow in his fifties with a remarkably full head of silver hair and an avuncular smile. Anneka unglues herself from Nigel's side and curtsies to him: 'Sir! May I introduce the Right Honorable Nigel Irving, Secretary of State for Defense? This is Dr. Raymond Schiller, Chief Executive of GP Services and its subsidiary GP Security.' She stands between them, clutching her hands and smiling anxiously as if unsure which master she wishes most to please.

'Jolly pleased to meet you, Dr. Schiller.' Nigel dials up the Old English Bonhomie to 11 and offers his hand as a ritual sacrifice. Schiller shakes it with the expected transatlantic nut-cracker grip. 'I've been hearing a lot about your operation lately. Number Ten is keen.' He smiles. 'I hear we have you to thank for solving our problem with a certain loose cannon agency.'

'Oh, call me Raymond. And thanks aren't necessary: we're pleased to help out!' Schiller sounds appropriately discreet. 'We're used to handling these matters for the State Department and we have all the clearances. That's why we were able to make a head start on getting assets into position for the spin-up of the new agency next week. But of course we're committed to openness and transparency in service to government, and I couldn't possibly ask for any favors, much less special treatment.'

Schiller says this with such dead-pan sincerity that Nigel almost believes him despite his better judgment. From what Adrian was saying he'd been expecting some sort of dry stick of a fire-and-brimstone preacher man, but Raymond is speaking his language with note-perfect accent. 'I look forward to talking later,' he says.

'Yes, absolutely.' Schiller glances around: 'But this really isn't a business meeting! It's a party, and if you'll excuse me, I need to play host and ensure everyone is having a good time.' He smiles broadly. 'I gather you've made Anneka's acquaintance?' The girl has her back turned as they speak, offering a pretense of privacy: Nigel's gaze lingers possessively over her naked shoulder blades, follows the elegant line of her spine down into her dress. 'She's been my executive assistant for the past three years, you know. A remarkable lady: I'm so sad she's leaving in a couple of weeks, to take up a post as special advisor to Norman Grove.' A minister without portfolio: Nigel feels a flash of jealousy, even though his own post is stratospherically senior to Grove's. 'She can take care of all your requirements, and if you let her know what you want, she'll make sure it happens.'

'Really?' Nigel is almost amused, but slightly on edge. *And I thought she was* – he stifles the thought. 'She has hidden depths.'

'She seems to have taken to you,' Schiller assures him, then winks. 'I must circulate, see you later?'

'Indeed! Until later.'

As Schiller turns away Nigel begins to follow up the uneasy realization that Schiller's words jogged loose in his mind. But then Anneka turns to face him, a flash of thigh tantalizingly visible through the slit in her gown. She beams brilliantly, then she steps inside his reaching arm and wraps an arm around him. 'Mm-hmm! And now you've fulfilled your obligation to your host we're free for the rest of the evening! Let me show you upstairs? You'll *adore* the Old Earl's bedroom,' she promises.

'*This is ridiculous!*' Cassie swears quietly. There's a hiss and crackle of static as she rubs a fingertip inside her collar, disturbing the hidden microphone. '*How am I supposed to not spill the drinks if they keep groping me?*'

I glance across the table. Alex is glaring at the battered laptop in front of him but his fingertips are white with tension. His expression is livid. Mhari is making notes on her tablet next to the floor plan 3-view displaying the location of the tagged wine glasses Cassie has handed out. Everyone in the living room of the holiday rental property in the neighboring village that we picked for a field office is uncomfortable. 'Situation?' I ask.

Mhari clears her throat. 'That was His Excellency, Prince—'

I cut Mhari off – 'So the wandering hands don't belong to one of ours,' I say pointedly.

'No,' she snaps. Aside: 'But please don't let her have a snit about this, we've got nobody else who's remotely as good at this job ...'

'From your lips to the Black Pharaoh's ears,' I snark. But she's absolutely right: this wasn't in the risk matrix we drew up for the mission as originally scoped. When Schiller rented a posh country pad as a venue for boozed-up receptions for business contacts it looked like a good idea to put some of our people on the inside wearing wires. Rooting the vacation cottage and getting a router-level packet monitor on the leased line to the country house wasn't a huge problem, and that gave us access to the CCTV and a carrier signal for our own roving commentators. The wine glasses are a neat trick. They're tiny bluetooth transmitters with resonant contacts that turn the goblets into microphones, reporting back through a couple of rooted smartphones, like the gizmos we planted in the BBC newsroom an eternity ago. It's the sort of Maxwell Smart hack that used to cost the CIA black budget half a billion to develop in the '60s but is off-the-shelf from a Chinese toy factory these days. Where we ran into trouble was in getting past GP Security's vetting. It's dismayingly professional, and the weak corner of our coverage envelope is the human factor. In the end our ability to kibitz on Schiller's shindig was entirely dependent on us being able to get an experienced infiltration asset who wasn't on any national databases (fingerprint, DNA, Immigration, or other) and who could sweet-talk – or englamour – their way past the door and replace a contract catering body. Subtype: unskilled, or at least trainable at a day's notice.

People like that are hard to get at short notice, but Cassie Brewer, the Queen of Air and Darkness herself, fits the bill – at least in her previous capacity as Agent First of Spies and Liars. She can steal your face and your memories, change her appearance to match if she's got enough thaumic mojo on hand. Convincing everyone she comes into contact with that she's just a waitress working for a contract agency barely qualifies as a warmup exercise. Persuading her to re-bind her command of the Host so that Alex is the fallback All-Highest if anything happens to her, was the hard part: but don't underestimate the incredible motivational power of the boredom that arises from being bubble-wrapped in a government detention block for a couple of weeks.

So here we are, huddling together around a bunch of computers in a safe house down the road from Nether Stowe House, recording and tracking a bunch of smart bugs around the ground floor and listening in on Cassie's subvocalized stream of consciousness as she ferries trays of champagne flutes, white wine spritzers, and the occasional apple juice between the scullery and the function spaces of the mansion. And I find myself drifting off, trying to put myself into her head in order to get a better feel for what's going on ...

This sucks – but it sucks slightly less than being stuck in that camp, thinks Cassie, as she backs through the entrance to the scullery carrying a mostly empty tray swimming in spilled bubbly.

When Alex's sometime boss put his proposal to them both, she'd been very excited. The camp on Dartmoor was tedious and lacking in amenities – no Internet access, not even cable TV: just a DVD player, a chess board, and the rain. They'd given up questioning her after the third interrogator's break down and focused on Alex, who had sworn horribly at the manual typewriter but persisted in writing up an extensive report. But that left her with nothing to do – well, aside from being with Alex, and you can't stay in bed all the time. Her offer to organize an amateur production of *The Great Escape* using the knights and officers of the Host billeted in the other wings of the camp had been received with an inexplicable lack of enthusiasm by Captain Marks, and for their part, her sworn vassals seemed to be trying to *avoid* her. It was almost as if they blamed her for this mess, rather than her father! So Mr. Howard's offer to get them both out of the camp and find something useful for them to do sounded like a really good idea, even before the nasty soul-parasites and their castrated *urük* slaves turned up, though Alex had been a total wet blanket about it until she very firmly told him it was going to happen.

But now ...

'What a mess! Dump that in the sink and take this one – try not to spill anything this time!' Lisa, the woman running the scullery, points her chin at a waiting tray of glasses on the side-table and gives Cassie a pointed glare as she continues to fill glasses, a spare bottle clamped in her left hand. 'Why did you – no, don't tell me.' She shakes her head. 'Where do they get these people from?' Lisa demands of the ceiling; 'The local JobCentre?'

Cassie ducks her head submissively and reaches for

the next tray just as the door behind her slams open and another waiter called Ben prances in, holding a tray of empties. She nearly jerks the tray but manages to stop herself just short, waits for Ben to pass on his way to the dish washer, then picks up the fresh load and turns towards the exit. 'Take those upstairs,' Lisa snaps at her, 'back staircase, round past the kitchen, snap to it!'

Live-action *Downton Abbey* cosplay spying had sounded like *fun* when Mr. Howard suggested it, but now Cassie's having second thoughts, it's too late to back out. It seems to be all about being shouted at by horrible people while wearing a ridiculous uniform, avoiding sleazy old men's wandering hands, and trying not to stumble and spill the drinks in heels. And if 007 is here he's keeping a low profile.

The servants' corridors snake around the back of the grand house, a late eighteenth-century addition to keep the below-stairs staff out of the way of their betters. The floors are uncarpeted boards and flagstones, the passages narrow, and the back stairs are steep and poorly illuminated. Cassie takes up her dozen champagne flutes and climbs to the first floor where there's a landing with a deeply recessed window ledge. She breathes deeply and puts her tray down, then reaches into the pocket of her apron for a sheet of what look like shiny self-adhesive stickers the size of 10 pence pieces. She peels off four of them at a time and transfers each one from her fingertips to the base of a glass until she empties the sheet. It's only the work of a minute, but she's sweating nervously by the time she finishes, because there's no way to deflect suspicion if anyone spots her doing it, and while it'd be easy enough to make them forget, the signs of mental tampering may be evident to the security staff. There are adepts here, maybe even magi. However, nobody interrupts her, and a minute later she straightens her dress, picks up the tray, breathes deeply, and carries on up the staircase.

The upper floor of the house is laid out around a long corridor with a landing opening onto the grand staircase, with shorter passages trailing up each wing of the house from either end. Cassie slips through a concealed panel in the wall of the main corridor and walks along it, glancing through open doorways. (On her last trip she made the mistake of opening one of the closed bedroom doors in the east wing. It was educational, but it's not a mistake she'll make again.) Most of the open-doored rooms are empty, so she nips inside and replaces any empties among the refreshments on each side-table. The doorway at the back above the ballroom opens onto a balcony with sofas and occasional tables. It's open and there are guests, so she enters and makes a circuit, face frozen in an ingratiating smile.

Half a dozen of the guests have made it up here: all middle-aged to elderly white men in dinner jackets. A couple have lit cigars, and all are in need of refreshments – both for themselves and their much younger escorts. 'Hey darling—' one of them flashes her a gold tooth – 'why don't you lose the tray and come join me? You're wasted as a waitress!' He's happy but somewhat unhinged in a way that Cassie associates with coke or meth, so she widens her smile, shakes her head, and sways her hips around the edge of his wobbly arm's reach. 'Come here!'

'Got a job to do,' she says mildly, and steps away.

One of the girls takes mercy on her. She grabs two full champagne flutes, and turns to face the grabby guy. 'Here you are, sweetie, let *me* be your waitress,' Cassie hears the companion tell him before he has time to flip from bubbly to sullen. Then Cassie turns the corner of the balcony, only to find herself face to face with an elegantly groomed copper-haired woman. She manages to stop dead without spilling the drinks, which is a good thing because *this* woman clearly thinks she's someone in authority, and the dry-cleaning bill for her gown would wipe out Cassie's pay check for the night. 'I don't remember hiring you,' the woman says accusingly. 'Why are you here?' She speaks with a faint Irish accent; her eyes are as cold as camera lenses, and Cassie feels her hackles tense, for there is something subtly *wrong* about her.

'The agency called me up this afternoon.' Cassie is defensive, her pulse speeding. 'Something about one of their regulars being off sick? Vomiting bug? Who are you?'

The woman studies her for a moment, scanning and categorizing. 'Bernadette McGuigan of GP Security Systems. I'm in charge of personnel here. You're serving for Lisa Geissler, is that correct? What's *your* name?' Cassie notices that she wears a discreet undecorated cross on a plain silver chain around her neck: the symbolism seems oddly out of keeping with the rest of this party. A reek of occult power hangs about Bernadette, unsettling and sweetly rotten, but Cassie doesn't dare to open her mind and look: if this woman is a practitioner, she'll spot the intrusion.

'Lisa – I don't know her family name?' Cassie ducks her head again. 'I'm Cassie Daniels, ma'am. Is everything all right?'

McGuigan's expression is unreadable. 'I don't like surprises,' she says evenly. 'You are not on my checklist. Wait here. Do not move.' She produces a drab-looking phone from her evening clutch and speed-dials a number. 'McGuigan. Temporary manifest, I want you to verify a name, Cassie Daniels. Yes, please. Full work-up.' Cassie shivers: McGuigan is the one with the bare shoulders but Cassie feels unaccountably naked before her gaze. There is *mana* here, and a powerful coiled intellect, something unnatural and alien that reminds her of something she's seen before, and recently – 'Oh, good. That will be all.' Ms. McGuigan ends the call and returns the phone to her bag. She frowns at Cassie. 'Your collar is wrinkled. Fix it before you carry on,' she says offhand, then picks up her skirts and marches away to find other members of staff to terrorize.

As Cassie watches her back recede she finally opens her inner eye, then closes it hastily and breathes a sigh of relief. 'Yikes,' she subvocalizes, 'that was *much* too close, YesYes!' McGuigan turns the corner of the balcony, taking her aura of unclean power with her. Cassie pats at her forehead, then runs a finger around the inside of her collar. 'The brain-worms are here and they're hungry.' Then she picks up her tray and continues around the balcony, looking out for conversations that might be worth planting an ear on.

Now not many people know this, but: Q-Division, SOE, has – or had – a Board of Directors.

I, personally, am not acquainted with the directors. Most of us aren't – they keep a low profile, even by the standards of Mahogany Row, where it's not unusual for certain senior personnel to keep such a low profile that only the payroll computers in HR can remember their names. It's not as if the organization doesn't have a well-understood charter and protocols for day-to-day and month-to-month operations: it's self-governing, most of the time.

As I implied, I don't deal with the board myself. But I know for a fact that Dr. Armstrong, as the seniormost Auditor, reports directly to the Board on occasion, as do the heads of other major departments: Human Resources, R&D, IT, Countermeasures, and Demonology, among others.

But sometimes conditions arise that demand active governance, with new policy directives and regulations a priority. Under such circumstances, we rely on the Board of Directors to do their thing. And if one situation is *guaranteed* to call for executive action, it's the sudden appearance of an order in council calling for the agency to be dissolved.

Unfortunately there are certain emergent problems with the Laundry's BOD.

The Board gave up trying to appoint external directors a long time ago. For one thing, the security clearance process is protracted and most candidates are rejected for one reason or another. For another, experience teaches us that when they are first apprised of the purpose and structure of the organization, a majority of external candidates assume they're the butt of an elaborate practical joke. And for a third, even when they find someone sufficiently open-minded enough to take it in but not so open-minded that they pick up every memetic infection that drifts past – well, it takes a long time to come up to speed.

So what we end up with is effectively an emeritus board of very senior members of Mahogany Row, trained up in management or oversight roles once their utility as practitioners goes into decline due to impending K syndrome, who are now semi-retired but still have enough experience and cognitive function remaining to be useful. They fill a variety of roles, acting as high-level emissaries to external agencies we liaise with, reviewing the big picture and our responses thereto, keeping us on track to deliver our mission objectives . . . and occasionally going to bat for us with head office, viz. the government of the day.

This is why that evening (although I don't know it at the time) a distinguished former professor of mathematics called Jack Berry – to which we can append: MA(Cantab),

DPhil, PhD, FRS, OBE, KCMG, and prefix 'Lord,' for he has indeed been appointed to the House of Lords – is sitting in the anteroom to the Prime Minister's private office at Number Ten, waiting to be invited in for a laptop-side chat with that august presence. Lord Berry is one of those academics who has aged well, despite his white hair and male pattern baldness: his eyes still twinkle and he exudes a keen interest in his surroundings, despite a dismaying ataxia that could be taken for the early stages of Parkinson's disease. He joined Q-Division in the late 1960s, an internal Civil Service transfer from GCHQ where he'd worked with James Ellis on what was then called non-secret encryption. After a distinguished career he officially retired in 2008, but took a part-time appointment to the Board. It's in that capacity that he's now here to see the PM. 'Not that it'll make any difference,' Mr. Redmayne reassures him sympathetically, 'I'm afraid his mind is made up. But at least you can say you made your case, eh?'

Professor Berry's expression is foreboding. 'Of course. But I really must say, in my experience inflexibility and excessive speed on these matters makes for poor policy. One wouldn't want to have to reverse oneself after a couple of years, what?'

Redmayne nods, but his smile is on hold. 'Of course. But my advice would be to pick your fights carefully. I'm afraid you won't be knocking on an open door. And as for the Treasury report ...'

The inner door opens, and Andrew Jennings, the PM's spad, high-steps out. He's dressed for the squash court and waving his racket alarmingly close to the paintings adorning the walls of the outer office. 'Oh hi, Ade. His Graciousness is ready for his next appointment right now; see you back here in an hour?' Jennings is bald, intense, and wears spectacles with such thick black rims that they appear shatterproof. He's also in his late twenties and almost offensively bumptious. 'Boss man says he doesn't need me for witch-doctor duty,' he adds, with a dismissive nod in Berry's direction. 'You can go in now.'

The professor glances at Redmayne, who smiles self-deprecatingly and settles back in the chair beside his desk. 'I'll be here when you're done with,' he murmurs.

Berry levers himself creakily out of his wing-backed chair. 'Thank you for arranging this,' he says, then approaches the study door.

The PM's office is not particularly large, but impeccably furnished with impressive antiques from the national collection. Unlike the Oval Office in the White House, the PM's den is not usually used for public appearances. Its window casements overlook the walled garden at the rear, but are protected on the outside with bulletproof glass; those parts of the walls unbroken by windows are fitted with tall bookcases, and the floor is broken up by a cluster of armchairs at one end of the room and a small meeting table at the other.

The PM is sitting at one end of the meeting table, reviewing papers from an open ministerial red box. He's wearing reading glasses and using a pen to scribble brief marginalia, his expression set in the intent mask of a schoolboy racing against the clock in an examination room. As the door swings shut behind Professor Berry, he walks slowly forward into the middle of the room, and waits.

Jeremy Michaels, the Prime Minister, finishes with one Treasury-tagged memo, places it face-down in the other half of the open box – then picks up the next paper. 'Well?' he says, offhandedly, as if talking to himself: 'Make it fast.'

Lord Berry knows a provocation when he sees one, and a hostile audience, not to mention a fix-up. Just the fact that he requested this meeting on Monday when the news broke and Number Ten only offered him a slot on Saturday speaks volumes. 'All right. I wouldn't be here if you hadn't already been briefed against my agency. I asked for this meeting to give you the other side of the story and explain why the course of action you've embarked on is incredibly unwise – if you're listening.' Needling the PM is a risk, but he's already so closed-off that it's not a huge one: if it jolts him into paying attention, it's worthwhile. And indeed, Michaels pauses in his reading of the memo on his blotter. Then, with exaggerated deliberation, he puts down his pen and makes eye contact with the professor.

'You have ten minutes, your Lordship, to explain why I should reinstate an organization that has demonstrably shat the bed in the most public manner imaginable, seriously embarrassing this administration, and the termination of which has already been announced. What makes you think there's anything on earth that will change my mind?'

Berry fixes his gaze on the wall behind the PM. 'Well, two things, really. Firstly, Q-Division shat the bed, as you put it, because of a long-term shortfall in recruitment, funding, and coverage. Bluntly, they're overstretched and we were unable to do our job properly. So my first message is that you can shoot your guard dog if it displeases you – but you're still going to have to secure your back yard. The threat hasn't gone away: if anything, we got off lightly this time. The order as issued made no provision for continuity or handover of existing projects: as such there are some, shall we say, *very worrying* gaps in coverage now. Firing the executive would have been one thing, but dismissing the line staff all the way down to the cleaners is going to cripple the replacement agency for months *and* lead to catastrophic loss of institutional knowledge. As to the second message, it's a bit uglier. Obviously you need to be seen to be doing something, and a major reorganization is the obvious thing to show you're a strong leader cleaning house. But we have a long habit of not using private sector contractors in this business. So there's nobody local to take on the job. Other governments do things differently, and doubtless you've been wooed by certain security conglomerates who can boast of esoteric specialities. Our advice to you is that we already vetted these contracting agencies with a view to using them – and rejected them with extreme prejudice. They come with some extremely questionable baggage attached and they do *not* have this nation's best interests at heart: it'd be like outsourcing the Army to Russia.'

One minute. Berry pauses and takes stock of the PM. His heart sinks: it's not looking good. Michaels's head is slightly tilted, as if he's trying to drain the water out of one ear – by all accounts he's a good swimmer – and he's wearing a slightly pained expression as if an annoying mosquito is buzzing around his head. Berry doesn't dare to use his not-inconsiderable thaumic skills these days – not unless he's willing to court an aneurysm – but he is pretty certain that the PM is not wearing one of the wards SOE supplied to the Cabinet Office. But neither is his mind undefended. There's only one conclusion Berry can reach, and it's an unpalatable one.

'Your Lordship,' the PM begins, then pauses. 'You've just threatened me *twice* in one minute. Firstly, with unspecified nasty beasties from the vasty deeps: "last time was bad, next time will be worse." And secondly, you're casting aspersions on our American friends' preferred contractors. I have it on very good authority that the corporation we're talking to is specifically rated as best-of-breed by our transatlantic colleagues. As there is *no* domestic equivalent, I have to conclude that you're trying to put the frighteners on me in order to stop the restructuring and reform of the failed agency dead in its tracks.'

Michaels started slowly but is rapidly gathering momentum, and shifting gear from patronizing lecture to bully pulpit as he goes: 'I will *not* be told what to do by a jumped-up maths teacher turned civil servant who bears partial responsibility for the worst disaster on British soil since the Battle of Hastings!' An expression of disgust steals over his face: 'I'm fed up to *here* with you people spinning all sorts of bizarre lies to justify your feather-bedding and special status within the Civil Service. As of now, that's ancient history. SOE will not be reinstated. Instead it will be replaced, and its replacement will be integrated with the rest of the defense apparatus, with sails trimmed to fit *our* policy position, rather than made-up mumbo-jumbo about alien gods and magic.' He snorts. 'Get out of here. We're done.'

Berry stands slowly, then nods. 'Of course. If that is your final word, sir, I have no alternative but to respect it.' The specialized ward he wears under his shirt collar is buzzing like a trapped wasp, desperate to escape. He can feel the pressure bearing down on it, the hostile intent of the Prime Minister's master. He needs to leave and bear witness while he can. 'I doubt we'll meet again. Goodbye.'

7: AUDITION FOR APOCALYPSE

Now pay attention:

As you will perforce be aware if you've read this far, the Laundry has been aware for a couple of years that our oath of office is subject to various workarounds and contains loopholes.

I gather that, historically, certain individuals in Mahogany Row were aware of these weaknesses but, for reasons now becoming evident, thought that the risk of third-party exploitation was outweighed by the benefits of being able to work around the outside of our normal constraints in event of an existential crisis.

The oath is a *geas* – a thaumaturgically enforced compulsion – that maintains security by compelling the sworn party to work in the best interests of the agency, as defined by its charter established by royal prerogative, etcetera. Note that royal prerogative bit: the *geas* in question draws its power from the sum over time of the entire loyal British population's faith in the Crown since that charter was established over four centuries ago. Which adds up to something like ninety million person-centuries-worth of belief. Hence the, shall we say *drastic*, consequences of violating one's oath.

Iris Carpenter got around it by convincing herself that with CASE NIGHTMARE GREEN imminent, the best way to maintain operational continuity was to adopt the methods of the other side. Call it the Edward VIII Approach if you like: if you're convinced you can't beat 'em, join 'em. (You might call it treason: I couldn't possibly comment.)

There are other weaknesses, of course. The definition of the Crown is not constant over time: Does it mean the Crown-in-Parliament, the absolute Monarchical Privilege of Elizabeth I, the whatever-the-hell-it-was exercised by the Lord Protector during the Commonwealth, or what? The twenty-first-century Crown as defined by the Constitutional Reform and Governance Act is not the same as the Crown as implied or assumed by the Treason Act (1800), which is not the same as the Treason Felony Act (1848), and so on. The oath works best on plain ordinary human brains. Those of us who are no longer entirely human are variably resistant to it. PHANGs are better than 50 percent likely to be immune to regular *geases*, as we discovered the hard way thanks to Basil. I gather the V-parasite infestation confers resistance. Even the *alfär* invaders, who have a lot more experience at controlling PHANGs than we do, use other methods to ensure docility. And then there's Angleton's special case ... which I have inherited.

But 95 percent of the time the oath of office is pretty good at binding us to obedience, and by the time you read this file it will have been superseded by something *much* better, so that's water under the bridge, right?

Well, no. Because in addition to the lift-bridge itself having mechanical vulnerabilities, the foundations are deliberately weakened. Not enough to count in most circumstances, but with the right leverage ...

... Like Dr. Armstrong's plan ...

... The entire system can be destabilized.

During normal operations (before it was dissolved so

abruptly) the agency operated as part of the Civil Service –
a secret part, but nonetheless, staffed by civil servants.
However, our charter was established by royal prerogative
of Her Majesty Queen Elizabeth I in 1584. It was renewed
by King James VI and I in 1611; and more or less swept
under the rug by King Charles I during the disastrous
period of Personal Rule that preceded the Short Parliament
and the subsequent descent into civil war. For entirely
understandable reasons, the small, collegiate body that saw
to the nation's magical defenses kept a low profile during
the Wars of the Three Kingdoms and subsequent Puritan
rule. And by the time the modern British constitutional
framework took shape in the early eighteenth century,
nobody thought to check the dusty archives for fine print.

So when Chris Womack's researchers went digging a few
months ago, in order to prepare the groundwork for bringing the agency under the aegis of the Constitutional Reform
and Governance Act, they discovered a loophole the size
of the one that allows the heir to the throne to play with
buckets of instant sunshine.* Which came as something of
a surprise, to say the least.

Most people live under the misconception that the United
Kingdom doesn't have a written constitution. Ignorance
is bliss, as they say. The UK does in fact have a constitution – but it's written up in about thirty different Acts of
Parliament, and Parliament reserves the right to tear it up
and redraft it pretty much at will. In a republic, the source

---

* As a result of prerogatives and exemptions written into laws dating back
to 1377 and subsequently grandfathered into newer legislation, the Duke of
Cornwall – in the person of the Crown Prince – has accidentally acquired the
right to use atomic weapons without facing prosecution under the Nuclear
Explosions (Prohibition and Inspections) Act (1998). Thereby promising a
different and alarmingly unsatisfactory outcome in event of another civil war
between Crown and Parliament.

of state power is the people. In a monarchy, the source of state power is the Crown – an abstraction that represents the power vested in the person of the monarch. (Monarchy demonstrably travels faster than light, for the instant one monarch dies, the next in line to the throne inherits the power of the crown: indeed, if we had a sufficiency of petty kingdoms to mess with we could use it as a basis for time travel, causality violation, and thereby an ironclad proof that $P = NP$. But I digress.) In the British system, ever since Charlie's unfortunate haircut, the monarchy delegates its power to the Crown-in-Parliament, which is to say, the successors to the chappies who administered the severe shave: but that's the post civil war settlement.

Our royal prerogative is a bit less abstract: it just says we owe allegiance to the monarch and his or her heirs and appointees. It completely misses out the indirection operator of referring to the Crown, so instead of a sophisticated royalty virtualization system we've been handed a raw, unprotected, bare-metal loyalty pointer leading straight back to the King or Queen.

Oops.

Under normal circumstances this wouldn't make any difference to the day-to-day business of running the agency as an arm of government: it's pretty much a legal abstraction. We do as we're told and leave the policy-making to people at higher pay grades because we're civil servants and we're supposed to be politically agnostic, loyal to the government of the day.

But it turns out that we're not actually *required* to be loyal to the government of the day, to the Crown-in-Parliament: we're loyal to the person of the monarch.

Which is why Continuity Operations was able to so easily ignore the dissolution order issued by the Cabinet

Office, drop a new oath on everybody, and carry on as if the agency was still authorized to exist.

And I think you can guess where this is going. It's going to be a wild roller-coaster ride: better hang onto your hat!

By midnight, the reception at Nether Stowe House is in full fling. While Cassie was taking a five-minute toilet break it surged past raucous, and as she exits the below-stairs quarters with a new drinks tray – this one loaded with vodka martinis – she finds the party well on the way to orgiastic excess.

A younger, glitzier crowd arrived after the capital's more of-the-moment venues closed for the night. They're bright young things with connections to the older and wealthier fixers Schiller invited as his primary guests: trust fund kids and heirs to family fortunes, here to party and not ashamed to let it all hang out. They're less likely to grope but more inclined to stumble drunkenly into Cassie's path, forcing her to swerve: servants are simply part of the furniture. She's expended all her bugs now, but she can't leave until her shift ends at three o'clock. 'Schiller is going to throw at least two more of these gala evenings,' Mr. Howard told her during the briefing the day before. 'We really need you inside all of them, if possible. I know it's a tough job: can you do it?'

Should have said no, shouldn't I? she tells herself as she reaches the side-table in the ballroom and starts methodically swapping full glasses for empties. *Too late now.*

The band has packed up for the night, leaving a sound system playing old eighties synthpop hits, and the air smells of sweat and weed. She's just finishing with her tray when something catches her attention. An older man with immaculately coiffed silver hair walks past her, chatting over his shoulder to another fellow, portly and balding, with a nose that bespeaks a fondness for spirits: '... don't care if it's proving difficult to find a workaround,' the silver-haired man is saying, 'I need them available as soon as possible, in this country, regardless of how you go about the import arrangements. Tell Major Riley if you encounter any difficulties, logistics is his speciality ...'

The fine hairs on the back of Cassie's neck rise, but not because of his words: the silver-haired male reeks of *mana*, and as she turns her inner eye on him she sees huge reserves of thaumic power bound at the cardinal points of his body, at heart and tongue and crotch. It has the same subtly unclean taste-feel-look to it as McGuigan's. He walks past Cassie, deep in conversation with his colleague, and she pretends not to notice, focusing on her tray – but she notes the direction his feet take, and feels a sharp pang of regret for having spent her last listening tag on a random piece of glassware. 'Yes, sir, Mr. Schiller,' says the fat man, 'I'll get them here in plenty of time, don't you worry. There'll be enough hosts to go round when you need them.'

Cassie shakes her head, then follows the pair at a discreet distance. They head towards the west wing of the building, at ground level, approaching a door marked PRIVATE. Cassie approaches it, steeling herself –

'Where do you think you're going?' Cassie startles, nearly shedding her load but getting it under control herself at the last second. It's Ms. McGuigan.

'Lisa said to collect all the empty glasses,' she says artlessly, 'I thought ...'

'You don't go in there.' McGuigan's tone is chilly. 'Leave that area alone. I'll arrange for it to be cleaned. Is that understood?'

'Yes, miss.' Cassie bobs in place, avoiding the woman's eyes. 'Where should I—'

But the security supervisor is already off, heading up the main staircase. *That was close*, Cassie thinks. The PRIVATE doors are off-limits to hired help? *Mr. Howard will be interested*, she decides as she turns to take her tray back to the kitchen, paying no attention to the pair of discreet CCTV camera balls overlooking the entrance to the off-limits area of the west wing.

'Yes, but what is he doing in those back rooms?' demands the Senior Auditor.

We're in a no-shit formal meeting of the GOD GAME INDIGO management team, convening in a safe house I've never visited before and will never see again.

'I can make a guess,' I say. 'So Schiller's spraying cash like there's no tomorrow. And there's the matter of these new leech-things he's come up with, and it's pretty clear he's got something to do with the Cabinet Office decision to shut down the agency. But what about the business contacts from other industries? And the bright young things? Is there something more to this? Because it goes beyond that DELIRIUM playbook the Comstocks leaked to us.'

'Stop speculating, Bob,' Persephone tells me. 'Unless you've got anything concrete – Doctor?'

Dr. Armstrong shakes his head. 'Bob's right in that it goes beyond simply shutting down a rival agency. This has got to be some sort of major power play. His burn rate is unsustainable, and that's the smoking gun. The question is, what *kind* of power play is it? He's already in a good position to mop up a hugely lucrative outsourcing deal and replace the agency. But is he after political power, or something else? Could he be piloting an end-game run for the Sleeper in the UK rather than on his home ground?'

We're sitting in a hunched-over circle inside a temporary summoning grid which has locked us into an isolated
pocket universe of our own for an hour, a camping lantern
on a tripod in the middle providing lighting. The glow
of LEDs gives everybody a weirdly washed-out, bleached
appearance, underlit with the tops of heads in shadow. It's
just the SA, Persephone, me, and Mo this time around.
Vikram's fighting administrative fires – money laundering
rules make it surprisingly hard to boot up a small covert
agency without anyone noticing, even if you've got access to
the House of Lords black budget – Mhari is keeping Alex
out of trouble and riding herd on Cassie – an unenviable
job – and Boris is running the monitoring suite upstairs
from Schiller's city apartment.

'Let's see.' Mo flips open the paper organizer she's carrying around and consults her notes. 'He's on the hook
for a million and a half so far for the use of Nether Stowe
House. Based on the contract caterers' invoices it looks like
he's paying just under three hundred thousand for each
party – but that's just the official entertainments budget;
the hookers and blow probably cost twice as much on top.'
Her lower lip curls in concentration. 'Two so far, another
planned for next week, it's *ridiculous* – if he kept it up for a
year his spend would exceed fifty million quid on partying.
Let's see. Add another fourteen thousand a week for the
Docklands apartment, and ten thousand for personal transport – three armored luxury limos, helicopter on call to the
tune of eight flying hours per week, plus drivers and flight
crew – yes, this is all petty cash by Schiller's standards, but
it adds up. Salary and wages for his entourage: he has at least
three senior female PAs and four male bodyguards or minders with him. Plus the chauffeurs. As he brought them with
him they're presumably members of his Church, but even so,

on American pay scales, ten bodies plus payroll overheads adds up to at least another eight thousand a week.'

'Exactly,' Dr. Armstrong says heavily. 'He's blowing between five and ten million pounds on wild parties this month.'

Persephone has been scribbling notes on a legal pad. Now she taps the cap of her pen against her teeth pensively. 'How much is Golden Promise Ministries worth? And the GP Services subsidiary?'

'Not enough,' says my wife. She flips pages rapidly. 'We got our hands on their last filed accounts. They're both privately held organizations but his Church is a 501(3) C body, income-tax exempt – we had to pull strings, but the Treasury were remarkably helpful – Golden Promise Ministries reported gross income of about forty-eight million dollars a year. Their subsidiaries are more interesting: GP Services actually made a loss in 2012, but it's an artificial loss, they would have been in profit to the tune of seventeen million dollars if they hadn't plowed it into, uh, "business development" and some heavy real estate and capital expenditure acquisitions. Like that Gulfstream Schiller flies around in.' She frowns in distaste. 'Gross turnover was two hundred and sixty-nine million dollars in 2012. There are some other activities – Schiller runs a talk radio station and a cable TV channel, all firewalled from the rest of the business because media outlets are subject to regulatory scrutiny – and then there's some stuff the Treasury people couldn't get us. A couple of business units with their own limited-liability setup and some sort of federal contract.'

Persephone whistles quietly. 'All right. Call it three hundred and fifty million dollars a year in turnover, and the black budget. That will be cost-plus if he's subcontracting for the Black Chamber. Why is that not sufficient, Michael?'

'Because.' Dr. Armstrong crosses one leg over the other and laces his fingers around his knee. 'How do you spend ten million dollars a month on entertainment on income of three hundred and fifty a year, without it damaging the rest of your business empire? It's thirty percent of gross turnover! Obviously you can't do that: it's a short-term strategy. He can afford to do it for a month or two, maybe three, but he can't keep it up indefinitely. So, let's work it through. If he's greasing palms in order to win outsourcing contracts from the new ministry, *he's doing it too early.* The temporary agency MOD is provisioning next week per order in council is a holding action. It'll take nine months to draft a proper legislative framework, rush it through committee, and get the new portfolio established. Even with the usual large government contracting agencies handling things at our end and Schiller plugging his GP Security people into them as specialist subcontractors. If he's here to grab a chunk of our work, he should be planning for a long haul, one to two years. So he's running a short-term plan, people, and he's going to reach the pay-off soon. Which means it has to be something huge enough to justify that level of expenditure, that pays off really fast.'

'There are other loose ends,' Persephone adds in the silence. 'Why his people tried to snatch Bob off the streets. And the attempt on Cassie and Alex. The new parasites, the segmented worms.'

'They're like nothing of his I've seen before,' I add, shuddering. 'And how did he come back from the Temple on the Pyramid? He's supposed to have died there. The gate was closed. He shouldn't be here *at all.*'

Mo speculates: 'Let me take a stab at it? Schiller Mark One was a charismatic evangelical preacher. He's still running the Church but he's not so visible on-air these days and he's not throwing any stadium events. So he's not looking for broad grass-roots public support and outreach. Instead he's making lots of friends among the point-one-percenters, he's hobnobbing with MPs and Cabinet Office insiders and providing hookers and blow to the elite.'

Persephone joins in. 'These parties. Two so far, another next week. I've met Schiller. Before the Pyramid he was a true believer: he believed in saving souls from the fiery pit. But he's also a, a moralist. A quiverful dispensationalist Christian, just with some extra baggage. If Ms. Brewer's report is remotely accurate the parties are swimming in sex, drugs, and rock and roll. Isn't this a doctrinal contradiction? I could see him as he used to be, hiring a Christian rock band and having lots of wholesome young Church members to encourage his guests to come to Jesus – his version of Jesus, sleeping in a tomb on a dead alien planet – but this is all *wrong*. I can't believe this is the same person. Something has reoriented his moral compass.'

'The Sleeper,' I say baldly. 'That's got to be the answer to how he came back here and it's probably the reason he's behaving like this now.'

The SA looks at me intently. 'Explain your reasoning,' he says.

'Gut feeling: our man exhibits behavior type A, goes somewhere weird, returns, and exhibits behavior type B, where B and A are, on the face of it, incompatible. If he was a teenager having a crisis of faith I might credit it, but Schiller's a middle-aged, wealthy Church elder. He's thoroughly invested in his world view. People like that don't bend, much less do a U-turn: they stick to their path or they break. Ergo, whatever is in Schiller's head isn't Schiller any more. At a minimum it's Schiller-plus.'

'We need to know what's going on around the Pyramid,'

Persephone says, her lack of enthusiasm for this chore glaringly obvious. Not that I blame her. Visiting the tomb of the Sleeper in the Pyramid is on my bucket list of things to do before I die, right between holding a tea party inside the sarcophagus at Chernobyl and infecting myself with Ebola Zaire. 'Is the Squadron available ...?'

'Not flying this year,' Dr. Armstrong says shortly, 'our ground crew got laid off.'

I can't contain myself: 'Oh *great*, that's just peachy. We spent how many hundreds of millions back in the late seventies acquiring a top secret aviation capability and now it's grounded because they can't top up the brake fluid and lube? What is the world coming to?'

'They were on the books under the Nimrod MRA4 program,' the SA reminds me. 'And look what happened to *that*.' I nod. Unhappy but true: the MRA4 upgrade program was summarily scrapped during the 2010 strategic defense and security review because of 'cost overruns.' Ahem, that wasn't us, there were no witnesses, you can't prove it, mate ... but if it means the White Elephants are grounded while the MOD hunts behind the sofa cushions for pocket change to keep them ticking over, we're stuffed. 'And anyway, high-altitude reconnaissance overflights are beside the point at this time, given that the Sleeper is clearly active to some extent.'

'Someone's going to have to walk over there and poke it with a stick. And this time, it's *not* going to be me,' Persephone adds.

'Me neither!' I squeak.

'Stop derailing.' Mo gives me one of her more repressive stares as she continues: 'Schiller came back, and he's got some sort of short-term goal that justifies pointing a firehose of money at making friends and influencing people *right now.* To say nothing of these horrible parasite worm-things. What if the attack on the agency is misdirection—'

'– It'll be a Plan B,' 'Seph interjects.

'– A Plan B, then his Plan A is an even higher priority. And we have to disrupt it at any cost because we're dealing with a proxy for the Sleeper, and if the *Sleeper* is playing an end-game we are in deep trouble.'

The SA rubs his forehead. 'Dr. O'Brien, do I understand that you're proposing we should go full Watergate on this?'

For a moment my wife looks incredibly uncomfortable. But then her face sets in a mulish expression, almost harsh, and I shiver: this is the Mo whose pieces I used to pick up after jobs gone wrong, the increasingly brittle face of a nightmare hunter. 'This is already a black operation, isn't it? Because of the findings about the . . .' She inclines her head in Dr. Armstrong's direction.

'What?' I ask.

He smiles that saintly, terrifying smile of his at me, and says, 'Whereof one cannot speak, thereof one must be silent.'

I glare. 'I hear your Wittgenstein and I raise you one Alfred Korzybski: the map is not—'

'Boys!' Persephone snorts loudly. 'Dr. Armstrong, please stop patronizing Bob. Bob, there's—' her eyes flicker to take in both Auditors – 'a sandbox, and you're in it. Because some-body has to come out of this without blood on their hands.' She glances sidelong at Mo. 'Oh yes, while I remember: we need to talk later. In private,' she adds, with a look back at me.

I'm about to ask *about what* but then what she said a moment earlier breaks through: I shudder, cold sweat breaking out in the small of my back, and do a double-take. 'But there's plenty of blood on my – already—' I stop and look at 'Seph. 'You're serious, aren't you?' She nods. *Jesus, she's serious.* 'More blood than a tank crew or a couple of hit teams?' *And she's got something to talk to Mo about without me around?*

She nods again. 'We're irrevocably compromised, Bob. When the SA took direct control over this operation his impartial status as an Auditor was thereby compromised, the *whole* of Audit is compromised, Continuity Ops is a rogue team working on our own blind intuition without effective oversight—'

Dr. Armstrong shrugs. 'Some knowledge is inherently corrupting,' he says forebodingly. 'And there are things you don't need to know. You might speculate about why the Black Chamber chose to run the operation described in the DELIRIUM briefing against the Comstocks *at this time*, for example. Just don't talk about it, because I can't give you any answers.'

'Should I even *be* here?' I ask the lantern despairingly.

'Yes,' says the SA. 'I assume full responsibility, Mr. Howard. You're just along for the ride.' He comes to a decision. 'I want you to go away and talk to Ms. Murphy, Dr. Schwartz, Ms. Brewer, Mr. Choudhury, and the rest of the non-exec team. I want you to draw up an action plan. During the next reception Schiller throws at Nether Stowe House, I want simultaneous searches of Schiller's apartment and his corporate HQ out at Heathrow. I want us to get people into the off-limits area of the mansion to find out what he's doing that's worth spending a million pounds an hour on that he doesn't want us to see, and I want to disrupt it.'

'But I can't be in three places at once!'

'Tough,' says Mo, and that shell-like expression cracks into a grin, 'you're management now: isn't it time you learned to delegate?'

*

So the SA has cast the dice and determined that we're going to disrupt Schiller's scheme – whatever it is – by hitting him from three directions at once; and that I, in the absence of full information about what the SA *suspects* Schiller is up to, am going to come up with an operational plan and manage this clusterfuck-in-the-making on the basis of what *I* suspect Schiller is up to (which is clearly No Good).

Happy joy.

I've been involved in field operations for over a decade, and I can tell you that there's a single golden rule that governs these junkets, and you already know it: no plan survives contact with the enemy. A corollary of this rule is that contingency planning is, if not futile, then of questionable utility. If you let it it'll eat up 90 percent of your planning capacity and your targets will still find some creative and unanticipated way to balls things up for you. And another corollary is that as an op grows more complicated, the number of ways it can go off the rails explodes exponentially. What Dr. Armstrong has so kindly dropped in my lap is responsibility for planning, not a single op, but an intricate three-way dance-off competition with an experienced team of adversaries (*mutter grumble* corporate security who subcontract for the OPA, our American counterparts) *who are already engaged in a counter-operation against us*, using only the resources made available to me via Continuity Operations, viz. the organizational equivalent of two blokes I met down at the pub and their whippet on a string.

This is not just asking for trouble: this is like walking up to a baby grizzly bear and punching him on the nose in order to get momma's undivided attention. It's so inadvisable that under normal circumstances I'd kick up an extreme stink if someone tasked me with organizing such a circus. Unfortunately the present situation is not normal, and – I am unhappy to admit this – I can't think of a better alternative. Schiller is trailing such a very scary threat profile in front of us (fox taking over contract to provide hen-coop security services, hit squads on the street, alien crotch-worm mind parasites as door-to-door evangelists) that it's only the red ink in his cash flow that's suggestive of it being cover for something even worse – something that justifies a burn rate that will bankrupt his organization within months if he keeps it up.

We need to find out what he's up to and stop it dead, and that means getting the drop on the operation he's running. It has three obvious centers on British soil: the posh mansion where he's wining and dining his marks, the corporate headquarters building where presumably the legwork gets done, and the apartment he's camped out in with his retinue. The obvious thing to do is to hit all three of them simultaneously (and without warning): he can't be everywhere at once, can he? Schiller himself is far too dangerous to confront face-to-face, so that will be a black-bag job. Given that he vanished in the Sleeper's Pyramid and then *came back*, the worst case possibility is that he's a mindhost for the Sleeper itself, a being which compares with your typical feeder in the night the way ... you've seen *Ghostbusters*, haven't you? We're in Twinkie Singularity territory here.

So I hole up in a safe house in Hemel Hempstead and get stuck into making some pretty overhead projection charts – Lord Acton said power corrupts, but PowerPoint corrupts absolutely – then draft a Gantt chart and draw lots of dotted lines on it. Finally I think up a codename for the op. INDIGO HUMMINGBIRD seems memorable enough. INDIGO because it's part of the GOD GAME portfolio, and HUMMINGBIRD because, well, that's a name for an ill-omened operation that's memorable enough to be a caution and obscure enough not to be an instant giveaway.

And two days later I take a small risk and call a face-to-face meeting of the designated team leads. The Lamplighters make it happen in public in a hotel conference room at Hinckley, of all places, everyone wearing suits and presenting as boring sales managers having a jaw-jaw about their regional targets.

'Okay, people, here's the outline plan. INDIGO HUMMINGBIRD will hit three sites in parallel, with different objectives at each. Target One is Nether Stowe House. During Schiller's next rave we will get people into the area his security folks have locked down and find out what's going on inside and put a stop to it if it's possible to do so while avoiding a direct confrontation with the Sleeper's avatar-in-person. The Target One side of the op is open-ended and requires maximal flexibility: it might be a simple look inside a security ready-room, or ... well, who knows? It's also maximally sensitive: there will be VIPs and celebrities present, and while we want no witnesses who can identify us we can't strong-arm them either. Because Schiller himself will probably be present, Target One is off-limits to those of us who were involved in the mess in Denver the other year – me, Persephone, and Johnny. Our current agent in place is—' I swallow – 'Her very Eldritch Majesty, Cassie Brewer. So far she's been running solo with a wire back to her off-site support team, notably Alex Schwartz.' I swallow again: the next bit is difficult. 'Mo, I don't think Alex is remotely ready to run HUMMINGBIRD, so I'd like you to take over Target One Control. Alex can stay and provide analysis support – also if you need a PHANG for backup he's on-hand and motivated.'

Mo nods thoughtfully. I'm not sure whether it's the plan she's holding judgment over, or me. I move swiftly on.

'Our friends from the Artists' Rifles are badly short-handed right now thanks to the business in Leeds, but they're still talking to us on the down low, and given the size of Target One I've asked the SA for a full OCCULUS team. They're the backup if it turns out there's something in the basement that wants killing with fire. They'll be deployed in Police drag rather than Fire/Emergency on this occasion and it'll be spun as an exercise if anyone asks, and they're nothing to do with us ... but at least they'll be there. Oh, and you get to ask for any other warm bodies you think Target One requires, once I get through divvying up the rest of the work.'

Now she smiles in my direction, and I'm very glad it's the notion that the gloves are coming off that merits this particular smile rather than something I've done, because if otherwise I'd be clutching my wedding tackle and looking for a window to jump through.

'Target Two is the GP Services office compound out at Heathrow,' I announce. 'Schiller almost certainly *won't* be there, but it's got solid security and it's where we'll find his backup resources. If we're going to black-bag his office we need a pretext to get inside without alarming the Airport Police. I'm going to lead this one, with Johnny riding shotgun. We're going to look like an HMRC customs inspectorate team serving an Anton Piller order – a court-ordered no-knock search to prevent the destruction of evidence. Our cover story will be that we're investigating a tip-off about VAT fraud and we're there to seize IT equipment and accounting records, but there'll be a second-level cover story: someone in his organization is believed to be using GP Security's internal post system to smuggle cocaine. This will justify a quiet poke around the rest of his facility. I've asked for another OCCULUS team, but if only one is available it'll be allocated to Target One.'

Mo nods. Johnny, who has been sitting silently but intent throughout the briefing, snorts quietly and leans back.

'Target Two is high risk,' I add, trying to keep a slight tremor out of my voice, 'because there is a risk that it'll draw the attention of the Police.' Which, in this context, does not mean a friendly community constable, it means hordes of guys in body armor with automatic weapons who train daily for shoot-outs with terrorists. Which in turn is why I have assigned myself to it, and just one of the reasons why I'm having trouble sleeping nights in view of how everything went pear-shaped on Dartmoor: it's more than possible for an operation to be both a technical success and an utter blood-drenched clusterfuck.

'Target Three,' I announce, 'is a bit different: it's Schiller's luxury apartment in Docklands. Unlike the other two, it's not public and it doesn't call for high-end force. We have a monitoring operation two floors above it. We want to get in, take a look around, and get out clean while Schiller is busy at Target One. Ideally they'll root any electronic devices on the premises and scan any documents. There's a safe, and we can get the manufacturer's schematics and see if there's a maintenance backdoor while we're at it. Now, the problem with Schiller's pad is that it's got security suitable for a visiting head of state – sparrowfart territory, remote controlled sensors on all the approaches – and some really nasty booby traps on the in-building approaches. Yes, I know booby traps are illegal: nevertheless. This is going to call for social engineering skills rather than the blunt approach or infiltrating a catering company.'

The people in the front row are looking thoughtful, except for the one I've picked to lead this particular hit, who just seems sleepily amused. 'Persephone, I believe you have a little bit of experience with this sort of thing? Great, because you're running Target Three and your main job is to figure out how to get Mhari inside.' 'Seph looks pleased; Mhari looks startled.

'But I'm not a covert ops asset—' She stops, then looks around apprehensively. *Right.* The vampire has just realized she's in a meeting populated exclusively by spooks and people who go bump in the night. (What she hasn't clocked yet is that she's not out of place in this company.) 'What?'

'Short of widening the magic circle, Bob's running short of bodies,' Persephone points out. 'Continuity Ops is already almost fully committed – at least, the part of it the SA has given me to play with while he's busy doing other things. If we hit a billionaire condo in London's Docklands with an OCCULUS team, somebody might notice, not to mention the other parallel ops going short-handed. So we're going to work out how to get you in and out under cover. Don't worry, if it goes off the rails I'll come and fetch you.' She grins. 'It's going to be *fun*.'

Q-Division SOE was not the Prison Service. While we sometimes had to detain people subject to our terms of operation, and sometimes provided security for the Black Assizes, who are called upon to rule in criminal cases dealing with the occult, we didn't actually run any prisons as such. (Camp Sunshine was a special case – it's a detention center, but most of the people there are theoretically on remand until they can be deprogrammed and released. And Camp Tolkien is less than a month old.) But sometimes needs must, and when that happened, when it became necessary to lock up someone who we can't simply bind to silence with a *geas* and place in the general prison population, we have access to a very special facility indeed, operated by the Prison Service with staff trained by us. And even after Q-Division's wind-up, this particular lock-up is still in business.

Let me give you a clue: it's the oldest still-functioning prison building in the UK, if not Europe. (Built in the thirteenth century, in fact.) It has hosted a number of extremely famous prisoners, although it fell out of regular use in the 1950s; its last inmates were the Kray Twins, who were banged up in 1952 for a couple of days for ignoring their national service papers. While it has a bloody reputation, only a couple of dozen people have been executed on the premises since 1900 – most notably spies and traitors during both world wars. Today, it's mostly preserved as a museum (and the headquarters of the Royal Regiment of Fusiliers), but Her Majesty's prison in the Tower of London still has a couple of cells tucked away in Beauchamp Tower, for our occasional use.

For the past six months, Cell Block Q (as it is unofficially known) has been occupied by a single guest. He's in solitary confinement, on lockdown twenty-three hours a day, no visitors allowed – and if you think that's harsh, it gets worse. The prisoner is guarded by four very special Prison Service employees. They're not youngsters (one of them is over seventy), and the one thing they have in common is that they're profoundly deaf. Two of them have cochlear implants: but they're required to physically remove their microphones and leave them at the door before reporting for work. Our prisoner is not allowed paper or writing materials, or internet access, or any way of communicating more complex than a board with carefully pre-selected words to point to: food, water, heat, light, toilet paper, TV remote, batteries.

Communication is a basic human need. Deprive us of the ability to make a connection with our fellow people and we become depressed or upset within a day or two. Solitary confinement prolonged for more than two weeks is viewed as torture in many enlightened nations. We don't keep the special prisoner in Cell Block Q incommunicado and under lockdown lightly. But if we don't, he'll slip through our fingers within hours, and questions *will* be asked.

So it causes no little consternation when, one evening, Dr. Armstrong signs himself in and communicates to the shift supervisor his intention of visiting with the prisoner.

'I'm sorry, sir, but you can't do that.' The senior prison officer crosses his arms uneasily. 'We've got strict orders here that direct communications aren't permitted under any circumstances. I'm sure you know why that is.' Prison officers are trained to be assertive, to own any confrontation just as police officers are, but Mr. McCubbin – mid-fifties, graying, a veteran of Wandsworth and Pentonville – clearly finds the Senior Auditor an intimidating figure. 'No exceptions, I'm afraid.'

Dr. Armstrong nods. 'The segregation order was made at my suggestion, and signed off by Mr. Justice Gilpin. As you can confirm from the prisoner's file, if you double-check it. Now, unfortunately a situation has arisen in which it is necessary for somebody to ask the prisoner some questions. I'm here because I have some, ah, natural resistance to the prisoner's wiles.' He pushes his warrant card across the tabletop, in the direction of Prison Officer McCubbin, who reacts to it as if to a bird-eating spider. 'I propose to go in there under your officer's supervision, for a thirty-minute period, after which I shall leave. Your officer will ensure that I do not pass anything to the prisoner and that I leave alone.' He touches the legal document he brought to back up his warrant card: 'As you can see, Mr. Justice Gilpin has signed off on this waiver, as has the Intelligence Services Commissioner. So an exception *does* exist – for me, and me alone, for a period of half an hour.'

McCubbin picks up the court order and sighs heavily as he rereads the first page. 'I'll need to read this all, and verify its authenticity,' he warns Dr. Armstrong.

'Take your time.' The SA smiles faintly as he picks up his warrant card. 'I believe there's a cafe adjacent to the gift shop. Will an hour be sufficient, do you think?'

(The court order is indeed genuine, although the signature on the ISC waiver is somewhat questionable; it's certainly the Commissioner's scrawl, and a copy is on file at the MOD, but if asked he'd swear blind he can't recall signing it. But in the absence of an actual operational OCCINT agency, it is distressingly easy for a former SOE Auditor to walk in off the street and charm the right executive assistant, literally as well as figuratively – especially with the extraordinary powers vested in him by virtue of his oath under Continuity Ops.)

An hour and a half later the visitor's cafe has closed for the evening and the lights are on in the supervisor's office as Dr. Armstrong returns to a more obliging reception. 'Good evening, sir. You'll be pleased to know that it all checks out. If I can see your ID again ... ? I'll log you in, then Barry can show you to the visiting room. We'll still have to search you, I'm afraid ...'

Eventually Dr. Armstrong is admitted to the visiting room. Which, Cell Block Q having but a single occupant, doubles as a day room. There are two cell doors at the opposite side, one of which gapes open. The day room is furnished with an elderly floral three-piece suite, a coffee table, and a smallish TV with built-in DVD player. Prison Officer Hastings positions himself to one side of the entrance and adopts a relaxed, waiting posture. He's profoundly deaf, but from where he stands he can trigger the wall-mounted alarm button instantly in event of trouble.

As the SA enters, the prisoner is leaning over the coffee table. A gridded board lies open atop it, dotted with rows of black and white stones, and the prisoner is studying them intently from the sofa. It's a game of Go, and as Dr. Armstrong watches, the prisoner places a black stone on the board, completing the encirclement of a line of white stones; he scoops these up and replaces them, then looks up. 'Ah, Michael! To what do I owe the honor?'

'Fabian.' The SA nods affably, then perches on the edge of the armchair. 'Are you free to talk?' As he speaks the prisoner's name he feels a prickling in the fine hairs of his arms, and a stinging from the ward around his neck: the prisoner is probing, of course, restlessly seeking an advantage. It's in his nature, of course, which is why the SA has taken additional precautions.

'Oh, I have *plenty* of time these days.' Fabian leans back and stretches, then smiles lazily. 'As you should know.'

The weird thing about the prisoner's smile is that Dr. Armstrong recognizes the expression but can't be certain what it looks like: whether Fabian is displaying a pearly white row of teeth or keeping his lips sealed, whether his eyes are blue, green, or brown, whether his hair is curly or straight. He can look at the prisoner and try to memorize his appearance and an instant later all the details will have slipped his mind. 'Well, yes.' Dr. Armstrong crosses his legs and matches the prisoner's recumbency. Mirroring posture is a trick human interrogators use to put their subjects at ease in their company, although whether it'll work on this particular prisoner is anybody's guess. 'How are you keeping?'

'So-so.' The smile slips away like spring rain. 'The lack of communication is a little frustrating, if I may say so. But this, too, shall pass.' He gestures towards the board, and a white stone hops neatly out of its wooden tub and lands a couple of grid intersections away from the nearest black eye. 'Hmm. White resigns in sixteen points, I think. It's a long game,' he adds conversationally: 'I find those are ever so much more stimulating, don't you think?'

'That's not the word I'd use ... but I take your point.' The SA nods. 'Is there anything I can get you? Anything to make life more comfortable?'

The prisoner chuckles. 'A by-election in a three-way marginal would be most amusing, but I don't suppose that's on offer yet, is it?'

'Not yet, no.' The SA pauses. 'But you never know. Questions are being asked. Do you have access to the news on that thing?' His glance takes in the TV set.

'Oh, I have Freeview, all the public-to-air channels.' The prisoner's disdain is clear. 'Is this something to do with that business up north? I gather the Intelligence and Security Committee is all in a tizzy. What on earth did your people do to get them so worked up?'

He's *playing* with Dr. Armstrong, almost taunting him. The SA frowns momentarily, then forces himself to relax. 'I think you know perfectly well what just happened.'

'Oh, you'd be surprised how far out of the loop it's possible to be when you're banged up in the Tower of London, Doctor. It's frustrating, I will admit. The first few days were relaxing enough, but ... I have *so much* to contribute.' He sighs unhappily. 'An elven invasion indeed! Then a cabinet reshuffle and a panicky order in council!

That would *never* have happened on my watch, you may mark my words.'

'Yes, but you didn't exactly start off on the best footing, did you?' the SA says with some asperity. 'Perhaps a little more respect for institutional procedures and a little less ambition would have stood you in good stead.'

'Mistakes were made,' the prisoner says blandly, letting the admission slide. 'Won't happen again, I can assure you.'

'I'm very glad to hear it. Not that you're going to get the chance to make any mistakes.'

'Oh, really?' The prisoner smiles blindingly, like the sun rising: an unshielded nuclear holocaust beyond a distant horizon. 'Why are you here, then?'

'I'm here to ask what you want, Fabian. It's as simple as that.' The SA laces his fingers around his knee and rocks forward slightly, his expression intent. 'Good governance is in short supply these days, but it has to be trustworthy or it's valueless. Obedience to the law, respect for the rule of Parliament, loyalty to the Crown, that sort of thing.'

'I note that you are not referring to the Crown-*in*-Parliament.' The prisoner looks amused. 'Leviathan has a lot to answer for.'

The SA sniffs. 'The Crown that binds our oath is older and bloodier than that, as you well know.' He pauses for a moment. 'But back to the business in hand. What do you *want*?'

'I want—' The prisoner turns his face towards the ceiling and smiles ever wider, beatific – '*everything*. You know what I want: a parliamentary mandate and a seat of power. The respect and envy of my peers, the adulation of the masses, and the authority with which to enact my destiny. Which as you well know is to become Prime Minister of these sceptered isles, by hook or by crook, and to shepherd this nation into the future it deserves.

'The fate of this nation does not lie in the choice between a Labour government or the Conservatives, or in the membership of a Labour cabinet or that of the current Coalition. What I am contending against is not the form of politics as such, but its ignominious content. I want to create in this nation the precondition which alone will make it impossible for our enemies – the iron grip of the enemies you and yours stand against – to be removed from us. To this end I wanted to restore order to the state, throw out the drones, take up the fight against the ancient nightmares, against our whole nation being overrun by the Quislings of alien evil, against the destruction of the agencies of our struggle – such as your own – and above all, for the highest honorable duty which we, as free citizens, know we should be held to – the duty of collective self-defense against the monsters from beyond the stars. And now I ask you: Is what I want high treason?'

Fabian pauses in his peroration and fixes the SA with a stare as unblinking as a laser's beam. 'Is it?' he demands, voice booming, an ancient and terrible power stealing into it as he sounds forth. 'Because if that be treason, the courts of this land may pronounce me guilty a thousand times, but the Goddess who presides over the Eternal Court of History will with a smile tear in pieces the charge of the prosecution and the verdict of the court! For she acquits me.'

Dr. Armstrong rises to leave. 'I've heard those words before, in another mouth,' he says drily. 'They ended in tears last time around. Why should they end any differently this time round, if we let you out of your box?'

'Because—' The prisoner's expression is fey – 'you have no alternative.' He smiles again, in evident pleasure. 'I won't fail you, Michael, if what you want is to protect this nation from the true threats that beset it. I've learned my lesson and I won't make the same mistakes twice, I assure you. Unlike the public-relations-obsessed opportunist currently running the show, I understand the coming storm better than *anyone* in politics – and once I move into Number Ten, my top priority will be to attend to the parlous state of the nation's occult defenses. After all, there's not much point in my being PM if all I have to rule over is ashes, is there?'

The SA pauses. 'Promise me you will stick within the letter of the law,' he says, 'and I'll see what I can do.'

'Is that all?' the prisoner snorts. '*Of course* I promise to obey the law! As you made perfectly clear, it was very shortsighted of me to ignore that requirement earlier. I, Fabian Everyman, also known as the Mandate, swear by my true name to obey the law of the land.' He swears. 'There! Satisfied?'

'It'll have to do.' The SA nods at the prison officer, and mimes turning a door handle: the fellow nods back and rests a hand on the doorknob. 'Be seeing you, Fabian . . .'

Nearly a week has passed since Johnny and I broke Cassie and Alex out of Camp Tolkien. I'm parked in a different ex-council maisonette in Hemel, courtesy of Airbnb, and I'm sleeping badly. It's my guilt: whenever I'm not working I feel as if I'm going up the wall, but there's a limited amount of work to be done, and I can't run away from the back of my own head. While I can hide from the police I can't hide from my own guilt. I'm effectively under house arrest, and I'm sinking a bottle of cheap supermarket plonk before bed-time each night to try and wash the taste of dying soldiers and brain-bruised friends out of my cortex.

Then the doorbell rings.

This is no immediate cause for concern, because my

meals are being delivered in supermarket pre-packs off the back of a delivery van, but I'm pretty certain today's drop-off isn't due for another couple of hours, so I approach the front door with caution. I open my mind's eye and see that there's somebody on the doorstep, the only person within a dozen meters (if you don't count the neighbor's bored and whiny King Charles spaniel, depressively chewing on a shoe as it awaits its owners return from work) ... and they're warded, but there's something familiar about them. *Very* familiar. In fact ... with a stab of apprehensive excitement I yank the door open and Mo stumbles into my arms. She's wearing a cardigan over a frumpy maxi dress and the wig doesn't suit her but she's still the loveliest thing I've ever seen.

'Quickly! Inside.' We stumble-waltz sideways as I kick the front door shut again.

'Bob—' She hugs me tight.

'What are you—'

'— Stand down, I *finally* convinced the SA to give me permission to come and visit, I'm clean – they're not hunting for accountants yet – and nobody followed me, and I've got a surprise for you.' I hug her back and then without warning she kisses me as if she's trying to make up for all our lost time in a few stolen seconds, and I kiss her right back. Everything – and I mean *everything* – goes out of my head except for the desperate lonely need to bury myself in her arms, and from the way she's responding she feels the same way.

We hold each other tight for a while, and one thing leads to another and we end up upstairs, and what happens next isn't going in my work diary.

(To clarify: we have been together and/or married for nearly a decade, albeit lately separated, but the cause of our

separation is not a lack of love but of safety. Her violin –
now, thankfully, banished – tried to kill me. And in the
other direction, I sometimes sleepwalk, or levitate, and my
eyes glow when I'm not home in my own head. The thing
I've become, or the thing that is becoming me, is quite capable of lashing out and killing, and while I don't know what
I'd do if I woke up one night to find her lying dead beside
me, I know that it wouldn't be anything good.)

More than an hour passes before we're ready to talk at
greater length than urgent monosyllables. We're spooning
on what's left of the bedding, me wrapped around her
back, nuzzling her neck with one palm pressed between
her breasts. There's a pile of discarded clothing and a wig
on the carpet and I can feel her pulse, butterfly-fast but
gradually slowing, the sweat sticky on her thighs.

She sighs.

'I know,' I say, and cuddle her closer.

(It's surprising how much meaning you can unpack from
a tender intake of breath when you know the other person
well enough.)

'It doesn't get easier. Still don't think I should stay, but . . .'

'Here.'

(Interpreting monosyllables is a lot of work, so from now
on I shall unpack them for you.)

'Sleepy, only mustn't. Bathroom?' ('I want nothing more
than to drift off to sleep in your embrace, only I'm terrified
that the psychotic death-clown who stalks your dreams will
take you over in the middle of the night and eat my face.
Also, my crotch feels disgusting and I want to shower.')

'Derp.' ('Derp.')

She elbows me in the ribs. 'Seriously, now!'

I sigh ('If you must'), and let go of her. We pull apart, the
drying sweat itching, and as she rolls to her feet my eyes are

drawn to her behind. 'Turn left, it's the second door along.' I begin to sit up. 'Oh *fuck*.'

'What?'

'The johnny burst.'

'Fuck!'

Of an instant we're both wide awake, tense, and not feeling even remotely monosyllabic. It's been around a year since I had to move out, and staying on the pill at her age without a good reason isn't a great idea, but we're sensible grown-ups, and suddenly I have a sick sense of doubt in my stomach. I pulled out afterwards, but now I see that the condom's tip has split neatly, as if razored, probably while we were at our most joyfully inattentive, which is why I didn't notice at the time. 'Shower,' I say on autopilot as she stumbles out of the bedroom and I follow, then divert into the cramped toilet cubicle to ditch the treacherous rubber.

(Personal hygiene interlude.)

Listen, there is a *very good reason* why Mo and I agreed never to have children. Leaving aside the fact that she's forty-three – dangerously late to even try – there is the small fact that we are both Laundry operatives and we know the fate that lies in store for any child of ours. Maybe if we'd met when we were twenty and ignorant things could have been different, but if there's anything that could make facing the probable end of humanity together even worse, it would be the sheer reckless stupidity of bringing new life into being at a time like this. So we clean up with gritted teeth, holding our tongues – recriminations would be pointless, we both know the score – and I fetch out a clean towel for her and we get dressed before traipsing downstairs again in guilty complicit silence, as if nothing had happened.

'Morning-after pill?' I ask.

She grimaces. 'There's probably no point; at this age I'm well past it, I'm about as likely to conceive as that—' she gestures at the kitchen table – 'thing.' She takes a deep breath. 'But I'll try Boots tomorrow. Or today, if they're still open later.'

Well fuck. This isn't what I wanted, but we don't always get what we want, do we? 'Mo—' I move towards her tentatively, then pause.

'I know.' She blows out her cheeks, momentarily resembling a frowsy hamster. 'Not your fault, not my fault, nobody likes me, everybody hates me, guess I'll go eat worms.' She manages a wan chuckle.

'Other than that, how was the play, Mrs. Lincoln?'

She drags out a kitchen chair and sits down. I sit down opposite her. 'Loved the climax, could have done without the ending. Oh Bob.' She shakes her head at my answering grin.

'Was this—' I steel myself – 'just a conjugal visit while I'm under house arrest, or was there anything else?'

'Anything else? Oh, yeah, *that*.'

'That?'

'We're homeless, dear.'

'*What?*'

She drums her fingers on the tabletop, gazing pensively past my shoulder. 'We're losing the house. *Technically* we've got until the end of the month, but we're supposed to get out as soon as possible, seeing we're no longer entitled to a key workers property owned by the Crown Estate via our doesn't-exist-any-more employing agency. But—' she nibbles delicately on one fingernail, and that's how I know the news is *really* bad – 'the police want a word with me about bookkeeping irregularities, so I'm couch-surfing with the aid of the SA's little helpers right now.'

'But, but—'

She misinterprets: 'Spooky is going to be all right; I've parked him at your parents' place.'

'But Dad doesn't *like* cats—'

'Tough.' In the face of Mo's implacable lack of sympathy I can see even my father sucking it up and hitting the antihistamines.

It all hits me at once. I take a deep breath. I'm homeless, jobless – at least, officially – on the run from the Police who have good and sufficient reasons to drop me in a hole and throw away the key, separated from my wife who may be – but almost certainly isn't – pregnant (which is just pregnant enough to be *really disturbing*), one of my worst nightmares seems to be taking over the country from the top down, and I can't sleep properly at night because of the things I've done. I take another deep breath, and another.

'Bob—'

'Can't—'

'I know how this script plays out and you're not going there love, too many of us are depending on you,' she says fiercely. 'Bob! Come here!' She stands up and leans over me and I grab her and bury my face between her breasts, feeling about four years old, and I begin to grizzle like a toddler with a grazed knee, letting it all hang out. 'Not letting you go,' she mumbles into my hair, and suddenly I'm sobbing, grief for all the souls I've eaten and the untimely ends I've brought to those who didn't deserve it, all of that swamping my own fucked-up life. 'Don't need to, not any more, that's why the visit. Being an Auditor gets me into – got me into – lots of closed files. And I went digging and I found what they used to bind TEAPOT back in the 1920s. So I pestered Persephone until she made me a better ward, just for you.' She fumbles in the pocket of that ridiculous cardigan and pulls out a pouch on a leather thong that hums with some kind of unearthly energy. 'Had a long heart-to-heart with her. Should have done it ages ago. I owe her for this.' She pushes me gently back for just long enough to drop it over my head and the world around us goes numb and quiet, peaceful even.

'What?' I look up at her face and blink, puzzled.

'It's a new ward,' she explains. 'Necromantic immobilization. Wear it when we go to bed.' She's speaking clearly and slowly as if I'm a very small child. 'We can stay together.'

'But if it doesn't work—'

'It's going to work. It's the same schematic they used when they first summoned the Eater of Souls, before they bound it via the oath of office. See? It's been tested.'

'But I might take it off—'

'You won't.'

'But I'm too dangerous, I'm not sure I'm even human any more . . . !'

'Bob!' She steps back and glares at me with her fists on her hips. 'Are you trying to drive me away?'

(Reader, this is why I married her.)

As Terry Pratchett observed, inside every eighty-year-old man is an eight-year-old wondering what the hell just happened to him: in my experience this remains true even if you divide his age by two. While my inner four-year-old is having a meltdown and Mo explains that love can find a way (with a bit of technical help from one of the most powerful occult practitioners in London), events are marching on.

This week, the cabinet reshuffle continues. A minister, Norman Grove, has been appointed to head a shiny new Department for Paratechnological Affairs, which exists entirely as an org chart with lots of empty directorship-sized bubbles, a bunch of PowerPoint presentations, and a press conference. Most of DPA's immediate needs are to be outsourced to private-sector contractors and indeed two of the usual large outsourcing conglomerates are supposed to be prepping shiny new offices to hold the 3000-odd civil servants that DPA will eventually employ. Grove optimistically declares that this will be a clean-sheet exercise in developing a leaner, more agile, twenty-first-century organization. In the fine print below the announcement it is mentioned that anyone who held anything above a surprisingly low grade in the predecessor agency will be barred from hiring until their background, culpability, and share of guilt for the fiasco in Leeds can be established, sometime after the Commons Select Committee Enquiry delivers its findings. (Early in the twenty-second century, then.)

In the meantime, private-sector contractors have been identified entering the New Annex. Presumably they're having some issues with site security – Residual Human Resources, being dead, are not on payroll and were not covered by the shutdown order – but after a couple of days the new arrivals no longer wear body armor, and body bags stop leaving in ambulances so the GP Security people must be assumed to have the free run of the building. I wish them much luck dealing with some of the more baroque and deadly non-Euclidean spaces such as Angleton's office, the eldritch singularity in Briefing Room 202, the hole where Andy's lab used to be, and so on. Babes in the wood, babes in the fucking wood – and I'm not shedding any tears over their screaming.

But none of this can make up for the fact that we've lost access to the archive stacks, Angleton's Memex, our in-house network and labs, and a bunch of other vital resources. Some of that stuff is priceless. Ditto a bunch of less obvious facilities. Persephone's top-floor lab, for example, with the humongous containment grid – I don't think it's safe to drop round there right now. All the remote facilities that have gone dark represent an imponderable hit to our ability to resume operations. And some of the side effects are worse.

There are a couple of rays of metaphorical sunlight. Mhari has apparently found a source of blood for the PHANGs. It may not last for long, but they're not going to starve or go feral. (The last thing we need on top of everything else right now is a V syndrome epidemic in London.) The crumblies from St. Hilda's have apparently bluffed their way into some sort of sheltered living half-way house arrangement by pretending to be senile, and I am informed that they're cautiously, gradually, showing signs of re-engaging with the cutout who's serving as their minder from Continuity Ops. Likewise, our drinking buddies from the SRR are still on speaking terms, and willing to see that the odd OCCULUS unit shows up should we need it (on an entirely deniable it's-just-a-routine-readiness-exercise basis – and this is a card we can play only once). And on a purely personal note, everything is coming up daisies.

But otherwise it's darkness, darkness, as far as the eye can see.

Something bad *is* happening in Assyria, but our last stringer on the ground was beheaded live on YouTube by Islamic State. There's a marked upswing in terrorist atrocities in that part of the world and some of the incidents … they're not being allowed to hit the mainstream media channels, let's put it that way, nobody wants a mass panic. Da'esh propaganda websites are fulminating about Western devils and if you drop the compass angle they're not entirely wrong: the *djinn* are restive, and I am not talking about the goatee-and-turban three-wishes Disney remix of the dark and bloody legend.

In Mexico there's been a mass kidnapping and disappearance of student teachers – forty-two of them – at Iguala in Guerrero. No bodies have been found. It's being blamed on a drugs syndicate with help from corrupt local police officials, but as I read about it in the daily flash briefing that someone working for Continuity Ops is still putting out via secure departmental email I'm not giving that much credit. Worshippers of Tezcatlipoca, the Cult of the Smoking Mirror, are no neophytes at the human sacrifice game, let's put it that way.

The United States is still disturbingly quiet. A couple of resignations and retirements of deputy assistant secretaries of this or that, a couple of new appointments to the Republican National Committee, nothing terribly visible to outsiders. We used to use the Kremlin as a reference point for politics utterly opaque to external observers, but the complexities of DC and the depths of the waters there are breathtaking. The only obvious sign of the power struggle in progress is that the number of actors represented by the United States Intelligence Community clearinghouse has dropped from eighteen to sixteen in the past month, due to mergers – and it's only obvious that a titanic and brutal struggle for supremacy is in progress if you know what signs to look for. There are other symptoms (our thaum flux distant monitoring array is picking up twenty or thirty intermittent titanic power spikes per day, as if someone or something is working major summonings in diverse states across the continental US), but it's frustratingly hard to tell what's going on from the outside ... and our few remaining stringers on the ground have stopped filing reports.

In our absence, a lot of the low-level occult defense

tasks we took care of are falling apart. There has been an outbreak of 'demonic possession' in Aberystwyth, claiming the lives of two pensioners at a Pentecostal Church. Séances have become markedly dangerous, with eighteen survivors being sectioned under the Mental Health Act in the past week alone, but so far the Health Secretary has stayed mum.

And finally there's the catastrophically bad news from back home. Due to the lack of anyone running routine security maintenance tasks on the Laundry's server farms – eighty percent of which are still running, at least until the power bills come due – a failure to install a critical patch for a zero day exploit that came out a week ago has resulted in the firmware blobs that install SCORPION STARE capability on one of the nation's most common outdoor camera systems being leaked. The first word we got was when it turned up for auction on the usual darknet sites, with a £25M opening bid: activity has been fierce. It'll take a while before anyone works out how to decompile the deep observing neural network code, much less figures out how it works.

But when they do?

Oh dear.

PART 3

SURRENDER

8: BETRAYAL

Euston Station, London, marks the southern terminus of the West Coast Main Line, one of the two main north-south railway arteries that tie England and Scotland together. Right now it's horrendously busy. The East Coast Main Line runs through Leeds and will not be back in service for at least two weeks; while some passenger services are diverting around the devastated city's station, all the freight and a good proportion of the foot traffic are using the west coast route instead.

Around the same time Mo and I are re-bonding over a pizza, a bottle of wine, and a pile of broken yesterdays, a Virgin Voyager slides into Euston and wheezes to a halt. Doors streaked with dirt after the two-hundred-mile run from Liverpool rattle and hiss open and passengers spill across the busy platform.

Concealed within the crowd of weary travelers is a middle-aged woman. Her dark blonde hair is streaked with gray and frizzled; her face is lined and there are crow's feet around her eyes, but she's trim and her posture erect. Wearing boots, jeans, and a sweater, with a waterproof and a small day pack over her shoulder, she might be on her way home from a hiking holiday in the Lake District. But as she casts around, looking for someone, there's an anxious, haunted aspect to her expression, and whenever she spots the anonymous black bubble of a camera she tenses slightly and hunches her shoulders.

Iris Carpenter is coming home.

Her instructions were clear and comprehensive, from the token to get her past the unsleeping alien guards to the road directions to Kendal. The train ticket in the wallet took her to Liverpool, and then onwards via a reserved seat on the express to Euston; there'd even been some petty cash for food and drink on the four-hour trip. She'd bought a couple of newspapers at Lime Street Station and spent the journey luxuriating in the unfamiliar sensation of uncensored, unrationed text at her fingertips. Little things kept tripping her up. The simple act of opening a door required a conscious act of will, the recollection that she was allowed to do whatever she wanted. Merely existing in motion was a constant tightrope walk across the infinite chasm of free will. The habits ingrained from six years spent deep in the penumbral constraints of Camp Sunshine would take more than a railway trip to shake off.

Enroute, Iris gave serious thought to the possibility of fleeing. The Hazard woman frankly scared her. One of the big eldritch beasts of Mahogany Row, she presented a coolly composed cosmetic mask to the world which concealed screaming depths of ruthlessness that dwarfed anything Iris recognized from her own esoteric order. Persephone was capable of *anything*, that much Iris could see at a glance, like that old creep Angleton. Iris merely saw the agency as a storm cellar against the tornados of the abyss.

If I had any sense I'd have gotten off in Birmingham and gone to ground, Iris tells herself as she looks around the platform, following the milling crowd towards the automatic ticket barriers. But the newspapers have convinced her otherwise, with the rising hysteria and demands that something must be done, the picking over of the wreckage and the post-mortem in parliamentary committee. The sum of all fears has come to pass, and her own attempt at furnishing a storm shelter has already failed. If the news out of Leeds is in any way accurate, then it's only a matter of time before things go from bad to unimaginably worse. And it isn't just Leeds: the world news pages tell their own story, of things better left undisturbed stirring in unquiet death on all sides, from Chile to Alabama, Kamchatka to South Sudan.

Iris feeds her ticket to the barrier – new since she last passed through this station – and walks up the ramp from the platform's end into the crowded station concourse. Being able to go so far in a straight line without facing a barbed wire barrier is disorienting and feels unreal, like a dream of walking on the moon. A quick mental audit reminds her that she has precisely £19.23 to her name. Not enough to run anywhere in London: buying a one-day Travelcard valid for the three inner zones would eat nearly half her remaining money. They've been careful not to leave too much slack in her leash. *Proceed to the front of the station, turn right onto Euston Road, go to The Rocket, and await contact.* The instructions are explicit and simple and fill her with dread. *Await contact.*

It's unseasonably cold on Euston Road, the street clogged with double-decker buses and taxis as night falls. The pub is easy enough to find, but busy: the benches out front are full of smokers, and there is only standing room indoors. Iris pushes wearily through the miasma of dying cigarettes and stale beer that haunt the entrance and walks towards the bar. Almost in spite of herself she feels a frisson of anticipation: it has been *years* since she last tasted beer. It feels like an indecent luxury. She orders a pint of Younger's Best and glances around just in time to spot a knot of braying loose-tied office yahoos breaking up, abandoning their empty glasses at a table with a couple of high cast-iron stools. Old reflexes die hard and Iris hastily moves in, then settles down to wait.

In just ten minutes she politely fights off two attempts to join her – not pickup lines at her age, just pushy oafs with no sense of personal space – and manages to refrain from lowering the level of her beer glass by more than a centimeter. (If she finishes it and has to return to the bar she'll lose her seat.) It's a hard, personal struggle, for the sharply fruity and somewhat sweet taste of the ale is a revelation, dragging old memories out of storage and marching them across the dusty proscenium of her attention. But there's no sign of her contact, and she's debating whether she should in fact be waiting here at all, when someone looms over her shoulder. 'Do you mind if I sit here?' he asks.

'Sorry, I'm waiting for—' She swallows the rest of her automatic brush-off. 'Oh.'

'Yes.' He smiles faintly and slides his overcoat off his suit jacket, folds it neatly, and places it on the stool beside her. 'I shall be back presently.' And then he ghosts across to the bar to order a drink.

Iris stares at Dr. Armstrong's receding back, blinking furiously, then takes a deep mouthful of beer. As she puts her glass back down she spills a little across the table-top: her hands are shaking. *Nobody expects the Spanish Inquisition*, an inner voice chirps inanely. For some reason she'd been expecting Angleton, or maybe someone senior from field ops. The presence of an Auditor is deeply disturbing, as if she's been walking down a staircase in the darkness and her foot has landed where a tread should be and is not. He has the power to bind tongues to silence and to coerce loquacious confession with a word. Worse, he carries the full power of the oath of office. He can make a traitor's tongue catch fire in their mouth. And even if he has stepped down from the Audit Commission and returned to his previous role within the organization, he cannot be described as anything less than formidable.

Dr. Armstrong somehow manages to be served immediately. He returns from the bar before Iris, still vacillating, can decide whether to stay or go. He's carrying a beer glass and two tumblers with a tall measure of amber liquid in each.

'Cheers,' he says, sliding a whisky glass in front of her.

'Oh for . . . ' She sniffs the tumbler, wide-eyed. 'What's *happening*, Mike?'

'I thought you might like a little celebration. Your release, your return to service, or something like that.' Her fingers tense, preparing to throw the drink in his face. 'Although I would quite understand if you'd prefer to take early retirement. It's the least we can do for you.'

She takes a sip of the whisky. It's a very good Speyside. She puts the glass down with exaggerated care. 'What—' her voice is shaky – 'is going on?'

Dr. Armstrong shrugs regretfully. 'We owe you an apology.'

Suddenly, refraining from throwing her whisky in his face seems like a bad decision. 'It's been six years!'

'Yes, well.' Dr. Armstrong is discomfited. 'That mistakes were made only became clear a couple of weeks ago. Along with the nature of the mistakes, I might add. Ends and means, Iris. Ends and means.'

'I've lost—' She takes a deep breath. '*Fuck*.' It trips off her tongue more easily than the alternative, the explosive, *everything*.

'Yes.' He looks at her, stone-faced. 'I take full responsibility.'

'*Why?*' she cries quietly.

'Iris. Look at me.' Dr. Armstrong reaches across the

table and takes her beer-sticky hand in his. 'Listen to me. *Grimalkin, Septangle, Concorde, Wolf.* Execute Sitrep One, Mrs. Carpenter.'

Iris defocuses. The world around her loses texture as she hears herself reciting words from a very great distance, as far away as Camp Sunshine. 'Subjective integrity maintained. Subjective continuity maintained. Subject observes no tampering.'

'Exit supervision.' Armstrong glances at her whisky, deceptively casually. 'That concludes your role in Operation CONSTITUENCY. You might want to drink that now.'

'Why?' she asks.

'Because it's the best they had in the house, and shouldn't go to waste. Nothing less than you deserve.'

Iris looks at the glass for a moment, then glares at him and tosses the entire measure back in one defiant, convulsive gulp. Dr. Armstrong watches for the entire duration of the ensuing coughing fit, but holds his counsel.

'What now?' she finally asks hoarsely. 'Why now? Why me?'

The SA makes a steeple of his fingers. 'Are you up to date on the news from Yorkshire?'

'I think – I read the papers on the train down – is it as bad as it looks?'

'It's worse. Infinitely worse. Everything we've been working for, all the sacrifices you made – it's all going to be in vain. The idiots in Whitehall are trying to sell us down the river. They liquidated the agency and they're trying to outsource the remains of ops to a fellow called Raymond Schiller, who just happens to be the current host of the Sleeper in the Pyramid. The Prime Minister belongs to him. The Cabinet Office is his plaything. His followers have riddled the Black Chamber like maggots in a coffin, they're making a power play in Washington, DC, and now it very much looks as if they're trying to take over here as well.'

'No. That can't be. It's not possible.'

'I'm afraid it is,' he says gently. Her shoulders are shaking as she reaches for her other glass. 'All the good work you did, all the sacrifices you made – running the CONSTITUENCY honeypot, all the sanctioned horrors – all thrown away by the idiots who run the country.'

Iris begins to tear up. 'Not possible. Damn them!'

'I am informed that there's still time to turn it around, but we're going to have to act fast and it's going to be very ugly indeed. There are some delicate negotiations to be undertaken, and the question of a new chain of command. The agency has provisions for Continuity, but for now most hands are raised against us.'

'Well fuck ... what do you want me to do? I assume that's why you brought me here? Do you want to swear me in again, bind me to this Continuity thing? You know there's no love lost between my Master and the Sleeper?'

'Yes, and you are correct: you're an escaped detainee, on the blacklist if any of the bumbling cretins who're going through the agency's files think to look: clearly not one of us. So I'm going to administer a new oath – there's no conflict of interest – and tonight you're going to check into a hotel. Your choice, I don't need to know which. There's a clean credit card, ID, a smartphone, and a few little extras, and a PIN for the card in here—' Dr. Armstrong hands her an envelope ' – and you're going to catch some sleep, because tomorrow you're going to play tourist.' He gives her a crooked smile. 'Have you ever visited the Tower of London? There's some fascinating history there – some of it still in the making.'

*

It has been a busy month for Raymond Schiller. Organizing and supervising the special parties at Nether Stowe House is a grind, even after his direct oversight is no longer required all the time. Bernadette McGuigan, herself now a hand-maid and initiate of the Inner Temple, is able to run most of the proceedings, with the assistance of security supervisor Dan Berry and Phil in the Events Management Department, but Schiller is the prize draw, the golden handshake that attracts the guests like moths to a flame as word about the private prayer sessions gets around – and a certain amount of seduction and flesh-pressing still falls to him.

This is as nothing compared to the mechanics of setting up the UK arm of GP Security to handle the operational respon-sibilities of the vanquished enemy, and to contain the damage spreading from the rogue occult intelligence agency that has been allowed free rein for too long. The mop-up is proceed-ing to plan, although a worrying proportion of the target's senior personnel are still missing, having scuttled into dark corners like vermin: but with their lines of funding severed at the source they won't remain effective for long. Schiller has been spending too much of his precious time at the complex near Heathrow, chairing committee meetings and establish-ing lines of control. Luckily he has been able to delegate: Anneka, busy working with Minister Grove, has actually inserted herself into his staff as a special advisor (with a nod and a wink to Adrian Redmayne in the Cabinet Office for seeing to it). Greedy, ideologically driven, and a fellow trav-eler by inclination, Grove is almost too good to be true: the sooner Anneka initiates him into the Inner Temple the better. But they have hit an obstacle: Anneka has determined that Grove is not going to be an easy initiation. Political zeal and shared interest in turning a profit is all very well, but personal matters have stalled progress towards his induction –

'It's not my fault he's a sodomite,' Anneka interrupts Schiller's musing from the other side of the enormous and luxuriously appointed living room. She leans back on the sofa and stretches, then smiles a come-hither smile. Pencil skirt, high heels, silk-sheathed legs converging: Schiller forces himself to look away, his pulse speeding. 'You see?' she adds; 'most men can't help it, the pupillary reaction is there even if they point their gaze somewhere else. Grove simply isn't interested. But when he sees a hunky young man—'

'– Enough, please.' Schiller waves his hand as if attempting to disperse a foul odor. '1 Corinthians, 6:9 is incontrovertibly—'

'– Superseded by the Third Revelation of St. Enoch?' Anneka smiles lasciviously and slowly spreads her knees.

Schiller takes a deep breath. 'Now is not the time, for the mortification of the flesh draws near ...'

Anneka hisses irritably and for a moment her host glares at him. 'I'm *hungry.* The prey merely leads me on a longer pursuit than usual: I'll reap his soul for our Lord in the end. In person, or by taking for myself a vessel, a Ganymede who will ...'

'*Stop.* Stop right now.' Schiller glares at his unruly hand-maid. He has overindulged Anneka disgracefully since initiating her in the back of the BMW the month before, he realizes. After the initial shock and pain she has grown to take delight in her new power, and more: for as the Third Revelation explains, to those of the Inner Temple no delight will be forbidden once the kingdom of the Lord arrives on Earth, and that's the work they are engaged in right now. If Schiller wasn't queasily troubled by his own imagination when he visualizes what it would be like to slowly undress Grove himself, the remains of his Baptist indoctrination wouldn't have bubbled to the surface, with its legacy of hellfire and damnation. 'Enough. We'll get to Mr. Grove in due course. Make sure he's on the special invite list to the next party.' That's the list of those who qualify for the full VIP cost-no-object treatment, helicopters and cocaine and oiled, nubile bodies: access all areas. Schiller's own host takes over, and he hears his throat forming words in a language no human larynx was meant to speak: *I will take him for mine own if it comes to it, Daughter.*

Anneka's host retreats. She sits up primly, knees together. 'Yes, Father.' She pauses. 'What else?'

Schiller glances at his wrist watch. 'It's almost eight. Where are they?'

'I can check.' Anneka's laptop sits atop her briefcase, on the coffee table. She clicks away for a minute. 'Not far, they should be here within ten minutes. Traffic diversions near the Blackwall Tunnel, I think.'

'Well and good.' Schiller breathes deeply. 'The next party is the last one before parliament is due to go into recess. I think we should strive to induct our friends Grove, Redmayne, and Irving. The PM will be an adequate bellwether, I believe. Their personal security might be problematic, however ...'

'I believe I can take care of that,' Anneka volunteers. 'They'll only be accompanied by two bodyguards at most for an event at a private estate on the Foreign Office cleared list – it's not like the United States.' (Public officials in the United States of America are unusually (even uniquely) well-guarded by the standards of other democratic nations.) 'I'll have Dan slip them the roofies and Bernadette can store them in a warded cellar until we can Elevate them. In extremis we could send them to Heathrow for initiation into the Middle Temple. If our Lord will provide, I'm sure a couple of our people under cover of a suitable glamour will be able to replace them with no one the wiser, at least for an evening.'

'Hmm.' Schiller thinks about it. 'As long as the substitution takes place as close to his induction as possible, I believe it will work. Once our friend Jeremy has joined us in the Inner Temple his guards are surplus to requirements.' He smiles. 'It is asking a lot of you, though – of you and of Bernadette and of my other handmaids – to bring your grace to so many men.' Schiller has only brought five handmaids into the Inner Temple since his arrival in the UK. The question of who he can trust is troubling, as is the not inconsiderable effort and pain of growing new distal segments after each initiation. Obeying the injunction to be fruitful and multiply is distressingly time-consuming: at this rate it could take months of doubling cycles before the entire adult population of the British Isles have been blessed by the Lord of the New Flesh.

'Can you Elevate some more sisters to work alongside us?' She smiles back at him. 'I'm sure your host is nearly ripe again.'

'There are no suitable—' Schiller changes tack – 'but that won't matter any more, will it.'

'Not once our Lord numbers the most important members of the cabinet among his faithful congregation?'

'Indeed.'

Anneka gives him a long look. She is unusually perceptive, for a handmaid, Schiller notes. All too often the shock of induction damages something, renders them incurious or dreamily withdrawn, as if soul-burned. But not Anneka, the jewel in his crown. When he installed her host, bringing her into direct communion with the Lord without an intermediary, it seemed to awaken something in her. The arrival of the millennium has freed her from her feminine sense of sin and shame, but it has also unlocked her potential. If it wasn't the host of the Lord himself that she nurtures within her womb, he might almost take her for the Scarlet Whore of Babylon: she is insatiable for converts, zealous in her pursuit of the mission, and frighteningly ambitious. 'Are you sure,' she asks slowly, 'that you are not unconsciously delaying the inevitable because it suits you to be the only man in our Lord's house?'

'I wouldn't—' Schiller meets Anneka's amethyst gaze, lips suddenly dry. Someone else looks back at him, the bell-like clarity of her voice striking echoing chimes in the back of his head. His Lord is surfacing in her mind, finally awakening to perceive itself through the prism of her soul. The Sleeping God's noösphere expands with each Inner Temple initiate who achieves this state of enlightenment and grace. 'Do you think so, my Lady?' he hears himself asking, and anticipates her answer before she gives voice to it.

'I will provide new converts for your baptism,' the half of him that speaks through Anneka replies, 'and you will plant your seed in their wombs so that they may be born again as handmaids. I will mold them from high-priced sex workers rather than from the daughters of the Church, and they will spread the good news far and wide: it is time to rapidly expand the ranks of the Lord's army rather than slowly growing the hands and hearts of the Inner Temple.'

Schiller's head bows. His host twitches sleepily in his trousers, reminding him who he serves. He can feel the truth in her words, the voice of the Sleeping – slowly awakening – God speaking through her. The Lord is awake, but desperately weak: it needs to broaden its congregation, to gain new worshippers through the holy act of initiation in which a communicant receives the segmented wormlike host that can bond with their central nervous system and join them to the Lord's growing distributed brain. He has focused over-much, he now realizes, on penetrating and defeating the only agency of government that might react effectively to the Sleeper's arrival on British soil. Already weakened by an earlier incursion and governed by crass materialists who scoff in the face of God, this nation will be much easier to take than the United States, where rival powers are emerging from the unhallowed shadows. All that remains is to roll up the remnants of the hostile indigenous power and the Kingdom will be his. But, intent on seducing their rulers and milking the venom from their fangs, he has deliberately kept the number of hosts in his team under tight control. Anneka is right. They stand close to triumph: they will soon need more bodies, an army of them to bring about the Kingdom of the Lord on these isles, and the time for restraint is past.

'*You are right, Daughter.*' He lapses into English, the common tongue. 'The party is still a priority, but once you and Bernadette have taken Redmayne, Grove, Irving, and Michaels, there will be no point in holding back any more. Bring them to me here and I shall convert them, and you may direct them to bring more sinners to the Lord.' He smiles when she tuts at him, an impishly conspiratorial expression on her lips. 'Now where are the others? We have a meeting to run.'

While much of Mahogany Row is on the run, hiding underground in scattered safe houses under the aegis of Continuity Operations, some sections are still relatively free to come or go as they will. The haste with which the Cabinet Office abolished the agency led them to make mistakes. Not only have they mistaken the Auditors for mere accountants, they appear to think that the office of the Chief Counsel, and the Black Assizes themselves, are merely an eccentric and obscure appendage of the Ministry of Justice. Not being on the Laundry payroll as such but accountable to the Supreme Court (formerly the Law Lords), Policy and Legal still occupy offices on Fetter Lane, not far from the Royal Courts of Justice, in a cramped but picturesque building just slightly older than the United States of America. This is where Chris Womack has her office, and this particular morning she is receiving a visit from the Senior Auditor. Even priests need to confess to someone, and the SA is no exception: as Chief Counsel Chris is in a position to give him a reality check on the lawfulness of projects under his supervision, and in turn to provide an unbiased progress report to the Board. (As an Auditor, when monitoring other operations Dr. Armstrong would report to the Board directly, but when managing an operation himself, other rules must perforce apply.)

'So how did it go?'

'I really couldn't say yet.' Dr. Armstrong sits hunched in his chair, cradling his teacup protectively. His eyes are shadowed and slightly bloodshot: he's showing signs of stress or sleeplessness. 'The cutout listened to me. I believe she'll do as I asked. There's a lot ... a lot of residual loyalty. More than we have any right to expect. It's what saw her through her time in the – on the outside.' He chuckles unhappily. 'The sunk cost fallacy makes us so easy to predict, sometimes.'

'How long was she in that place?'

'Most of six years.' Dr. Armstrong nods at Womack's sharp intake of breath. 'Yes, exactly. At first it was just for the duration of the COBWEB MAZE wrap-up, but when we couldn't get a lock on the scope of the mole problem everything dragged on. Unconscionably so. Then OPERA CAPE came up and there was the throw-down between Basil and Old George and it became clear that being penetrated by the Cult of the Black Pharaoh was the least of our problems. And now there's this.'

'Are you sure she's still loyal?'

'Yes, absolutely. Which is to say, her overall objectives have always been aligned with those of this organization. She was flexible enough to square her oath of office with leading a congregation of a forbidden faith, but then, we always knew that was possible, didn't we? And she volunteered in the first place. It was the only way to make sure, at the time . . . '

'And she's not embittered in any way by her treatment?'

Dr. Armstrong winces. 'You know, when this is put to rest I intend to recommend that we make special accommodations for her. The restoration of her full back pay with interest, for starters. An additional component to recognize promotion and grade increments she missed out on. Some sort of formal recognition. I think the incoming management will see fit to sign off on it, under the circumstances.'

'I thought we already had?'

'No. In order to make it look good we bypassed the usual escrow arrangements. Everyone except you, me, and Persephone can swear under oath and compulsion that she's a disgraced traitor. And Persephone doesn't count.'

'So the Board is insulated. For how long?'

'We haven't passed the final go/no-go gate yet. Our candidate is still in the Tower and Iris is still on the "wanted" list. If you tell me to, I can still stop it in its tracks with a single phone call – until tomorrow morning.'

'All right. And in practical terms, how likely is she to get through? What about the Ring of Steel? Might the police spot her going in?'

'Oddly enough, it turns out that we didn't have an up-to-date photograph of her on file that's suitable for biometric extraction. And therefore neither do they.'

Womack nods. With no biometrics on file, the police camera network around the City won't be able to automatically identify Iris Carpenter – or the Mandate, for that matter. The credit card Iris is using is a prepaid disposable card purchased overseas by a foreign tourist, and her phone is sterile. Iris's tradecraft is about as good as can be expected, and she's in her home city. The only way she's going to get picked up is if she's run over by a cycle courier or has the terminal bad luck to be spotted by one of the Met's handful of super-recognizers – who will be working from a blurry ten-year-old picture if Persephone and the SA have done their job properly. 'So tell me what happens next?'

'It's going to go down like this ...'

'We serve an old man in a dry season, a lighthouse keeper in the desert sun ...'

Iris moves among the tourists like a fish swimming with her school, humming lyrics under her breath in time with the tune playing on her iPod.

After her meeting with Dr. Armstrong the night before she did as she was bid: checked into a hotel, ate dinner, slept, showered, broke her fast, and checked out. But then she had a morning at liberty before her meeting, and time to fill. When she couldn't work out how to put music on her locked-down and paranoid phone, she went into an Apple store and took a certain malicious delight in the purchase of an iPod Touch, some headphones, and a gift card which she used to buy back the sounds of her teenage years. *Misuse of funds – fuck 'em, they can dock my pay.* It enabled her to combine an acoustic nostalgia trip (there was no music in Camp Sunshine) with tradecraft cover: no sane agent would render themselves situationally unaware by screwing in the earphones and grooving to The Sisters of Mercy, so that was exactly what Iris chose to do.

'... *Dreamers of sleepers and white treason, we dream of rain and the history of the gun.*' And as the queue shuffles forward past the ticket desk she pays for admission and a tour guide, thinking of lighthouses and what it means to have nothing to lose.

Not wanting to stand out, she takes an hour to make her way around some of the historical exhibits – not including the Crown Jewels: the queue is out the door and halfway to Tower Gateway station – before drifting towards the cafe. She took the precaution of withdrawing a bundle of cash so now she's able to pay for coffee and a croissant without leaving a transaction trail. She sips at her drink slowly, mentally revisiting her plans for the next couple of hours. After that, who knows? The SA implied that after doing her bit she should go to ground and await further orders. Which is all well and good, but it could be days before anything happens. It occurs to her that she quite fancies the idea of a spa treatment, and resolves to go in search of one this afternoon, assuming she survives.

Time slips slowly away until Iris's coffee is a memory of bitterness dusted with cocoa, nothing left save a rim of scum adhering to the inside of an empty cup. She flicks pastry crumbs from her lap and stands, slightly creaky but as ready as she'll ever be. A raven caws somewhere outside, baristas chatter behind the bar – the cafe seems to have hit a slow patch – and sunlight glints off the damp cobblestones beyond the doorway. Which, she reminds herself, she is allowed to walk through without heed for locks or wards.

On her way to the Beauchamp Tower Iris passes the site of the former firing range used by the Fusiliers during both world wars. They executed spies and traitors by firing squad, she remembers, and dips her chin in passing, feeling a momentary frisson of connectedness to those long-dead men. But she's no longer a spy, she reminds herself, having taken a very long leave of absence from the Laundry's org chart, and treason is a movable feast, as Seneca, or maybe John Harington, observed.

If she gets through this, she'll treat herself to a spa session and a pedicure, she decides. And once the situation stabilizes she'll move heaven and earth to find out where her daughter's gone to ground. She doesn't blame Jonquil for not visiting her in prison (the girl's scatty but not that stupid), but once there's no more reason to hide . . .

It's not just her own life that she sacrificed on the altar of operational necessity, and for *that* she feels truly guilty.

The entrance to the Beauchamp Tower is coned off from the areas open to the public, and a discreet sign on the door says NO ADMITTANCE – PASSHOLDERS ONLY. Iris straightens her back and palms the identity card from the SA's envelope. Her fingertips prickle as she touches it, and a moment later her scalp itches and she shivers violently as she crosses an invisible line just outside the threshold. Then she opens the vestibule door.

'Can I help you, ma'am?'

The guard behind the transom smiles politely – he probably gets the odd tourist blundering in every day, it's easy enough to take a wrong turning – but he's clearly an old screw and his scrutiny isn't remotely casual. Nor are the locks on the door at the other side of the guard room. She smiles right back. 'Iris Carpenter, from Q-Division. I'm here to interview the inmate. Following up on Dr. Armstrong's visit a week ago.'

'I don't think so,' says the guard, glancing at the computer screen on his desk, 'no visitors expect—' Iris zaps him with the SA's 'little extra something.' It came pre-loaded on the company phone, a gadget that she still periodically boggles at – phones have come a long way, while she was in prison – and she holds the tiny tablet screen-out towards the man and he instinctively looks at it and then he slumps forward across the tabletop, sending his in-tray skidding. Iris intercepts it before it can shed its load – a bizarre mix of papers and what appear to be hearing implant transducers – then checks on the guard. He's still breathing, but he's deeply unconscious. She loosens his collar and tie, then fumbles for the ward he's wearing on a chain – standard issue, heavy duty – and takes it for herself. (Not that she expects the prisoner to try and take her, but there's always an element of risk.) Finally, she rummages along his belt for the inevitable keychain and adds it to her collection.

Two minutes have passed by the time Iris works out which key to use in which lock on the inner door. She takes a deep breath, holds her phone up, and pulls the door open.

'Hey, you—' The other screw slurs oddly as he collapses. Iris steps over him. There's another door ahead on the left and she opens it.

'Why, hello!' The man-shaped thing in the armchair beams at her as he raises his teacup: 'I was just wondering where you'd got to. Would you care for refreshments?'

'My Lord.' Iris goes to her knees creakily, then bends

low, as low as a fifty-three-year-old can manage. 'It is an honor to serve you.'

'I suppose so, but there's no reason to stand on ceremony here, what? Get up, get up, have a seat. Do you take milk in your tea? Sugar?'

Standing up takes far longer for Iris than prostrating herself, and she catches her breath before replying. 'Whatever you think suitable, my Lord.'

Her Lord appears to be in remarkably good spirits considering his circumstances, jovial and at ease with himself, but Iris is not misled. He is a mercurial being, capable of flashing from cheerful to icily furious and vengeful in a second at a perceived slight – or even on impulse, should he become bored. 'I think you take your tea white, no sugar,' he announces, and, picking up the teapot, pours her a cup accordingly.

'Thank you, my Lord,' Iris says, careful not to spill a drop as she accepts the beverage and takes a seat in the other chair. He is eerily correct: when she drinks tea, this is exactly how she takes it. 'I believe we will be free of interruptions for at least ten minutes.'

'Jolly good! So all is well with the world, I take it?'

'I ... couldn't say, my Lord. I've been out of touch for quite a long time.'

'As you will. That's an interesting new *geas* you're under; I assume your presence means that Dr. Armstrong is amenable to proceeding?'

Iris nods, not trusting herself to speak. She sips her tea for cover: it's really very good, a perfect brew.

The prisoner picks up his cup and sips from it thoughtfully. 'Would you like me to release you from your oath?'

Iris looks at him evenly. 'As you will.'

Her Lord smiles. 'Then I shall leave the *geas* in place:

it suits you, you know, and it's not as if it will make any difference. Time is short, I take it?'

Iris nods. 'Dr. Armstrong told me to tell you that, ah, the party is to be held on Saturday at the usual venue.'

'I see.' He puts his cup down. 'Then time *is* short, too short for a by-election. Hmm. So it will be necessary to join the government by the non-parliamentary route. Hmm again.'

'The non-parliamentary route, my Lord?'

He smiles again, sunlight flashing on teeth like wavetops. 'The Prime Minister may appoint a non-parliamentarian to the cabinet, but by convention ministers must be members of the House of Commons or the House of Lords. So I will not only have to persuade him of the pressing need for an interim appointment, but then obtain the Royal Assent for my elevation without waiting for the Queen's Birthday Honours List. Although as that's due to be announced next month I imagine an appointment could be expedited? A Dukedom will do at a pinch . . . '

'Yes, my Lord.'

He chuckles at Iris's use of the honorific. 'Not yet, Daughter, not yet.' Then the smile fades. 'How am I to proceed?'

'Do you have any luggage?' He shakes his head. 'Then we can leave as soon as you're ready.'

The prisoner looks at her, and then through her, and for a moment Iris feels that her body has turned to glass beneath the thunderous scrutiny of a godlike gaze – 'ah, I see. Carry on then.'

'Thank you, my Lord.' Iris stands, a little shakily, waits for the prisoner to also rise, then walks along the short corridor. The door has swung to in front of her. She unlocks her phone, turns it so that the rear camera faces the door, and brings up the standard OFCUT countermeasures app. The ward appears in the middle of the door, limned in false-color balefire. Iris presents the shiny new warrant card from the SA's briefing package. '*Attention. By the power vested in me under my oath of office, I deactivate this ward.*' Her Enochian is very rusty, but she manages not to stumble over the words. There's a brief flare of light and a crackle as the ward fades away. 'The way is now open,' she says over her shoulder, trying not to think too hard about what she's just done.

If nothing else, she has just confirmed the wisdom of locking her up and throwing away the key – at least, to anyone not cleared for CONSTITUENCY, the honeypot operation under which she had established and run a chapter of the Cult of the Black Pharaoh. But looming above and beyond that are the frightening implications of the SA's gambit – and of the depthless pit of despair that must have motivated the Board of Directors to approve it.

Above my pay grade, Iris tells herself nervously, as she opens the front door and leads her Lord blinking into the daylight.

Thursday evening finds Mhari working overtime with the tiger team monitoring Schiller's apartment in Docklands.

Things have changed quite a bit in the weeks since Persephone and Johnny McTavish first rented the apartment and subsequently parked Bob in it in the wake of the snatch attempt. Johnny has been spending a lot of time there, as has Mhari. The living room is now an operations room, staffed by former tech ops people who Continuity Ops have vetted, cleared, and recruited. Johnny is managing the team, who keep the apartment two floors below the safe house under 24/7 observation. The kitchen is stocked with microwave meals and coffee, the office desks in the living room support a comprehensive array of surveillance receivers and loggers, and go-bags sit in the hallway awaiting the mission to black-bag Schiller's residence.

Working out how to enter Schiller's flat without falling foul of the elaborate alarm system has been tiresome and problematic. For one thing, there's a one-floor air gap between occupied apartments, with empty but alarm-covered rooms in the way. For another, the flats are shielded against electromagnetic leakage, with their own cellular picocells and secure internet land lines to carry the traffic. The ops team have brought a StingRay to the party but it's remained stubbornly silent apart from logging all the team members' own phones. Schiller's staff have some top-notch infosec discipline. GP Security employees sweep for electronic bugs daily, there's a white-noise generator coupled to every window frame to defeat laser microphones, and whoever configured their internet firewall is frustratingly competent.

If Johnny was still able to call on GCHQ's resources via Q-Division's liaison desk, they could doubtless find a zero-day that would get through the cordon downstairs, but under the circumstances that option is off the menu. It's also targeting a state-level adversary – a private-sector contractor that works for the Laundry's American equivalent agency. So Johnny is already feeling a little defensive when Mhari beckons him into the second bedroom – repurposed as a break room by the surveillance team – and sits him down for a head-to-head.

'It's not goin' well, love,' he shakes his head. 'The StingRay's getting nothing – Schiller's people turn off their mobile phones when they go inside. Roz thinks 'e's got 'em all using some kind of encrypted voice-over-IP app on the suite wifi, which is stitched up like a kipper.' Roz is the team's white-hat hacker. 'She cracked the wifi password but says they're just using it for a VPN. She also figures they've got a bunch of intrusion detection sniffers. Snooping on them is like blind pogoing in a minefield, she says.'

'Well, bum.' Mhari picks up a can of caffeine-free Coke from the cooler on the dressing table and plants herself on the side of the bed. 'How are the mikes coming along?'

'Gazza's done good.' Johnny scratches his head. ''E made a few false starts with the drill but 'e finally found a stud wall downstairs yesterday and drove three fiber runs through it.' The empty flat below the safe house is a major obstacle: the non-load-bearing internal walls are deliberately offset from the floors above and below, so that attempts to run a wire or fiber-optic cable straight down through the ceiling will be glaringly obvious. 'One came out in the bog, one's in the kitchen, but the third – 'e thinks 'e got the living room, but it's not over the conference table.'

'Is there any take?' Mhari sips at her Coke. She's tired and irritable, having spent the day holed up in a cheap hotel room with noisy neighbors, and has come here to take over the night shift.

Johnny smiles crookedly. 'I was just gettin' to that.' Mhari resists the urge to strangle him, but flashes him a little fang. The smile vanishes. 'Gazza's got us a passive optical pickup embedded about half a millimeter inside a ceiling tile diagonally across the room from the conference table, just over the sofa. Optics are really hazy but we can see when someone's sitting there – not who, though. The audio is better: we can bounce an infrared laser beam down the fiber and amplify the take, so there's no EM noise for their bug sniffer to pick up. Only trouble is, nobody's been in there during the daytime 'cept the agency cleaners, so there's no intel—'

'Wait. Agency cleaners.' Mhari cocks her head to one side. 'Are you thinking what I'm thinking?'

Johnny whistles quietly between his teeth. 'Risky, love, very risky.'

'Who logged them?' Mhari persists.

'I think Steve was on the morning shift ...'

Mhari puts her can down and stands up. 'Let's see how thoroughly he did his job.'

Gary – the bugging tech – is working at the desk with the rack of recording gear; Roz the pen-tester is getting ready to leave, leaving Mhari and Johnny to take care of the evening hand-off. Mhari goes over to the other desk, where there's a PC running case management software developed for the Police, who do a lot more covert surveillance operations than an agency usually more busy suppressing things with the wrong number of dimensions, never mind limbs. 'Let's see.' She logs on and pokes around for a bit. 'Okay, user SteveG reports from today, 1124 hours, two POI entered target lobby. Hmm. Okay, that gives us a time window to pull the CCTV and the front desk register.' Mhari pokes around some more. 'Yes, they look like contract cleaning staff.' She glances at Johnny. 'Can you nip down to the front desk and ask who they are?'

Johnny raises an eyebrow. 'You want me to flash it around ...?'

'You've got a warrant card for now, use it while it's fresh.'

Johnny raises a lazy finger to his forehead. 'On it.' The source of occult authority that binds the Continuity Ops warrant cards gives them some of the mind-warping mojo of the dissolved agency's ID, and Johnny is on the inside. He heads for the door as Mhari sits down to trawl through the past day's event log.

She's just reached the record of the cleaners leaving – they took just under two hours – when Gary clears his throat. 'Ms. Murphy?' he calls, half-turning in his chair. 'Got something.'

'What—' Mhari is across the room so fast he barely has time to flinch. The spare pair of headphones he's offering her falls from his fingers: she catches them. 'Yes?'

'I'm putting this on a sixty-second delay.' Gary recovers and scrubs back through the digital recording. 'I think you'll find this interesting.'

Mhari listens. The sound from the omnidirectional passive mike is muffled to begin with, and it picks up every sound in the room, from the white noise of the air conditioning to the thud of the bedroom door and the shuffle of feet on carpet. Furthermore, people in conversation use their bodies and their faces as much as their words. Gradually she begins to decode the discourse. ' – Hosts will be ready – two days – next party primary – yes, Grove and the, the Prime – induction. I'll supervise – Back here. Invite them—'

Gary is tormenting the speech transcription software on the laptop next to the desktop with the audio capture card. 'That's Schiller,' he says quietly. 'What are hosts?'

Mhari has read the GOD GAME BLACK report. 'Keyword clearance. Keep listening for more, it's important. Also names and dates.'

She stands up, elated. Not that she expects Schiller to be so indiscreet as to twirl his nonexistent mustache and tell one of his minions, *we shall enact our dastardly scheme to take over the Prime Minister's brain upon the hour of midnight, hah hah!* – But just picking up the terms *host* and *next party* in the same conversation is a big win. It's something concrete, and she already knows from other sources that Schiller's next big knees-up at Nether Stowe House is due this Saturday night.

If Johnny can unearth the personal details of the cleaners who are servicing Schiller's apartment, and Mhari can confirm that Schiller will be running the party in person, then the outline of a plan for Site Three is beginning to come into focus.

They meet back in the same bar on Euston Road at three o'clock in the afternoon. It's midway between the lunchtime rush and the afterwork crush; this time Iris has no problem finding a padded bench seat with a view of the doorways via the big mirrors behind the bar. She orders a pot of tea and a burger. It's not exactly a gastronomic extravaganza but it's available and she's hungry and it gives her an excuse for occupying a booth by herself. And the tea keeps her from drinking anything stronger, because she has a twitchy feeling that if she gets started now she won't stop until the world goes away.

She's drunk most of her tea and is working unenthusiastically on the burger when a presence appears on the seat opposite her. Irritated, she keeps on masticating regardless until he has finished shedding his overcoat and clears his throat. 'Yes?' she says.

'How did it go?'

'You know how it went or you wouldn't be here.' She puts her fork down. (Iris is too jealous of her remaining dignity to eat with her fingers if she can avoid it.) 'He accepted your offer.'

'Good, I think.' To his credit, Dr. Armstrong looks slightly queasy.

'It's too late to back out now.' Iris picks up her fork again and goes to work on her chips. 'I hope you know what you're doing.'

'Riding a tiger.' Dr. Armstrong has brought a pint of beer to the table; now he takes a mouthful. 'Mmm. The question is whether the tiger prefers to eat the monkey on his back or the juicy, fat buffalo in front of him. Better eating on the buffalo. I think.'

Iris finishes her burger in silence before moving on to the next question. 'So what do you have for me to do now?'

'Liaison work: consider yourself his personal assistant for the time being. It's not as if we have a management role for you right now anyway. Just be on hand in case he wants something arranged: call on me if you need agency resources for it, but bear in mind we're extremely limited right now.' Reaching under his overcoat, the SA pulls out a travel document organizer that bulges slightly. 'We have an unallocated safe house – it's out in SW17, I'm afraid – and I took the liberty of having it set up for you. Because you aren't anywhere on our org chart you're safe from the current adversarial situation, and we've taken steps to ensure that you won't be reported as an absconder. Six months private lease, furnished, security system certificated to level three, no strings attached. Council tax paid up until November, utility bills chargeable to an offshore account where the paper trail vanishes. Here are the particulars and the front door keys. The rest of the paperwork is on the kitchen table.' He pauses.

'What paperwork?' Her expression is stony.

'I took some liberties. Some of us remember the good work you've done: funds equivalent to your payroll continued to be deposited while you were away and you have, hmm, a not inconsiderable bank balance awaiting you. Once the agency is reconstituted – if we are successful – I checked your personal progression profile and, if you choose to take the requisite courses, we can bump you four grades up from where you left off within a year. Assuming you wish to resume your employment.'

'Assuming I don't choose permanent deactivation. And assuming there's an agency to come back to.'

'If there isn't, we'll all be dead. Or worse.' They sit in silence for a couple of minutes.

'There will be obstacles to me returning,' she says at last.

'Which ones?'

'You know perfectly well—' She stops dead and squints at him, red-eyed, then takes a deep breath. 'Dr. Angleton, for one, and his gofer Bob, for another. They think I—' She stops again – 'What?'

'I'm sorry to be the one to break this to you.' Dr. Armstrong glances down at the table. 'Angleton's dead. Nothing to do with your – I mean, it was an entirely different threat situation. There were other changes, while you were away.'

'Other changes.' Iris frowns. 'Such as?'

'Mr. Howard is James's successor.' At her double-take, Armstrong adds: 'Not only in post but in practice – he's coming along very nicely.' While she's absorbing this, he continues: 'Andy Newstrom, Doris Greene, Judith Carroll, and a bunch of others died during an incursion last year. Gerry Lockhart is suspended – arrested, in prison on remand awaiting trial – following events in Leeds. Most of our senior personnel – Mahogany Row – are currently avoiding spurious arrest warrants arranged by the enemy. Dr. O'Brien, Bob's other half, is our newest Auditor. Right before we came under attack we were integrating new and unexpected add-ons on the org chart: vampires and elves and other strange creatures out of legend. Dragons, even. And that's barely scratching the surface.'

Iris snorts dismissively. 'Next you'll be telling me were-wolves are real.'

'No, of course—' He shakes his head – 'that is to say, I really hope not.' For a moment he almost musters up a smile, but it slips away. 'But we're currently running Continuity Operations in the absence of a mandate from Parliament. We're very short-staffed. The enemy attacked us from the top down, very suddenly, while operations were already disrupted by the crisis in Yorkshire. If a sister agency in the United States hadn't tried to warn us we might have missed it completely. First they destroyed our legal standing with the rest of the Civil Service by getting the PM and the Cabinet Secretary to announce our dissolution, then they attacked our budget via the Treasury – not just cutting off our funding overtly, but aiming the Serious Fraud Office anti-money laundering teams at our fallback resources. They generated spurious crime reports targeting individual members of Mahogany Row, starting with those who were already known to them and then adding names from the files they obtained when their subcontractors went into our recently vacated offices. They already did this once, in the United States – they used the same protocol against the Comstock Office, and only the fact that a very brave man leaked their transcripts to us has enabled us to keep ahead of the ball.'

She shakes her head in disbelief. 'It's hard to credit. You're certain the attackers all work for that *thing*? The Sleeper in the Pyramid?'

'As certain as can be.'

'Well,' she mumbles, 'now *nothing* makes sense.'

The SA sighs. 'There's a historical precedent.'

'Oh? Do explain, please.'

'Japan, in August 1945.' He frowns. 'The popular wisdom is that after the USA dropped two atom bombs on Hiroshima and Nagasaki, Japan surrendered to avoid being nuked into oblivion. But that's not actually the whole story. A few days before the first atom bombing, the Soviet Union declared war on Japan, and within days the Red Army had shattered the Japanese army in Manchuria. It's hard to exaggerate how devastating the attack was: it was one of the biggest, most successful land offensives of the Second World War, although it's virtually unknown in the West. The Americans and British were preparing to invade Japan in November, which was bad enough, but the Japanese government was even more frightened of the prospect of an invasion by the USSR. The atom bombs allowed them – gave them an adequate excuse – to make their peace with the lesser evil.'

'You're telling me—'

The SA straightens, his eyes angry: 'The Sleeper is *not* the lesser evil! It's—' He catches himself. 'There are no good guys in this war,' he says, forcing himself to measure out his words calmly, 'but at least your master wants us alive. *Some* of us,' he corrects himself grimly. 'Your master is happy to indulge his willing servants with a semblance of freedom, and to ignore the rest; the Sleeper leaves only soul-raped slaves and walking corpses behind.'

Iris gives him a sidelong look. 'Trust me, Doctor, currying favor isn't going to work. He'll see right through you. He's not just a sharp suit and a witty quip for the cameras, he's one of *them*. He's totally out of your league. If you try and play games ...'

'He'll win, yes, I know. We're not stupid, Iris, we are Mahogany Row and we are aware that the only way to win this game is not to play. Nevertheless.' He tilts his head towards her. 'We have been dragged, kicking and screaming, all the way to this scaffold: all that is left is to do the thing gracefully. Take the house and the money, Iris. Think about what I said. The new agency is going to need sound leadership, and you, at least, have no particular reason to fear our new Lord and master.'

It's the Friday before HUMMINGBIRD and Mo and I have sallied forth from the safe house *together* to attend a meeting. I am in a good mood, and even the constant urge to look over my shoulder and cringe at the sight of CCTV cameras can't dampen it. She holds my hand: she's in a good mood too, I think.

So I book us an Uber to the railway station, then take a taxi for a trip around the block fetching back up at a bus station, then take a beaten-up old Stagecoach over to the next town, then she orders an Uber on *her* account to break continuity ... and eventually we fetch up in a rented hotel office with the other waifs and strays (Mhari, Johnny, and Persephone), drinking coffee from a thermos and chatting about nothing in particular while Johnny checks the room out for listeners and other occult bugs. The jitters only cut in when he gives us the all-clear and then nerd-boy vampire and his maniac pixie dream girl slip through the door; she gives me the stink-eye for no reason I can establish, and Mo raises an eyebrow at me. *She* looks tense now. The gang's almost all here, for values of gang that approximate to the active members of the INDIGO HUMMINGBIRD team. A couple of other bodies filter in and stack against the wall – we're up to standing room only – then the SA arrives, closes the door, and bars it with a word that makes my back teeth ache and my vision blur. He clears his throat.

'Johnny, would you mind pulling back the curtain? Yes, it's just the television, if you please.'

Dr. Armstrong looks as tired as I feel, as if he's been up all night struggling with his conscience. Mo takes hold of my wrist. 'This is going to be tough,' she whispers in my ear. 'Try not to sound off until you've heard him through, okay?' She sounds tense, and that in itself is enough to curdle my stomach.

'What's going—' Alex is immediately shushed by three different people, including Cassie, who wraps a hand around his mouth.

'*Parliament Live*,' says the SA. 'The Public Administration and Constitutional Governance Committee in session, as of half an hour ago. Norman Grove, minister without portfolio, is addressing the committee—' he fiddles with the remote – 'aha.'

'– Honorable friends, is why we have commenced the structural rationalization and replacement of SOE, anticipating the recommendations of the review process in light of the findings of the enquiry into April's events in Yorkshire—'

Why is he showing us this? I wonder, because this is all old news—

'– Utilize a statutory instrument in accordance with the provisions of the Civil Contingencies Act (2004) to transfer those roles associated with the defense of the realm to the Ministry of Defense, and support and infrastructure responsibilities to—'

Statutory instruments are administrative orders that the government can use to implement secondary legislation, bypassing debate in Parliament. The CCA is the emergency powers law governing the UK in time of war or natural disaster, and it basically allows a designated minister to make it up as they go along. It's tantamount to a declaration of martial law. I didn't know the government had invoked the CCA, and I'm about to open my mouth to say so when Mo squeezes my wrist again –

'– Dangerous rogue agency is a thing of the past. Luckily we have the legislative instruments and, more importantly, the assistance of our American allies and their experienced private sector contractors to fall back on during the necessary period of upheaval that this restructuring will cause—'

Click. The SA freezes the livestream. 'Observe.' He points at the screen with the knobbly remote, then fiddles with some buttons. The screen jumps, zooming in on Grove. He's standing in the middle of the horseshoe-shaped table, but behind him I see a blonde in a power suit. 'Seated, behind the minister's left shoulder. Known to the public as Anneka Overholt, the minister's special advisor. And known to those of us who have been keeping an eye on Target Three—' his cheek twitches – 'as the Reverend Raymond Schiller's former personal assistant, lately promoted to his deputy.'

The SA takes a deep breath. 'I'm showing you this to demonstrate just how desperate the situation has become. A few years ago, some of you were instrumental in denying Raymond Schiller access to the cabinet. This time he – or the thing pulling his strings – has succeeded in suborning Parliament. This isn't simply an attack on the agency and an attempt to place its operational assets under the control of a new ministry. We – that is, the Board – believe this is an active Category One swarm attack by the Sleeper in the Pyramid, that as before, the Sleeper is using engineered brain-control parasites to co-opt slaves. However, this time the parasites are rather more effective than the previous generation of neurotropic tongue-eating isopods, and the enemy's plan is to amplify, exponentiate, and go pandemic. The parties at Target One are being used as cover for induction or implantation of individuals with a high degree of connectedness in their social graphs – the ideal vector for transmission. We thought until yesterday that we had about three months, that they were still keeping it to a recruitment gambit for the so-called Inner Temple of Sleeper cultist-slaves, but then we got hold of the guest list for tomorrow's event. We were over-optimistic.'

Mhari clears her throat. 'Schiller will be throwing another of his big parties this Saturday. He'll be attending in person, and inviting half the cabinet by the sound of it – the half who aren't already infested.' She sounds almost apologetic.

I'm still trying to get my head around his last words when he walks across to the TV screen, turns, and says a word that refuses to stick to the insides of my ears. I blink and see other people shaking their heads. It's very quiet all of a sudden, and it takes me a moment to realize that the usual subliminal hum of minds all around has died down, so that I can only sense the people I can see in this room, not the rest of the building. I look round for confirmation and see a blank expanse of wall where the door I walked in through used to be.

Dr. Armstrong straightens his back and looks at us. 'What I have to say next is not to be discussed outside this room: nor is it recorded or written anywhere. This agency has assets you are unaware of, deliberately so – compartmentalization is a fact.' He doesn't even manage a self-deprecating smile, and that's when I feel, in my guts, just how serious this is. 'You will shortly be given orders of questionable legality, to the extent that, taken at face value, they would appear to violate the Treason Act. Measures are in train elsewhere to ensure that a separate statutory instru-ment is fast-tracked to retroactively grant immunity for any actions you are required to undertake in compliance with these orders.' (There are sharp intakes of breath all round.) 'Moreover, whatever Mr. Grove thinks, this restructuring is not going to happen because Mr. Grove is not going to be around to carry it out.'

My mouth is open. I manage to close it before I catch any flies; meanwhile Persephone speaks up. 'We aren't in the business of overthrowing the government,' she enunciates very carefully.

Dr. Armstrong stares at her. 'Of course not.'

Cassie sits up very straight. 'It all depends what you mean by the government, doesn't it?' she chirps, doing a very good impersonation of a teacher's pet. I stifle the urge to strangle her. Is it my imagination or is Mo actually *relaxing* next to me? 'There is the Crown-in-Parliament, and there is the Queen, the person in the central seat, but there is also the government, as in Parliament, YesYes? And it is the individual members of the Parliament who have been suborned?'

She sounds really alien when she puts it like that, a green-haired Martian invader with pointy ears trying to get her head around humanity.

'Yes,' says Persephone. 'What is our operational objective? Our exit strategy?'

'Your objective is to sterilize the source of infection.' The SA looks straight at me. 'Secondary objectives are to rescue any members of the cabinet or other VIPs who have not yet been parasitized, and to verify that Schiller, or his people, are controlled by the Sleeper in the Pyramid – but we are already certain of this beyond reasonable doubt: it's icing on the cake if you can do it. Other hands are taking care of the broader constitutional issues in the background; you need trouble yourselves no more over the niceties of the situation. I believe you have a plan, Mr. Howard?'

Gulp. 'As directed, I've established and kept up-to-date an operational plan for simultaneous attacks on Schiller's UK footprint,' I hear myself saying. 'Is this the go/no-go point?'

'Yes,' the SA falls silent.

'Right.' I pause. 'So if Schiller's hosting his big push in the countryside we can be certain he won't be in his apartment in Docklands. And it's out of hours, so the facility at Heathrow will be empty or short-staffed. I assume we're in a position to disrupt cell and phone service to Nether Stowe House, or at least prevent alerts from reaching Schiller's staff during the black-bag stages of the operation. Anything else?'

'It's those fucking cock-worms, isn't it?' says Johnny. 'Anything else we should expect?'

'Alas, yes.' Dr. Armstrong looks deeply uncomfortable. 'Expect the worst. PHANG-like superparasites or other soul riders, class 3 or higher. I've arranged for backup from a class 5 or higher for the assault on Target One, but there's no guarantee the Sleeper won't be able to match or exceed it.'

The classification of occult parasites is esoteric and terrifying: the SA is referring to a logarithmic scale of power. Feeders in the night and tongue-eaters are class 1 occult parasites; they eat minds retail, not wholesale. PHANGs are at least a class 2 and sometimes higher; I'm not sure what the Hungry Ghosts are, but the Eater of Souls is at least a class 4, maybe a 5. I have no desire ever to meet anything higher on the scale but I'm pretty sure the Sleeper, the Black Pharaoh, and their ilk start at a 6 and go up from there. It's that Twinkie Singularity problem again.

'Happy joy!' Cassie seems delighted by this. 'Can I come on this one, too?'

I can feel Mo forcing a poker face, trying not to roll her eyes. 'Sure,' I say, 'you're on the roster for Nether Stowe House. Waitressing again.' I manage not to smile at her evident disgust. 'But it's a vital job. We're relying on you to guide the door-breakers on their way in ...'

9: INDIGO HUMMINGBIRD

Mid-afternoon on Saturday finds Raymond Schiller relaxed and calm, back in the Docklands apartment after a lunchtime excursion to Claridge's for an interview with a journalist from the *Daily Telegraph*'s financial pages (over lobster bisque followed by veal and wild mushrooms in red wine sauce). The luxury apartment is a convenience, close to hand for events in the city but sufficiently secluded that he can retreat to it for solitary contemplation and prayer, unlike Nether Stowe House where he is always the center of attention. But he can only retreat for so long. Therefore, after a brief nap he showers in the master suite's bathroom and prepares for the ride back to this evening's party and communion service.

When he steps out of the bathroom he finds his freshly dry-cleaned tuxedo waiting in the adjacent dressing room. He can sense Anneka and Bernadette beyond the warded bedroom door (there are four other bedrooms, and they have their own rooms) but the handmaids are sensitive to his dignity. To save time, Bernadette booked a visit from a stylist and a cosmetician. Schiller has little patience for such superficialities, but he understands the need for them to make the right impression, and is willing to pay.

As he adjusts his bow tie, Schiller hears the muffled chime of the doorbell. Listening, he hears captive minds buzzing and humming beyond his door, moving to intercept the visitors. He opens himself to his handmaid's perceptions while he finishes up. Anneka is answering the door, gowned and immaculately coiffed for her greeter's role at tonight's event. Her visitors are three men in dark suits, dark glasses, and earpieces from the Personal Protection department. 'You're early,' she tells them tersely. 'This way.' She leads them into the lobby. They follow her silently, their faces immobile. One of GP Security's money-spinners on the side is providing security for VIPs and stars, and over the past week they have all been initiated into the Middle Temple, gifted with the Tongue of God behind their lips and the peace in their souls that they'll need to see them through the more distasteful stages of the mission ahead.

Schiller gathers the reins of their hosts – the isopod-like parasites that have replaced their tongues and now control their higher functions – and sends them over to wait at the window side of the room.

'Father?' Bernadette asks, uncertainty in her voice: she senses the weight of his attention through her host. (Inner Temple initiates are *far* more useful than those of the Middle Temple, Schiller reflects, although the process of Elevation is painful and time-consuming.) 'You have additional instructions for me?'

'Pack an overnight bag. After the party, you will stay at Nether Stowe House. You can take charge of the morning-after crew.' (Wild humans, uncaptured and uncut: little better than animals.) He feels her apprehension and adds, gently, 'I have distasteful business to attend to after the party that would only add to your discomfort. Best that you are elsewhere.'

She nods, relieved. 'I'll pray for you, Father,' she says, and hurries into the bedroom to prepare. Schiller glances at

Anneka and nods minutely. Bernadette had a poor – emotionally traumatized – reaction to her host implantation: once Schiller was able to inspect her soul he realized that she harbored weaknesses that were not obvious until too late. Her induction was a mistake, but not an irremediable one – her host will break her to her role eventually. But in the meantime, she is simply unsuited to tasks that require ruthless detachment. Anneka, made of sterner stuff, returns his nod, then accepts the reins of the protection crew and gives them their detailed instructions.

'We will depart for Nether Stowe House shortly. Jack will ride shotgun in the car. Olaf, Barry, you will go to the room at the Hilton. Your task is to book the services of one of the contractors on the list—' she hands over a sheaf of laser-printed papers, ads gleaned from the internet, several already checked off from previous occasions – 'get them to show up, verify that they match the description on their publicity material, then bring them here, and prep them for Dr. Schiller's return. It is anticipated that we will be back no later than 3 a.m. tomorrow, at which time you may go off-shift.'

They incline their heads to Anneka simultaneously, like a string of puppets. Bernadette returns, clutching a slightly incongruous day pack. Schiller smiles. 'Ladies. Shall we be on our way?'

It's early evening on the Saturday of Schiller's big party, and the Target One team are taking up their positions. Cassie is aboard the minibus ferrying agency waiters from the west London hinterlands to the big house, incommunicado for now (the agency insisted on everyone turning in their mobile phones for the shift, ostensibly to prevent unauthorized photography as well as to reduce goofing off). The bus has already dropped off two loads of shift workers; Cassie is part of the late evening shift, on duty until the early hours. But she won't be alone once she arrives on site. A mobile support truck and two cars are parked half a mile down the road at Nether Stowe itself. Alex shelters from the remaining sky-glow in the back of the truck, along with the special backup people Dr. O'Brien introduced him to earlier that afternoon. Brains, who has come from nursing his injured partner, Pinky, in Leeds just to help with this caper, swears at the array of receivers and data loggers in the rack beside him while Alex fidgets edgily. 'Cheap cables, kid.' He wiggles an ethernet patch experimentally as one of the speakers crackles. 'Bane of my life.'

Meanwhile, Mo is differently nervous. She sits in the back seat of a Bentley, checking her foundation in a makeup compact for the third time. She wears her one black evening gown, with borrowed jewelry glittering at throat and wrists. In her clutch she carries a gilt-edged card acquired – at some personal risk – from a certain high-flying Metropolitan Police officer with a guilty conscience. Cassie's way in is below stairs, but hers is strictly ballroom. 'If you can score me an invitation I can go in separately and rendezvous with Cassie once we're both on-site,' she pointed out in one of the planning sessions. 'It has the advantage that it gets Zero in too.' (The uniformed chauffeur behind the Bentley's wheel, taking a catnap while they wait for the go signal, has been Persephone's Oddjob for as long as I've known them both. I've never seen him wearing a steel-brimmed bowler hat but there's always a first time, and it's the sort of thing that would appeal to his sense of humor.) 'Nobody will think twice about us stashing our driver round the back, so we'll have muscle and a rapid evacuation route if it all goes to shit before the cavalry can reach us,' she added, sealing the deal.

But despite all the planning, despite the backroom crew and the extraction team, when she finds herself dressed to the nines and waiting in the car for London Central to fire the starting pistol, she's jittery. Stage nerves. 'I'm getting too old for this *Mission: Impossible* crap,' she tells the microphone concealed in her corsage.

'Could be worse,' Zero chirps; 'you could be prepped for *Mission: Impossible* and find yourself in a teen slasher movie instead.'

She shudders and pulls her silk wrap closer around her shoulders. 'Don't even *think* that.'

'Mind you, the way things work around here *The Prisoner* is more likely than either ...'

Mo screens him out – Zero is an aficionado of spy thrillers – and glances at her phone again.

'Alex. Talk to me?'

'Dr. O'Brien.' He sighs noisily. 'What can I do for you?'

'How are you feeling?' Mo isn't nervous on her own account – she's done this sort of thing plenty of times before, although not as frequently since her CANDID cover was wrecked on national TV – but she gets edgy whenever she knows that *I'm* in play, and she's very aware that Alex has gotten into deeper waters far faster than she or I ever did. It's not some sort of mother hen instinct: she's just concerned that the least experienced member of her team might be out of his depth.

'Mostly worried about Cassie.' Alex pauses. 'Huh. Tracker on the Transit says the minibus is about three kilometers out. As long as it doesn't go off the road, or—'

'That's not going to happen. She knows what she's doing, Alex. How about you?'

'What about—? Sorry. I'm easily distracted.'

'Don't be.' Mo pauses to collect her thoughts. 'Worrying

about your girlfriend won't help. You've got a job to do – focus on that, and you'll make everyone safer, her included.'

'Yeah ... I guess so. How long until it's time to go in?'

Mo glances at the dashboard clock. 'Zero and I will probably be on the move in about another ten minutes. You don't move until you get the signal, but it won't be long, I promise.' Not unless there's an abort on Target Two or Three, and that doesn't bear thinking about, but she decides against reminding him of this. Nervous PHANGs make everyone else extra-twitchy, and it's a vicious circle. 'Hang tight, try to chill, and call me if anything comes up. Bye for now.'

Mo leans back, closes her eyes, and sighs. The SA has taken her into his confidence and explained just how high the stakes are. If he is right about the real agenda behind Schiller's parties and backroom meetings, then the cost of failure is too nightmarish to contemplate. So, with the heavy-hearted assent of the Board, he has made a deal with the devil: and the hell of it is that she can't see what else he could have done. It's up to her to keep the Laundry's side of the bargain tonight, and to that end he's given her a blank check to do whatever she thinks necessary. *Time to face the music and dance,* she thinks mordantly, feeling a reflexive stab of nostalgia for the eldritch strings of an instrument she's lost forever, then she begins once more to go through the trigger words for the summonings and wards that her smartphone is keyed to activate on command –

'Why's the kid nervous?' asks Zero.

'Someone back at HQ thought giving him a cup of coffee to make him extra-alert this afternoon – he usually works nights – was a good idea. He thought it was decaf. Caffeine and PHANGs – most of them – go together like bankers and cocaine. He's still coming down and twitchy.'

Zero does a double-take in the mirror as Mo opens her eyes again. 'And his girlfriend is point on this? Is that entirely wise?'

Mo swears softly. 'No it isn't, but it's our least-bad option right now. We're short-handed, and he's one of the few halfway-trained combat thaumaturges we've got, even if he *is* wet behind the ears. Anyway, he's not the only field support we've got in play tonight.' Her phone vibrates and a message bubbles up on the screen. 'Okay, that's our go signal. Showtime.'

Zero pushes the *go* button and the big V8 purrs to life. 'Death or glory. Break a leg. Your next mission—'

'Stick a cork in it and drive.'

'Yes, ma'am.' He peels out of the parking slot and turns the limousine towards the tree-shaded lane that leads towards the mansion as Mo takes a deep breath, and wonders how many unpleasant acquaintances she's going to have to smile at before the night is over.

As Schiller's car heads towards the M40 and Mo's Bentley drifts up the long gravel drive leading to Nether Stowe House, I am sitting in the back of what appears to be an airline caterer's truck while the guys from the Artists' Rifles check their weapons. Every thirty seconds or so there is a titanic growl of jet engines as a couple hundred tons of airliner throws itself along the runway and claws its way into the sky, passing directly over our heads. They're low enough to rattle the panels of the truck. This is Heathrow, one of the ten busiest airports in the world, and we're inside the perimeter fence, parked just to one side of the general aviation stand.

The boys from Hereford have finally gotten the message that I don't like guns: praise whoever you believe in, it's a huge relief not to be expected to tow one of the bloody things around and make sure I don't accidentally drill a hole in my foot. Instead, I'm strapped into a Kevlar-and-ceramic corset, otherwise known as a bulletproof vest. Along with a helmet, night vision glasses, and a spare set of fatigues, that's me kitted out. Well, it's that and a Hand of Glory (pigeon-surplus, lab produce), a heavy-duty defensive ward, a booklet of Angleton's patented door-stoppers, a brace of memorized Old Enochian couplets. Plus of course my phone and a two-inch-thick attaché case full of legal paperwork.

'Are you sure this is all in order?' I ask Chris.

She smiles at me tensely. 'It had better be: if it isn't, the judge will tear me a new one.' *She's* wearing a business suit. Her only concession is that she's in sensible shoes rather than heels, the better for stepping over broken glass and groaning bodies to serve the court order. Otherwise she looks as if she's ready for a day in court, minus the gown and wig. It's not every day I get to go on a raid team with a barrister. 'Captain, where are we at?'

Captain Partridge, predictably, is paying attention to the job at hand, namely making sure that the snake eaters have all brushed their teeth, combed their hair, and remembered to pack stun grenades rather than frag or Willie Pete. After a final mike check to confirm they're all dialed into the correct troop frequency he turns to make eye contact with Chris and myself. 'We're ready when you are,' he says mildly. 'It's coming up on 1800 hours, so the day staff will be clocking off in the next—' He raises a hand, pausing, and listens. 'Roger that.' Turning back to us, he continues – 'minute, the front door's open.' He keys his microphone: 'Driver, proceed to objective. Team Red, take point on arrival. Team Blue, follow through. Civilian staff, stay with me.'

Johnny gives the back of the captain's neck a mulish stare, but holds his tongue. He's not taken the Queen's shilling so he's a civilian for legal purposes. We shall draw a polite veil over the utterly illegal pistol he's packing in a shoulder holster. I'm sure the folder Chris gave me to carry has a suitable piece of paper to cover that, too.

The engine grumbles into life and we drive forward. 'What level of risk do you anticipate?' Chris asks.

I remember that she has some kind of military background. I'm not sure what it was, but it means she's less likely to freeze or panic than a raw newbie – like I was when I first got dragged into this, too many years ago for comfort – so I give her my unvarnished best guess. (She'll already have read the briefing.) 'Schiller's operation is a security company. One of their jobs is personal protection; another is trans-shipment of munitions. Also, he tends to employ true believers in security-critical positions. This is the UK and we're inside the terminal security cordon so we're *probably* not facing firearms, but it's a really bad idea to make assumptions. So we're prepared for the worst case – aggressive resistance by deeply unreasonable men with guns. Say, ten percent probability. In which case, get down, stay back, and leave Captain Partridge and his merry men to clean house before you call in the scene-of-crime folks to nail down the evidence.'

What I'm *hoping* for – say, with twenty percent probability – is a janitor with a jobsworth attitude. That leaves a seventy percent likelihood of something in between (for example, a deeply unreasonable janitor). I console myself that at least Mo can expect a polite welcome when she gets to make her big entrance: it's one less thing for me to angst about. Last time I went on a door-breaking run with an OCCULUS crew I ended up picking bits of sergeant out of my hair for days because I didn't anticipate armed resistance in Watford. Won't fool me twice: these are Schiller's people, I've had a run-in with him before, and if there's any sign of trouble I'll ... well, there's a reason I don't carry a gun on armed raids, it'd only slow me down.

The truck grumbles and sways as it trundles around the taxiways and service roads of Heathrow Airport. Eventually we come to a security gate leading to a fenced-off section of the cargo terminal. This is where they keep the warehouses, many of them guarded and separately fenced because they contain high-value bonded merchandise or military cargo – munitions and explosives, supplies for overseas missions, that sort of thing. Not far from here is the site of the old Brink's-Mat warehouse, where thirty years ago thieves carried out what was then the biggest robbery in British history: three tons of gold bullion, plus diamonds and cash worth a few million on top.

Cops with automatic weapons who had their sense of humor surgically excised at birth patrol the airport: you do not want to pick a fight with SO18. However, if everything is going according to timetable, then about half an hour ago they were told in no uncertain terms to go into three wise monkeys mode with respect to this particular corner of the facility. Presumably the Board burned one of our rapidly dwindling stock of one-time-only party favors, otherwise this op would be impossible, and if the Aviation Security unit turns up while we're going in there's going to be blood everywhere.

But as it happens, we drive right up to the front door and park outside without any trouble. The door opens, and there is a cry of 'Go! Go! Go!' as Partridge's gang jump out and serve their no-knock warrant – a shotgun with a breaching round into the front door lock, followed by a size twelve boot. This is not Anytown USA and our guys aren't a steroid-enraged SWAT team, so they do not follow through with flash-bangs and indiscriminate gunfire, but there is a lot of shouting and brandishing of automatic weapons as they rush the lobby.

Chris and I watch the streaming camera feed from Sergeant Harry's helmet as he grabs a look around the corner of the door. It opens into a corridor with other doors – offices, by the look of it – to either side. The walls are flimsy partitions with windows backed by venetian blinds: not exactly defensible. I'm climbing down from my seat when someone finally opens one of the doors, takes a look up the corridor, and slams the door with a muffled shriek of terror. Okay, so not a janitor, but not a suicidal gunman either. The sergeant followed by Johnny and three soldiers race into the corridor and take up defensive positions while two more apply boots to the door, which the presumed-harmless occupant vanished into. And then I'm out of the truck, Ms. Womack tagging along behind me, and we get inside.

'Police!' shouts one of the soldiers, which is not *entirely* untrue – several of them hold commissions in the Royal Military Police – 'on the floor, get down! Who's in charge here? No, stay on the floor and don't move!' There is much thundering of boots as doors are slammed open to either side until the sergeant and his backup confirm that there is nothing here but offices, and that the only person they've found is – surprise – a very confused janitor.

'I think this is my cue,' Chris comments as she steps past me and addresses the janitor: 'Ah, hello there. Are you the only person here right now, or is there someone in charge? I have a court order to serve—'

I stay in the corridor because something is not quite

right. I can tell it by the prickling in my thumbs and the whispering voices in the back of my head. The guy Chris has pounced on is harmless enough, but the crackling paper-dry dreams of the deep-dwelling tongue-eaters that have haunted me ever since Denver are close to the surface here.

'Are the records we need here?' asks Captain Partridge. 'Or are there more offices deeper inside?' He catches my expression and shrugs. 'Had to ask. Smith, McIntyre, up here: Mr. Howard, could you help Mr. McTavish check the floor—'

'Got a feeling about this, 'ave we?' asks Johnny as I approach the end of the corridor, where he's crouched beside Sergeant Harry.

I raise a finger, then close my eyes and *listen*.

Without the distraction of other senses, it's a lot clearer. Beyond the end of the corridor there's a larger space, and wards, and beyond the wards I sense the faintly discernible flavor of decomposing souls, minds half-dissolved by the parasitic hosts that have captured them. 'Contacts thataway,' I murmur, pointing off to the left of the door, then moving my hand to indicate an upper floor. 'Multiple contacts, at least three groups moving, and there's a, a spawning pool—' I can hear the narcotic crooning of the host-mother surrounded by her immature offspring, a giant underwater woodlouse from hell. It wants me to open my mouth and take it in so that it can make me complete, to bring me into communion with its god. 'Ward up, it's going to be messy.'

'So that's a yes, then,' Johnny says grimly, shouldering his monstrous assault shotgun.

My sense that things are about to go *wrong* suddenly comes into sharp focus. The sources of chittering white noise are moving, and while some are upstairs there's something below us. 'Take cover!' I shout, and stop being Bob as I open myself to the Eater of Souls. And then everything goes to hell.

'HUMMINGBIRD One confirms Schiller's party has arrived at their target,' Gary announces. 'He's out of the game for now.'

'And the guards?' Mhari leans across the desk towards him.

'Guards could be problematic,' Persephone comments from the far side of the lounge area, near the short corridor leading to the lobby. She's peeled back the carpet and underfelt and is marking out an intricate circular design about a meter in diameter on the exposed concrete with a conductive pen, connected by wires to a couple of small project boxes stacked neatly to one side. She's swapped her usual couture style for a cut-price ninja outfit: black leggings and sweater worn under a military webbing vest slung with equipment pouches. 'I'm nearly through here. Could do with a hand, Madge?'

'Don't call me that.' Mhari's voice is even and over-controlled.

Persephone flashes her a feral grin. Her eyes sparkle: she's clearly having the time of her life. 'Got your attention, didn't it? Johnny was right.'

'I will strangle that man, I swear it.' Mhari stalks over to the circle. 'What do you need?'

'A drop of your blood.' Persephone produces a sterile needle.

'You cannot be ... *eep!* Serious!'

'Can and am.' Persephone holds Mhari's finger over the

circular grid until a drop of blood splashes onto it, then passes her a pad of cotton wool and a plaster. 'My turn.' She stabs herself with a fresh needle, baptizes the grid, then flicks a switch on one of the small black boxes. 'This is really neat: it'll only let as many people come back as go down, so if we land in a nest of hornets we just climb up again and they can't follow us. It's good for about two hours.'

'Then?' Mhari stares at her as the silvery lines inked on the concrete turn black and begin to glow and warp, as if sucking the light out of the air around them. A faint chittering tickles her nerves, rising from the trapped cognitive parasites in the storage ring.

'Then the batteries run down and I have to set it up all over again. Only the next time it'll take rather more blood.'

'How much more?'

'About three PHANGs full. So let's not do that.'

Now Persephone plugs the other breadboard box into the first one, and adjusts a dial on the front. 'Underfloor space is fifty centimeters, then there's twelve of cement, then under-ceiling space of thirty, then a three-meter air gap to the next concrete level, twelve centimeters of rebar and cement, then another under-ceiling space of thirty, then we're into Schiller's suite – call it two-fifty centimeters to the carpet. I make that six eighty-five. If I set this for a drop of four-fifty that should bring us out about a third of a meter under the ceiling. Advantage of that is that it'll be too high for us to decapitate ourselves if we walk into it edge-on by accident. Disadvantage: we'll need a chain ladder. Like, oh, this one I packed earlier.' Persephone gives Mhari a grin that is every bit as sharp as a PHANG's canines. 'And it *completely* bypasses the ghosties and ghoulies roaming the floor below us.'

Mhari nods cautiously. 'Ghosties and ghoulies.'

'Technical term. Don't tell me you can't hear them? Nice doggies, those Hounds, just don't let them touch you or catch you in a rectilinear killing zone.'

'Oh yuck.' Mhari pauses. 'So it's show time like, now? I'd better change.'

'No, really?' Persephone raises an eyebrow: 'And here I thought you were planning on attending a cocktail party.'

'Bah.' Mhari stalks back towards the spare room where her kit bag is stashed. She's still dressed for the office, and after an afternoon of meetings she's not in the mood for Persephone's pre-caper ribbing, even though she knows it's the other woman's way of psyching herself up. This evening Mhari would rather be anywhere else than playing live-action Portal against a mad billionaire who might be possessed by an undead god. She changes quickly into an outfit similar to Persephone's, except for a lack of offensive weapons that she isn't trained to use anyway. 'Walk a mile in the other guy's boots indeed.' According to Mrs. MacDougal it makes for better human resources asset management, but she can't help wondering if she's the butt of an elaborate practical joke as she clips on the last of her supersecret agent outfit, pulls on her shoes, and heads back out to join Persephone.

'I started the count,' Gary volunteers, hovering. 'We're at four minutes. I'll give you a call at thirty, sixty, and ninety minutes, then at one hundred. If you're not out by one hundred and ten, I kill the grid and activate the emergency plan.'

'Correct.' Persephone frowns, focusing intently on the telescoping steel bar she's holding. The chain-link ladder with its lightweight treads loops around the bar, and she makes sure both ends rest across the full diameter of the circle and the treads are stacked in a mound in the middle of it. Above them, Persephone has set up a low metal frame that straddles the circle. Mhari notices that she's wearing heavy-duty insulated gloves, and shivers: she can feel the hunger of the things trapped in the swirling vortex of power. 'Okay, dialed in for a four-fifty drop, the ladder is six meters long, that should work fine. And go.'

Persephone presses a button on the second box and the circle of floor within the grid abruptly vanishes. The chain-link ladder unrolls with a silvery clatter until it dangles, wobbling side-to-side above a carpet. Everything Mhari can see looks perfectly mundane – except that it shimmers slightly, as if glimpsed through blue-dyed water. 'Okay, I'm going first. Headset on.' Persephone taps her headset's microphone, then grabs the frame above the portal, raises a foot, and places it on the ladder, taking care not to touch the energized circuit as she does so. Then she descends into shimmering turquoise light.

Mhari swallows as she waits. At last Persephone says, 'Clear,' in her headset; the chain-link ladder wobbles wildly as she drops free. 'Portal is about one-ninety centimeters up, ladder comes to within a meter of the carpet. Come on down, the water's lovely.'

Mhari climbs down the ladder, copying Persephone's extreme caution in avoiding the energized portal circuit. *This is* so *childish*, she thinks. *If we get busted doing this I'm going to die of embarrassment! What am I doing, playing make-believe like I'm some kind of secret agent?* The field ops specialists have always struck her as living in some sort of *Boy's Own* fantasy world, a looking-glass universe where they get away from the boredom and the office politics by playing games without frontiers. Even a six-month stint with the Home Office, wearing a glorified police uniform, working with genuine card-carrying superheroes and punching lunatics with a Lycra fetish, hasn't given her a taste for adventure – quite the opposite, in fact.

As her head passes below the level of the grid her vision blacks out. She's overtaken by a ghastly and appalling hunger, a pointed reminder of the life-altering infection she's been living with for the past year, that has forever excluded her from normal life and relationships. For a moment she begins to panic, but then she keeps climbing.

She counts her way down twenty rungs and then her vision abruptly returns. The hunger subsides: spill-over from the trapped V-parasites in the portal. She's hanging from an emergency ladder in an entrance lobby almost identical to the one upstairs, except for the color of the carpet and the darkness hovering above her in midair. She resists the urge to giggle and concentrates on finding the next rung down. Eventually her questing foot can't find anything. 'Uh. 'Seph?'

Persephone's face appears at the end of the hall. 'You've bottomed out, lower yourself by hand or jump, it's not far.' She speaks softly, relying on her headset.

'Right.' Mhari steels herself and lets go. 'I'm down.'

'Over here.' Persephone beckons. As Mhari follows her into the living room she glances back. The ladder dangles in midair in blatant violation of the laws of physics, but when seen from anywhere other than directly underneath it, the portal is almost invisible, a hair-thick slice of darkness in the air directly below the ceiling.

'Sitrep?' Gary asks in Mhari's ear, startling her.

'Sit – oh, I'm down, 'Seph's down, I think—' Mhari listens hard – 'we're alone here.'

'Confirm,' Persephone echoes. 'Raise the ladder until I call for it.'

'Raise the—' Mhari catches her eye.

'Yep. If we have a visitor, you hide, I'll take care of them. If they open the front door and see the ladder, the game's up.'

'Right.' Mhari swallows. 'Sweep the suite?'

'You go for the bedrooms and bath, I'll tackle the living room, hall, and closets.'

'On it.'

The layout of Schiller's suite is identical to the one the Laundry rented two floors up, and intimately familiar from a month-long stake-out. There are four bedrooms, the largest one with an en-suite bathroom and sitting area, all of them equipped with walk-in, mirror-fronted wardrobes along one wall. There are two secondary bathrooms and a robing area with stool and dressing table. There's a compact kitchen with fridge, microwave, and cupboards. So Mhari pulls on her blue latex gloves and gets down to searching them.

Two of the secondary bedrooms show signs of being occupied by women; closets hung with business suits, blouses, and a couple of formal gowns in carriers; chests of drawers with underwear, suitcases empty and stashed neatly in the wardrobes. Dress shoes lined up neatly two by two. Toiletries and makeup boxes in the dressing area tell their own story, as do in the wardrobes. Schiller's handmaids have clearly settled in for the long haul, but their rooms are frustratingly free of anything approximating signs of independent personality: both of them have bibles out and prominently positioned on the bedside table, but that's about it. The kitchen shows signs of a succession of takeaway meals, and there are coffee supplies and soft drinks in the fridge but, again, there is absolutely nothing that betrays any sign of personality. There are no casual clothes, no magazines or newspapers, no games or distractions or stuffed toys or jewelry or ornaments. Mhari shudders for a moment as a chilly flush washes over her. It's almost as if they come home from a day at the office, read the bible, then climb into bed and switch off like robots.

She moves swiftly on to the master bedroom. Again, it's bereft of personality. A rail of men's suits – conservative but expensively tailored, if she's any judge of quality – fill the wardrobe, along with a row of shirts and a rack of ties. The same bible, this time with a somewhat dog-eared look. Mhari picks it up, then puts it down again hastily when it stings her fingertips. *That's* unusual: PHANGs don't have any kind of reaction to religious symbols – contra popular vampire mythology – so she takes out her smartphone and calls up the OFCUT app. 'Schiller's bible is contaminated,' she tells Gary and Persephone, 'medium-high thaum count.'

'If you can bear to check it, can you tell me if it contains the Apocalypse of St. Enoch?' Persephone replies after a moment. 'Should be near the back.'

Mhari flips it open: 'Huh. Weird ... you're right, there's a lot of stuff here I don't remember from RE classes.'

'Okay, at least we've been bugging the right guy.' Persephone sounds edgy.

Mhari closes the book and continues. The en-suite bathroom contains more masculine toiletries: after shave, a razor and accoutrements, and a bag full of medication. Schiller is on a bunch of stuff. Mhari photographs all the labels, just in case they're useful to someone. 'Cialis – is that what I think it is?' she asks over the open circuit.

Gary chuckles nervously. 'Weekend get-it-up drug, you mean?'

'Schiller's on a bunch more stuff. How old is he again? Fifty-five?'

'Wouldn't surprise me.'

Persephone cuts in tonelessly: 'Focus, please.'

'Yes, mum.' Mhari puts the medications back where they were, then starts checking the luggage at the bottom of Schiller's walk-in wardrobe. 'Oh my.'

'What is it?'

'Is our man into the mortification of the flesh, or what?' Mhari blinks at the contents of the second suitcase, then pulls out her phone for some more candid snapshots. 'I see a, a ball gag, some kind of bridle, manacles ... is that a chastity belt? Kinky!' She zooms in. 'Uh. That doesn't look right ... there's blood on it.' Suddenly it's not remotely funny. 'Something's wrong here. These aren't, they're not toys. I mean, if Schiller's into consensual BDSM he's *really* hard-core.'

'Schiller's hard-core all right, but it's the no-sex-except-for-procreation kind of hard core that gets him up.' Persephone sounds distracted. 'Mhari, come into the kitchen and tell me I'm not hallucinating, please?'

'The kitchen?'

Mhari finds Persephone leaning against the full-size refrigerator with her eyes closed. 'What?' she asks.

'Check out the thing in the fridge.' She steps sideways to give the other woman access.

'Okay.' It takes Mhari a little while to take inventory. Milk, a box of Coke cans, various food products. 'The Mason jar?' She peers at it. 'What's *that*?'

The one-liter Mason jar on the shelf is full of a cloudy, turbid liquid that at first conceals her view of the contents. The thing inside looks like a pickled dead fish – about five centimeters in diameter and twenty centimeters long – but it's banded or segmented along its length, and something about it makes her skin crawl. There are no fins, but membranous attachments dangle from its lower end. She can feel something faintly, like static on a dead radio frequency, plucking at her nerves.

Then the fish squirms and turns the tip of its head towards her, lamprey mouth-parts puckering in concentric toothy rings that scrape at the glass. She squeaks and jumps backward, fangs sliding out defensively. '*Fuck!*'

'Yeah.' Persephone pushes the door shut. Her face is pale and pinched. 'My ward's holding up, but it's hot. That thing, it wants ... wants to be *inside* someone.'

Mhari can feel it now: its flesh-hunger is slowed by the chill of the fridge but not entirely dampened, the urge to squirm and thrust, to pump deeper into a warm and yielding cavity, a chewing, eating, drive to move forward ever deeper in orgasmic lust, until it swims in screaming blood and sprays eggs from every pore into the victim's abdominal cavity –

'*Gaah*. I feel sick.'

'Not here. Bathroom.' Persephone leads her out of the kitchen.

Back in the living room Mhari breathes deeply for a minute, forcing her stomach to settle. It's not fair: becoming a vampire should, she feels, have rendered her immune to feelings of queasy disgust. 'What, what *is* that thing?'

'If I had to guess, it's the new type of host that Schiller's got his hands on. Johnny said the goons he and Bob took down at the camp on Dartmoor had them – segmented wormlike body and cartilaginous teeth, with added mind control capability. You've read the GOD GAME BLACK transcript. This is like the tongue-eating isopods, only it's a hypercastrating parasitoid: one that lives inside its victim, eats the victim's gonads, and repurposes their reproductive drive to spread itself. The Sleeper has a lovely library of parasite-derived biological weapons it uses to control its victims, and evidently Schiller has been helping it refine its choice of human-specific vectors. Evidently this is one he was saving for later.'

'Uh, can we kill it with fire? Like, right now?'

'I approve of your instincts, but—' Persephone freezes – 'Incoming! Get in the master bedroom, *go hide right now*. Leave this to me.'

Because of the churning in her stomach it takes Mhari a moment to register what Persephone has just heard: that in the hall, the doorknob is turning.

Mo's arrival at Nether Stowe House goes smoothly, despite her last-minute stage fright. Part of her discomfort, she realizes, is a side effect of her single status. She has no escort: Bob can't be here – Schiller would recognize him instantly – and it would be inappropriately out of character for her to turn up with a boy-toy. Her social unease is ancient programming instilled in childhood, a Victorian sensibility that good girls don't go to parties on their own or bad things happen to them. So as Zero pulls up outside the front steps and a uniformed police officer steps forward to open the door for her, she manages to disguise her snarl of self-directed irritation as a smile. 'Good evening, ma'am. Your invitation, please?'

'Good evening.' She pumps a little more sincerity into her smile as she hands over the card and the officer stands to attention. 'At ease.' She's still on the roster as a director at the Transhuman Police Coordination Force. The officer – he's from the Diplomatic Protection Group at the Met, she sees, but in dress uniform and not carrying – doesn't have to know that she's a non-exec now, and on indefinite leave, sliding sideways into irrelevance as the Home Office digests the TPCF and replaces its original staff with their own loyalists. *Might as well see what he knows*, she thinks. 'How's everything shaping up this evening?' she asks as she climbs out of the Bentley.

'It's fine so far. The perimeter's secure, the contract staff passed their checks, and none of the VIPs have kicked off: we're here for Number Ten and Number Eleven, and once they've been and gone we can pack up and go home.'

'Good luck.' She smiles again, then turns and heads towards the open front door and the uniformed but clearly civilian greeters waiting for her.

The distinguished-looking man in the thousand-dollar haircut who is greeting everyone who enters must be Schiller himself, she decides: the photos in the briefing pack don't do him justice. He's wearing a wire with his tuxedo, and as she approaches him he rolls out a smile that displays dentistry as expensive as a Porsche: 'Dr. O'Brien, from the TPCF? I'm so pleased you could be here tonight! Wonderful to meet you, I've heard a lot about your agency. Perhaps we could talk later?'

Mo smiles and nods disingenuously, then says something politely noncommittal; of course TPCF will be on Schiller's hit list, but it's a much smaller and less important target than the Laundry, one for the mopping-up round. Another car is already drawing up outside the door and from the stance of Schiller's companions – an ice-blonde in a designer gown and a shaven-headed mook whose dinner jacket fails to conceal his assault-course muscles – it's somebody important. 'Later,' she adds, and Schiller is already turning back to the red carpet as she slides sideways around the welcoming committee. There is no reason to be resentful. She's definitely B-list in this glittering company, and very glad of it. Schiller has managed to rope in the Prime Minister, the Chancellor of the Exchequer, the Secretary of State for Defense, and half the cabinet (including the new Minister of Magic). Mere directors of supercop agencies and GovCos are small fry compared to the rock stars of national politics. For which she is deeply grateful. It makes her job much easier, which is to remain invisible until she's needed.

Mo has done enough formal events in her other role as an academic – and a couple as a diplomat – to be familiar with the drill. You swipe a glass of bubbly, mingle and smile and chat politely, identify targets of interest for later, do not grimace when your feet remind you that you don't normally wear high heels on marble floors for hours on end, and above all do *not* mistake the refreshments for hydration fluid or vitamin supplements.

The house is hopping tonight, if somewhat sedately – if you ignore the arm candy and the hospitality staff, the average age would be somewhere north of fifty – and the party has spread out through the linked rooms of the building. It's old enough that with the exception of the grand hallways the only corridors seem to be for servants; the ballroom and the drawing room and the dining room are all linked by wide doors, currently open, and there's a pavilion on the lawn where a band is playing. There's a finger buffet and standing space to one side, seats and low tables for conversation to the other, and dancing in the central ballroom – although whether the pretty young things shaking their moves are hired dancers, escorts, or the children of some of the older guests is hard to tell. Mo glances at the ceiling, past the enormous chandelier and baroque cornices, and spots a musician's gallery upstairs. As Cassie indicated, it has been turned into a discreet retreat with an overview of the dance floor.

Mo makes her way around the big public rooms, fading in to smile and chat briefly with those she wants to investigate, then stepping back gracefully and allowing them to forget her presence. She makes sure never to stand still for more than a couple of minutes, and she is on guard constantly: while her singular talent for enhanced middle-aged invisibility works perfectly face-to-face, the house is certain to be under continuous CCTV monitoring and if she slips out of character one of the supervisors might notice. This sixtyish fellow *here*, who is friendly enough if you make allowances for eyeballs that point thirty centimeters below your face, is the managing director of one of the bigger outsourcing contract agencies – Mo gives him an extra-ingratiating smile before she makes herself scarce and moves on – while the seventyish balding gentleman *there*, with a stunning Italian or Brazilian companion clinging to each of his arms like it's their life savings, owns at least sixteen regional newspapers. That man there has something to do with investment banking, a half-familiar face from the financial pages. The party is like a who's who of the new elite, the ascendant stars of the British constellation within the global capitalist firmament. Not a composer, artist, or academic among them – that's for little people – although going by the sounds emanating from the pavilion Schiller has paid a globally renowned chanteuse for the evening.

Mo moves on, quietly dictating notes. Her gaudy earrings are there to distract attention from a minor technological miracle, a bluetooth headset so small that it resembles a pair of hearing implants. The flesh-colored earplugs pick up everything she says via bone conduction, and her phone is running a background app that relays her comments to Brains in realtime and records them locally in event of loss of signal. With the gain turned up even subvocalized comments work. ' – *Sleazebag Number Three is the chief financial officer of Telereal Trillium, who handles—*'

Her chain of thought is rudely interrupted by an excited crackle in her ears: '*CHIPMUNK to CANDID! CHIPMUNK to CANDID! Whee, does this thing work?*'

Mo manages not to startle as she does a hasty scan. Nobody is watching her. '*CANDID here,*' she subvocalizes. Then she remembers to pull out her phone and hit the button for push-to-talk. '*CANDID to CHIPMUNK, you really don't need to use the silly codenames all the time, Cassie. Sitrep, please.*' She holds the phone to her head and fades back against the drawing room wall, between a concealed servants' doorway and a swag of curtain, as if deep in conversation.

'*I'm fine! There's a new woman in charge of the kitchen tonight, instead of Lisa: I like her, she's much calmer and easier to work for. Oh, I just saw Ms. Overholt go inside the private corridor under the main staircase! I caught her PIN!*'

Mo is instantly on full alert. 'What was it?' she asks aloud.

'*1-3-3-7! YesYes!*'

Someone is not as smart as they think they are, and it's not the Queen of Air and Darkness. Maybe Schiller's security think the presence of a PIN-pad lock on the door will deter intruders, or perhaps they just don't care, but using LEET as the password for a secure installation is just dumb. The nasty possibility that perhaps they want to sucker intruders inside occurs to Mo barely a second later. 'Uh-huh,' she says aloud, then, subvocalizing: '*CANDID to MADCAP, did you copy that?*'

'*Copy that,*' Brains replies.

'*Cassie, will you be noticed if you disappear for a few minutes?*'

'*Maybe, but I can tell them I had a stomach bug and*

had to rush to the little room. Ms. McGuigan will sack me, but who cares? The minibus won't be back for at least two hours!'

Mo speaks aloud: 'I am moving my lips for the benefit of the cameras, ignore me, rhubarb rhubarb bet you wish you'd hired a lip-reader ... okay, back to business. *Cassie, I need another hour here to trawl the party. Also, I bet Schiller's people will all turn out when the main guests show up. So once the PM goes in, that's when we'll make our move. Do you copy?'*

'YesYes! How do you want to do it?'

'I'll call you five minutes ahead of time. If you're with people, run your stomach bug excuse. Go into the bathroom under the stairs and await my call. I'll go in, look around, and if all's well I'll come out and give you the all-clear. If I call you or if I'm out of contact for more than ten minutes, come in and extract me. Is that clear?'

'Clear as moonlight!'

'MADCAP, relay to ZERO. CANDID out. Thanks, dear, you're a star, now go and fix yourself some rhubarb rhubarb. Bye.' Mo returns the phone to her clutch, then straightens her back, permits herself a momentary wince as she shifts weight onto her back foot, and heads towards the staircase. The night is young, the Prime Minister hasn't arrived yet, and who knows? There might still be useful intel to extract from the guests before it's time to start looking behind locked doors.

I can't *stand* fucking zombie movies.

Well okay, I'll make an honorable exception for *Shaun of the Dead*. But the point stands: zombie flicks strike too close to home – and too far as well. Ever since I did my own star turn in Brookwood Cemetery (and *don't* get me started on my perfidious ex-boss, Iris Carpenter, and her happy clappy friends-and-family Black Pharaoh cult), I've had an uncomfortably close relationship with the reanimated. We don't say *undead* because there's no such thing. Zombies are just corpses that have been activated by an Eater that wants to go walkabout and chow down on other folks' souls. Our Residual Human Resources would do just that if they weren't locked down tight by Facilities' *geas*. PHANGs are living people who have been infected by a terrible commensal symbiote or parasitoid. K syndrome victims are living people who are dying of an extradimensional parasite infection. The Eater of Souls is *sui generis* but I can confirm its host has a heartbeat and still enjoys a plate of spaghetti bolognese, and so on. The thing is, I can deal with them all, kinda-sorta. (Zombies are easy, PHANGs really *don't* get on well with UV laser pointers, and K syndrome isn't a threat, except to my emotional stability.)

But Schiller's mooks, the ones with giant isopods in place of their tongues who dream of drowning in their god's mind, give me the willies. And right now they're trying to give me lead poisoning, too.

While Captain Partridge, Johnny McTavish, and I were working this scene like it was a corporate storage unit and office inside the Heathrow fence, and while Chris Womack was serving an Anton Piller order on the janitor, a silent, many-legged alarm began sounding in the depths of the warehouse. There is a brood mother here, and while Schiller's been taking care of business at Nether Stowe House (and presumably at his apartment near Jamaica Wharf) the brood mother has been busy happily infecting the airport staff and Schiller's regular employees. It's after six o'clock on a Saturday night and most normal people would have somewhere better to be than hanging out at Heathrow, but no: the Middle Temple of the Golden Promise Ministries is holding a revival meeting, and the theme of the event seems to be that when you're speaking in tongues you can never have too many guns.

As I open up my mind's eye the world fades and I find myself standing in a gray-scale maze on an infinite plane, the walls of which are chest-high charnel racks of human bones. An invertebrate the size of a grizzly bear rears up above the piled femurs and skulls on dozens of tiny legs and clatters its chitinous mouth-parts at me. The silvery slug-trails of hundreds of half-eaten souls trail away from it in all directions, too numerous to count, like strings of drool. It's tugging on them – I register this just as a real-world someone brusquely grabs me by the scruff of my neck and yanks me down onto the floor, hard, just before the airspace previously occupied by my skull is shattered by the percussive banging of gunfire. We are indoors, so it's deafeningly loud, at least until Johnny lines up his AA-12 and starts laying down an artillery barrage, at which point it feels like I'm being punched in the eardrums by an angry woodpecker.

I sprawl backwards and try not to scream. I can feel the hosts around us, some upstairs and some in the basement, and a bunch more out front. *The basement*, I think, con-fused – something about the basement, like a flash of déjà vu to the second *Alien* movie – *oh, right*. I crunch down *hard*, and find myself sucking up the debris of what's left of Ollie Jackson, 27, single male, born again into the mind of the Sleeper by way of its loyal many-legged servant. Ollie was downstairs with an MP5 pointed at the ceiling, just like those guys in Grozny during the Russian invasion of Chechnya, getting ready to shoot upwards through the floor we're lying on. Well, not any more. His mind is a bitter and watery-thin gruel, much of his individuality already digested by the Sleeper before I ended him. I cast the net wider, feel two more above us and off to one side, and another raising his gun on the emergency stairs from the basement –

Nope, can't be having any of that.

'Can you do something about these guys?' Someone is shouting in my ear. It comes through as a thin, high-pitched buzzing.

'Working on it—' I manage, but it feels as if I'm drowning in second-hand death: the thing is, I can kill at a distance just by willing it so, but I also get to live through my victims' experience of dying, and – 'I'm not a fucking machine gun. Got one below, three upstairs. 'Nother below—'

There's another burst of gunfire from a soldier's G36, then shrieking that doesn't stop but fades into gasping for seconds at a time before it comes right back at full gut-shot volume. No more shooting, though. Someone is giving orders, boots are pounding past me. I struggle to sit up, but I still can't see anything except the host-mother's bone maze nest. 'Host-mother!' I call. 'Get the host-mother!'

'Bob? How many fingers?' It's Johnny. He sounds calm enough.

'Can't see. Inner eye.'

'Oh bollocks.' Someone grabs my right arm so hard that I gasp, then they're lifting and after a moment I flex my leg muscles. It's at this point that I realize there's a sharp pain in the middle of my sternum, as if I've been punched. 'Eh, looks like your vest caught it.'

'What. Have I been ...'

'Yeah, mate, you're gonna 'ave a lovely bruise. Also a nice little souvenir an' a story to dine out on once we're finished 'ere.'

I've been shot, I realize, *but the body armor worked. Okay, that and I'm blind.* With a massive effort of will I withdraw from the odd corner of my attention that I've been locked into, and force myself to open my physical eyes again. 'Whoo,' I gasp. 'Johnny, there's a host-mother stashed about thirty meters thataway. Mooks are guarding it and I've got a, a sense that it's concealed storage. They were setting up to pincer us from above and below. They've got guns—'

'We'd noticed,' he says drily. 'You comin'?'

'Got to: if we don't nail the mother it'll summon all its offspring, and it's rooted the Airport Police . . .'

10: A VERY
BRITISH COUP

Being a PHANG, Mhari has blindingly fast reflexes and superhuman strength, and during her time with the Transhuman Police Coordination Force she got regular workouts and practical self-defense training, thanks to the police college at Hendon. It's a habit she's kept up, because even though she doesn't have much time for super-heroics she's come to appreciate a good workout. So she's out of the kitchen door before Persephone has finished speaking; she bounces off the living room wall and spins through into the master suite, pulls the door closed behind her (cushioning it at the last instant), and skids to a stop in front of the mirrored doors of the floor-to-ceiling walk-in wardrobe.

'Fuck! Hide. Where?' Her palms are damp, and she forces herself to slow down, reaching for the rail rather than shoving the door aside by hand – it wouldn't do to leave a sweaty handprint in the middle of the polished surface. She slides it to one side and confronts a hanging wall of a male occupant's suits and shirts. Below them, suitcases. She cranes her neck back. There's a shelf, about two meters up, entirely suitable for boxes – and it's empty except for a couple of spare pillows in plastic storage bags. 'Perfect.' She reaches up, gives a tentative tug to check that it can take her weight, then pulls herself up by her fingertips, rolls smoothly onto the shelf, and slides the door shut behind her.

It's the work of a couple of seconds to squeeze behind the bagged-up pillows and excavate just enough space between them to breathe, hear – and if the door opens again, to see what's going on. Then she gets comfortable, and waits.

Doors bang and more than one pair of heavy boots thud across the lobby. There are no shouts of alarm or other signs that the arrivals have seen Persephone. But after a few seconds the sound of heavy breathing and muffled swearing filters through the barricade as someone opens the bedroom door. It sounds like they're dragging a sack of potatoes with them. 'Over ... on the bed. Carefully, don't drop her.'

The bed in Schiller's room has a memory foam mattress so there are no springs to squeak, but the muffled thud of someone depositing a heavy load reaches Mhari's sensitive ears. She waits, heart in mouth, for their next move. *Shouldn't they have searched the flat first?* she wonders. Schiller's goons are sloppy, to be so trusting of a burglar alarm. Gary blocked the suite alarm system between the control panel and the outside world using the StingRay – intercepting the high-end burglar alarm's GSM modem was about the only thing the box of tricks was good for – and once she got inside, Persephone installed a dodgy firmware upgrade on the in-room control panel. That sort of thing is above and beyond the call of duty for regular burglars, but even so, it's still poor practice for security guards to believe the story the alarm head unit is telling them.

'That's harder than it looks in the movies.' A younger voice, male. There's something odd about it, a flatness of affect.

'Put her in the recovery position while I prep her,' says the other man – older, gravelly voice – then the wardrobe door nearest Mhari's feet slides open without warning. She manages not to flinch as halogen light floods in. Her lower legs and feet aren't concealed, but she's far enough back on the upper shelf that unless he looks up, above head height, he won't spot her. And indeed gravel-voice does not look up. Instead, he pulls out one of the drawers from the storage unit adjacent to the suit rail and rummages around. A silvery clattering tells Mhari that he's after the bondage gear, and she dry-swallows, choking back rising bile. 'Yes, like that. Wrists behind her. Ankles, like so.' More clanking of fetters. 'No, not the ball gag – use the bridle instead. If you obstruct the airways while she's unconscious, she might inhale her vomit. Nausea's always a risk with Rohypnol when it wears off.'

'Are we done yet?'

'Nearly.' A clicking of metal on metal suggests a padlock to Mhari's imagination. 'That should hold her. Yes, we're done here.'

'What if she—'

A snort. 'That's between her and our Lord and Savior. She's still got time to repent. Anyway, she's a whore: if she wasn't, she wouldn't be here, would she?'

'I don't like this. Can I go?'

Another snort. 'Go on, wait in the living room. I'll finish up here. We're not supposed to leave until our Master is on his way back.' The door opens and closes. Mhari hears the older security guard walking around, a rattle as he tugs on a chain, then the light goes out and the door opens and closes again.

'Fuck,' Mhari swears very quietly, and worms her way round until she can pull her phone out. She listens intently, holding her breath, but hears only the faint whispery breathing of the drugged woman on the bed. Lying on her back she pulls up the camera app on her phone, switches off the flash, then slowly drags the wardrobe door open and snaps away. What the camera sees is what she expected, and she swears some more. A skinny blonde in an off-the-shoulder dress and stilettos lies on her side on the bed. They've pinioned her ankles and wrists behind her back, and there's some sort of gaglike contraption hugging her head, but she's out for the count.

Mhari hits the push-to-talk icon and whispers: 'Gary, got a developing problem here. 'Seph and I have gone to ground, there are guards in the living room, and they just stashed a prisoner in the master bedroom. She's incapacitated and unconscious and I *really* don't think their intentions towards her are good. What's our countdown at?'

'Checking ... you've been down fifty-nine minutes. Are these the same guys Schiller sent out before he left? Because they're supposed to clock off after their last assignment of the evening.'

'Tell *them* that,' Mhari says grimly. 'I overheard boss-man tell his assistant they can't go until they hear that Schiller's on his way home.'

'That's unfortunate.' Gary sounds rattled. 'Let me check something. Maybe Ms. Hazard can suggest a solution. I'll text you back.' He drops the call, leaving Mhari alone in the darkness, trying not to count the minutes until the portal back to safety closes.

Mo takes another seventy minutes to ghost around the perimeter of the party, kibitzing on a conversation here, exchanging a smile and pleasantry there, graceful and cour-teous and forgotten within seconds everywhere she goes. She's working the middle-aged invisibility field – carefully nursing her power, feeding it with all the skill she's learned over years as a practitioner of the eldritch arts. It's a talent she first mastered during the previous year's close encounter with a nervous breakdown. Women of a certain age tend to be overlooked, unless they go out of their way to make themselves look younger or kick up a stink. Normally it's a nuisance, but when you have the ability to amplify it to the level of a preternatural power it's even better than a cloak of invisibility. True invisibility would be a disastrous nuisance (people walk into you; photons travel right through your retinas without stopping, rendering you effectively blind), but Mo's self-effacing superpower renders her anonymous and uninteresting. Onlookers simply dismiss her and walk on by. Burglars would view her with envious regard – if their eyeballs didn't slide past her without stopping.

It's probably a good thing that she's socially invisible at this event, Mo decides as she pauses to pick up a glass of unadulterated orange juice: the risk of running into people who know her professionally would otherwise be unacceptably high. The Home Secretary isn't on the guest list – she's probably at home in her burrow, laying eggs in a paralyzed illegal immigrant or something – but Mo recognizes a deputy commissioner from the Met, the Dean of Music from one of the second-tier London University colleges, several knights and dames and sundry other members of the House of Lords, and a couple of other hangers-on and power groupies. She slinks around in the shadows, avoiding eye contact with intent. Anyone who is here at Schiller's invitation must be considered a potential recruit for the enemy, if not yet actually possessed. That excludes Cassie, with whom she exchanges a quiet smile and nod in the gallery overlooking the ballroom, then carefully avoids. Mo is the invisible woman, wryly amused – or perhaps just slightly bitter – about the way the world passes her by (although that's all to the good right now). Having confirmed that everything is in place, Mo continues to whisper her running narrative to the analysts back in the safe house. And as she does so she realizes with a sinking heart that Schiller has woven a sticky spider's web indeed.

He's not just after power brokers, ministers, and business contacts in the outsourcing and security sectors: the newspaper magnates are a clue, and as the evening rolls on a sprinkling of reality TV stars, actors, and pop celebrities arrive to leaven the mix. *Mouthpieces*, she thinks. What are the consequences when the government, the media, and the leaders of commerce all speak with one voice? Why, it means that if you hold opinions other than the ones you are told to, you are out of step, and if so, it is best to bite your tongue and be silent. The most efficient kind of censorship isn't the heavy-handed black inking of the secret policeman: it's the self-censorship we impose on ourselves when we're afraid that if we say what we think everyone around us will think us strange.

Mo looks around, and what she sees is the embryonic outline of a new national order taking shape in a salon hosted by a charming, magnetic personality who intends – somehow – to weld them into an establishment that serves his will. It wouldn't work under normal circumstances (politicians and celebrities are as easy to herd as cats: that's how the Chief Whip earns the residence on Downing Street), but these are strange days indeed, and if Schiller is the channel that brings the Sleeper's power to bear on a couple of hundred movers and shakers ...

She's making a second, more leisurely pass along the second-floor corridor when she notices a gaggle of discreet private security staff and police officers forming in the grand hallway at the bottom of the staircase. This is of interest: it's unlike anything she's seen so far. '*CANDID to MADCAP, do we have any VVIPs inbound?*'

'*Please hold – yes, we have the PM and the Chancellor's motorcade about two kilometers out. Four cars and four police outriders. Why?*'

'*I'm seeing preparations at reception. Will update on arrival. CANDID out.*' The police and security are dispersing. Most of them exit through the front door, but two take up discreet positions below her, and one armed officer turns and briskly climbs the stairs.

Mo comes to a halt near the top of the staircase, opens her clutch and palms her warrant card. The uniform has seen her – she makes no attempt to conceal herself from him – but as he sizes her up she pulls her ID. 'Security Service,' she tells him, pushing power into the card from Continuity Ops. 'Should I assume the PM is arriving?'

Suspicion dissolves instantly beneath the impact of the warrant card's *geas*, backed up by Mo's conviction that she is, in fact, supposed to be here: it's the unvarnished truth, in fact, for there's still a Mo-shaped box on MI5's org chart. 'Yes, ma'am. If I can ask you to clear the landing for a few minutes while we conduct our sweep?'

'Certainly. I'll be in the viewing gallery above the ballroom if you need me.' She turns on her heel and walks towards the balcony, having installed herself in the officer's awareness as a member of the home team. She sits at one of the tables to take the weight off her feet for a few minutes while a pair of SO6 officers discreetly check the upper floor of the house before taking up positions at the top of the stairs. They're carrying the usual – MP5s, Glock 17 sidearms, and bulletproof vests – just in case Hans Gruber decides to crash the party. Neither of them notices when Mo pushes back her chair, wraps herself in night and magic, and walks back towards the landing. She leans against the wall behind their backs, smiling at a private joke, as the front door opens and Schiller and his gowned and tuxedoed greeters move in to welcome the two high-value assets and their attendants.

The Prime Minister enters, accompanied by the Chancellor of the Exchequer – both in ordinary evening suits rather than white tie and tails, for this is an informal event – and there is hand-shaking and greeting, as Schiller introduces them to his handmaids. 'Pleased to be here tonight,' Mo overhears the PM saying, 'and very pleased to meet you at last! Norman sings your praises, I must say—' Mo's eyes narrow. It's the ice-blonde, of course, the Special Political Advisor to Norman Grove, *soi-disant* Minister for Magic: Anneka Overholt. She's all teeth and smiling eyes in the presence of Jeremy Michaels, MP for Witney and leader of Her Majesty's Government. Mo senses something preda-tory and just slightly putrid around her, an unclean aroma of old blood and decay: but perhaps it's psychosomatic? It's inconceivable that Schiller would accept personal hygiene issues among his retinue –

'– You look lovely tonight, is that a—' Mo notices that the Chancellor is clearly taking a fancy to Schiller's other handmaid, whose mane of copper-orange hair hangs in carefully curated locks that artfully suggest wildness – 'you must show me the ropes! I must say, I'm really looking forward to—'

'*CANDID to MADCAP, Schiller, companion number two, auburn, one-sixty centimeters, who is she?*'

'*That sounds like Bernadette McGuigan. GP Security, Schiller's new PA, in charge of site security at Nether Stowe House.*'

'*Roger that. The Chancellor of the Exchequer just*

offered her his arm and they're—' Mo blinks rapidly – '*update, the PM is with Overholt. Is Schiller running a dating agency or something?*' (Both men are married with children, but they're also products of the English upper classes, pedigrees back before the Norman invasion and relatives in the Lords. They're children of privilege, still in early middle age and with enough connections that only an idiot would discuss their private affairs in public.)

'*You mean like Berlusconi? Uh, your guess is as good as ours?*'

As the new arrivals drift towards the ballroom Mo clears her throat quietly and walks towards the staircase, making no attempt to hide. The cops nod her through, then forget she was ever there. Schiller and his coterie of assistants are following along in the wake of the two senior politicians and their arm candy: the road is now definitely clear. As she reaches the bottom of the stairs and glances at the discreet door with the keypad and the sign saying PRIVATE she taps her left earpiece and subvocalizes: '*CANDID to CHIPMUNK, time for your toilet trip. CANDID to ZERO, go to alert state amber. Over.*'

Then she calmly and confidently walks up to the door, punches in the combination, and lets herself inside.

I don't know what I expected to see beyond the entrance to the warehouse zone, but a cubicle farm surrounded on all sides by airline cargo containers is not it. A cubicle farm from which Schiller's minions have been shooting at us. Cubicle farms make really good mazes, even though the partitions aren't bulletproof, and if Partridge's merry men didn't have thermal imagers we'd be pulling back and looking to smoke them out with tear gas at this point – but partitions aren't terribly heatproof. Nor are the flimsy aluminum airline shipping containers. As Partridge's piratical crew race through the cubicles and confirm nobody is left to twitch a trigger finger at us, I persuade Johnny to follow me around the edge of the farm until we come to a breeze-block wall. I stop. 'Other side,' I tell him. 'About five meters thataway there's probably a fish tank full of something well and truly fucked-up. A big one – think in terms of a saltwater woodlouse the size of a sheep, surrounded by baby critters.'

'Huh. Can you kill it?'

I wince. The thing's already nibbling on the edges of my ward. I can hear its demented singsong lullaby, broadcasting calm and love and worship at me. 'I think I can do better,' I tell him. 'I just need to get close.'

I brought along Angleton's happy fun sticker book of doom. They're blocking wards, able to lock out just about anything if you can get close enough to apply one. The mother-thing is in semi-permanent communion with the Sleeper. What I'm hoping is that if I can lock it down with a blocking ward I can cut off all its children simultaneously. Friends don't let friends try to conquer the world using an army that has a single point of failure, right? I'm pretty sure Schiller's immune, and the hideous crotch-worms he uses for controlling and coordinating his Inner Temple insiders are probably not so vulnerable – the tongue-hosts were pretty clearly a version one demo program before the real pod person app release – but if I can shut down the gun-toting mooks with one shot we can get to work applying that Anton Piller order for the preservation of material evidence. And the fun begins.

Last time I ran into a brood mother it nearly got me: they're stronger and much more insidious than their tongue-eater offspring and I was falling under the influence until

Persephone nailed the fucker. But I'm a lot stronger these days and I know what I'm dealing with. It's like having the world's most annoying ear-worm on auto-repeat inside my head, a ghastly remix of 'Things Can Only Get Better' by way of 'I Kissed a Girl,' performed by Rick Astley's evil twin. So I push back, forcing the rhythmic chatter into one corner of my skull, and as Johnny slows down, mouth drooping open, I step around the corner into the loading bay. As I expected, there's a bloody great fish tank sitting on a forklift pallet. It's plugged into the electricity mains and a water hose next to a sluice, and I briefly consider the Hazard approach to cleaning out fish tanks – a gallon of concentrated bleach – but you never know: I might need the thing alive. The glass walls of the tank are scummy with algae, but not so opaque that I can't see the gigantic carapace humping up inside. It knows I'm here, and the mindless chittering rises to a crescendo. It *loves* me, it holds nothing but benevolent compassion towards me, it's inviting me to join it in the warm bath of God's goodwill –

I grit my teeth and slap a self-adhesive sticker on the nearest side of the tank, then tear off another and move around to repeat the process on each side. The tank sits on a box containing pumps and filtration kit, and it's capped by a lid, and each time I slap a ward on it the love gets fainter and the chitinous crackle of mandibles scraping glass gets more audible. Finally I stick the last ward down on the lid, and the inside of my skull falls silent. It's lovely, like the moment of stunned disbelief immediately after you finally snap and tell the world's most annoying office-mate to shut the fuck up – the moment of silence when they have no come-back and you finally had the last word. I take a shaky breath and turn as Johnny shuffles through the doorway, whey-faced. 'You did it,' he says breathlessly. 'Fuck me.'

'No thanks ... hang on a moment.' I've unconsciously fallen into a crouch under the weight of the mother-thing's loving regard. Now I straighten up and open my inner eye again. There are bodies out on the warehouse floor, and in the windowless three-story office block at the opposite side of the shed from where we entered – that's a nasty surprise, it's not on the floor plan from the airport security office – but they're comatose. 'I can't feel any hostile actors right now, though that could change in a hurry. Let's clean them all out, then begin the search.'

'Begin?' Johnny raises an eyebrow and nods at the tank. 'I'd have thought this would do for starters. Ain't there regulations banning the import of invasive species?'

'Yeah, that's a good angle to start with: Chris will know. And there's the office complex. It's not on the airport map: that's a planning infringement for sure and probably an offense under the Air Navigation Act and maybe the Terrorism Act.'

None of this is giving me the warm fuzzies, but we already knew there were a bunch of tongue-eaters in London: this is just joining up the dots for the prosecution, proving the connection to Schiller. It's a start, but it's not enough to hang him – especially with the friends he's made.

There are three levels of offices tucked away in this high-security bonded warehouse. He could be hiding literally *anything* in there, including a haystack of paperwork – and I'm worried that we might not have time to unearth the poisoned needles before he counterattacks.

The rattle of the front door keypad is what Persephone remembers most vividly afterwards. 'Get in the master bedroom, *go hide right now*. Leave this to me—'

Mhari is already gone in a living blur, thudding as she caroms off the wall opposite the kitchen door in a crazed exhibition of indoor parkour. Persephone scans quickly. The under-sink cupboard space is promisingly empty but it's too small and too low. She makes a snap decision and follows Mhari out the door, trusting that the geometry of the main living room will shield her from the entrance unless the guards enter at a run. The nearest spare bed-room door is closed but unlocked, and she smoothly spins through the doorway before it's half-open, and has it softly closed behind her just ahead of the shuffle of shoes entering the lobby.

Moving from memory in the darkened room, Persephone hunkers down behind the far side of the bed, underneath the window frame, in the gap between the mattress and the wall. Staying out is a calculated risk, but she doesn't think the guards are likely to snoop around Anneka Overholt's bedroom and it gives her two possible exits: through the doorway and past the guards, or through the window. Neither of them are terribly good prospects but she's been in worse fixes before. While she waits, she loosens her hair from its elaborate knot, removes the ebony hair clip it was held with, and re-ties it in a ponytail. The hair clip is a small, lead-weighted dumbbell, and she hopes she won't have to use it. Contrary to movie mythology people don't always recover from head injuries, and it's not her intention to kill the guards if she can avoid it.

But they're between her and the escape portal – and she can't use the front door unless she takes one of their key-cards, not with the hounds patrolling outside – and she'll just have to hope that Mhari has enough common sense to handle them if they stumble across her.

As the minutes tick by, Persephone gradually becomes

worried. She recognizes the sound of a body being dragged or carried, and hears the low voices from the master bedroom. There are no sounds of fighting, which is good, but a body complicates things. Schiller told the guards to clock off after running their errand, so she waits patiently. But it gradually becomes apparent to her that they're waiting for something.

Her phone vibrates. Mhari has sent her a photograph. It's grainy and somewhat out of focus but it raises the hackles on Persephone's neck. A few seconds later Gary texts her an update: *Mhari is in the master bedroom closet, they've passed the one-hour mark, the woman in the bedroom has been roofied and is out for the count, and what do you think we should do about it?*

Persephone closes her eyes and tries to relax, then opens her inner eye to the other place. She's an experienced ritual practitioner, and the ability to see into the soulscape comes easily to her. The guards are obvious – she's seen the host-ridden initiates of Schiller's temple before – as are Mhari (chilly, cold, not entirely human, surrounded by a swarm of buzzing hunger) and the woman on the bed (alive, unconscious, fully human). The hungry nightmares patrol the floors above and below this one, and the corridor outside the residence's door: there's no escape in that direction. She can feel Gary's unease two floors up, just as she senses the private security guards in the lobby, five floors below. Casting her perceptions further she feels the hum and blur of the vast metropolis spreading out around her in the vibrant evening twilight.

She opens her eyes again and considers her options dispassionately. A thought occurs to her and she texts Gary: *Did the StingRay grab the guards' IMSIs before they entered the flat?*

All cellphone transmissions within Schiller's flat get diverted through his tame picocell and the VPN it's feeding back to his base in Colorado. But the guards, and the call girl they kidnapped, came in through the public spaces, the elevator and the corridor outside.

Stand by, Gary replies. A couple of minutes later: *I have three new candidate IMSIs in past 25 minutes.*

Persephone is too professional to feel a flash of triumph at this point – *wait until it's in the bag* is her motto – but she nods unconsciously. *Can you identify the devices from their carrier settings?* she asks. The carrier settings are a small chunk of data that cellphone companies send to phones to tell them the best frequencies to use for that network's base stations, and they vary from phone to phone.

Phone 1 is an iPhone 5S. Phone 2 is a Galaxy S3 Mini. Phone 3 is a Galaxy S3 Mini. Why?

Persephone smiles humorlessly in the twilight. She's half-surprised that Schiller's men haven't been issued with Blackberries, but perhaps there's some sort of company-side secure messaging app ... the odd phone out is the current Apple flagship phone, a luxury item that low-rent security guards aren't likely to carry. *Please copy and send the next message to both Galaxy S3 Minis via SMS,* she instructs Gary: *Schiller returning to apartment early, your services no longer needed, you can leave now.*

She settles back to see if they'll rise to the bait.

Once upon a time – a very long time ago – there was a wine cellar carved out of the chalky rock below the foundations of Nether Stowe House.

Over the years, as wings were added to the house, collapsed through neglect or fire, and were refurbished and replaced, the wine cellar was also extended and refurbished and replaced. During the middle years of the twentieth century it was converted into a bomb shelter, and then a Home Guard bunker; then the bunker was forgotten about. In the 1970s it was rediscovered and part of it was fitted out as an on-site spa and sauna: but it fell out of use in the 1980s. Then in the late 1990s, during the most recent renovation of the house and grounds, an impish echo of a folk memory of the Hellfire Club and other eighteenth-century distractions of the rich and powerful caught the fancy of the architects. And so to the most recent renovation and reincarnation of the cellars under Nether Stowe House – this time as an underground venue for very exclusive parties.

After all, Nether Stowe House caters to any and all requirements – just as long as the customer has enough money to pay.

Mo finds herself in a low-ceilinged corridor, paneled in antique oak and well-lit. Paintings of seventeenth- and eighteenth-century aristocrats line the walls in lieu of windows, punctuating the gaps between doors. The doors are labeled: some mundane (CLOAKROOM), others less so (BONDED STORE). Near the end of the passage, a staircase leads down into the cellars. Mo descends carefully, acutely aware that she's moving beyond the bounds of the easily explained. *I got lost* will only carry you so far when you go wandering around the private spaces at this kind of venue. Also, she realizes, she's underground. If she needs backup and her phone loses signal, this could be a problem.

She is on edge as she reaches the bottom of the stairs, so she startles as an usher clears his throat. 'Ma'am, the chapel is nearly ready for communion, but it will be another five minutes. Would you mind waiting in the club lounge?'

She smiles instinctively as she assesses him. He's another of Schiller's security guards, but he wears a surplice over his dark suit, an unadorned silver cross dangling from his collar. His eyes track her incuriously. 'Certainly, if you'd show me where it is,' she replies. 'Which service is it to be, first?'

'The Communion of the Inner Temple,' he states. 'The lounge is that way.' His movements are slightly off, as if an unseen puppeteer is pulling his strings. Mo nods and follows his direction, trying not to shudder. She's read the GOD GAME BLACK report and knows about Schiller's parasites packaged as communion wafers. *But isn't the Inner Temple something different?* She strolls along another low-ceilinged corridor, towards a lounge furnished in oak and red leather with brass fixtures, all wingback chairs and gentlemen's club ambiance.

She's not the only partygoer here; *there must be another staircase*, she realizes. But this is a different crowd, older and expectant. The media stars and party people and escorts Schiller had invited for the event upstairs are absent: this is a more select gathering, although the bar is open and a bartender is offering wine by the glass to all comers. Mo accepts one, then does her best to fade into the wallpaper between prints of a Stubbs racehorse painting and an aristocrat who wears an identical expression to the steed.

'*Cassie, where are you?*' she subvocalizes tensely. Opening her clutch she sneaks a quick glance at her phone. It's showing one bar of signal, a tenuous connection at best. '*Sitrep.*'

'Here I am!' The breathy voice next to her, in her ear, nearly makes her jump. 'Am I late-late?'

Mo gives Cassie a hard stare. 'Not yet.' She's still recognizable, but the *alfär* woman's glamour has lent her waitress uniform the semblance of a black cocktail dress. She's done something to her hair and added face paint, too, or more enchantment so that she looks older, elegant, and less out of place than she might otherwise be. 'Whatever they're doing, they're going to start soon—'

Very soon, as it happens. Mo hears jovial laughter and bonhomie as a new party approaches by way of the corridor she used. Eyes turn, conversations temporarily dampened, for the arrival of Jeremy Michaels, arm-in-arm with the Minister of Magic and the Chancellor of the Exchequer. All three of the ex-public-school types are somewhat tipsy; the outer two are trailing bottles of Bolly. 'Party on, ladies and gentlemen!' The Prime Minister is avuncular, his smile magnanimous. The small talk starts up again on all sides, but there's an edgy note of pleased anticipation to it, and Mo feels her ward heat up, prickling the skin of her chest like a nettle rash. All of a sudden the lounge feels sultry and small, the background noise pulsing with turgid expectation.

'Oh this is not good.' Cassie clutches her left arm. 'FuckFuck!'

'Yes,' Mo says tightly. Despite her ward she feels a tight heat growing in the pit of her belly. She clenches her thighs together instinctively, unsure whether she's resisting or complying. Around the room, middle-aged men are shedding their jackets and loosening their bow ties. And now a peculiar pilgrimage emerges from the staircase: gorgeously muscled and toned young men and shapely women wearing not very much at all, most of it underwear of a kind normally reserved for bedroom games. Overholt and McGuigan, Schiller's handmaids, enter the lounge from the side-passage that Schiller's usher was guarding. They're wearing sheer white gowns, their movements languid and hesitant, as if they're sleepwalking. Four more women follow them, all statuesque Valkyries: they converge on the ministers of state, take them by the hand and offer them dreamy smiles and air-kisses as they lead them towards the chapel.

Mo taps her left earpiece. '*MADCAP, get Alex down here right now. OCCULUS, go go go. ZERO, red alert, extraction imminent.*'

Cassie's grip on her arm tightens painfully. 'What are they *doing*?' she asks shakily. 'There's something in there, something horrible—'

The alpha males are whooping it up, stripping off their clothing and grappling with the Middle Temple communicants Schiller has brought in to service them. They don't seem to notice that none of the youngsters are speaking or smiling as they press breasts and crotches up against the VIP guests.

Mo feels the strength of a host-mother's will beating down like tropical sunlight, a glowing benign lust that floods every body and moistens the driest soul. 'Schiller's end-game,' she says quietly. 'He's going to plant those parasite things in everyone here. Cassie, we need to leave *now*.'

But Cassie is staring at the passage to the chapel. 'YesYes, but there's something *different*—'

'Different?' Mo stares at her. 'Didn't you hear me?'

Cassie's eyes blur momentarily as her glamour slips; for a moment her pupils seem to stretch vertically, becoming catlike. 'I – I've heard of this,' she says, and Mo realizes her younger companion is shaking: 'Don't you see?' Abruptly she releases Mo's arm and darts towards the chapel.

'Cassie!' Mo hurries after her. The rich chords of organ music swell from the open door ahead, liturgical and naggingly familiar. The usher stands before the doorway and moves to intercept Cassie, but she reaches out to touch him lightly and he crumples to the floor. Mo swears, then runs after her on throbbing feet. But she doesn't have far to go, for Cassie stops just outside the chapel.

'Look,' says Cassie. She points, her eyes and mouth wide.

Mo presumes the chapel was added by the current owners of Nether Stowe House in order to make it easier to host private VIP wedding ceremonies. But this evening it's being put to a use that the owners are hardly likely to approve of. The altar is the central prop in a communion service the like of which Mo has never imagined. Behind it stands the Reverend Raymond Schiller, surrounded by his handmaids; before the altar forms a queue of semi-naked politicians. The air is rich and heavy with the fumes of an incense that throbs with lust and the sickly sweet floral scent of opium. Two of the handmaids swing thuribles as they chant prayers in a language that Mo recognizes as a dialect of Old Enochian, invocations and invitations to a God who was already ancient and feared before the rise of Egypt. As each of the communicants approaches, Schiller utters a brief prayer and seats the communicant on the altar, then directs one of the handmaids forward to meet him: they strip off their robes as they mount the new initiate, bucking and moaning beneath their open thighs.

Mo tries to look away, but there is an erotic compulsion here that has her itching to throw caution to the wind and join in the bacchanalia. But then Cassie – whose expression is one of wide-eyed horror rather than heavy-lidded lust – pinches her arm. 'Look at the altar!' A dark fluid stains the front of the tablecloth, darker than wine and dripping from beneath the lovers locked in communion. The moaning takes on a keening note as the current handmaid kneels over her victim and pulls herself away from him. His penis pulses, fat and segmented and maggot-white as he continues to keen and the blood drips from between his thighs. The other handmaids come and carry him down to the pews before the altar, legs twitching in the grip of what might be a protracted orgasm, or the clonic spasms of a hanged man. Meanwhile the handmaid who initiated him kneels, gasping, beside the altar, her face purple, blood trickling down her thighs.

'Let's go, *now*,' Mo whispers, the spell slipping away in a cold wash of terror as she focuses on the Minister for Magic's newly installed host, its cyclostomic mouth squeezing rhythmically as it draws his penis fully into its digestive tract and begins to suck blood from the dorsal vein.

'YesYes!' Cassie turns away from the open doorway and Mo leads her aside gratefully. The occupants of the chapel are so focused on their ritual that they appear not to have noticed their audience. Mo takes a grip on Cassie's arm and pulls her shroud of invisibility tight around them both, then leads her back towards the lounge area on shaky legs. 'It's them,' Cassie whispers, horrified: 'the monsters that hunted my people. They must have followed my father hither—'

'No,' Mo reassures her, 'they were already on their way. But we—'

She stops dead. While they spied on the occupants of the chapel, the guests remaining in the lounge have relaxed into orgiastic excess, sucking and kissing and squeezing and in some cases enthusiastically fucking. The sweet, floral scent of the incense is chokingly thick in the lounge. The air is heavy with sighs and moans and happy chuckles at first – but as Mo and Cassie reach the threshold of the room, a sudden silence descends as all around them the youthful initiates of Schiller's Middle Temple collapse in stuporous piles. Someone has cut the master puppeteer's strings, and as Mo watches the guests raise their heads and start to look around, seeking the source of disruption.

From behind the altar in the chapel, the being calling itself Raymond Schiller – for there is increasingly less of Schiller and more of the Other inside him, with every new Inner Temple communion rite – makes eye contact across the room with Jeremy Michaels, who is watching the initiation of his cabinet peers from the sidelines. 'The mother of the Middle Temple has been cut off,' he rasps, the human tongue no longer coming easily to his mouth and throat. 'Something is *wrong*. Fix it.'

The Prime Minister stands and marches stiff-legged towards the exit, led by the will of his recently grafted New Flesh. If he is slightly glassy-eyed, the party-goers upstairs will merely think he's been hitting the Bolly. As he walks, he smiles experimentally, then runs through a series of facial expressions before settling back to his usual assumed superiority.

Meanwhile, Schiller addresses his handmaids: 'Gina, activate the perimeter ward, the Middle Temple appears to be under attack and we may be next. Anneka, do we have intruders here, too? Find them!' Anneka Overholt nods; eyes glowing pale green, she stalks towards the downstairs lounge, mouth silently forming words in an ancient tongue. A handful of new initiates stumble after her. Behind the altar, Bernadette McGuigan pulls out her mobile phone to contact the site security office.

At the top of the stairs, Michaels finds two police officers standing guard. 'There's been some sort of incident,' he tells them in clipped tones, then holds up a hand: 'No, no, not *here* – there's been a break-in at Dr. Schiller's business premises at Heathrow. Armed robbers. Would you send someone to deal with it? Our host is quite annoyed.'

By the time he is halfway down the staircase back to the chapel, one of the officers is already reporting to the inspector in charge of the PM's security detachment; by the time he resumes his seat at the ceremony, the inspector is briefing the desk officer in the airport station at West Drayton.

And the jaws of a trap begin to close.

I'm standing in an office full of computers and filing cabinets, swearing under my breath as I try to figure out where to start, when my phone vibrates. *Not now*, I think. Chris has holed up in the supervisor's office in the corner and is working the phone to the Transport Police, and a bunch of corporate crime folks from the National Crime Agency are apparently on their way in the next hour, but I'm increasingly worried that we've blown it. Knocking out Schiller's host-mother will have blown all of his communicants' little minds, and he's bound to notice and come running. So why *isn't* he running, come to think of it? It's been over five minutes since I locked down the fish tank and the remaining warm bodies among the defenders – the ones the OCCULUS crew put on the floor in warded restraints, instead of shooting – all went sleepy-bye at once. It's a real mess out there: six dead bodies, two injured and unconscious, four more unconscious. In fact, we're about three live victims short of lighting up the local hospital's major incident plan, and if this doesn't make headlines tomorrow I will be very much surprised. So who –

Oh, it's the SA. Of course. So I answer the bloody phone.

'Sir?'

'You need to pull out, Bob,' he says, with no warmup, no preamble, no social nattering. 'Let Chris hand over to the NCA when they arrive, deal with the fish tank, then get Johnny and the OCCULUS crew out of there. We've got a developing situation.'

I resist the urge to swear. 'Change of plan, why, exactly?'

'I want you to get up to Nether Stowe House to support the Target One team ASAP. Schiller's making an end-run and the evidence from Target Two is frankly irrelevant at this point – nothing short of a bloodstained altar and a pile of bodies would do. The take from Target One is deeply alarming and we've run into problems – Cassie and Dr. O'Brien appear to have sprung a trap and are boxed in. They need a distraction and the special backup I arranged for is late.'

Shit! Here I am at the far end of the M25. 'I'm at least an hour away by road, with blues and twos.'

'Not if you hit on the ASU. I've put in a request and India 97 is enroute to Heathrow to ferry you out there. They should be landing in about ten minutes. Get moving.'

I don't waste time arguing. If Mo is in danger it's not just a screaming emergency, it's personal. And these days she doesn't carry a white violin. I know she's an Auditor and anything but helpless, and she's got the All-Highest of the Host of Air and Darkness with her, but they're up against the Sleeper's living avatar. This is what I've been afraid of all along, and I get a weird shivery feeling in my stomach that it takes me a little while to recognize as gut-wrenching fear.

I stride briskly back towards the cubicle farm and nearly walk into Johnny coming the other way. 'What's eating you, guv?' he asks, raising an eyebrow; he looks pleased with himself about something.

'I'm needed at Nether Stowe House an hour ago. The SA's sending a chopper.'

'Oh right.' Suddenly his expression is as sober as a heart attack. 'Yer other 'alf ran into trouble?'

'So I gather.' I start moving again, and as soon as we

reach the cubicle farm I fill Chris Womack in on the situation. 'So Johnny and I need to be on the other side of the airport in ten minutes—'

There is a thunderous *bang* from the front door and as I try and munch carpet tiles Johnny tackles Chris. 'What—' she tries to speak, but my ears are ringing and I can barely hear anything. Boots rush past the cubicle from behind us, with much shouting – the OCCULUS team responding to a perimeter breach – and there's a brief crackle of automatic gunfire, still painfully loud through the building wall and the cubicles. I close my eyes and *look* around, outside at the mindscape around the warehouse and the terminal building and the bright, shining hard-focused minds with their wards and their guns –

'Fuck, it's the Police!' I yell.

'On it,' Johnny says tensely, and he's away.

Fuck, this is the *very worst* outcome, or close enough: there are cars outside and men and women with guns converging on the building and up against the walls outside the loading bay, a dozen of them already and more coming and that's an airport fire tender bulling the OCCULUS truck away from the entrance –

Mo is in trouble. I could end this and be on my way –

I force the panic back down but it keeps bubbling up. It shouldn't be anything new but just because she's been in danger before and I haven't been there doesn't make it any easier: this one's different because *the SA told me to go* and I can't, not unless I –

There are fourteen of them outside and they're in my way and all I have to do is grab their minds and *squeeze* and their crappy little wards will fracture like glass –

Another gunshot. Shouts: 'Disengage! Stand down! Stand down!'

I'm shaking. I swear I'm shaking, lying here on the carpet feeling the warm, soft, crunchy things all around the building, flickering lights against the infinite darkness of un-life, and it would be so easy to kill them all, the constellations in the neighboring warehouses and the distant galaxy of Terminals 1–3 and beyond them the M25 motorway: and I could extinguish them for her, I *would* extinguish them all in a heartbeat and go flying to her rescue if I couldn't already see the look on her face when she learned what I'd done –

(Does this make me a monster?)

Seconds that feel like minutes slide into minutes that feel like hours as I lie there shivering, not trusting myself to move a millimeter or twitch a finger, silently weeping with the strain of holding back the infinite hunger. I distantly realize that I'm overloaded, irrational, and suddenly unable to cope. The breakdown on Mo's shoulder in the safe house was a warning temblor, not the earthquake itself: I don't trust myself not to kill thousands of people by accident and I'm paralyzed with fear of what I have the potential to become, if I haven't become that thing already.

Hasty footsteps. 'Bob? Can you hear me?' It's Johnny.

Someone else, voice full of concern: 'Oh fuck, did he catch a bullet—'

'– No, something worse, seen 'im get it bad but never like this before—'

I push back at the voices in my head and try to block out the hungry awareness and force myself up until I'm kneeling and braced against the floor on my palms. My head is spinning. I want to throw up.

'Bob—' It's Johnny, kneeling beside me – 'it's going to be all right.' His voice low-pitched but urgent. 'Someone set the airport police on us but the skipper's on it—' He means Captain Partridge – 'telling 'em it's an unscheduled exercise, crossed wires – standin' off while they confirm, then we're gonna get you out of here—'

'Get me to. Nether Stowe House,' I grate, and Johnny and whoever else is there with him recoil from whatever they hear in my voice. Flying will be good: flying will get me up above and away from all the souls laid out so invitingly like a giant buffet in all directions.

'What's wrong with—' a hushed voice asks Johnny.

'Not sure, mate, but I think 'e's leveled up from tactical to strategic and 'e needs 'is personal Auditor bad only she ain't 'ere—'

'– But his *eyes*—'

I concentrate on my deep breathing and the whole mindfulness shtick and on trying not to casually squeeze the contents of a taxiing aluminum tube of intercontinental goodness into my imaginary mouth – *it's a Boeing 777 or Airbus 330 and it's nearly two miles away*, a distantly rational part of me realizes –

'Get me out of here,' I tell Johnny, working hard to make my voice as normal as possible, and then I push myself up and stand. Cubicle farm, office, a worried-looking warrant officer in airport firefighter drag (spoiled slightly by the MP5 with Basilisk sights he's carrying): he takes a step back behind Johnny, but Johnny is made of stern stuff and stares me down calmly enough. Johnny's mind ... if I let my inner demon off the leash I think it might actually break a tooth on Johnny. 'I'm not safe, and the SA wants me at, at Target One.'

'Right.' Johnny's eyes narrow. ''Scuse me for saying this, mate, but you're in no condition to go anywhere right now.'

'But she *needs* me—' Anxiety rises and surges over my defenses: I feel the pinprick popping of defensive wards deflagrating all around, unprotected minds wriggling like so many shell-shucked tasty oysters as their bodies fall, retching, to the ground for a hundred meters in all directions –

'– Don't.' Johnny raises a warning hand as the soldier behind him keels over in a dead faint. '*By right of oath I bind you*—' Verses in Old Enochian salted with English code-words roll out, and the thing in the back of my head listens incuriously – '*Ruby. Seminole. Kriegspiel. Hatchet.* Lock down and make safe—' In the background I hear a hollow bang, very different from an explosion, and the crunch and crackle of a vehicle impacting a building, its driver uncon-scious. The part of me that's still me, still Bob, feels a stab of guilty remorse, but the part of me that's the Eater of Souls doesn't give a shit, being more irritated (if anything) by Johnny's use of my oath's override facility. ' – Abstain from feeding, feel no hunger—' The great hollow anti-pressure inside me recedes slightly – 'be calm, all is in hand.'

My eyes close. Johnny recites the override words again. 'Bob. Can you hear me?'

'Yeah.' I feel tired. Desperately tired. So tired I could sleep for a thousand years.

'Bob, open yer eyes. Come on, wake up! We need you.'

I open my eyes. On the floor behind him, a soldier lies as if asleep except for a trickle of blood running from his left nostril. 'Oh shit, did I—'

Johnny bends over him: ''E's breathing but 'e's out for the count.' He rolls the body over into the recovery position, then stands up. 'Come on, we've got a chopper to catch.'

'But I can't—'

All of a sudden Johnny McTavish is up close, right in my face, doing his best drill sergeant act, and as he used to be a sergeant in the French Foreign Legion it's not exactly an act: 'Howard you miserable worm, get your fucking shit together *right now* and *move it*! Because the next time I

hear you say *can't* I will take your *can't* and shove it so far
up your ass you can give yourself a tonsillectomy by biting.
Is that understood? *Do you fucking hear me?*' With every
fuck he shoves me so that I'm constantly off-balance and
then he's behind me and grabbing my shoulders and aiming
me at the doorway. 'We have a fucking helicopter to catch
and if you want to see yer trouble and strife again you will
quick march double-time—'

We're going, my rational brain realizes. We're going to
Nether Stowe House. We're really *going*. The paralysis and
terror falls away behind me, replaced by uncertainty.

I'm not sure what we're going to find when we get there,
but it can't be anything good.

Mhari lies on the shelf in the walk-in wardrobe, count-
ing the minutes. After rather too many of them pass for
comfort, her phone vibrates again. It's a message from
Persephone: *I'm trying to dislodge the fleas. Hold on.*

Dammit, what now? she asks herself, gritting her teeth.
She waits a while longer, then she hears the muffled, vaguely
familiar chimes of unsilenced phones receiving incoming
messages in the living room. There are voices, low and hard
to interpret – then the bedroom door opens abruptly. She
cowers back inside the closet as the bedroom light comes
on. 'She's still out,' says the older guard.

'Look, we can go now,' the youngster says from outside
the door, 'can't we?'

'Huh. I suppose so. You got it, too.'

''S'what I said.'

'Well, then.' The guard pauses in the doorway for a few
seconds, then switches out the light. 'Nighty-night, and
may the Lord have mercy on your soul.'

The door closes and Mhari relaxes infinitesimally. *That was too close*, she thinks shakily. For a while she'd considered jumping down and looking for somewhere more comfortable to hang out. But still she waits: and after another minute she hears footsteps, and then the beeping of the neutered burglar alarm followed by the rattle of the front door closing.

'All clear,' Persephone calls quietly through the bedroom door.

'Don't turn the light—' Mhari jumps down ' – on. Okay, you can do it now.' Persephone flicks the switch, and Mhari sees her expression: the older woman looks as if she's swallowed a live mouse. 'What is it?' She follows Persephone's gaze, and turns to look at the bed. 'Oh. Fuck.'

The beeping from the suite's burglar alarm stops as the alarm hits the point in its cycle where it would normally arm itself but, thanks to Persephone's firmware crack, lapses into catatonia. 'You can say that again,' Persephone says grimly.

'What do we do now?'

'We get the civilian out—' Persephone stops and takes a deep breath. 'What a mess.' She takes another breath. 'I think I saw her handbag on the living room table. Go see if she's got a phone or any ID in it while I look for the keys to this crap.'

Mhari does as she's told without arguing because Persephone's expression frightens her. Society ladies aren't supposed to do homicidal rage in public. 'Seph is doing a good job of bottling it up, betraying it only through a certain tightness about the mouth and her unusually clipped diction, but Mhari can tell she's boiling. Truth be told, Mhari's pretty upset, too. She'd read the report and knew what Schiller's Church did in their compound in Colorado to runaway teens who wouldn't be missed, but there's a difference between reading the dry facts and interrupting a kidnapping in progress. There is indeed a handbag in the living room that hadn't been there earlier: a Louis Vuitton, *not* counterfeit if Mhari is any judge, and the contents tell their own story. In addition to makeup and tissues there's a purse containing the driving license and credit cards of an Angela McCarthy, MSc. She also carries university ID and a couple of library cards in the same name – also condoms, lube, iPhone, and a slim business card wallet. The cards carry just her name, a Gmail address, and usernames on Tinder and Ashley Madison. So, a postgrad student who's hard up for cash, moonlighting in an older profession. London is a horrifyingly expensive city to study in: most students need to work, and a surprising number of the prettier ones try sex work.

Mhari takes the bag through into the bedroom. Persephone has found a bunch of keys in the drawer full of restraints, and as Mhari enters 'Seph manages to unlock the leg irons. Angela is still unconscious, her shallow breathy inhalations telling their own story. 'We've got to get her out,' Mhari says. 'Shall I call an ambulance?'

Persephone pauses. 'If we do that, we blow the mission. Traceless infiltration, remember? And the portal's only good for two bodies.'

'Can we get her up to the safe house in the lift or fire stairs, then? I think I can carry her—'

'Under the eyes of whoever's monitoring the cameras in the corridor? I don't think so. Anyway, we don't have a card key for the lift and taking the fire escape would be a *really* bad idea – too many right angles, and the hounds are out upstairs. The only way is the lift, and for that we'd need to get a card.' The collar padlock releases with a metallic click and Persephone gently pulls it away from Angela's neck. 'How do you feel about extemporizing?'

'About—' Mhari looks at Persephone and sees the older woman watching her, poker-faced. 'What. You're thinking of extracting her through the portal and leaving one of us here? To do what?'

'Schiller's expecting to find a drugged-up helpless woman on his bed, waiting for him to apply the, the thing in the fridge, or something like it.' Persephone's eyes are burning. 'Those guards – we can grab the recording of them bringing her in, we captured them discussing leaving her, we're miked up, there's the thing in the fridge – we've got the evidence we came for. This is what we need to nail him, once we've cleaned house. Assuming he gets away from Nether Stowe of course.'

'– Right, but if he isn't alone—'

'– I've got a booster to install for Gary's optical bug, and some transmitters like the ones Cassie was passing around at last month's party. We put in a call for the OCCULUS crew at Site One as soon as they've wrapped up there. They can get here before Schiller. So, there'll be backup—' Persephone slows. 'Shit.'

'What?' Mhari raises an eyebrow at her expression of frustration. 'Are you going to unlock that gag-thing or am I?'

'Oh, sorry.' Persephone goes back to testing padlock keys. 'I wanted it to be me,' she explains. 'I've got unfinished business with the preacher-man. But he'll probably remember me from last time we met, and anyway, I'm not blonde.' She finds the right key and unlocks the bridle and bit. Angela's breathing evens out, then speeds up slightly.

Mhari clears her throat. 'Am I not blonde?' she asks rhetorically.

Persephone looks at her dubiously. 'Yes, and you're absolutely fabulous, sweetie, you're exactly Schiller's type, but you're not trained for Field Ops, you're a Human Resources manager—'

Mhari hisses and extends her canines – 'And you know what they say about HR, don't you? Let me do it, 'Seph, you get her out of here and I'll be your bait. If Schiller tries to fuck with me he'll regret it, that I can promise you. We've still got twenty minutes to set it up – you can patch the OCCULUS team into my headset when they arrive and I'll take it—'

'Set *what* up?' croaks Angela. She clears her throat. 'Who, who *are* you people? Ow. My head. Where—'

Persephone nods at Mhari: 'Let's do it.' She turns her attention to the other woman. 'Uh, Ms. McCarthy? I'm afraid you've been roofied and abducted. We're from the security services and we're here to arrest the bastard who did it.' She looks past Angela, who is making an uncoordinated effort to sit up, and shakes her head silently at Mhari, who is mouthing words at her vehemently: *cardiac arrest.* 'Can you move? We need to get you out of here. Mhari, I'm going to update the SA on what we're doing here. You should go and check the wardrobe in the other rooms, see if you can find something more suitable—' McGuigan's little black dress is a far cry from Mhari's webbing vest and combat pants – 'otherwise he might suspect something. Angela, can you stand? I need you to stand up, if you can, so we can get out of here—'

Mhari hurries next door to rifle Overholt's wardrobe for a disguise. The clock is ticking, the game's afoot: and she surprises herself at how *hungry* she is for Persephone's improvised plan to succeed.

11: NIGHT AND MAGIC

'Don't let go,' Mo tells Cassie; 'whatever you do, *don't let go* of my arm.'

'ButBut—' Cassie is so tense she's vibrating. All around the lounge angry and concerned voices are rising. Bodies sprawl and glasses roll and smash on the floor as hands slacken in release.

'They can't see us,' Mo tells her, although it's a prayer as much as it's an assertion of truth. 'No, really. We need to go back up the stairs, Zero is on his way with the car, if anyone tries to stop us leaving Alex will cover—'

The rising shrieks of damned souls resound from the open doors of the chapel. Mo tries to turn, but Cassie is rooted to the spot. 'Come *on*.'

'*Feeders*,' Cassie says in a dialect of Enochian that Mo can just about make out. Looking at the middle-aged movers and shakers as they struggle to extricate from beneath the insensate bodies of their host-ridden seducers, Mo sees immediately that she's right: the abortive ritual has opened the way for an infestation. Heads turn, directing a luminous green gaze on their surroundings: hands rise before faces for the curious inspection of the newly incarnate.

'Okay, we are leaving *right now*,' Mo says firmly. She grabs Cassie's wrist with her free hand and turns, forcing her to move. 'Quick march, work that catwalk, whatever gets you moving—' Something has clearly gone very wrong indeed with Schiller's project. The tongue-eaten communicants have collapsed and Schiller's ritual has been damaged. That invocation has in turn attracted an invasion of feeders, whose nibbling at the walls of the universe has been repaid with sudden success and a breakthrough to the rich buffet pickings in the lounge. 'Come on!'

Cassie breaks into a trot and nearly leaves Mo behind – her feet are sore from the unaccustomed strappy heels, while Cassie, as catering staff, gets to wear sensible shoes – but Mo leans on her and manages to keep up. With her free hand she taps her earpiece. 'Zero, extraction now! Alex, front gate, cover us! Backup, I need backup—'

Behind them the naked dead are rising, struggling to control their unaccustomed bipedal locomotion and to navigate their peers. The feeder-possessed are little better than zombies until they learn control, but once they're fully integrated they can run – and their touch is lethal: the feeders can transfer by skin-to-skin contact. And Mo is coldly certain that her ability to go unnoticed only works on conscious, self-aware beings: the effect happens in the observer's mind, not their eyes. As Cassie rushes towards the stairs Mo recalls the usher. 'Stop,' she commands, holding the younger woman back. 'There'll be guards—'

'FuckFuck.' Cassie stops dead and Mo barely manages to stop in time. 'Can't go there.'

'– There's got to be a fire exit,' Mo tells herself. 'Where . . . of course, it'll be at the opposite end of the lounge. Past the toilets.' She glances round, taking stock.

They're in the wide corridor leading to the staircase, cloakroom, and the side-passage to the chapel. The screams of despair and agony from the communion ceremony beyond the chapel door tell their own tale: the other parasites, the hosts of the Inner Temple – segmented worms, suckling off the rich gonadal blood supply as they control the minds of their mounts – writhe directionlessly, as if cut off from whatever ghastly fount of will directed them. 'Where—'

Cassie grips her arm. 'The toilets are beyond the lounge, along another corridor.' She points back the way they've come, through the lounge and the orgiastic feasting feeders and the screaming, panicking guests. Cassie's features sharpen as her glamour falls away: she's gathering her *mana*, and Mo feels a spasm of relief at the quivering, barely restrained power she feels through the *alfär*'s wrist. 'We must choose: we can go through the feeders, or past the worms, but—'

Mo instinctively raises her free hand to the glittering borrowed necklace she wears. 'This ward's good for about three minutes. Can you handle the feeders?'

Cassie bares her teeth in an expression that is very unlike a smile: 'Watch me.'

'Good.' Mo's necklace is one of Persephone's specials: a tiny thread of pearls dangles from the central diadem, and she tugs it viciously until it comes free. She remembers something Bob once said, jokingly, as he lit off a Hand of Glory: *Once you pull out the pin, Mr. Hand Grenade stops being your friend*. 'Let's go,' she says as the concealed high-end ward lights off, making her teeth buzz with a taste of electricity and regrets.

Cassie lets go of her wrist and doubles back towards the lounge. The wall sconces and spots have gone out, replaced by dim emergency lights, and the first couple of feeders are staggering towards the corridor, still getting used to controlling their fleshbodies. As Cassie approaches they look up, green-glowing eyes casting hollow shadows across their cheekbones: a B-list pop starlet and a posh boy in a half-unbuttoned dress shirt, bow tie dangling. There's nothing human about their expressions, just a shared feral hunger. They lurch towards her, and Mo, still invisible, murmurs the macro to release one of the canned exorcisms stored in her bracelets. The pop starlet drops like a puppet with severed strings; the boy's body collapses across her. Cassie glances round. '*Waste not thy ammunition,*' she says, in the horribly accented dialect of Old Enochian that is the *alfär* High Tongue.

'But you—' Mo scans swiftly: they're still in the corridor and Cassie is concealed from most of the lounge by one wall— 'I'm warded, you're not.'

'Oh, but I *am*.' In the gloom, Cassie's smile is terrifying. 'My magi can feed my will from a distance, you know.'

Mo bites her tongue. The *alfär* magi are castrated PHANGs, bound to service, and the power they can deploy or funnel to Cassie is fueled by blood and lives. '*Damn.*' She supposes she's wasted an exorcism macro. But this is not the time for cost-value calculations; swallowing her gorge, Mo shelves the matter for later. 'Let's go,' she says tensely, 'clock's ticking.'

Cassie slithers along the wall like a human shadow, renewing some of her glamour to mimic Mo's invisibility. She glides, feet not leaving the ground, and sways to avoid a stumbling body in the dark. Mo follows close behind, a trigger word ready on her tongue. There's a sharp scream, suddenly cut off, from across the room as one of the few still-living humans succumbs to a feeder.

They're halfway across the room when Mo hears a crash from behind. She looks round and sees a side-door banging open across the lounge: an emergency exit from the vestry room attached to the chapel. 'Shit,' she mutters, then looks back just as Cassie comes face to face with another feeder. It begins to reach for her, and Mo's heart hammers madly for a moment as Cassie leans into its killing embrace – then the glowing eyes go out and the dead body collapses at her feet. 'Go,' she urges, 'Schiller's people are coming!'

Men and women, mostly naked, are spilling into the lounge from the chapel. Mad-eyed and bloodied about the crotch, the men sport impossible, grotesque erections that writhe and squirm like elephantine trunks, cyclostomal mouths opening and closing in a crunch of needle-sharp teeth. The handmaids are Maenads, blood spattering their legs, the engorged heads of their parasites peeping out between their thighs and gnashing at the air. They're only recently inducted and not yet fully under the control of the Lord of the New Flesh, but they are far from mindless as they fan out into the room and work their way into the crowd of feeders, banishing them with a touch. Some of the feeders are aware enough to try to flee, and this leads to a crush at the entrance to the passage to the toilets – directly in Cassie's path.

Cassie scythes into the milling crowd of feeder-possessed bodies, cutting a path through them like a bowling ball through skittles. Mo hurries to keep up. Behind her she hears a cry: 'Catch them!'

'Go,' she urges.

Cassie is slowing. 'It stings, in my *head*,' she complains. 'Like wasps!'

'Well, fuck.' Mo swallows, then drops her invisibility and utters the macro to release another blast of banishment at the bodies crowding around them. She's running out fast. 'Coming through! Clear the toilet! Ladies first!'

The remaining feeders shuffle aside, almost as if her

urgency means something to their tiny, abhumanly hungry minds – then there's a crack of gunfire, painfully loud in the confined space, and an answering wet thud and a spray of blood from one of the bodies. 'RunRun!' Cassie shouts, and leaps forward. Mo hikes up her gown and kicks her shoes off as she scurries after, and the next shot goes wide, missing her shoulder. Then Cassie is at the end of the corridor and slams into the crash bar on the emergency exit, and Mo follows her onto a steep steel staircase and keeps going.

The emergency stairs tops out in a small vestibule with another crash-barred door, this time warning that it's alarmed. Mo grabs Cassie's shoulder before she can open it. 'Listen,' she says, panting, 'we know what's behind us; who's in front?' Footsteps clang from the lower flight.

'Don't know don't care just *go*.' Cassie is febrile, bouncing from foot to foot. 'Follow me close!' And before Mo can say anything else she shoves through the exit.

Mo's earpiece begins to hiss as the door opens: '*MADCAP to CANDID, hard contact with SO19! Shots exchanged! CANDID, respond!*'

'CANDID here, I've got Cassie, exiting via the kitchen block at rear.' Cassie is creeping along a narrow servants' corridor, windows onto the back garden admitting a wan moonlight glow. 'Bad guys in pursuit, shots fired. What's your position?'

'OCCULUS pinned down at front perimeter, active shooters engaged. Zero is round the back but not responding.'

The corridor has evenly spaced doors, all closed. Cassie pauses between the second and third, then darts forward and shoves the third door open. It's a pantry, walled-in, open-fronted cabinets displaying fine china. Mo closes the door behind them. 'Come on!' Cassie hisses.

'Coming—' She taps her earbud again – 'We're going to try and escape through the woods at the rear.'

'We *are*?' Cassie squeaks as she stops dead again in a darkened, empty kitchen. 'WaitWait – *fuck*, can't go there!'

'Why not?' Mo demands edgily.

'We're cut off! I can't—' Cassie hyperventilates – 'can't feel my *geasa*! The Opener of the Way is also the Closer of Doors and *owww*—'

Mo doesn't have the senses of a strong ritual practitioner but she's plugged into her oath of office and the more esoteric binding of the Auditors besides: she senses it as a stillness in the corner of her mind that is normally aware of her duties, and as a bubble of pressure expanding around her mind, like an airliner repressurizing during descent. 'MADCAP to CANDID, do you copy? Some kind of ward just went up around the perimeter. Do you copy?'

'CANDID here, I copy.' She licks suddenly dry lips. The stillness in her head is pounding like the absence of giant drums, an alien heartbeat coming closer. 'Cassie just lost her *mana* stream. Are we cut off?'

'Yes. Suggest you find Zero and the car and try to drive out: it's shielded—'

A brief stutter of gunfire some distance outside the building rattles the window panes. 'Ri-ight,' Mo says slowly. Cassie is doubled-over as if in pain. Mo hears footsteps beyond the pantry. '*Move it!*'

She grabs Cassie and tugs her towards the big kitchen doors. These rooms are a trap, even with her natural invisibility. She hears a shout from behind as she throws herself against the door and sprawls through it into one of the side rooms, shoving up against a snowy linen-draped table bearing a half-eaten buffet of finger food. It's part of a horseshoe surrounding the center of the room, the open side facing gaping French windows and a terrace open to the night and magic. Cassie moans as Mo drags her down under the tablecloth and crawls on hands and knees away from the doorway. '*Shut up*,' she whispers, and hunkers down, clutching the *alfär* woman. For a miracle, Cassie falls silent.

Behind them, the kitchen door opens. Footsteps squeak on the polished parquet floor of the morning room. A man speaks, his tone dull and oddly atonal: 'They are not here, Mistress.'

A woman – Overholt, Mo thinks – replies, her voice ringing: 'They ran up the stairs, they must have come out on this level! They have not crossed the boundary therefore they're hiding. Find them! You, you, and you: take the function rooms. You two, search the service areas. Work front-to-back and flush them out into the pavilion. If you see them, know that our Lord does not require the service of their kind: you may shoot to kill.'

Heathrow is a big airport, but luckily the Transport Police are already here: most of them are lying on the ground or kneeling and variously groaning or throwing up, but Johnny knows what he's looking for and takes the Airwave handset from a supine inspector, then calls up the dispatcher. He explains what we want using yet another bloody codeword nobody has seen fit to confide in me – how the fuck was I to know that we have a backdoor liaison with them, and why didn't the boys on the ground know about it in time to avoid this clusterfuck? – and then we get a fast ride in the back of an SUV driven by one of Captain Partridge's men, right around the perimeter with blues and twos going.

India 97 is already on approach when we arrive at the chopper terminal. It's a twin-engine Airbus Helicopters H145 in police markings, a Nightsun and thermal imager slung beneath its nose like a gun turret. 'C'mon,' Johnny says, and briskly shoves me out of the SUV.

'The cops – they weren't told about this target because the SA was afraid they'd been rooted by Schiller's bunch? But we're supposed to be their best homies *now*?' I ask incredulously.

'Shaddup and run, kid, we can chew the cud later.' Johnny is unusually tense and I am increasingly pissed-off at being kept in the dark about what seems to me to be an important aspect of an operation I'm supposed to be in charge of, sandbox or no sandbox. But the skids touch down just long enough for us to run across and climb on board – ducking instinctively even though the spinning blades are too far overhead to be a problem – and then we're off, climbing out and turning towards the center of the capital at low altitude until we clear controlled airspace.

He passes me a headset. 'We kept it quiet to avoid tipping our hand prematurely, but now Schiller knows something is up. Chris got through to the dinosaur's head, but the tail was already knocking on the door.'

'Fuck.'

'Yeah. Best laid plans'n'all that.'

I hate being out of touch, but it's too loud for a phone conversation in the back of the chopper. I propitiate my inner demons by sending the SA a stream of peevish instant messages, but he's old school: it's far from certain he'll even read them today. I'm taken by surprise when a couple of minutes later he begins to update me on what's going on. But then he sends me the photograph Mhari took in the bedroom, and I give up on the not-swearing thing – and when he gives me Mo's latest sitrep on what she and Cassie are doing I learn the real meaning of fear.

Anneka Overholt is blazingly furious, and the splinter of the Lord's soul that pierces her mind like one of the nails that joined Christ to the Cross burns with a painful echo of her rage.

Things have been going well, almost too well: Father Ray's plan has run as if on rails, and she has had reason to bask in the warm satisfaction of the Lord at a job well done. But Schiller is prideful and has allowed success to go to his head, thinking that he could take his time and that Elevating his own person could somehow be made part of the Lord's plan for this apostate land. Anneka knows better and has tried to steer him towards the path of righteousness, but it hasn't been fast, or easy, to get his attention, and now they are paying the price.

Who were those women spying on the initiation ceremony at the back of the chapel? She barely noticed them at the time, her mind skittering away from them like a willful child avoiding her chores. Her initial suspicion that they are just confused party-goers, easy enough to silence, is clearly wrong, disproven by the shockingly rapid collapse into silence of the entire Middle Temple chorus (who have been a constant whisper of praise in the back of her mind ever since her own Elevation). They must be spies in the house of the Lord, hostile witnesses to the Gospel work. And then they ran *towards* the chaotic mass of feeders at the orgy (a messy and wasteful arrangement for cleaning up the leftovers, in Anneka's opinion), and the feeders *died*. Black magic indeed! Anneka mustered the new initiates – barely serviceable, still suffering from blood loss and shock – then hastened after them, gathering the Lord's power even as the ward around the estate powered up. But they're devilishly hard to find, and at the back of her head she can hear Father Ray on the jittery edge of panic, shouting orders at the other congregants that barely make sense. He's *frightened*, and he's putting on an ugly display of cowardice in front of the flock, and Anneka is unsure whether she is more angry at him or the unwelcome intruders. Until the congregation grows large enough to open the way again and bring forth the Lord in all his majesty to fill the mortal vessel that is Raymond Schiller's body he is, indeed, vulnerable to the infidels and heretics – and she, his chosen handmaid, is vulnerable beside him.

Anneka storms back through the service corridors towards the grand hall at the front of the house. As she erupts from a concealed doorway she finds the premises in chaos. Guests are milling around aimlessly, demanding explanations from harried police officers who are trying to herd them away from the doors and windows. Other officers are taking up firing positions behind whatever cover comes to hand, as if expecting armed intruders. '*What* is the meaning of this?' she demands of the inspector in charge.

'Get back we have shooters—' The man barely looks at her other than to push her back with the rest of the flock.

Furious, Anneka reaches out and touches him with the majesty of the Lord's will. He stumbles and groans and she grabs his elbow, forcing him to stand. '*Report. Obey,*' she instructs him, nostrils flaring at the stink of burning skin and ash rising from the ward he's wearing.

'*Urk* – shooters on the loose, my men are deploying to defend – probably terrorists got wind of the PM and half the cabinet—'

Anneka releases him and frees him from the attention

of the Lord and he drops like a stone, soul torn. She bends down and scoops up his weapon, a Glock semiautomatic. Then she opens her senses wide and calls out to Father Ray. '*There are armed intruders within the perimeter, Father. The police are confused and obstructive. I require support.*'

She senses his fear and confusion through the communion of the hosts, under his actual speech. '*Take those you can and defend the front. We must leave no witnesses behind! I must flee as soon as the way is clear: the Lord warns that the old enemy is approaching, and if it catches me that will be a lesser ending—*'

He's losing it, she can see, and she sniffs as she walls him out. Schiller is good when the going is good, but goes to pieces when faced with real opposition. Anneka considers herself to be made of sterner stuff. She spreads her awareness out across the grounds, taking stock. Up front, half a dozen armed police take aim from cover, waiting for the unseen hostiles who made their presence known barely two minutes ago to reveal themselves. (Presumably the hostiles are doing likewise, both sides engaged in a lethal game of hide-and-seek.) Back in the house she can feel her three brothers and sisters in the Lord sweeping cautiously through the access passages and service areas. They are debating extending the sweep to the upper floor, and she nudges approval at them. Out in the grounds she senses the other two swinging around the lawn and flower beds from the east, near the stable block. *That* is where her people are weakest. She signals her intention to join them, then stalks back towards the crowd of alarmed party-goers clogging up the ballroom behind the entrance, drawing a glamour around herself to hide her pistol and render the disarray of her robe unnoticeable. Behind her the dead police inspector's body sprawls across the checkered tile floor, a trickle of blood leaking from ears and eyelids. He has gone to meet his maker, and in what little consideration Anneka holds for him she feels a brief, bitter stab of envy: for her Lord will know his own.

Mo waits, heart in mouth, as Overholt and her minions sweep through the morning room. She keeps a tight grip on Cassie's ankle even as a shod foot kicks underneath the draped tablecloth, narrowly missing her. But the searchers are in too much of a hurry. They don't systematically check under the furniture before they move on: or perhaps Mo's invisibility is working in her favor. She hunkers down low, imagining herself into the semblance of a mouse that has wandered in from the garden, frightened and lost and frozen in place in its effort to avoid the attention of predators.

It takes less than a minute but the wait for the Inner Temple initiates to leave feels like forever. Cassie quivers with fear or perhaps an unreleased, restless febrile energy. 'We're trapped,' she says quietly, voice pitched for Mo's ears only. 'There is a net-of-summoning around the palace, newly erected while we were below. What do we do?'

Mo sits up under the tablecloth. She taps her earpiece. 'CANDID to MADCAP, please copy.' She glances at the other woman. 'It's a defensive grid. Which means we're winning – we just have to stay alive until our backup arrives. Whatever it is. CANDID, MADCAP, please copy.'

'*MADCAP, CANDID. Sitrep.*'

'Both in hiding indoors. Schiller's got some kind of perimeter ward and his Inner Temple are searching the building and grounds for us. Tongue-eaters are all down and there are a bunch of feeders in the night on the loose. If we make a break for the car we may be spotted. Please advise.'

'*Alex is in the driveway. As soon as the defensive ward drops he'll be straight in. Your special backup is still on the way, got delayed in traffic. ETA twenty minutes, estimated. A chopper is enroute to collect TEAPOT as well; confirmed ETA forty minutes. If you can hide out that long—*'

'CANDID, will comply. Over. *Fuck,*' she adds. 'Good news and bad news,' she tells Cassie; 'the seventh cavalry is riding to the rescue, but they won't get here for thirty to sixty minutes. We need to find somewhere to hide out.'

Cassie shakes off her hand and crawls out from under the table. After a few seconds Mo follows her, wincing slightly: her knees aren't happy about crawling over hardwood these days. Cassie is standing up, holding a tray of champagne flutes and Mo does a double-take as she realizes the girl's got her waitress glamour back in place. '*One* of us needs to find somewhere to hide out, YesYes?' Cassie winks at her.

Mo thinks fast. If Schiller's people decide things have gone irretrievably wrong they won't leave any witnesses behind, but it'll take the Sleeper cultists time to organize a large-scale conversion – or a massacre – without triggering a messy panic. If she and Cassie can blend in with the guests – 'This will buy you ten or fifteen minutes, but it's worth a try.' She takes stock of herself. Her hair's a mess and she's lost her shoes; she smooths down her dress and tucks a straying lock of hair back as she prepares to rejoin the party. 'Let's split. You go left, I'll go right, they're looking for two fugitives not a waitress and a guest. Aim to meet me at the Bentley parked behind the stable block.'

'YesYes, on my way.' Cassie taps her ear – Mo blinks as the tip twitches, then disappears from her vision again – and walks away in the direction of the French windows onto the terrace out back, tray held high. Mo wastes no time but heads for the side-door opening into the ballroom.

The instant she slips inside she realizes that something is very wrong. The band plays on in the pavilion on the lawn, but the guests aren't dancing – they're clumping in corners, agitated and upset. The doors to the grand hall are half-closed and an armed policeman stands in the open half, blocking the exit and shooing away anyone who approaches. More and more of the guests are drifting towards the terrace and the gardens beyond.

Mo approaches a small cluster of silverback banking executives and their younger, prettier partners. 'Do you know what's going on?' she asks, deliberately cutting into a mansplaining monologue.

'There's some sort of incident out front—' the sixty-something with the five-hundred-pound haircut leers down her cleavage unconsciously – 'police are handling it, nothing to worry about, I'm sure.'

Mo stares at him. 'I heard shots.'

'I should think that was the police—'

Silverback's partner is tugging at his arm and giving Mo a very obvious side-eye, one second away from escalating, so she nods and turns away, dismissing the guy even as he carries on monologuing at her back. She heads across the room towards a side-table and picks up a glass of bubbly for social camouflage. As a single woman in this crowd she's going to stand out, but Silverback and his company were just too sleazy to put up with. She casts around and sees two men and women of roughly comparable age near the French doors, glancing nervously at the guarded entrance. Arts people, she guesses, not pretty enough to be rock stars or actors, slightly unconventional and thus unlikely to be politicians or business magnates. She plasters a smile on her face and minces over.

'Hi. I'm terribly sorry about this, but do you mind if I stand with you people and pretend to be making conversation?' She tilts her head, briefly indicating Silverback and his friends: 'I just ran into my ex and he's a lot less likely to be a nuisance – make a scene – around other people.'

'Oh, honey,' one of the women smiles sympathetically – thirty-something, fifties-vintage butterfly glasses, and cherry red hair – 'been there, done that, join the club.'

'Thank you.' Mo glances at her companions. Tall, thin, academic-looking guy in a bow tie and tweed jacket rather than a dinner jacket; bald bloke with a beard and a ruddy wine-drinker's nose in a dinner jacket that is at least a decade out of date; and an older woman with distinguished silver hair and a purple velvet frock. 'Sorry to be a nuisance. I'll just stand here and smile and nod if you don't mind?'

Red-nose speaks: 'If he's trouble, do you want me to talk to the cops—'

'– I don't think that would be a good idea.' Mo thinks fast. 'He has lawyers. I just wasn't expecting him here.' Across the room, out of the side of her eye, she spots a blonde woman in a white shift stalking past. She's got something in her right hand down by her side and for some reason trying to focus on it makes Mo's eyes hurt and a prickly sweat stand out on her forehead. *Right*. 'He tried to screw me over the settlement,' she extemporizes. At the other side of the room, a jacketless man, his tie draped around his open collar, dark stains on his trousers (which are tight around the crotch). She looks away hastily. 'He's the over-controlling type.' She has no idea whether she's libeling the silverback executive or not but she's desperate to keep talking because now her conversational gatecrashing gambit has paid off and her four companions are nodding and looking sympathetic, as if she's been here all along. She smiles at Red-nose: 'What brings you here?'

'I think I'm part of the comic relief,' he says self-deprecatingly, before launching into a purportedly amusing anecdote about internal politics between dueling BBC directors who can't decide whether his next show should be a sitcom about government bureaucrats or a horror series – Mo tunes it out, nodding and making encouraging noises at appropriate intervals as she scans the room for threats.

Two more handmaids slip into the ballroom behind the back of the policeman, who pays them no attention. Mo pulls out her phone. 'Excuse me, I think someone just texted,' she says, smiling as she glances down at it and fires up a scanner app. She turns away from her companions and raises it to eye level, seeing the telltale flares of light limning the heads and crotches of the possessed. 'Sorry, my son wants to see what it's like,' she says, turning back.

Woman in Purple raises an eyebrow. 'Really? I thought you were playing Ingress.' Mo suppresses the urge to scream: Purple must have glimpsed the scanner display.

She makes a snap decision: she can't rescue everybody but she'll save as many as she can. 'I don't expect you to believe anything I say, but it would be a *really* good idea if we all stepped outside onto the patio before the people who have just come in start to herd everyone into the basement.'

Purple's eyes narrow. 'That's not your husband—'

The jacketless man is approaching. 'Sorry to interrupt, but we have a security situation. There are intruders in the grounds. Please go into the main hall, then take shelter in the basement.' He doesn't make eye contact or wait for any acknowledgment but proceeds to the next knot of conversation, evidently unaware of the effect of his writhing priapism. The eye-warping blur at his right hand stings Mo's eyes for a moment, then resolves into a squat-looking machine pistol.

'Well, *that* was special!' Purple's eyes are wide.

Mo reaches into her purse and pulls her warrant card. 'MI5. If you go downstairs you will die: this is a terrorist incident. We need to leave *now*.'

'I say! You're—' Producer Guy nearly crosses his eyes until Butterfly Specs takes his arm.

'Come *on*, Gary, if it's a joke you can write a letter to the *Guardian* tomorrow,' she hisses, giving Mo a wide-eyed look as she hauls him towards the open French windows.

Purple looks Mo in the eye. 'You're not MI5, you're one of *them*,' she says with a gleam of recognition. 'But your agency was dissolved weeks ago. What's happening?'

'Come on and I'll tell you.' Mo takes her arm and tugs. 'I suppose you *are* MI5.'

Purple follows. 'Have I seen you ... oh. Home Office briefings last year?'

Mo nearly stumbles but manages to keep going. 'Transhuman Police Coordination, and yes, it was an SOE false flag op. I'm not kidding about the danger, the bodies herding everyone into the cellar are the reason we were officially shitcanned.'

'That man, there was something in his pants that looked like, like – and his eyes—'

They make it across the threshold and onto the flagstones. They're chilly and rough beneath Mo's stockinged feet; she looks around for the steps down to the lawn. 'He's under a mind-control parasite. So are Schiller's other people. I don't suppose you're carrying?'

Purple looks at her as if she's insane. 'Going armed at a reception for the Prime Minister? Do I look mad?'

Mo sighs. 'Well, fuck.' The crowd in the ballroom is already thinning, mostly drifting back into the great hall and the stairs beyond. She taps her earpiece. 'CANDID, MADCAP, sitrep.'

'MADCAP, OCCULUS *is pinned down outside the perimeter. Still awaiting support; you're on your own. Sitrep?*'

'In the garden with civilians, Schiller's people are herding everybody into the basement and sending out armed patrols. I don't anticipate a hostage situation or siege, it looks like a Jim Jones setup.' Purple's face is wan in the glow shed by the floodlights on the terrace. Mo gestures impatiently towards the lawn. 'I'm going to try and find Zero. Over.' She heads towards the lawn, meaning to circle round behind the stable block.

'Wait! Where are you going?'

'Follow me and find out.' Mo regrets it instantly. 'Look, we're in big trouble. Stay back, don't make any noise, and if anyone shoots me, run away as far as you can, then hide. Better still, find your friends' – they've moved away and are standing around in the middle of the terrace, looking gormless – 'and get them to do the same.'

Without waiting for a reply she turns and heads for the steps, then down onto the grass (it's cool and slightly damp, a welcome balm for her sore toes), and heads diagonally away from the house, skirting the big pavilion on her way towards the stables.

But she's only halfway there when a pulse of released occult power sweeps across her – and then the shooting starts.

Driving is a lot like riding a bicycle, Iris finds: it feels very strange at first, but the skills come back rapidly, and within an hour it feels almost as if she hasn't taken a six-year break.

Of course, this is a dangerous delusion, and Iris is very aware that she's at risk. Before everything went wrong, culminating in the fiasco at Brookwood and her arrest and trial, she'd driven an older Honda. The new hire car is a Jaguar – only the best will do for this job – and it's fifteen years newer, a gleaming, streamlined, black and chrome monster that seems to be about fifty computers flying in loose formation. Everything is computerized, including the controls, and it's totally bewildering, as if sixty years rather than a mere six have passed her by.

At least the basics are in the right place – steering wheel, go pedal, stop pedal, indicators – so she resists the urge to fiddle beyond working out the basics of the satellite navigation system, and sticks to concentrating on moving forward and not hitting anything.

'I say, are we nearly there yet?' Her passenger sounds archly amused, but she still cringes slightly at the faintest implication of dissatisfaction.

She checks the satnav for an updated projection. If they hadn't hit tailbacks due to a contraflow on the M40 they'd be there already. 'Five minutes, sir.' She squeezes her right foot on the accelerator and the big cat purrs very quietly and pushes forward, nosing into the darkness faster than she's entirely comfortable with.

Dr. Armstrong had told her to take it easy: *just a light liaison role*, he said. But her Lord had other plans. Plans that involved a brisk afternoon's shopping for clothes – both his *and* hers, for he has firm ideas about appropriate business attire for his personal assistant – then a friendly chat with a luxury car rental agency. No money or credit cards pass hands when her Lord wishes to buy a suit or a phone or a helicopter: Saville Row tailors and Bond Street jewelers practically queue up to throw their wares at him and his entourage. 'One must make the right impression: first appearances are *important*,' her Lord explained, 'and my staff's presentation reflects on me.' So Iris, an old biker girl, finds herself encased in a black Hugo Boss suit, white shirt, and matching heels – which are playing hell with her pedal control.

'I do believe the festivities have kicked off without us,' her Lord says, faint disapproval evident underneath his light tone. 'Too bad they couldn't wait, say I.' He snaps his fingers and the darkness beyond the reach of headlamps roils and cringes away, giving her a clear view forward. Iris doesn't need to be told: she floors the accelerator and the Jaguar snarls forward, around a tight bend telegraphed with illuminated chevron signs, then uphill into a 30 mph limit – the village nearest their destination. 'I do so *hate* to be late to a party,' Fabian sighs.

Iris takes the high street at eighty, then hammers the brakes and yanks the car into a tire-screeching turn into the estate driveway leading to Nether Stowe House. She passes a 20 mph signpost, still doing upwards of double the speed limit, but reluctantly brakes as the drive snakes between trees. The planting is thinning out ahead, under the moonlight, when she sees a big fire truck parked athwart the drive and barely has time to stand on the stop pedal. There is a juddering of antilock as the Jaguar skids to a standstill just short of the OCCULUS truck, and very scary men with guns materialize from the darkness to either side and she finds herself staring into the grooves of a machine gun barrel.

The door is yanked open abruptly – they've got some kind of remote locking override – and a hand grabs her shoulder roughly. 'On the ground *now!*' says the soldier.

'I don't *think* so.' Fabian Everyman, also known as the Mandate, unfolds himself from the back seat and stretches as he steps clear of the car, his voice a low singsong that nevertheless wraps fingers of steel garroting wire around the throats of everyone who hears him. A nerdy-looking young man in jeans and a hoodie appears out of the darkness and blurs towards him; but he merely snaps his fingers and the youth collapses to the gravel, motionless. A faint popping and stench of burning skin betrays the disintegration of every military-strength defensive ward within hearing range. 'Captain Stevens, make yourself known to me. Everyone else, be still—' he pauses – 'you may breathe,' he adds, as if it is an afterthought for the benefit of the human statues frozen on every side. 'You too,' he nudges the fallen – civilian? Laundry operative? – with the brightly polished toe of one dress shoe.

Iris is perturbed to find that she is free to move. Clearly her Lord's intent privileges her. She steps out of the car and walks around to his side as one of the soldiers stumbles, almost sleepwalking, away from the big truck. Beyond it, something sparks and crackles in the gravel – a line bisecting the road, and the plantation of trees. A ward of some kind, and a big one if she's any judge of things.

'I'm – I'm Stevens. H-he—' A faint gesture at the ground – 'Dr. Schwartz, our Continuity liaison.' He stops moving.

Fabian smiles in the darkness. 'I did wonder about him – not terribly military, is he? I believe Dr. Armstrong told you to expect me. Report, Captain.'

'Yuh ... yessir.' Stevens clearly finds it a painful effort to speak, much less to think. 'The, the police marksmen inside opened fire as we approached. One injured, condition stable, then the big ward went up around the house. Our K-22 shows a thaum field off the scale and the cops aren't answering on Airwave or mobile phone—'

'I can clear the ward for you, Captain. Tell your men who I am and I will release them.'

'Yessir. Men, this is our back-up-up . . . new Masterrrr . . .' Stevens sounds as if he's having trouble enunciating the words. One side of his face is slackening as Iris watches. His voice drops an octave, slurring drunkenly but gaining an uncanny echo: 'All glory to the Black Pharaoh!'

'That's enough.' Fabian snaps his fingers again: 'Be free again to serve me, soldiers of England. You too, Doctor.' The unseen grin fills the darkness again: a million blind, many-legged things cringe in reverence before him in the woods. 'Ah, hmm. I shall take care of the crude barrier presently. You and your men—' He nods at Stevens – 'will deal with the police and the handmaids of the False Pretender. You will find the worst of their works in the cellars. My priestess will go before me: I shall grant her the power to deal with the Pretender's minions.' A vast and airy power clamps itself around Iris's mind and it is all she can do not to cry out in terror and awe as the night falls away before her strange new senses. 'I grant *you*—' his gesture takes in the soldiers – 'protection from what you will face this night.' Muffled swearing tells Iris that she's not the only recipient of her Lord's weird benediction. 'I shall wait in the grand hall. When you find the Prime Minister, bring him before me.' He pauses. 'Iris? I want you to leave the car open and the keys on the driver's seat.' A grinning skull wreathed in flames of darkness howls with mirth before her inner eye: 'A little jape at the expense of the Pretender.'

Iris hastens to prepare the car as her Lord directs. A soldier climbs into the cab of the big fire incident control vehicle, and a moment later its engine grumbles and it rolls away from the driveway. Her Lord stands in its wheel tracks, facing the curtain of eerie green radiance that blocks the steps to Nether Stowe House. Other soldiers disperse to either side, behind the tree line.

Does he think he can – she begins to think, just as Fabian makes a gesture and the defensive ward bursts, pulsing outward into the night like a breath of wind from the abyss.

Then the shooting starts.

The former stable block is a three-story stone building facing onto a cobbled courtyard at one side of Nether Stowe House. The courtyard itself is reserved for parking at these events, both for the catering suppliers and for those guests whose status extends to chauffeur-driven limousines. Here the drivers wait with their cars, awaiting a call to drive round to the front of the house to collect their passengers.

Mo trots around the back of the pavilion and is halfway across the expanse of lawn when the hair rises on the back of her neck, a moment before a crackle of automatic gunfire thunders out from beyond the front of the building. She flops to the grass, swearing and frightened, pulling her invisibility tight around her like a shawl: but invisibility won't make a blind bit of difference to a random bullet, and all she can do is pray that all the shooting is around the other side of the house.

'CANDID, MADCAP, *shooting just started, is this you?*'

'MADCAP, CANDID, *can confirm perimeter ward just dropped, OCCULUS moving forward, defenders returning fire. Can you take cover?*'

Mo risks looking up, briefly. The floodlights cast long, razor-edged shadows across the lawn she's lying on, revealing it to be as flat as a crepe. 'I'm in the middle of the lawn. How about I head for the cars?'

'Do it. Alex is inbound with help. I'll direct him your way.'

'Over,' she murmurs, rolls to her knees, and hikes up

her skirt – the gown is ruined, but it'll help her blend in with the shadows if she loses her invisibility – then knots it out of the way, and lurches into a crouching, erratic run, breathing heavily. 'I'm too old for this stuff,' she pants under her breath.

The cars are parked in a neat row before the barred stable doors, gleaming in the moonlight like black and silver beetles – only bridal corteges come in white, and for some reason it strikes Mo as ludicrous that nobody ever drives a lime-green or purple candy-fleck limousine – the drivers are either snoozing at the wheel or have gone elsewhere. She steps off the lawn, wincing at the sharp-edged tarmac and gravel underfoot, and casts around for Persephone's Bentley. There it is, at one end, windscreen a silvery sheen in the night –

Something tickles the edge of her senses. She focuses, relaxing her invisibility as she peers into the night. The sheen on the windscreen doesn't shift as she walks forward, it's as if it's part of the windscreen, not a reflection: and there's a black dot at its heart –

She hears the clack of a gun being cocked directly behind her: 'Freeze!'

The woman's voice is harsh and full of a dangerous tension. Mo isn't stupid. She freezes.

'Hold your hands straight out to either side, palms up. Speak or move and I'll shoot you.' American accent, mid-continental twang.

Mo's heart hammers thunderously. She can see the hole in the center of the cracked windscreen laminate now. She can't see beyond the crazing, can't tell if Zero's dead body sprawls behind the wheel or if he somehow got away, but the driver's door is closed so the odds are looking bad. *Cassie doesn't drive, does she? Where is she, anyway?*

Mo subvocalizes a macro, feels a tingle of power and sees ghost-lights in her mind's eye, dotted around the courtyard. Two, in particular, might be crouching human forms, half-obscured behind a parked Maybach.

'Turn around slowly. Face me.'

Mo obeys. The woman is one of Schiller's valkyries, a straight-haired, blue-eyed blonde in a bloodstained white shift, her face a rictus of barely suppressed rage. There's something faintly familiar about her. Any hope of escape withers at the sight of the Glock she holds in a two-handed shooter's stance, five meters away: it's aimed directly at Mo's chest, and a red speckle of laser light from the tube clamped to its barrel tells its own story.

'You're one of *them*, aren't you?' the woman snarls. 'Heretics and infidels! Servants of the Old Enemy! *You* did this!'

Mo licks her lips and takes a calculated risk: 'Did what?'

'Everything!' the woman shouts. 'Violated the Inner Temple! Shattered our Lord's sanctum! Made me look like a fool in front of my boss and half the cabinet!' The penny drops: Mo is facing Ms. Overholt, the special advisor to the Minister for Magic. She's working herself up into a frenzy of self-righteous hatred and Mo is absolutely certain that she's going to pull the trigger in the next few seconds, but she's clearly trained – the muzzle of the pistol never wavers. Mo works her suddenly dry mouth, reading a last desperate command –

Gravel rattles by her feet, and a fey, singsong voice calls out: 'Over he-ere!'

Overholt spins and fires rapidly into the darkness as Mo dives for the grass behind her and yanks her invisibility around her like a caul, putting everything she's got into it. The pistol is a rapid pulse of thunder, three rounds at a time – *she must have an extended magazine*, Mo realizes, and that's *really* bad news: Glocks start at fifteen and go up from there –

Cassie's silvery laughter echoes from the stables. 'I know what you did!' she sings at Overholt. 'You thought you could keep us out with your silly magic circle but we're faster and smarter and better than you-hoo!'

Another three-round burst goes wild as Overholt spins round again and fires over Mo's prone shadow-shrouded body. She grabs at the sod, terrified to release her grip on invisibility for long enough to speak another word of command before Overholt looks away. Where *is* Cassie? What's she playing at? Then Mo realizes: when the barrier came down, Cassie reacquired her connection to her fount of power, and the OCCULUS team will be on their way in, with Alex and some unspecified heavy backup. All she has to do is stay alive –

Overholt turns to scan once more, then, without warning, throws back her head and shrieks. It's an unearthly scream, appallingly loud: tendons stand out on the side of her neck as she vents a noise not meant for human lungs. Gooseflesh prickles on Mo's body as Overholt's hair begins to fan out in a halo around her head and she stretches onto the tips of her toes. Then she begins to rise, her eyes glowing as she gathers an aura of *mana* around her like a huge static charge prevented from seeking a path to earth. The muzzle of her gun is glowing now, the eerie green of a feeder's eyes, and Overholt's scream dopplers down into a ground-shaking roar of thwarted rage.

'*You!*' The thing that animates her howls at the night, at something or someone approaching across the lawn. Mo dares not look round, but raises her hand to her ear and taps her earpiece. 'OK Google, tell application OFCUT active ward maximum strength now,' she mumbles.

'Hello, I don't understand that—'

Fuck. Computers. 'OK Google, tell *app* OFCUT active ward maximum strength now,' she speaks and scoots backwards as fast as she can on hands and knees, but Overholt is paying her no attention and she can't tell whether it's because her invisibility shield has held or because the unseen thing she's reversing towards is so pants-wettingly terrifying –

'Yes, I can do that!' her phone warmly assures her, just as she stubs her left big toe painfully on someone's shod foot and suppresses a yelp.

'Ah, Chief Inspector! We meet again!' says a posh, avuncular, and utterly unwelcome male voice. 'Having a spot of bother, are we? This is your lucky day: your Dr. Armstrong asked me to stage an intervention on your behalf.' He raises his voice and addresses Overholt in a tone that drops several hundred degrees in temperature. 'This is *my* fiefdom. Your False Pretender is banished. Leave now in peace, or I will not be merciful.'

'You!' Anneka Overholt rumbles. Then the thing speaking through her larynx switches to Old Enochian, inflected in an accent like fingernails scraping down a blackboard and the drowning screams of waterboarded prisoners: '*Emperor of Centipedes and ruler of corpses! I will eat your slaves and shit worshippers and you will rue the day you challenged me!*' Then she begins to chant, uttering noises that periodically overload Mo's hearing so that the horrific phrases seem to stutter and stumble between bursts of static.

'Oh, *do* shut up; you're boring me.'

Mo can't help herself: she whimpers. Every hair on her body is standing on end with the backwash from the thaumaturgic firepower converging on Anneka and the Mandate. She tries to crawl away, but her limbs aren't answering her brain's most urgent commands. The loss of control is mortifying and fills her with the horror of the bone-white violin. *Going to die now*, she realizes, despairing. A mind-numbingly powerful blanket of sorcerous power sweeps past her, rippling through the earth like the tracks of a main battle tank rumbling past her head at a range of centimeters; then the night lights up the green-white of a lightning strike with a pulse of noise so loud that it feels like a door slamming on her head.

The Mandate giggles. 'Is *that* the best you can do?' he demands. 'Why don't you go back to sleep?'

Then he snaps his fingers and the world ends for a few seconds.

Darkness. A smell of burned hair. Mo moans quietly. She hurts, everywhere.

'Mo? Can you hear me?' She recognizes the voice. Pain rasps across her right shoulder. 'Mo?' Someone prodding her.

'Hurts,' she manages.

'I'm not surprised.' Alex sounds worried.

'Is she alive?' Cassie demands excitedly.

The pain is subsiding. 'Backwash.' She tries to open her eyes – they sting, but she succeeds with the second attempt. As the pain recedes she begins to notice other things. The back of her left arm is sticky. Her eyelids don't want to stay open. Redness. 'How bad. Am I?'

'It's *just* like that movie!' Cassie is ebullient: 'So spectacular!'

Mo groans again, then pushes herself upright. Her arms and legs are evidently working again, but she feels disgusting, and there's a stench of voided bowels and warm dampness. *Did I just wet myself*, she wonders dismally, then decides to ignore the question. She raises a finger and taps something brittle and moist and a lump of something unspeakable falls from her ear: 'OK Google—'

'I think your phone's toast,' says Alex, wiping his fingers on the grass. 'I mean, your handbag's on fire. Did you have it running as a virtual ward? If so, it died to save your ass.'

She pushes herself to her feet and tries not to retch at the stink. 'What's—'

'Just like *Scanners*!' Cassie enthuses. 'She totally *exploded* all over you! Well, all over everyone, actually, but none of it stuck to *him*,' she clarifies. 'Well, actually, her *worm* exploded, but as it was inside her—'

'Stoppit.' Mo gags. 'Just stop. Wanna. Be sick.' She has not, she realizes, pissed herself: she's just covered in Overholt. She doubles over and tries to keep her airways clear as her stomach spasms. It's not the proximity to sudden death that does it, but the immanent tank-track terror of feeling the Mandate's power crunching past, taking aim at a frail meatsack animated by the will of the not-fully-awakened Sleeper. That, and the ghastly stench of whatever she's covered in. 'Needa. Shower.'

'Come on, we'll sort you out.' Alex is solicitous, but inexplicably not solicitous enough to offer her his arm.

Mo staggers across the lawn between Alex and Cassie. They lead her past police and soldiers who are escorting dazed party-goers in the opposite direction, towards the pavilion which has been pressed into service as a triage station. Alex waves off an offer of first aid: 'She just needs a shower and a change of clothes,' he assures them, and the police are only too happy to focus on the non-walking wounded.

'And a stiff drink,' Mo adds, *sotto voce*, and Cassie giggles.

They are crossing the ballroom towards the door to the grand hall and the staircase beyond, carefully avoiding the paramedics and police officers laying out the dead, when a woman in a black power suit steps out in front of them. 'Ah, Mo. Long time no see,' she says, nodding congenially. 'And who's this?'

Mo boggles. 'Did *he* bring you?' she demands. 'I thought you were in Camp Sunshine.'

'I was: Persephone let me out, and the SA signed off on it.' Iris nods at her companions: 'Who are these? New blood, I see?'

Mo swallows. 'Iris, meet Dr. Alex Schwartz and Cassie Brewer, yes they work for us and I'll introduce you properly later but right now I need a shower and a change of clothes and we really ought to be leaving.' She has to raise her voice to be heard over the hoarse screaming echoing up through the open door leading to the basement lounge.

'I'd noticed.' Iris's lips quirk. 'You might as well make yourself at home: I'm sure Schiller's people will have left something that fits in their suite. West wing, second floor, room 309,' she adds. Something behind Mo wheezes, a long sighing exhalation like the air departing a corpse's lungs, and she begins to turn.

'NoNo—' Cassie says just as Iris raises her right hand and gestures at the drunkenly staggering green-eyed chief financial officer whose attempt at stalking them is somewhat impaired by the unshed trousers wrapped around his ankles – then there is a flicker of radiance and the body collapses, animating pattern banished back to wherever the never-living come from. 'Oh, that was neat! Can you do it again? May I watch?'

Iris gives Cassie the hairy eyeball. 'I think you'd better help Dr. O'Brien upstairs,' she suggests. 'She looks as if she's about to keel over.' There's a disturbance near the entrance to the chapel: evidently someone else is in a hurry to escape. 'Don't you worry about the feeders, I'll keep them contained until *He* gets everything wrapped up.'

Mo's shoulders slump. 'So it's true.'

'What? You're up against a greater evil and you *still* have qualms about making common cause with a lesser one?' Iris sniffs, but there's a twinkle in her eyes. 'Go on, get away with you.' More shamblers are heading their way: Iris steps aside to clear Mo's path and raises her hand again, to bar them.

'Come on,' Alex urges her. He looks slightly queasy.

'Let's,' Cassie says fervently, and nudges Mo towards the sweeping staircase. Nothing else blocks their way, and the upper levels look to be eerily quiet after the chaos below stairs. 'What *was* that?'

'If I had to guess, I'd say Schiller was trying to induct the government into his cult until you-know-who blocked him. Which means—'

They're almost at the top of the first flight of steps when the front door opens below them. Schiller's greeters are conspicuously absent as a solitary figure in top hat, white tie and tails, with silver-topped cane tucked under one arm, paces through the entrance and pauses dramatically.

Mo's knees turn to jelly as the new arrival turns its face upwards and directs the full weight of its vast, drily amused attention on her. 'What now?' she asks, a faint note of resentment in her voice.

'Just taking care of business.' He raises his top hat and inclines his head. 'Dr. O'Brien, I see you survived after all! And in such elevated company. You *do* know that your companion is not entirely human ... ?'

Mo's self-assurance is shot, but she pulls herself together just enough to put a brave face on things. 'Yes, I am aware of that. So, uh, your priestess is waiting for you down in the basement.' She waves at the door to the cellar stairs. 'You may need to know the combination to the lock, it's—'

'Entirely irrelevant.' The implicit force behind his awful smile will give her nightmares in the days and weeks to come. 'When I told you that you would serve me, I was giving you a true seeing: you are mine now, and forever more. However, I've decided that I don't want to be the Home Secretary any more. I've raised my game; what this country needs to see it through the coming stellar conjunction is firm government under an enlightened ruler, and I've decided I'm *exactly* the best possible candidate for the job!' The living avatar of the Black Pharaoh beams up at her, like a distant supernova blazing through mist rising from the liquefied atmospheric oceans of a frozen outer planet. 'Michael asked me, on behalf of the Board of Directors of your agency, if I could deal with the situation here. Give him my best regards when you see him, and let him know that thanks to Schiller's diligence in distributing those silly little hosts, I will have the cabinet *entirely* under control by the end of the night.'

'Eep,' says Cassie, as timidly as a mouse facing a rearing cobra.

'I'll be sure to tell him you said that,' Mo says snippishly. She takes Cassie's limp hand and tugs, gently. 'Goodbye!'

'Be seeing you!' the Mandate calls lightly as they trudge upstairs to help themselves to the facilities in the suite Schiller and his handmaids reserved for their own use. And Mo is so exhausted and frightened that she neither notices nor pays any heed to the beetle-black Jaguar spinning its tires on the gravel out front, in its driver's haste to evade the descending fly swatter.

*

Raymond Schiller flees for his life, screaming silently at the emptiness inside his head.

For the past two years he has never been alone within his skull: sleeping or waking, he lives every day in the mindful presence of divinity, of the sleeping god he awakened in the temple on the dead plateau. His first attempt at summoning the Christ-thing was thwarted, but his god is no longer comatose. Deities, like brain-damaged humans, can experience a locked-in state in which they are aware of the passage of time and of people around them. And if you try hard enough to gain such a god's attention, so hard that you loan them a part of your own brain, they may answer your prayers.

Schiller's prayers were answered on the third day, kneeling before the wrecked sarcophagus in the crypt beneath the temple – cut off from Earth by the severing of the portal through which he had entered – and his god made its wishes clear. It will take more than a handful of souls to bring the Sleeper to full awakening now – a number closer to fifty million, rather than the five thousand he tried with previously, will surely suffice – but the Sleeper is nothing if not subtle, and in its divine majesty it shows Schiller, through dreams, what tools and stratagems he must employ if he is to gain absolute control over such a cornucopia of sacrificial power.

And it was all going so smoothly, right up until the moment when Anneka, glassy-eyed and panting, lowered herself carefully onto Norman Grove's eager middle-aged erection and tensed, her pelvic floor muscles contracting around the sheath of scar tissue that surrounds the host that grows inside her in place of her womb and ovaries, and whose open cyclostomal jaws lie just behind her labia –

– *bit* down hard, then pushed herself up with her arms, gasping from the pain as half her host tears away from her, like the worker bee's barbed stinger that stays behind in its target –

– Schiller feels her moment of transcendent joy, and then the horror as, all of a sudden, the newly spawned host is ripped away from his soul, muted, blinded, deafened by the deadening numb silence that engulfs all his scattered organs. The other hosts, the eaters of tongues, have fallen silent too: what is this? What blanket of mutilation falls across his will? Why can he no longer hear the dreams of god resonating in his mind? Who has stolen his grace?

Chittering vile pests, icy parasites from outside the world, invade his empty vessels, stealing flesh and will and memories. Schiller tears himself away from the communion rite and runs. The newly inducted Inner Temple members – ministers of government one and all – are still functioning, and he sends them to the surface to aid Anneka in hunting down the intruders who have violated the glory of the coming of the Lord. But his beautiful handmaids are half-exhausted by the effort of shedding the new hosts and bringing so many to the faith, and some of them are stunned by the same assault that Schiller was barely able to resist. He flees by the emergency fire stairs at the back, and as he does so he feels a vast and horrifying sense of dread steal over him. It casts a shadow as large as his god, but penumbral and chillingly amused rather than warm and loving. The one who casts the shadow out of space is approaching the front of the house, and Schiller knows, with a flat sense of despair, that if the shadow bearer notices him then that will be all over –

Drenched in chilly sweat, shivering in the night air, Schiller yanks his surplice and vestments over his head and throws them to the ground. He stumbles down a narrow servants' passage at the back of the house, then through a scullery door and out past the stables yard at the rear. His car is parked there but he senses the presence approaching across the grounds and flees, heading away towards the front of the house. He knows he must escape, knows that any who fail to do so will be taken by the ancient foe. But he's still human enough to want to save those closest to him: If only Anneka hadn't –

There is a flare of green-white pain in his mind, a sense of Anneka's desperation and rage and love of the Lord, then the echo of a terrible voice asking, 'Is *that* the best you can do?' And he blanks for a few minutes. When he comes to himself he's in the driving seat of an unfamiliar car – a big cat snarling from the hub of the steering wheel – racing through darkness along a narrow road between hedges, overhung by the boughs of ancient trees. '*London*,' he tells himself. 'Got to get to London.' The Falcon is parked at Stansted, and if he goes there he can run for home – but maybe they'll be waiting for him? First he needs to visit the apartment in Docklands, check in with his people, see if it's safe to run and, if so, where. The climax of tonight's communion was to be his holy union with the CFO of a big internet search company in Europe. But he was to induct another new handmaid afterwards, in the apartment, wasn't there? A temple whore, a missionary, to bring the joy and the light and the host to as many powerful men as possible. He was saving himself for her – well, the part of him he shed and left in the fridge two days ago – but that's not necessary now. What *is* necessary is his passport: without it they won't let him fly home.

He ought to change into a regular suit, he realizes. And groom himself. A disheveled man in evening dress arriving at an airport with blood on his shoes and wild eyes and no papers, such a man *will* raise questions. Nor does he want to leave the hibernating host where his Lord's enemies might find it. They might *experiment* on it. They might try to *cure* it. They might find the link that binds it to his Lord and send a poison of the mind through it. If the new handmaid is waiting in accordance with his instructions, he'll take time to convert her before he leaves: but leave he must, before the new day dawns ...

Schiller drives feverishly, paying little attention to speed limits as he thunders towards the imagined safety of the city. Within the M25 he will be harder to see, he intuits, one more cell of human consciousness within the teeming, swirling dreams of the human superorganism slowly waking towards an apprehension of its own ultimate power – but here in the countryside, laid out on these strips of tarmac illuminated by the amber and unblinking gaze of streetlights, he's vulnerable to the predator that awakened and came to sniff around the edges of his ritual.

An hour passes, minutes trickling away like the rough-edged grains of crematory remains. The satnav – he can't remember having programmed it: he must have done so during the blackout when he felt Anneka die – directs him dispassionately, routing him around roadworks and blockages, and through the congestion charge zone where traffic consists almost entirely of buses, taxis, and delivery vehicles. London is a knotty rat's nest of streets but Schiller pays no attention, his mind fixed on the guide star of a higher calling as his hands manipulate the steering wheel and controls. Finally he turns the big car onto a narrow street and his robot guide recites, 'Turn left in twenty yards and you have reached your destination.'

'Praise God,' Schiller says fervently. The car park entrance looms, and he noses into it. Stops the car in the first empty space – a disabled slot, but he'll be gone before any fine can trouble him – and runs, gasping and clutching his chest, for the elevator entrance.

As the lift elevates him silently into the building, he glances down and sees that a fine mist of blood drops have soiled the gleaming tips of his shoes. Schiller shudders convulsively. Passport, papers, Anneka's briefcase and secure laptop – he remembers where she left them. One bag, that's all. He can be packed and gone in minutes, almost as if he were never here. His host twitches uneasily, squeezing uncomfortably at the crotch of his trousers. It hasn't fed recently: blood alone isn't enough, and if his men left the new girl here –

He's in the lobby of the apartment, shaking his head as the burglar alarm beeps. Punching numbers in, his hand shakes so much that he gets it wrong the first time and the beeping escalates angrily while he makes a second attempt. He double-locks the door, leans against the wall, and gasps for breath past the tightness in his chest. 'Slow down or you'll die,' he tells himself, then gasps some more. Finally he closes his eyes, and tries to recall the words to one of the prayers his Lord showed him. Peace of mind gradually steals over him as he hums the oddly alien phonemes. Yes, this is what he should do, he realizes. Leave the new missionary sister behind to work God's will on this dark island. Take the remaining host from the fridge, and the briefcase and the bible and the gun, and go to Stansted. Fly after the setting moon, to the mountains and hills of Colorado, and pray on his knees for forgiveness –

Briefcase. It's on the table. He opens it, trudges to the kitchen, and finds the Mason jar where he left it. The host within senses him and stretches languorously, comforted by proximity. And Ray realizes he can still hear it in his soul, thrumming contentedly: he's *not* alone. The caster of the shadow was a liar and his Lord is not dead. Smiling, he carries the jar back into the living room and places it inside Anneka's bag.

The bloody droplets on his evening shoes seem to mock him when he glances at the carpet.

Ray feels a stab of petulant resentment. Cometh the hour, cometh the man: but what if the hour cometh and the man is unavoidably detained? What if the man is detained indefinitely while the supplicant, the faithful worshipper, ekes out his life alone on an insignificant island where no gods tread? Or worse, where only the *wrong* gods move among the mortals? Disgusted, he walks towards the bedroom. He needs to get himself under control. Take care of business. Seal the deal. Live the dream.

He opens the bedroom door and turns on the light.

There's a woman on the bed, lying on her side, facing the doorway. She's an ice-blonde, perfect in every way but for her hair, which is cut in a flapper bob – ungodly, in his opinion, but hair can be grown out – and she wears a red silk minidress so short that her stocking tops are visible. Her wrists are cuffed and chained to her ankles behind her back. The guards gagged her, which annoys him (don't they know she could choke, unattended?) but she's awake now, staring at him with wide blue eyes.

Schiller smiles shyly as he sheds his tuxedo jacket. 'Don't be afraid,' he reassures her as he bends down to unlace his shoes. He unzips his trousers and lets them drop. 'I'm not going to hurt you.' His host flexes lazily, questing towards the future handmaid. She rolls away from him, over onto her back, muffled sounds coming from behind the leather ball gag. 'I'm going to show you something wonderful; it'll bring you closer to the Lord.' He steps out of his trousers and pushes down his boxers. 'Do you pray?' Almost shyly, 'Would you like to pray with me?'

The girl sits up, and the chains fall away from her as she spits out the ball gag that concealed her teeth. 'Yeth, but I spell it differently,' she says, lisping breathily as she leans towards him.

Schiller's eyes widen and he starts to retreat, but he's too late.

Mhari climbs across the bed, wraps uncannily strong arms around him, and leans her head against the cleft between his neck and his collar bone. 'I don't pray: you're *my* prey. *Mine*, motherfucker!'

And then she begins to feed.

EPILOGUE: THE QUISLING BREED

It's after midnight and the party's already over when I climb down the ladder from India 97's cabin, flinching slightly at the rotors whirling overhead, and walk across the field towards the garden and the floodlit mansion beyond.

The SA's waiting for me beside the open back gate to the paddock. He looks old, and gray, and so very tired.

'What,' I ask, 'the *fuck*—' voice rising – 'have you *done?*'

'Walk with me.'

He turns without waiting and walks through the gate, then along a narrow gravel path between flower beds. I swear some more, then follow him.

'Is she all right?' I call ahead.

He doesn't answer, and for a moment it feels as if my head's about to explode. I had her on speed dial and kept trying during the flight but the call went straight to voice-mail every time.

He bears right, towards a row of smaller buildings – cottages? stables? – around the side of the house, then casts around as if looking for something. Then he steps onto the lawn, walks halfway towards the yard full of parked cars behind the buildings, and stops.

'It happened here,' he says.

'What happened?'

'She should be dead.' He swallows. In the sharp glare of

the floodlights I see the shadow of his Adam's apple move. 'According to Forecasting Ops—'

'Fuck Forecasting Ops, *is she all right?*'

He cracks. 'Maybe. Probably. Not sure.'

'Why.' I take a step towards him. 'Don't. You.' Dr. Armstrong gestures at a smear of darkness near his feet. I take another step towards him and realize the grass is damp. I've just trodden in something squishy, and it smells horrible, fecal. 'Know?'

'Two class 6 or higher entities faced off at a range of five meters *right here*. You're standing in all that's left of one of them.' The light glints silver off his spectacle lenses. 'Your wife was lying right ... *there*.' He points to one end of the mess. 'Her ward was broken. According to Control's diagnostic monitoring she put her phone into Hail Mary mode just before the incident, but it would have been about as much use as an umbrella in a hurricane. Forecasting Ops projected that *if* this particular fork in the decision tree came to pass – it was only an 18 percent probability – she'd be a greasy smear on the lawn.'

I could strangle him. Fuck, I could eat his soul, except it's probably stringy and tastes of cardboard and spreadsheets. 'Is she all right?' I ask softly.

The SA takes a deep breath. 'She's on the second floor in room 309 – Schiller's guest suite – having a long, hot shower, according to Dr. Schwartz. Cassie is looking after her. She's *a bit shaken*, unquote, and she's had a very bad day. When we finish here—'

'– What—'

'– I want you to go to her.' He glances round. 'Walk with me,' he says again.

This time, I don't put up a fight.

'I made a bargain with the devil,' Dr. Armstrong says

as he picks his way across the blood-drenched grass in the direction of the car park, 'and part of the package deal is my soul. Your wife—' his voice falters – 'was going to be my successor eventually, assuming that she came through all right and passed all the tests. And assuming she did indeed survive whatever happened out here.' He raises a hand before I can interrupt: 'The person upstairs *thinks* she's your wife, Mr. Howard, the way *you* think you're still just Bob Howard, a bit of a lad who likes messing with computers and having a laugh over a pint of beer. But I want you also to be *very* certain, at the same time, that she has been at ground zero of a non-survivable event. Now, there are several various and sundry reasons – and some of them are even relatively innocent – why she might have come through; but it's also a remote possibility that she died, the way *you* died six years ago in Brookwood Cemetery – and I'm trusting *you* to work out what happened. You know what it's like to try and pay no attention to the papery whisper of the tantalizingly appetizing souls around you, so I trust you to go easy on her, but *the organization needs to know*. Because I don't believe she survived because her phone absorbed the entire force of the blast. She placed the Pale Violin beyond human reach some time ago and its master has subsequently shown no sign of interest in her, and I don't think the Black Pharaoh would have saved her out of the goodness of his heart.'

'The Black—' I blank for a moment as my brain reboots ' – the *Black Pharaoh?*'

'I said I made a deal with the devil, didn't I?' The SA shrugs. 'It was Him, or the Sleeper: who would you rather work for?'

Fuck. Fuck. Fuck. 'That's *treason*—'

'– Only if it be unsuccessful,' he says tonelessly. 'The fix is in. The fix was in even before you noticed there was a problem in need of a solution. That's why I had to keep you in the dark, in the sandbox, for so long. We work under oath to the authority vested in the Crown: but you didn't ask *which* Crown the new oath and warrant cards are sworn to. The PM's dead, Bob. Half the cabinet are brain-wormed castrati thanks to Schiller. Our biggest traditional ally appears to be in the throes of a takeover by something so much worse than the Sleeper that Schiller chose to flee and make his stand here. And the agency is in ruins. What else would you expect the Board to do?' Gravel crunches beneath my boots as we cross onto the car park. There's a big-ass pavilion on the lawn and I see ambulances with flashing lights loading up stretcher cases from inside it. 'We have to be realistic. Pick fights we can win.'

'You're beginning to sound like Iris.' I reflexively rub my right upper arm, the patch that still aches in bad weather.

'Speaking of whom.'

'Oh, you didn't ... please tell me you didn't?'

'Sorry, Bob, but that's how it's going to be, now. Meet the new boss: same as the old boss.'

A middle-aged woman in a black suit is heading our way. I recognize her and I feel a sick sense of dread. 'Michael, Bob.' She gives me a small, tight-lipped smile. 'The Leader is ready to see you now,' she tells the SA. To me: 'It's been a long time.'

'Not long enough.'

She raises an eyebrow. 'I won't hold any grudges if *you* agree not to.'

I look at Iris. I used to like her, once. That was before she sacrificed a baby in front of me. 'Life's too short,' I say, taking care to mind my words.

'I see.' She straightens her back and turns away. 'He's

waiting, Michael,' she upbraids the SA, and I experience a sudden nauseating perspective flip: *Iris* is bossing the *Senior Auditor* around? Is this what we're coming to, the shape of things under the reign of the Black Pharaoh?

'He'll deal with you later,' she tells me, offhand. 'I expect you'll want to visit your wife first.' Then she stalks away in the direction of the tent, clearly taking charge.

Dr. Armstrong looks at me.

'Why?' I ask again.

He shrugs, almost embarrassed. 'She's a good manager,' he says, almost defensively. Lowering his voice: 'If the Board had not authorized and I refused to cooperate with this, Dr. O'Brien and I would both be dead, along with the rest of the Auditors. Cassie Brewer would be dead, too, and the Host unbound, and the government in the hands of the Sleeper's Inner Temple by sunrise tomorrow. You and Johnny might have survived, if you had the wits to get on board the first flight out and not look back. This was *much* too close for comfort, Mr. Howard. We could have kept fighting, but we would have had to win every battle; they only have to win once. The Board voted to throw in their lot with a lesser evil so that a new binding *geas* could be installed. We just have to hope and trust that the lesser evil is in fact less deadly than the alternative.'

Behind him an older woman in a purple frock is picking her way towards us. 'You there! I say—'

Dr. Armstrong turns towards her. 'Can I help you?'

'You're—' She stops and peers at me – 'I saw *you* on television,' she announces, in much the same tone she might telegraph the discovery of a wasps' nest in her attic; 'weren't you disbanded? Home Office,' she adds.

I roll my eyes. 'Yeah, we were disbanded.'

'But not for long,' the SA remarks drily. 'Bob, you handle

this: I have to report to our new Master.' He walks away, whistling; he's so far off-key that it takes me a few seconds to recognize 'My Way': *I did what I had to do ...*

'What do you want?' I ask the woman from the Home Office, more brusquely than is strictly called for (because it is late and I am eager to make my way to room 309 and confirm that Mo is safe and uninjured and no more an undead thing of horror than I am).

She nearly recoils, but she's made of stern stuff: 'I was talking to a woman earlier, before the lightning strike – tall, red hair, something to do with Transhuman Coordination, I think she was one of your lot—' *Now* she recoils as I stare at her.

'Yes?'

'– So she *is* one of your people?'

'What happened?' I demand.

Home Office woman bends but doesn't quite reach breaking point: 'She went that way,' she points at the lawn, 'told me to follow. And I saw what happened. The lightning strike? The woman in white with the gun and the glowing jade eyes, and the man with no face and a laugh like dust swirling in an empty tomb – and *she wasn't there*, between the first stroke of lightning and the next—' She blinks rapidly and begins to shake – 'and I want to say, I need, if you're looking for her I'm supposed to tell you something, something like—' Her eye begin to glow and her voice changes as something hijacks her larynx: '*Aw der hal amedn aset, aw der hal amedn aset! Aw der hal amedn aset, aw der hal—*'

It's a feeder, of course. Dumb, but not so dumb you can't program them to loop a message, like a demented voicemail machine from hell. Fucker must have crept in while the cleanup crew's back was turned, and of course the civilians aren't warded. Being looped, it's too busy running her vocal chords to eat properly, so I crunch down on it and catch her body as she topples. She's still breathing, so maybe she'll survive the attack. But right now I'm so furious and frightened I hardly care.

I wave for a paramedic, then walk towards the steps up to the terrace and the open French doors to join the Black Pharaoh's court, leaving the last of the humans behind.

Look out for

THE LABYRINTH INDEX

by

Charles Stross

Britain is under New Management. The disbanding of the Laundry – the British espionage agency that deals with supernatural threats, has culminated in the unthinkable – an elder god in residence in 10 Downing Street.

But in true 'the enemy of my enemy' fashion, Mhairi Murphy finds herself working with His Excellency Nylarlathotep on foreign policy – there are worse things, it seems, than an elder god in power, and they lie in deepest, darkest America.

A thousand-mile-wide storm system has blanketed the midwest, and the president is nowhere to be found – Mhari must lead a task force of disgraced Laundry personnel into the storm front to discover the truth. But working for an elder god is never easy, and as the stakes rise, Mhari will soon question exactly where her loyalties really lie.

orbit

www.orbitbooks.net

extras

www.orbitbooks.net

about the author

Charles Stross is a full-time science fiction writer and resident of Edinburgh, Scotland. The author of seven Hugo-nominated novels and winner of the 2005, 2010 and 2014 Hugo Awards for best novella ('The Concrete Jungle', 'Palimpsest' and 'Equoid'), Stross's works have been translated into over twelve languages.

Like many writers, Stross has had a variety of careers, occupations and job-shaped catastrophes in the past, from pharmacist (he quit after the second police stake-out) to first code monkey on the team of a successful dot-com start-up (with brilliant timing he tried to change employer just as the bubble burst). Along the way he collected degrees in Pharmacy and Computer Science, making him the world's first officially qualified cyberpunk writer (just as cyberpunk died).

In 2013, he was Creative in Residence at the UK-wide Centre for Creativity, Regulation, Enterprise and Technology, researching the business models and regulation of industries such as music, film, TV, computer games and publishing.

Find out more about Charles Stross and other Orbit authors by registering for the free monthly newsletter at www.orbitbooks.net.

if you enjoyed
THE DELIRIUM BRIEF

look out for

EVERYTHING ABOUT YOU

by

Heather Child

Freya has a new virtual assistant. It knows what she likes, knows what she wants and knows whose voice she most needs to hear: her missing sister's.

It adopts her sister's personality, recreating her through a life lived online. This data ghost knows everything about Freya's sister: every date she ever went on, every photo she took, every secret she ever shared.

In fact it knows things it shouldn't be possible to know. It's almost as if her sister is still out there somewhere, feeding fresh updates into the cloud. But that's impossible. Isn't it?

1

The voice is young, buttery and upbeat. It settles against her skin and calls up something within her, some emotion impossible to place. 'Wake up,' it says again, and Freya obediently wriggles under her duvet. She looks around, seeing no one but hearing the echo of a tone compelling enough to make her move first and ask questions later. The blind is closed, January's blue-slush light no match for the luminous dawn spreading across her wallpaper: birds trilling and flitting above flower-fogged meadows, the sensory gradient she usually ascends to wakefulness over a period of thirty minutes or so. Now she is jittery, still tangled in the covers and struggling to sip her water. It was a mistake to install this app, the latest smartface, which is currently telling her she looks cold, that it will turn up the thermostat. She skims a hand along the roughened texture of her arms, wondering if it is clever enough to perceive her goose bumps through the wallpaper webcams.

'Why did you wake me? I'm not late, am I?'

'You will be,' says the invisible speaker.

This is outrageously cheeky. Freya snatches up the smiley-faced sphere from her desk and examines it, feeling the almost skin-like texture of the plastic. There is no need for this ball, but it means people who want to give a smartface as a gift have something to wrap. When she turned it on last night, her wallpaper exploded into balloons and the words *Happy birthday, Julian!* She had to reset it to factory defaults.

Replacing the object in frustration, she remembers Julian's father dumping the Smarti gift bag on the table the evening before, snapping, 'There's his present,' before storming out. It rattled her, and left the room sour with aftershave. Later, Freya watched Julian take out the two boxes, the very latest tech and off the scale in terms of price.

'Smarti tat,' he scoffed. 'Designed to speed up my job hunt.' To him it was just stuff his dad had brought home from work – a lazy option. The items were left on the table as he screwed up the bag disdainfully and went to the kitchen. When he returned, he registered that Freya was interested in the little red sphere and tossed it in her direction. 'You want it? Go ahead. I can't be assed with chatbots.' The larger box, a state-of-the-art Halo headset, he tucked under his arm before returning to the mulchy aromas of his bedroom.

Maybe he had a point, and she was wrong to be seduced by all the hype, or by her colleague Chris, who is virtually in love with his smartface. They are coming down in price, but Julian's model is the latest incarnation, super-intelligent and maybe – considering the 'beta' sticker – not even on general sale yet. The voice launches into a weather report, and because of the goose-bumps incident, she finds herself dressing between the screening doors of her wardrobe. Her red necktie, the most clown-like piece of her workwear, still looks wrong no matter how she knots it. She takes scissors from a drawer and snips raggedy bits from the hems of her trousers, which are too long and drag on the ground as she walks. It is only a matter of time before her supervisor spots the state of them, or he may have noticed already and is saving it up.

When the flat is this quiet, which is most of the time, she finds herself becoming silent too, padding carefully through the empty living room and into the kitchen. The toaster has timed it correctly for once and ejects a pre-spread slice into her waiting fingers, perfectly crisp. If she wants to talk to someone, there are always her African land snails. They slide along the piece of mirror in their tank, their pointed shells like the sails of extremely slow ships.

'Would you like some lettuce?' she asks, fetching a buckled leaf of romaine and placing it among the questing antennae. There is something calming about watching them move around their little glass universe. She has kept snails, and usually a lizard of one kind or another, since she was twelve. Following a sociable breakfast, Freya discovers the lid was ajar and one snail has escaped as far as the tabletop. It makes a sucking sound as she detaches it and returns it to the tank. 'It's for your own safety, mate.'

Back in her room, she pulls on her shoes and quickly checks Social – her wallpaper becoming a stream of comments – wondering if she has missed any interesting posts during the night. Something catches her eye, riles her and before she knows it, she is interjecting in an argument about snail eggs – the need to regularly check for and freeze them. When she shares a how-to video, the smartface voice rises gently from the speakers, complimenting her on the choice and suggesting another, offering to post the clip in her stead, as Freya is now very late for work. She looks at the time and leaps up, horrified. Trouser-hem fibres flutter down as she dashes from her room, throwing on her toggled winter coat.

Outside, her legs are repeatedly drenched as driverless cars slough through the puddles. In an ideal world they would stop and give her a lift in recompense, but there is about as much chance of that as there is of her supervisor failing to notice her lateness, or being cool about it. Even now he is probably checking his vintage watch and smiling, looking forward to dousing her with his scorn.

The monolithic concrete of the flyover looms up overhead and gives Freya a sense of her own smallness, hurrying along inelegantly in her ill-fitting uniform. For distraction, she unfolds her smartspecs, the pin-thin titanium sharp behind her ears before no-feel technology makes it vanish. Through her glasses, the flyover becomes a canopy, thick with flowers and succulent green leaves. The projection is semi-lucent, just a faint augmentation of her surroundings. A full virtual-reality immersion would be more than she could handle, but she enjoys seeing the graffiti turn into phosphorescent petals, mallowy buds opening as she passes, each road a river she will cross on stepping stones.

'Stop!' the smartface commands. Her outstretched foot hovers over the kerb and then pulls back, just as a bike whizzes past.

'Whoa,' Freya says, realising a collision was narrowly avoided. 'How did you know?'

'GPS.' The voice seems to shrug.

Freya removes the smartspecs, slightly concerned at her everyday special effects nearly resulting in an accident. Normally a cyclist would trigger them to turn off, but this one may have been travelling too fast. Her steps are cautious as she covers the last few hundred metres of pavement, the glass wall already in view, builders still in the process of converting a couple of acres of sales floor into flats.

It used to be fun at U-Home, back when they still had the showroom. Customers would get lost on the winding path through endless bedrooms, lounges and kitchens, and Freya would enjoy directing them through secret short cuts. The place was piled high with every kind of furniture, along with silos of polka-dot cushions or cuddly frogs, mountains of colourful mugs and fold-up storage cubes. There were forests of lamps, bunk beds, cupboards and other hiding places, and interesting colleagues whose true calling was a million miles from flat-pack furniture. She remembers a girl who could escape from twelve knots of washing line and a locked wardrobe in under two minutes, eventually fired for asking one too many elderly gentlemen – who couldn't believe their luck – to tie her up. Most of Freya's friends left during the refurb: Michelle, who always had a New Wave DJ playing inside her head, Kat the landscape gardener, and the two Moldovan students who claimed to live on caviar and high-end vodka but thought the store was a cool place to work.

The double doors swing closed behind her, and the sales floor flickers. The catalogue has been hologrammed, haptic gloves by each pedestal so customers can feel the texture of fabrics, open drawers and pat mattresses. Beyond these platforms, the springy wooden chairs of the café are oddly untidy, no sign of the catering staff. The only living creature she can see is Sandor, stalking past the cutlery island, his sideburns puffing up as he smiles. This puts her on her guard. Her supervisor's baseline is a mood of low-level bitterness, and any variation on this tends to mean he has something up his sleeve. She checks her necktie is still fastened, wishing she was on time. A cheese smudge has somehow appeared on her trousers. Where is Chris? Her colleague's usual style, especially if she is late, is to come in early, making her look even worse. It unsettles her not to see his tall, skinny figure, a stake she can cling to in the face of whatever storm is gathering.

Beside the largest pedestal, Sandor intercepts her, standing too close and rocking forward on the balls of his feet so his toilet-scented breath diffuses across the short distance.

'Freya.'

'Morning.' Her voice is full of brittle cheer.

He can hardly contain himself, grinning and twitching. He slinks around the pedestal so she is viewing him through a semi-transparent wardrobe, which morphs into a bookcase. He tugs back his shirtsleeve and brandishes a finger, like scissors at a ribbon-cutting ceremony, before reaching for the control pad.

'I have something to show you.'

Before she can frown at these ominous words, a geyser of light spurts up, startling her. The spectre stands smiling, saying something inaudible but enthusiastic, giving her its full attention. She flinches as a hand – smooth as a globule of oil gliding through water – reaches out and narrowly misses her arm. Lips move and she hears the words: 'I'll just look you up ... Ah, Freya! I hope you're having a great day. Can I interest you in new blinds?' The figure is female, about her height. Its shirt is blistering white, the necktie sculpted into that perfect ruffle Freya can never achieve. But here the wrongness starts: the eyes are too luminous, disproportionately large and electric blue. Then there is the cartoon skin, the healthy Vaseline glow. The whole figure is somehow weightless, free of scent or presence, but waiting earnestly for a response. Freya's throat has gone dry. Sandor looks on tenderly.

'Isn't she adorable?'

'What is it?'

'I've called this one Helpful Holly.'

It looks up, hearing its name.

Why have they brought in a hologram assistant? Freya wonders if Chris could somehow have quit, or been sacked, since they worked together on Saturday. Conceivably Sandor is about to sack her too; that would almost be preferable to being left alone with this. She has seen these projections before, but never so close, never wearing what she is wearing. It smiles with its milky, heart-shaped face. Her supervisor reaches out and slices a hand through its abdomen, laughing as the light-generated figure steps back and wags a finger playfully. It must be programmed to have faintly human reactions, though this hardly makes it seem normal. Just as she starts to back away, Chris appears from the kitchens.

'Ah, I was just making introductions.' Sandor's laugh becomes artificial as he realises he is the only one amused. He taps the control pad and the figure vanishes, along with several leaf-print blinds that have started rolling and unrolling in the air. 'So there we are,' he adds, as though everyone has been fully briefed. 'You'll both need to be on catering today.'

After administering this casual demotion, which Freya fears will be permanent, Sandor strolls back to his office. She wishes she was immune to him, like Chris, who is calmly directing a series of obscene gestures in his wake. Her colleague is wearing two PVC aprons, one on top of the other.

'What's going on?' she says.

The fabric crackles as he manoeuvres one over his head, careful not to mess up his blond spikes.

'Just take the apron.'

Seconds later, she is behind the food counters, hair imperfectly tucked into a net, plastic gloves on her hands. Chris is dumping sausages into a stainless-steel tray under the heat lamps.

'So we're supposed to be dinner ladies?' She gazes into the vat of grey-brown sauce.

'Why were you so late? Customer shows up, hologram is there bang on time.' He hits the counter on *bang*, making the trays of food rattle. One or two early shoppers look over, and Freya shrinks, wondering if the hooded counter amplifies what they say.

'What about Jacqueline? Isn't she coming back?' Her whisper is met with a shrug.

'Guess not, and this way they get to test the new tech.' Steam rises as he stirs the beans ferociously. They both know their contracts allow for pretty much anything, short of harvesting their organs. Freya clenches and unclenches her fists, testing the sensation of latex stretched over her knuckles. The apron reaches almost to her feet. When she blinks, constellations of light appear in the shape of the hologram assistant, shaking its balloon-satin head and stepping back as Sandor's hand passes through insubstantial flesh. Its voice is different to that of her smartface, higher-pitched, more synthetic, and skidding into each phrase as though from a laugh. This being will now be taking her place, talking to customers, placing orders, taking payments from smartaccounts. It makes her feel strangely empty, as though she is the one made of light.

'Why don't they get a robot to dispense food? That's the dumber job of the two,' she mutters to Chris, driving a spoon into the mashed potato. 'It doesn't make sense.'

A young couple appears at the counter, and it takes a

second to remember what she is supposed to do. Her body lurches into action and she scoops six chicken nuggets towards their plates, dropping them from too much of a height so she loses two and has to add another scoop. Even on tiptoes she struggles to hand the meals over the top of the Perspex. Her colleague watches the performance, entertained. Then he sighs. 'It does make sense, if you think about it. The holograms only have to talk, they're made of nothing, no expensive robotics, plus they can keep every detail of size or fabric in their sparky little brains ...'

'I was pretty good at that.'

'... tap into people's data,' he continues, prodding her, 'and find out what they've already bought for their house. Do you know what a customer's looking for as soon as they walk in? Or what goes with their phlegm-yellow sofa? Or whether they've got any money?'

She sinks back into silence, cataloguing the dealings she has had with hologram staff. They are often help-desk assistants or receptionists, taking the brand as their personality, their age and appearance tailored to the company's target audience. They are dirt cheap, reasonably effective and keep levels of graduate employment at record lows. In her mind, she hears her mum's entreaties to take an internship – Freya was reluctant to pay the fee – at any large company, because entry-level positions are dying out. Although U-Home has been focusing on its virtual catalogue, selling off the sales floors level by level, she never really imagined it would come to this. Freya looks down at herself. Apart from the odd lapse in timekeeping, she has always been professional, learning about new products, listening to Sandor's lectures and encouraging customers to fill their houses with as much furniture as possible. These two years of steady graft were supposed to lead to promotion, maybe even something that could be called a career.

Chris hands her a spray bottle and points to the tables, which are covered in half-dried streaks of ketchup and splashes of coffee. She gets to work, forcing herself not to sniff, though the cleaning product gets up her nose anyway, diffusing everywhere as she squirts too many times onto the chrome. There is a certain familiar fizz to it, and she examines the bottle. Lemongrass. She used to smell this same spicy citrus constantly when they were living at home. It was the incense favoured by Ruby to overwrite cigarette smoke on her clothes, though this is a more chemically version. *You wouldn't like it.* She closes her eyes as pinpricks of lemon settle on her cheeks. *You wouldn't like any of this.*

Back at the counter, Chris doles out kid-size burgers, scoops of mash and rectangles of lasagne, a salty steam rising from the food.

'Any sauce, sir?' He is brisk and courteous. A lot of people come here for breakfast, or for a cheap hot lunch, almost as though they have forgotten it is a furniture store. Several are already seated, cardboard cups brimming with orangeade, too-smooth mash being smeared onto their forks. When a long queue has been served and is lining up to pay at the thumb scanner, Chris places his hands above his buttocks and leans back, groaning. The hairnet stretched over his quiff is obviously bothering him, as is the apron. Outside work he dresses sharply, or at least unexpectedly. The recent incorporation of old tweed coats into his wardrobe has provided Freya with much amusement. More than once she has wondered what he is still doing here, as the work becomes less interesting and Sandor more unreasonable. Surely Chris has outgrown the place, extending upwards – as he does now – like a plant in search of light. He is twenty-one and full of ideas. When he turns, having stretched as much as he can, she is surprised to find his expression cloudy.

'It's true what you say,' he continues, ignoring the gap in their conversation. 'They could get bots for this too. Let's be on our best behaviour, do customer service till it's coming out of our eyes.'

She stares at him, searching for irony. When none appears, her expression changes to one of compassion. He must genuinely be afraid of losing his job. Perhaps it is money-related, a bad time to find something else.

'I'll be on my best behaviour,' she says, 'as ever.'

By late afternoon, it has quietened down, just a few customers flicking through furniture. She and Chris start picking up bits of food dropped by children and pouring out the mingling Coke and lemonade from the dispenser's over-spill trays. Towards the end of their shift, she remembers what she meant to tell him earlier.

'Hey, do you still have Prince George?'

'My sweet prince?' A doting look as he brings his beloved virtual assistant to mind.

'I've just got a smartface. The latest model.'

'What, a Smarti one? Not like you to splash out ...'

'It was a Julian cast-off.'

'I see,' he smirks, gathering an armful of cleaning products. 'All right for some.' As he swoops down to the cupboard, she resists the urge to twang his hairnet.

'It hasn't done the washing-up yet.'

'Trust me, you'll never look back.'

He continues rearranging the cleaning bottles, a dreamy

smile on his face. She can see the attraction of a virtual assistant, but there is something odd about hearing a voice from nowhere.

'What does a smartface do for you?' She yanks an empty stainless-steel tray out of the counter. The heat lamps are like tropical sun on her arms.

'Everything. Half the time I don't even have to ask; George just looks at my data and works out what I need. No more searching or decisions, that whole step completely skipped.' His hand leapfrogs over hers to help pull out the other trays. 'I just wish I had one of the newer ones, like yours, with the more powerful learning processors. But he learns. He can tell if I've had a bad day.'

'Can't we all?'

'Honestly, it's very liberating. Friday was my housemate's birthday, and I knew nothing about it until the present George had bought him – from me – turned up wrapped and ready on the doorstep.'

'He bought it with your money?'

'It was another of those war figurines he likes. Yeah, with my money, but the amount I'd normally spend. To the pound.'

Freya is quiet, uncertain about having someone dip into her funds. Chris is happy to let his smartface – or Prince George, the celebrity persona he has chosen for it – handle things. He allowed it to book him a holiday in Scotland in the summer, after the virtual assistant measured his blood pressure and found it high. She was jealous when he came back to work all ruddy-cheeked and relaxed, if somewhat poorer. Since then he has been completely besotted with Prince George, spending many an evening just talking to him, or even – he has confessed – trying to chat him up, and pretending the young royal has ditched his Cambridge halls for a crowded Catford house share.

'I don't think I need it.'

He dumps the trays with a crash, making her jump.

'If anyone needs it, you do. Or are you planning to live with your ex for ever?'

She is taken aback, but says nothing. Chris's disgusted face vanishes from view as he ducks under the counter to wipe up some gravy dribbles. 'Honestly, Freya,' he adds, 'you need to let it kick you up the arse.'

Later, the shift having passed to the evening staff, she peels off her gloves, noticing blotches on her wrists from the licks of hot fat. Chris's words have also made their mark. Her living arrangements are stale, the crust of her relationship having broken off to reveal a new side of Julian, fast becoming intolerable. Though her instinct is normally to wait and see, it feels like good timing to have this smartface fall into her lap. Perhaps she should grasp it with both hands and get it to help her with whatever degree of *smart* it can muster.

With new resolve, she puts on her specs, a pink map-line stretching along the road to indicate her route home. As she passes the bakery, a cartoon scone appears, floating like an alien outside the door, and says it looks forward to seeing her tomorrow. She finds this unusually irritating, and blinks to dismiss it, nearly bumping into a woman who adjusts the lapels of her tiny, fashionable jacket and flutters mocking eyelashes at the smartspecs. Most people use long-term contact lenses these days, but Freya prefers something she can remove. The woman resumes a conversation as she walks away, perhaps asking her own personal assistant to sort out her weekend or decide what movie to watch. It is one of those technologies that people are starting to find too useful to do without, the adverts focusing heavily on how smart-faces have helpfulness at the heart of their coding, and if the user is a little hazy about what they really want – either in life or in the next five minutes – the intelligent assistant will simply analyse their data and find out. It is something that has sparked debate in the media, though few can argue that everything you've ever said and done is not a reasonable guide to what you might want in the future.

'Okay, smartface,' Freya announces, 'I want you to think long-term. What can you offer?'

'Long-term?' the voice chirps. 'You mean life decisions, what diseases you might get, children's names, where you might be living—'

'That last one,' Freya turns off the road to cut through a wilderness of brambles. 'Wait, what do you mean, what diseases I might get?' She traces the lines on her palm with a finger, wondering whether to let this virtual assistant tell her fortune. The idea does not appeal. 'No ... let's stick to where I could be living.'

'You want to get away from Julian, right?'

'Right.'

It is pleasing how quickly the smartface grasps her meaning. While the algorithms crunch through her data and the complex choice of accommodation in a city like London, Freya's feet crush wet twigs and crisp packets. She discovered this short cut soon after she moved here, all overgrown hawthorn hedges and fly-tipped fridges, a rare strip of land undeveloped and never categorised as a greenzone. It is the nearest thing to stepping outside the city for a few moments. The thick grass is brown at the roots, rotting from beneath and sweetly malodorous. Images of apartments pop up on her smartspecs, projected a couple of metres ahead on the left of her visual field. The overriding impression is of beige carpets and corrugated iron, garage-like spaces that barely try to hide their bleakness. Day is bruising into night, the sky so heavy overhead it seems to bulge. For the first time, she recognises the weight of sadness that has been growing inside.

'You know,' she murmurs, 'I was downgraded today, replaced by a hologram.'

Just as she accepts the smartface is not going to reply, it says:

'I'm sorry.'

All day she has been hearing artificial voices offer her warm sentiment and best wishes. In a different mood she would take this sympathetic response and might even, with customary politeness, thank the computer. But her eyes are still smarting with the outline of Helpful Holly.

'The hell you are. You're not real.' The sharp words are refreshing, like a strong mint.

Her smartface's reply is measured, even indignant.

'Hey, if I were real, I'd be sorry.'

What is it about this voice? It has an irritating kernel of arrogance. What right does it have to be so overfamiliar, when prior to last night it did not even exist? She wants to uninstall it then and there, but Chris's words replay in her ears. If she keeps tossing opportunities away, nothing will ever change. Just give it one more try, she tells herself, look at the settings and pick a 'face' that is slightly less cocky.

'There are celebrity choices, right?' she muses aloud. Chris has his prince; there must be some actor with a voice she can tolerate.

'You can choose absolutely any celebrity and your

smartface will function based on their data. As it is, my personality was chosen using all the defaults available to this beta model.'

The first drops of rain land on her forehead.

'What does that mean?'

'So in a way I'm real. I'm based on the data of a real person.'

She cannot help being impressed that the smartface has this capacity to pursue an argument. There used to be a test, a Turing test, it was called, to see if a computer could create conversation indistinguishable from that of a human. It must be fifteen or twenty years now since the chatbots passed it.

'Who might that be?' She pictures some bland customer-services assistant, paid a token fee to let her cat-loving, microwave-meal identity be bundled and installed on a million smartfaces worldwide.

'Well, it's me, Ruby.'

Her feet come to a halt, wet grass plastering her ankles. There is no longer any need to breathe. She can just stand there and let the words fall against her skin, the touch of them, that sensation that has bothered her all day, hatching into shivers that crawl up and down her spine. A voice so familiar, so long unheard. Already her forehead is numb from the frozen rain, and the pink map-line startles into a timer icon, gutters and vanishes.

2

All the way home her mind spins like a centrifuge, scattering her thoughts. It is not until she is rubbing her hair with the kitchen towel that she can think straight. Flinging open cupboard doors, she locates a litre bottle of vodka, very old, just a couple of inches left. The way she is feeling, there is no need for a mixer, or even ice.

Her clammy, rain-wet skin is impossible to dry, and the shocking announcement from her smartface keeps replaying in her ears. The spotlights flicker, and Ruby is a sprite, hiding here and there in the kitchen, peeping from the empty space in the vodka bottle or the cupboard, crouching beside the fat digestive biscuits, identical to the ones she brought to the community centre when she made s'mores without a fire. With shaky hands, Freya takes these down too. *The biscuit is just the beginning.* Ruby's surprisingly large fingers, washed free of soil, the nails unpainted, holding one and smearing a knifeful of Nutella on top. Normally a s'more was a piece of chocolate and a marshmallow melted together, but the Conservation Hub considered campfires too dangerous. The risk of litigation had also cut short the day's activity of digging a wildlife pond – which Freya had been eagerly anticipating – due to the quantity of broken glass turned over by their shovels, the fact that ten-year-olds were flinging trowels of glittery soil at eye level. There was some other reason why she was angry, which escapes her now, but she remembers stamping off to the kitchen, hoping for some cake or a bit of chocolate, and finding Ruby already in the process of creating the perfect comfort food.

The older girl had not been around long, but was spending a lot of time at the Hub. Officially, she was in the naughty group, the girls who sat on the wall in tiny skirts, smoking, swiping through faces on their phones, laughing if a leader dared to suggest an activity. Most of them became typecast, but Ruby was different. If something caught her fancy, she would ease herself down from the wall and saunter off to mess about with seeds, or cut up bits of fabric, or string together CDs to make ridiculous jewellery. Youth workers latched onto her, the key to reforming the other rebels, but when they turned their backs she would be outside again, leading the call to tease some passing boy, or trying to get onto the roof, which drove their safety-conscious minds to distraction. She seemed self-contained, always wearing the same burgundy jumper that reminded Freya of a poncho. If you did not know her, or if she was not smiling, Ruby could look a little mean. But when her eyes creased, full of warmth, you would realise she was just very laid-back. Freya became familiar with her excessive yawns, arms splayed and jaw almost dislocating, gurgling like a zombie for brains, until limbs and lips regrouped and she would once again be an attractive girl, playful under half-closed eyes. Freya can still bring her facial expressions to mind, the way she would rub beneath her lip, paranoid that her lipstick had gone awry, or twist a lock of hair round her finger.

As the smell of nutty chocolate drew her into the kitchen, Freya saw the other girl look up sharply, and was expecting to be told to get lost. Instead Ruby gave a conspiratorial squint, sticking her knife straight from the Nutella into a jar of white foam.

'Where did you get the marshmallow fluff?' Freya wanted to know.

The question brought an impish grin to Ruby's face. 'My dad.' He was apparently in the States. Later, when they got to know each other, she admitted that all the goodies she used to bring in – the Lucky Charms, Hershey's and Oh Henry bars – were bought at great expense from a shop that sold American imports. It was a source of silent anguish that her dad had sent nothing, not a word, since he left.

This was outside Freya's experience, her mum having frozen her eggs and bought donor sperm in her late thirties when it looked unlikely that a suitable partner would show up. All the men were frightened as rabbits, Esther would say, before widening her eyes in a way that made her look slightly scary. When Freya related this tale to Ruby, she found herself sounding more melancholy than she really felt.

'So you never had anyone, babes?' Ruby asked, hugging her knees. By now they were sitting together on the wall, most of the other teenagers having been picked up already. When Freya shook her head – realising that mums didn't seem to count – the older girl passed her a half-squashed cigarette. The little stick was warm between her fingers and, though she only pretended to puff it, she took pleasure in the bond forming between the two of them. They were two atoms, the roll-up like an electron passed from one to the other, though Freya kept this geeky illustration to herself. At the time, she was in the habit of thinking in terms of scientific processes, designing experiments to see if she could fit in with London kids, or at least understand their weirdness. Things were starting to get desperate.

Up in Lincolnshire, where they lived before, she acquired friends at primary school without any particular thought. If there were times she had to question herself and her ability to fit in, they have vanished from memory. Peckham was a different story, a school full of individuals who could barely tolerate those around them. All Freya wanted was to find her place in their ecosystem, but it was like dealing with an alien race. They stood in dark huddles of headphones and screens, pale skin exposed numbly to the winter chill. She remembers going up to a girl with pink and white plaits and trying to start a conversation. The girl pulled back as though Freya were a sticky patch on a desk. 'What you talking to me for?' she said, staring her down. Other times she would perk up as someone turned to address her, only to realise that a mic was buried in their hair. Even when people at the school did interact, it was quantified in likes and comments, with anyone slow to respond falling from grace. Freya had been making do with old-school technology and was quickly painted a country bumpkin, or simply 'northern', no matter how often she insisted that Lincolnshire was East Midlands.

Her appetite for learning directed itself beyond the usual subjects, so she would grow mould on Tupperware lids, fascinated by the topiary she could achieve, but forget to do her English homework. Later she would wonder what was wrong with her, shut herself away and watch documentaries until she fell asleep. It was a lifestyle that worried her mum, who reacted by planning activities, trying to be a substitute for all the friends Freya expected to make at secondary school. When Esther's job became more intense, she indulged her daughter with as many pets as could feasibly be contained within a small Peckham flat, and enrolled her at the Conservation Hub. This at least gave Freya a place to go, two evenings a week, though since its funding relied on it sweeping together any 'youth' who might otherwise behave in an antisocial way, she was not typical clientele.

Neither was Ruby, though she was definitely a loiterer on street corners. After that first meeting, they gravitated together, finding things in common, and Freya started her next school term dusted with the kudos of hanging out with someone a couple of years older. Ruby did geeky stuff in a non-geeky way. She was interested in facts, in certain periods of history and in any kind of experiment, from roasting bits of plastic over her lighter, to seeing whether they could pass for eighteen (Ruby: always; Freya: never). They would be seen together on top of a bus stop, or with cans of Coke-Bull on the yellow grass of the Rye, oblivious to the rest of the world. Freya was stunned that Ruby wanted to hang out with her, and every now and then the older girl poked fun at her insecurity, sometimes managing to puncture it.

Though she did not see Ruby at school, Freya found things changing. In the echoing corridors, in those hitherto bleak gaps between lessons, people would seem to see her where they had previously looked straight through her. At first she put it down to the efforts she had made, with Ruby's help, to finally get a foot in the door of the most popular virtual hangouts. Ruby had some good tips on setting up reciprocal cycles of 'liking'. Later, with every new word spoken to her, she felt as though something new and physical was running through her system, as though she was more substantial now, transformed into a molecule with different properties.

Years have passed since her schooldays, yet the emotions come back fully formed. She cradles the mug in her palms and carries it to the living room, remembering that back then it would have been ceramic, easy to smash and impossible to recycle. Now every cup in the flat is made of resin, warm to the touch. She sniffs the vodka and takes a gulp. It is liquid cruelty, enough to burn her throat, but not sufficient to get her drunk. Across the room, her leopard gecko places a delicate five-fingered hand against the glass.

Though it wasn't something that could be said, she knows that if she had not met Ruby in that second year after moving to London, something would have happened. The unfairness of being plucked from village life and left without a friend was starting to grow like a hard ball, a gallstone of anger in her heart. In every sense, Ruby saved her, and Freya thought she would never get the chance to return the favour. Not until the following Easter, anyway, when she became aware that no one was picking Ruby up from the Conservation Hub. No one had ever picked her up. How could it have taken Freya so long to realise that all this time her friend just waited for everyone else to leave and then made her own way home?

Ruby did not like to talk about anything 'downbeat', so Freya knew almost nothing until that one June evening, when the older girl's usually serene eyes were turning red under their thick eyeliner. Her mum's alcoholism had been a closely guarded secret, and now it had advanced to Korsakoff's, which Freya understood to be a sort of dementia brought on by the booze. It was impractical for there to be a fourteen-year-old in her care. Ruby sat on the wall outside the Conservation Hub smoking half a cigarette, talking in a gravelly monotone about options for sleeping rough in the Peckham area: the big log by the children's play area on the Rye, the top floor of the car park or maybe one of the railway arches, if she could find a gap between the tapas joints and cocktail bars.

'Or you could just have a sleepover with me,' Freya said.

At this stage the council had not told Ruby for sure that she would have to move out, but it was only a matter of time. The only relative she had was a grandmother in Manchester, dependent on a care assistant. Ruby's plan, should they try and make her go up there, or into foster care, was to somehow get herself to America and go looking for her dad.

'I could get the money,' she said, although she did not explain how.

That first night Ruby gave in and came home with Freya. She started staying a few days a week, just while arrangements were made. By the time her mother was ready to move to a specialist facility, Ruby was in a state of agitation. While her general manner did not change, her eyes remained bloodshot and she would pinch fingernail-sized wisps of hair and tie them full of knots when she thought no one was looking. Freya knew her friend's thoughts were turning sinister, the idea of running away ripening fearfully in her mind. There was something troubling about the way she sat on the casement windowsill with one leg hanging out, her eyes yellow with evening light, as though she might jump.

So it was with great relief that Freya came home one day to find her mum stapling a market pashmina over the box-room window and moving the junk into storage cases so Ruby might be installed there more permanently. Esther bought a rail and clothes hangers, bedding that was not half eaten by moths and a paper star lampshade. With the practical approach of someone who had worked in healthcare all her life, she settled Ruby with minimal fuss, checking on her well-being, referring without awkwardness to her mother's condition, but not dwelling on it except to offer support if Ruby wanted to go and visit the facility.

'I don't,' Ruby would always say. 'But thanks.'

Whenever there were negotiations with social workers, Esther managed to intimidate them with her simplicity. Freya remembers one particular encounter, when a woman appeared at the door and introduced herself as something beginning with Mrs, the prefix making her sound instantly old-fashioned. She brought the drizzly morning into the house, a dust of rain on the shoulders of her mustard coat. Ruby took one look and, having not been spotted, escaped to her room. Esther stepped in, smiling benignly, a thick crocheted blanket wrapped around her shoulders.

'She can stay here for a bit, can't she?' The lightness in her voice was disarming.

'Well, yes, but there are a range of options ... a decision for her to make ... in time.' The woman peered into the flat, tugging at her coiled scarf. Esther let the pause grow.

'No rush, though.'

'No, no, of course not.'

Freya was grateful for her mum's ability to buffet people with her silences, gently ushering the woman from their threshold.

'Just doing her job,' she commented sternly to her daughter, the moment the door was closed.

After the first couple of weeks, something shifted; there were signs her mum was considering a longer-term arrangement. Freya was surprised how quickly it was happening. Phone calls started to be taken in the corridor, words like *guardianship*, *legalities* and *food budget* leaking through the keyhole. Esther took Ruby aside and had a serious conversation about whether she might choose them as a foster family. She was honest about everything, including the fact that they would receive money towards her board, and there was only the box-room to live in. It was in Ruby's hands.

They went to a posh coffee shop to celebrate. Hot chocolates for the girls, and a large cappuccino for Esther. Freya had not yet learned to share her mum's passion for good-quality coffee, but she liked the smell and the array of treats under the counter.

'She won't have a cake,' she explained to Ruby, 'but she loves these little caramelised biscuits you get for free.' She took hers and moved it to her mum's saucer. Ruby did the same, simultaneously starting to whisper some detail about the 'serious conversation'. It was something Freya would always admire about her foster-sister: through all of it, she never deceived herself. Once she accepted the offer of a home, she received the welcome and the affection without anxiety, with only a vestigial acknowledgement of being new to the family. Both Freya and her mum were surprised – happy, of course – that the process hadn't been as bumpy as anticipated.

Freya had long since stopped watching anxiously as her mum prepared three plates of food every evening, licking tahini off the spoon and scrabbling for cutlery. It seemed to suit her, to have offered a home to a homeless child. She had always been amenable to fostering, and had even taken in a little boy for a short time one autumn when Freya was four. Her leaning towards 'community' remained as strong as ever, and moving to this block of Peckham flats, so crowded together yet so isolated, left that part of her aching to be fulfilled. Now she had a livelier household, was giving back to society, and could lay claim to a slightly more radical self-image. Freya was fearful at first that something would go wrong, but Ruby was more skilled than she realised at getting on with adults, and would sometimes talk to Esther as though they were old friends. They would cook alongside each other, their hands smelling of garlic and ginger.

The box-room must have been partitioned off by some money-grubbing landlord in times past, its rickety stud wall cutting the window in two. Every morning Ruby would crawl over the bed, hook back the makeshift curtain and whisper through the hand-wide gap to Freya, who could see a small bit of Ruby's face if she pressed hers against the glass. The younger girl did not mind giving up her desk lamp so her friend could have a bedside light, nor was it any hassle waiting a bit longer to do her teeth, or finding the last strawberry-shaped vitamin foam gone from the packet. All this was nothing compared to the excitement of having Ruby just metres away.

A few months in, it felt as though she had always had this calm, slightly devious face beside her at breakfast, always waiting with her at the bus stop for their two different buses. 'You're my sister now,' she would say more times than she can remember. Occasionally she would backpedal, afraid of overdoing it and seeming too clingy, but Ruby would stick her tongue out and ask if that meant she could beat her up and tell her what to do, like any older sister. They did not look so impossibly different – both had a touch of gloom in their hair, though Freya's was a neat bob, with Esther constantly trimming her fringe, while Ruby did everything with her hair except cut it, leaving it wavy from plaiting and always a little damaged. Being among the more diminutive in her year, Freya had to stand on tiptoes to see Ruby eye to eye. 'You'll grow,' her sister said reassuringly. She was always complimenting Freya on her posture, her smile, denying the existence of her jutting incisors. It meant a lot coming from someone who could look stunning with the barest touch of make-up. Of course, Ruby could not resist turning flattery into a game, her compliments growing ever wilder until they became beautiful insults. When it was her turn, Freya would do an impression of her sister by letting her mouth hang into a pout, raising her eyebrows and lowering her lids, which Ruby said made her look paralysed or on drugs.

The gravitational force of Ruby's personality did not wane while she lived with them in Peckham; she still moved in her own circles, going out at odd times, restless if they went on one of their Brighton holidays or if the weather was bad. Yet the healthy shine in her eyes belied any crabbiness. Time was a new kind of pocket money, to be spent cooking pancake breakfasts, cutting up magazines to make Valentine cards, arranging and rearranging Ruby's tiny room, or going out to greenzones, or along the Embankment. It could be blissfully squandered, wrapped in duvets compiling video clips for each other, breathless with laughter. The supply of hours was unlimited.